A COLD
DARK PLACE

A COLD
DARK PLACE

Toni Anderson

A Cold Dark Place

Cover design by Regina Wamba of ReginaWamba.com

Contact email: toniannanderson@gmail.com

For more information on Toni Anderson's books, sign up for her newsletter, or check out her website (www.toniandersonauthor.com).

ALSO BY TONI ANDERSON

COLD JUSTICE – CROSSFIRE

Colder Than Sin (Book #2) Coming 2019

Cold & Deadly (Book #1)

COLD JUSTICE SERIES

Cold Blooded (Book #10)

A Cold Dark Promise (Book #9~A Wedding Novella)

Cold Malice (Book #8)

Cold Secrets (Book #7)

Cold Hearted (Book #6)

Cold in the Shadows (Book #5)

Cold Fear (Book #4)

Cold Light of Day (Book #3)

Cold Pursuit (Book #2)

A Cold Dark Place (Book #1)

THE BARKLEY SOUND SERIES

Dark Waters (Book #2)

Dangerous Waters (Book #1)

STAND-ALONE TITLES

The Killing Game

Edge of Survival

Storm Warning

Sea of Suspicion

'HER' ROMANTIC SUSPENSE SERIES

Her Risk to Take (Novella ~ Book #3)

Her Last Chance (Book #2)

Her Sanctuary (Book #1)

To Mary T, my most beloved friend.
And, no, it isn't a book about Guinness.

PROLOGUE

LINDSEY KEEBLE SANG along to the radio, trying to pretend she wasn't freaked out by the dark. It was one in the morning and she hated driving this lonely stretch of highway between Greenville and Boden. Rain was threatening to turn to snow. The wind was gusting so forcefully that the tall trees looming high above her on the ridge made her swerve nervously toward the center line. The back tires slid on the asphalt and she slowed; no way did she want to wreck her precious little car.

She worked evenings at a gas station in Boden. It was quiet enough she usually got some studying done between customers. Tonight everyone and their dog were filling up ahead of a possible early winter storm. You'd think they'd never seen snow before.

A flash of red lights in her rearview had her heart squeezing. *Dammit!*

She hadn't been speeding—she couldn't afford a ticket and never drank alcohol. She signaled to pull over and stopped on the verge. Lindsey lived responsibly because she wanted a life bigger than her parochial hometown. She wasn't some hillbilly. She wanted to travel and see the world—Paris, Greece, maybe the pyramids if the unrest settled down. She peered through the sleet-drenched glass as a black SUV pulled in tight behind her.

A tall dark figure approached her vehicle. A cop's gold shield tapped against the glass. Frigid damp air flooded the interior as she rolled down the window and she huddled into her jacket as rain spat at her.

"License and registration." A low voice rumbled in that authoritative way cops had. He wore a dark slicker over black clothes. The gun on his hip glinted in the headlights of his vehicle. She didn't recognize his face, but then she couldn't really see his features with ice stinging her eyes.

"What's this about?" Her teeth chattered. She found the documents in her glove box and purse, and handed them over. Her hands returned to grip the hard plastic of the steering wheel as she waited. "I wasn't speeding."

"There's an alert out on a stolen red Neon so thought I'd check it out."

"Well, this is *my* car and I've done nothing wrong." She knew her rights. "You've got no reason to stop me."

"You were driving erratically." The voice got deeper and angrier. She winced. *Never piss off a cop.* "Plus, you've got a broken taillight. That gives me a reason."

Lindsey's worry was replaced by annoyance. She snapped off her seat belt and applied the parking brake. She'd been shafted last year when another driver had sideswiped her in a parking lot and then claimed she'd been at fault to the insurers. "It was fine when I left for work this afternoon. I haven't hit anything in the meantime." *Goddamn it.*

"Go take a look." The cop stood back. He had a nice face despite the hard mouth and even harder eyes. Maybe she could sweet talk him out of a ticket, not that she was real good at sweet talk. Her dad could fix the light in the morning but if she had to pay a ticket as well, every hour of work today would have been for nothing.

She pulled the hood of her slicker over her head and climbed out. The headlights of his SUV blinded her as she took a few steps. She shielded her gaze and frowned. "I don't see anything—"

A surge of fire shot through her back. Pain exploded in a shockwave of screeching agony that overwhelmed her from the tips of her ears to the gaps between her toes. She'd never experienced anything like it. Sweat bloomed on her skin, clashing with sleet as she hit the tarmac. Rough hands grabbed her around the middle and hoisted her into the air. She couldn't control her arms or legs. She was shifted onto a hip where something unyielding bit into her stomach. She fought the urge to vomit even as her brain whirled.

It took a moment to make sense of what was happening.

This man wasn't a cop.

Still reeling from the stun gun, she couldn't get enough purchase to kick him, but she flailed at his knees and tried to elbow him in the balls. It didn't make any difference and she found herself dumped into the cold confines of the rear of his SUV. He zapped her again until her fillings felt like they were going to fall out and her bladder released.

The world tilted and she was on her front, face pressed into a dirty rubber mat, arms yanked behind her as something metal bit into one wrist, then the other. Handcuffs. *Oh, God.* She was handcuffed. A sharp pain ripped through her chest—if she didn't calm down she was going to die of a heart attack.

A ripping sound rang out in the darkness. She was shoved onto her back, and a piece of duct tape slapped over her mouth. It tangled with her hair and was gonna hurt like a bitch when it came off.

Something told her that was the least of her worries.

There was no reason for him to kidnap her unless he was going to hurt her. *Or kill her.*

The realization made everything stop. Every movement. Every frantic breath. Her heart raced and bile burned her throat as she stared into those cold, pitiless eyes. With a grunt he slammed the door closed, plunging her into a vast and consuming darkness. Rain beat the metal around her like an ominous drum. She was scared of the dark. Scared of monsters. Humiliated by the cold dampness between her legs. How could this have happened to her? One minute she was driving home, the next…

Where was her phone?

She rolled around, trying to feel it in her pockets. Shit. It was still in her purse in the passenger seat of her car. There was a crashing sound in the trees. She closed her eyes against the escalating panic. He'd gotten rid of her car. An elephant-sized lump threatened to choke her. She'd worked her ass off for that car, but finances and credit ratings were moot if she didn't survive this ordeal. This man was going to hurt her. She wriggled backward so her fingers could scrabble with the lock but there was nothing, and the panel above her head didn't budge even when she kicked it. *How dare he do this to me*? How dare he treat her as if she was nothing? She wanted to fight and rail against the injustice but as the SUV started up, she was immobilized by terror. All her life she'd fought to make things better, fought for a future and this man, this *bastard*, wanted to rip it all away from her. It wasn't fair. There had to be a way out. There had to be a way to survive.

She didn't want to die. She especially didn't want to die in the dark with a stranger who had eyes as cold as death. Tears brimmed. It wasn't fair. This wasn't fair.

CHAPTER ONE

IT WAS CLOSE to midnight and Alex Parker sat in darkness.

Edgar Paul Meacher had left three hours ago, driving the white panel van he kept for this purpose alone. Meacher would have switched plates along some quiet dirt road, before going on his own little hunting excursion.

Alex had searched the farmhouse—found enough evidence to confirm this guy was the real deal, but nothing else of interest. His chair was in the shadows, facing the doorway. The sound of an engine rumbled up the drive. He wasn't nervous. He hadn't been nervous since his first assignment back in 2005.

The farmhouse was about a mile outside the small town of Fleet, North Carolina; the walls pervaded by the slight sulfurous odor of rotten cabbage from the fields surrounding the property. No neighbors close enough to witness the wild parties held at the Meacher residence. No passersby to complain about the screams either. It worked for Alex too.

He tapped his finger against the cold metal of the SIG P229 fitted with a threaded 9mm barrel and suppressor, listened to the sound of a door slamming, then another door opening. A grunt of physical exertion as something heavy was dragged and hoisted.

The back door opened. Alex aimed the pistol, ready to end

this now. But Meacher trundled straight down to the basement, blind in his excitement to unwrap the latest present he carried in a dirty old blanket.

Alex climbed to his feet. Walked silently across the century-old farmhouse floors and glided down the stairs like a ghost.

The basement was dark and dusty, the faint odor of decay wafting through the air. Classic serial killer lair. A single bulb lit the corner where a camp bed was set up, all comfy and cozy except for the thick plastic sheet draped across it. The floor and walls were decorated in ubiquitous gray with flecks of rust-colored paint. Except it wasn't paint. It was blood. Blood of victims who ranged in age from nineteen to thirty-five. Women who'd done nothing more than wander into Meacher's field of vision. Ten that the FBI knew about; more the authorities didn't know about. Yet.

There was a conveniently placed drain in the middle of the floor. A bucket, a hose and a few big bottles of bleach—obviously bought in bulk. Several rolls of plastic were propped against the wall, and stacks of duct tape were stashed beside the furnace. Experienced and practical—the guy was an old pro at killing.

So was Alex.

Meacher was busy securing his latest victim to the bed. Handcuffs laid out in readiness, waiting for the next lucky recipient. The scumbag—a math teacher from the local high school—generally kept the women alive for about a week before putting them out of their misery.

Alex pushed thoughts of past victims out of his head. Dead was dead and thinking about them only added to his nightmares.

Meacher snapped on the cuffs, fitting them snug to the woman's wrists, the ratcheting sound loud in the otherwise deathly quiet of the basement. Having the woman incapacitated worked for Alex, so he let Meacher finish. He didn't want her mobile. He didn't want her getting in the line of fire.

The guy never turned, never looked away from the brunette. You'd think someone attuned to stalking prey might sense another predator in his lair.

Obviously not.

Meacher licked his lips and ripped open the woman's blouse. Buttons scattered and pinged across the basement floor. Alex's revulsion for the man grew with every despicable act.

"Edgar," he whispered softly.

Meacher turned, lips forming a surprised circle as he spotted Alex on the stairs. There was no time for the man to lunge or fight as Alex put another circle between his eyes. Double tap. The so-called "Snatcher" crumpled to the floor, too dead to bleed out.

Despite the suppressor, the sound of the gunshot made Alex's ears pound but he ignored the discomfort. Headaches plagued him from his time in a Moroccan jail, but he'd been lucky to get out alive and figured they were part of his penance. *This* was the other part.

He picked up both shell casings with a handkerchief and placed them in a silicone pouch he'd had custom-made. He removed the suppressor and slipped the SIG into the shoulder holster. Then he walked over to where The Snatcher's last victim lay restrained on the camp bed. Her head lolled from side to side as the effects of ketamine—Meacher's abduction drug of choice—wore off. As much as Alex wanted to release the cuffs and set the woman free, the vibration in his pocket told him it was time to leave. Her knights in body armor were about to burst through the door.

He touched her hair and spoke gently. "The feds are coming. You're going to be OK." Then he was outside, melting into the darkness as vehicles raced down nearby roads.

The FBI had once estimated there were approximately two hundred and fifty serial killers active in the US at any one time. Alex's job was whittling that number down, one murderous asshole at a time.

FBI SPECIAL AGENT Mallory Rooney held her government-issue Glock 22 flush against her thigh—round in the chamber, finger *off* the trigger—and crouched between her fellow agents and law enforcement officers. Her Taser was on her belt, and backup Glock 21 strapped to her ankle. The bulky flak jacket kept out some of the November chill and adrenaline did the rest. Her temple throbbed from an earlier altercation, but a couple of extra-strength Tylenol and judicious application of makeup had masked the problem well enough to get her on the team. No way in hell was she missing *this* because some gangbanger had smacked her in the face.

SWAT was tied up with another hostage rescue situation in Charlotte that was going downhill fast. She'd be lying if she said she was upset about that, given she now got to participate in this assault instead. They had some highly experienced agents and local cops with them. Sheriff's deputies manned the perimeter.

She was the only first office agent—FOA—on the team.

Two take-downs in one day might be a record for a rookie.

Sweat trickled in a cold line down her back. Her heart hammered but she breathed steadily and forced her pulse to calm. She'd trained for this scenario a million times over; kicked some serious butt in Hogan's Alley. But going after a serial killer who'd butchered at least ten women meant she couldn't help the tiny trill of fear that laced her nerves. Not that she'd show fellow officers that weakness. Nor would she show them the fierce sense of determination that surged through her bloodstream, to take this guy down, whatever the personal cost.

Play it cool. Do the job.

She wiped her left palm surreptitiously down the leg of her black pants, every sense on high alert as to what was going on behind the unassuming farmhouse door. She was so close to the agent in front she could smell his laundry detergent. Her best friend and mentor, Special Agent Lucas Randall, crouched behind her—probably scenting apprehension that no amount of deodorant could hide. Another four law enforcement officers mirrored their actions at the front of the building.

They'd examined the blueprints and knew the basic layout. She and Lucas were to take the basement with two sheriff's deputies covering the storm doors. The external doors and locks were shitty but they had a breacher with a battering ram prepared to open it up just in case.

She didn't move. She concentrated instead. They were waiting for the signal to enter the house of suspected serial killer, Edgar P. Meacher. Dubbed "The Snatcher" by the media, this guy had eluded authorities for four long years, taking women not only off the streets, but also from their homes, instilling terror into the heart of every woman in the

Carolinas and surrounding states.

Mallory understood that visceral fear better than most. She'd lived with it every day for the past eighteen years. Her whole life was shaped around the question of why someone had taken her sister but not her. What made one person a target and another safe? How did bad guys choose their victims?

But she didn't have time to think about that right now.

The Bureau's Behavioral Analysis Unit—part of the National Center for the Analysis of Violent Crime, NCAVC—based in Quantico, Virginia, had developed a sophisticated profile of The Snatcher. This guy, Meacher, fit it to a T.

An anonymous tip-off had been phoned in to their office just as she'd finished writing her FD 302 regarding this morning's arrests. A member of the public had informed her that the guy they were looking for was one Edgar Paul Meacher of Fleet, North Carolina. It didn't mean Meacher *was* their guy, but a woman matching this UNSUB's preferred victim profile had been abducted earlier this evening, and they didn't have time to sit around debating the best course of appropriate action. They were going in. They had to.

Her fingers tightened on the butt of her pistol.

Supervisory Special Agent Petra Danbridge gave them the order to "go" over the radio. Adrenaline surged through her bloodstream. The breacher rammed the door and with a loud crash they all raced inside. Speed was of the essence because stealth had been blown out of the water when they'd smashed down the doors.

Mallory and Lucas took the stairs to the basement. Sweat formed on her brow despite the cool air flowing up the stairwell. She caught the aroma of blood and that faint echo of death. Mentally, she braced herself for whatever lay ahead. Even so it shocked her.

Meacher lay crumpled in a small pool of his own blood. No weapon visible.

"Subject down, in the basement!" she yelled. Feet pounded the boards above them as the house was systematically searched.

She and Lucas cautiously approached the prone figure who sported a dime-size bullet hole between his eyes. Mallory peered closer. There were actually *two* bullet holes, so close together as to be almost indistinguishable. Whoever killed him had either gotten lucky or was a hell of a marksman.

She held her gun on the suspect as Lucas reached down to check Meacher's pulse. Her gaze flickered to the victim who lay perfectly still on the bed. It was Janelle Ebert, the woman who'd been reported missing.

Alive, or were they too late?

"He's dead," Lucas confirmed.

Mallory walked swiftly over to the woman, touched two fingers to her neck, searching for a pulse. A huge swell of relief burst through her at the feel of warm flesh and a solid beat at the base of her throat. "She's alive. I don't see any obvious injuries." Her voice caught and she stumbled through her own nightmares. *Put it away, Mal.* She scanned the restraints. "She's also cuffed. Who the hell shot Meacher?"

They went back on high alert, she and Lucas moving in tandem to clear the rest of the basement. It wasn't big. There was a massive upright freezer—Mallory could wait a lifetime to go through that sucker. Steps to storm doors off to the right. There was also a small room built into the corner, with the door firmly closed. A furnace fired up, making them both jump. She and Lucas looked at each other, nodded in silent communication, and stood on either side of the doorway to the small room. Lucas turned the knob and pulled the door outward. Mallory went in low, but there was no one there.

There *were* enough glossy photographs plastered to the wall that even if there hadn't been a woman handcuffed to a bed, Mallory would have no doubt Meacher was their UNSUB. *Sweet Jesus.* A choking sensation rose up in her throat but she forced it away. She quickly scanned the photos, searching for a sister she hadn't seen in eighteen years even as she told herself not to. Then she made herself stop. There were other things to deal with first.

SSA Danbridge came down the stairs; the woman's boots were lethal weapons but at least Mal always knew where her boss was.

"It's clear," Lucas shouted.

"Get the EMTs down here," Danbridge yelled behind her, stepping around Meacher's corpse and walking to where Mallory and Lucas stood staring into what had to be Meacher's trophy room. "I didn't hear a shot."

"He was already dead when we got here." Lucas looked disappointed as he holstered his weapon. "Which is a damn shame because I'd have loved to haul his ass off to jail."

The woman on the bed groaned and Mallory strode across to her, holstering her own weapon even though the creepy cellar made her scalp prickle. "Where are those EMTs? Can I take these cuffs off?"

Danbridge looked pissed but nodded, then, "Wait!" She pulled out her cell phone and took a series of photographs of the woman, the cuffs, the proximity of the bed in relation to the body. Meacher was a serial killer but he'd obviously been murdered. This was a crime scene on multiple levels but the safety and comfort of living victims always came first.

"Do you think he had a partner who tipped us off and then killed him?" asked Lucas.

"Meacher's only been dead a few minutes. You can still smell the gun powder." Mallory sniffed the air. "It would have been a hell of a risk to tip us off just before he killed him."

"I'll set up roadblocks and a search party." Danbridge spoke quickly into her radio.

"Someone might have set up Meacher to be the fall guy," Lucas offered.

"Maybe." Mallory grimaced. "But nothing about the profile suggested Meacher had a partner and those images"—she jerked her thumb over her shoulder—"only show one male subject in action. We should search for video footage. No way he'd be satisfied with just photographs."

EMTs arrived on the scene and pounded down the wooden steps. Danbridge herded them away from Meacher's body. "You don't need to worry about him." Tall and blonde, Supervisory Special Agent Danbridge put the 'bitch' in ambitious. Mallory had a great deal of respect for her boss as an agent, but she wasn't an empathetic being. No warm and fuzzies in the girls' restroom back at the office. "Touch anything apart from the woman on the bed and I'll report your asses."

Yup. About as warm and cuddly as a tarantula.

Both EMTs rolled their eyes as Mallory unlocked the handcuffs using keys Meacher had left tauntingly close to the bed, just out of reach of the victim. The woman started to moan, then blink and frown in confusion.

"You're okay, Miss. Can you tell me your name?" the EMT

asked, strapping a blood pressure cuff to her arm.

"Where am I? Was I in an accident?" Her voice was hoarse. "The man said I was going to be okay. Said the feds were coming. Why would the FBI be here?" She closed her eyes and rubbed her forehead.

"Lie still," the medic admonished.

"I feel dizzy. God, I didn't have that much to drink."

"Who told you the FBI were coming?" Mallory asked, exchanging a glance with Lucas. The trouble with Special-K was it could produce vivid hallucinations and often made witness statements not only inadmissible, but downright freaky. Still, right now they had nothing else to go on. Maybe she'd remember some detail about whoever shot Meacher. "Did you get a look at his face?"

"A really nice-looking guy. Unless I was dreaming." Dark brown eyes focused and unfocused as she squinted at Mallory's face. "Are you with the FBI? What happened? Where am I?"

But before Mal could answer, the woman caught sight of Meacher's corpse lying on the floor, and seemed to become aware of her ripped blouse, the crinkle of plastic beneath her. She half sat up, looked around at the cold dank basement, and started to sob. Then she started to scream.

SEVEN HOURS LATER, Mallory stood in the shadowy parking lot at the back of the hospital, sipping too-hot coffee and wishing SSA Danbridge would pick up the damn phone. Her feet were numb; toes tingling blocks of ice. Giving up on her boss, she stuffed her phone back in her pocket and jammed her free hand under her opposite armpit. She should have grabbed an overcoat to go over her black wool pantsuit before she'd left the division yesterday but had been too excited to even think of it. A hard layer of frost covered the ground—ridiculously cold for North Carolina even in November.

Danbridge had assigned Mallory the task of accompanying the victim to the hospital and getting a statement. If the "alleged" serial killer had still been at large there was no way a lowly agent like her would have gotten this job. Mal sighed. By the time a doctor examined Janelle Ebert's injuries and collected evidence from her clothes and person, it had been three AM. Then the poor woman had requested a nap while Mallory paced the hallway. Finally, Mallory had gotten a statement which told them nothing they hadn't already known. Janelle had been out for a drink in a bar and Meacher had snatched her from a poorly lit parking lot. She remembered nothing between leaving the bar to waking up in that basement.

She'd been reported missing by a friend who'd arranged to sleep over at Janelle's apartment and who'd worried when Janelle hadn't arrived to let her in. When the friend had gone back to the bar and seen Janelle's car still in the parking lot but the woman herself nowhere in sight, she'd called the cops.

Now Janelle was sleeping quietly with a local sheriff's deputy guarding the door to her room—more as a protection against members of the press than any unknown attacker. If the person who'd killed Meacher had wanted Janelle Ebert dead, he—or she—had had ample opportunity.

Janelle was a very lucky woman.

Mallory wanted to leave. Wanted to help search the house of horrors and see exactly who Edgar Meacher had killed. But she needed her job and pissing off her boss topped her list of things not to do if she wanted to keep it. She took another scalding mouthful of coffee and then watched her breath freeze on the exhale. The sun was rising over the eastern horizon lightening the gray of twilight to pale mauve and pink of dawn.

It made her pause.

Her twin sister Payton had loved watching the sun rise over the woods that surrounded their West Virginian home. At the time, Mallory had resented being poked awake with the birds, but nowadays she found it oddly reassuring—another fragile connection to the sister she'd lost. No matter what happened, the sun always rose. And until the day the solar system decided to implode and take this galaxy with it—it always would. It reminded her exactly how small a speck in the universe she really was.

Her colleagues had found photographs of twelve victims so far—one was even a former pupil of Meacher's—but no mention of anyone who resembled her identical twin.

Payton had been nine when she'd disappeared without a trace from the bedroom they'd shared in their West Virginian mansion. Mallory hadn't really expected to find evidence of her at Meacher's house, but there was always a tiny flicker of hope she and her parents would eventually get closure. The sheer number of monsters she'd encountered since she started working for the FBI stunned her.

Footsteps approached. A man ambled toward her.

She turned to face him, mentally mapping out her surroundings. Even though it was early there were too many people and too many cameras for him to be a real threat, but her right hand slid closer to her weapon anyway. Cataloging the man's big wool overcoat, nicotine-stained fingers, and razor-sharp eyes she knew exactly what he wanted.

He held out a pack of cigarettes. "Smoke?"

"Thanks, but I don't smoke."

"You a fed?" He'd accurately assessed her bullshit meter to be in the red zone and decided to be direct. Small mercies. "Know anything about this whole serial killer business?"

"You with a paper?"

"Charlie Fernier. The Post." He held out his hand, which she pointedly ignored.

She slugged back her coffee, wiped her mouth with the back of her hand. Silence was her best friend when it came to the press.

"Hey, don't I know you?" He angled his chin to get a better look at her face, his gaze lingering on her eye which had darkened overnight to form a nice blue-rimmed socket. "You look real familiar."

Mallory held her ground even though she wanted to run. Ice formed inside her chest. That old familiar cracking sensation when someone recognized her from her mother's annual campaign to keep her sister's disappearance in the public eye. Who needed computer-generated aging software when you had a readymade replica on hand?

Well, not this year. She was done with pretending Payton might still be alive, and done giving her abductor a thrill as she begged for information. She wanted to see *him* begging—for mercy as she held her Glock to his head. The image startled her out of her reverie. Too much coffee; not enough sleep.

"No. You don't know me."

"Are you sure, Special Agent...?"

She started to walk away. "I'm sure, Mr. Fernier."

"Hey!" His voice boomed off the glass and concrete of the hospital behind them. "You're that girl"—every muscle in her body flinched—"the one whose twin sister was taken all those years ago."

"Don't know what you're talking about." Her mother had a *lot* to answer for.

"It's gonna make a great headline, 'Senator's daughter still searching for justice after all these years.'"

She stuck her middle finger in the air without turning around and heard a strong male laugh behind her. Her life was more than a news headline. Tossing her coffee cup in the garbage she climbed into her car, checked her mirror and saw the reporter walking away, probably plotting how best to spin her involvement in this case. She started the engine and reversed out of her spot. By the time the story went to press she'd have either succumbed to a nervous breakdown or taken down Meacher in hand-to-hand combat and saved Janelle's life. How to piss off your colleagues and influence people. Like her life wasn't complicated enough.

Making an executive decision, she turned right out of the parking lot to head back to the farmhouse. Her phone rang. It was her boss. Mallory rolled her eyes.

"Where are you?"

"Still at the hospital."

"You not done there yet?"

Mallory bit down on a retort. "Just finished. Janelle's sleeping and I have the evidence locked in the trunk." Clothes. Rape kit. Although there was no evidence of assault.

"She say anything about the person who shot Meacher?"

"He had beautiful eyes and she thinks he touched her hair."

"Pity they haven't invented a DNA test that sensitive yet."

"Anything in the farmhouse?"

"Enough photographic evidence to suggest Meacher killed at least twelve women. We've found his video cache. There are probably more."

Mallory braced herself. "You want me to help look through it?"

"BAU is sending two agents to assist in the evidence collection and they specifically want eyes on the video and photographs to try and link unsolved murders."

Which meant, as the junior agent, Mallory would be reduced to fetching coffee. But it would be worth it to pick the brains of these people.

"I want you to go back to division and start tracing that anonymous tipster—"

"What?" She winced. Damn. She sounded like a whiny kid, but the tipster wouldn't lead her to her sister's killer.

"Somebody suspected Meacher was The Snatcher before we did. I'd bet the same person put a bullet in his brain. Whether it was an accomplice or an outraged member of the public, I want them brought to justice." Danbridge hung up on her.

Mallory tossed her phone on the seat. *Great. Just frickin' great.* Everyone else got to dissect the mind of a serial killer. *She* got to trace a phone call.

CHAPTER TWO

OUTSIDE THE FRONT of FBI Charlotte Division a light dusting of snow clung to the sidewalk. "What do you mean you can't trace it?" Mallory tugged on the small gold hoop in her ear as she looked through the window. "I thought you could trace anything."

"Not this." Mike Tanner specialized in communication systems. He was a super nice guy and everyone in the Bureau tried to exploit that fact. Ex-military, he'd helped design some of the software that used voice recognition to pick up suspected terrorists talking on cell phones during the Iraq war. "He bounced the signal off different servers *and* used a burner cell which has since been switched off and deactivated. I could possibly tell you where the call was made from—if I devoted the next six months to this one thing. Unfortunately, my boss will have other ideas."

Securing the phone handset with her shoulder, she checked her email. "What about voice analysis?"

"It was electronically disguised."

"So you've got nothing?"

"More specifically, *you've* got nothing."

"Ha. *Thanks*, Mike," she said it with enough humor that he laughed.

"Always a pleasure, Mal."

She hung up as Lucas Randall came into the room. His black hair stood on end, a day's growth of beard darkened his jaw. He was a good-looking guy and she was aware of speculation that they were secretly a couple. Not true. They'd been friends for years. He'd always been like a big brother to her.

"What's going on?" she asked.

"Unit briefing in the conference room in fifteen minutes. Two BAU bigwigs in attendance." He pointed his finger at her. "Danbridge was pissed to see you making an appearance on *The Post* website."

She pulled a face. "Like I planned that. Some journalist cornered me at the hospital, recognized me from my mother's yearly media circus and pounced. Believe me, I am *not* seeking any form of attention." She stood, stretched out her back, then followed him over to his desk. Her fellow agents had been processing the Meacher residence non-stop for the last eighteen hours while she'd been chasing her tail, achieving nothing. The tight cast to Lucas's lips and added weight to his shoulders suggested the day had taken its toll. "Bad?" she asked.

She'd only been in the FBI for twenty-two months and was still on probation, but she'd already seen things she'd take to her grave. As much as she wanted to be involved in the Meacher investigation she knew dealing with this sort of evil took a toll. It was one thing to see crime scene photographs; quite another to be in the lair of a serial killer, uncovering victims.

"We're up to fifteen women," Lucas's voice was gruff. The dark circles under his eyes added a worn-out quality to his grim expression. He answered her silent question with a shake of his head. "I didn't see any kids and no one who looked like Payton."

Mallory was torn between disappointment and relief.

"He kept more personal trophies in his bedroom. Whoever shot the sonofabitch did the world a favor." A flicker of unguarded emotion crossed his face. Then he buried it beneath six years' field experience and a flat cop stare. "You'll hear all the details at the briefing." He rubbed the back of his neck. "Lemme get a coffee and we'll head over together." He froze as a stranger wearing a visitor badge and carrying a laptop walked through the office doorway. "Alex? What the—?"

"You missed the meeting, asshole." The man's expression was fierce. "Thought I'd hunt you down and make you buy me a beer." His gaze darted to her. "Looks like a bad time though."

"That was today?" Lucas palmed his forehead. "Jesus, you're right. I'm an asshole."

"I already covered that." The man—Alex—grinned, and Mallory got a fierce blast of gorgeous.

The response wrung a reluctant smile out of Lucas. "Believe it or not, Mal, this is a good friend of mine, Alex Parker. I asked him to attend a Counterintelligence Awareness Group briefing I organized so he could tell us about some of the latest internet security measures being developed in the private sector. He runs his own company in DC. Does a lot of government contracts. We served together in Afghanistan." His gaze swung back to Alex. "I assume the meeting went ahead without me?"

Alex nodded. "We managed to fumble along without your incisive brilliance."

"Yet *I'm* the asshole," Lucas grinned. "This here is Special Agent Mallory Rooney."

The stranger held out a tanned strong-looking hand as they were introduced. His skin was warm, fingers firm as they squeezed hers.

"It's a pleasure to meet you, Agent Rooney." The self-deprecating smile was a killer. So was the short, ruffled light-brown hair and days' worth of scruff on his jaw.

Despite the tailored suit, he hadn't been intimidated enough by the high-powered members of that committee to shave. The contrast snagged her attention. He was different from the law enforcement personnel and political players she usually met. There was something underplayed and restrained about him that didn't mesh with the keen intelligence she saw in his eyes, nor the taut-looking muscles that filled out that suit. It intrigued her. She hadn't been intrigued on a personal level in a long time.

"You work in security?" she asked.

"Keeping Trade Secrets secret—or trying to. It isn't exactly running the gauntlet every day like you guys."

Lucas sat atop his messy desk. "Says the man with the Distinguished Service Cross."

Something vulnerable sparked in those slate eyes. "I got caught in a firefight and managed not to get killed. *I* got lucky." Those eyes of his weren't revealing anything now—all emotion banked. "I better let you get back to work. It's a long drive back to DC."

Their boss walked in and Mallory stiffened. Danbridge's gaze skimmed Alex with a cursory glance that notched up to feminine appreciation on the second go 'round.

"Special Agent Randall, I need a word." Then she walked into her office, heels tapping.

Lucas swore under his breath. "Alex, I owe you big time,

buddy. I'll be in touch. Will you show him out for me, Mal?"

"Sure," she said. The longer she could avoid her boss the better. The two men shook hands and said goodbye.

"I can find my own way," Alex said softly.

"No problem. I need to stretch my legs anyway."

His gaze flicked to her boots and up, the brush of it almost as intimate as a physical touch. An unfamiliar sliver of sensation unfurled inside her, nearly unrecognizable because it had been so long. Attraction.

Telling herself she wasn't deliberately prolonging their time together, she took the stairs as she led the way out. He was taller than she'd first realized. In her low-heeled boots she stood just under five foot nine and he was four or five inches taller. She frowned. Seeing him at a distance standing beside Lucas, she'd have described him as medium height and just *okay* looking. Up close, when you got the full force of those intelligent gray eyes and that perfectly proportioned masculine face, he was a hottie. Made you appreciate the inaccuracy of eyewitness accounts. No wedding ring either.

It was her job to pay attention to detail.

Even though she maintained a space between them she was hyperaware of him beside her. Outside the front entrance of the five-story, white concrete building he turned to her and asked, "Can I take you out to dinner sometime?"

"I don't date." The answer came out automatically before her brain engaged. Crap.

There was a long pause while those beautiful eyes of his wandered over her face, resting on her bruise from yesterday. He didn't argue or try to change her mind.

"It was nice to meet you, Special Agent Rooney." And then he walked away.

She squeezed her hands into fists. Damn, why had she said no?

Because she didn't date.

She watched Alex Parker climb into his car—a low-slung sporty job—and raise a hand before he drove away. His car disappeared and a familiar sense of loss rushed over her. She clenched her jaw, turned around and went back to work.

ALEX DROVE AWAY trying not to think about why Mallory Rooney didn't date. The sight of her in the rearview mirror made his chest tighten. It seemed a shame for someone so young and beautiful to isolate herself like that. Not that he'd have done more than take her to dinner—*you keep believing that, buddy*—but the flare of attraction had been instant and unexpected.

What made it truly ironic was he didn't date either. And he didn't like surprises.

The snow hadn't stuck; it scraped across the asphalt like cotton swabs and gathered with dirt in the gutter. The grimy edge of his reality bore down on him. He didn't like lying, didn't like killing. Didn't like death. But he had no choice. When his debt was paid he'd move on and rebuild a life to be proud of. In the meantime, he owed five hundred and forty-two days on his contract and had no right to be thinking about pretty women with sad amber eyes. His phone rang and he took the call, grateful for the distraction. Work kept him busy. Too busy for regrets.

MALLORY HEADED BACK into the building and went straight to the briefing room. Two serious-looking guys in suits sat at the head of the table next to the Special Agent in Charge of the Charlotte division. He eyed her over his glasses and she gave him a weak smile. Damn that reporter.

"Who're they?" she whispered to Lucas as she sat next to him.

"Supervisory Special Agents Hanrahan and Frazer from BAU."

These guys were legendary in the Bureau. Hanrahan was silver-haired with tanned craggy features. He'd interviewed serial offenders from every state in the Union and wrote the book on profiling the sick bastards. Mallory always wondered how much you could expose yourself to these people without some of your morality wearing off. Frazer was much younger, gleaming blond hair, arctic blue eyes, and Ryan Gosling handsome—if you liked that sort of thing. He was a rock star in law enforcement circles. In Afghanistan he'd tracked down a serial killer who used the war to hide his crimes. After that he nailed a black widow who'd been on husband number four—who just happened to be billionaire Robin Greenburg who owned media companies across the globe. Needless to say, Frazer never got bad press. Polished and perfect, just looking at him made her teeth ache.

The image of Alex Parker flashed through her mind and she wished she hadn't brushed him off. There was a rugged quality to his looks that appealed to her. But she hadn't had time to date since she'd joined the academy and didn't have time now. She drummed her fingers on the wooden conference table, irritated and frustrated with her lack of life outside work.

SSA Danbridge strode in on her black-heeled boots with a toss of her long blonde hair. She shot Mallory a narrow-eyed glare that made her want to squirm in her seat. Mallory held still. Danbridge looked more tense than usual, though she'd taken the time to change into a fresh power suit. Mallory's gaze shot to the two men as she finally got it. *Duh.* Danbridge had applied for an opening at Quantico and was hoping to impress these guys enough to make it happen. Mallory's throat went dry because she had nothing to say that was going to make her boss shine.

Danbridge started the meeting and outlined what had happened last night.

"How did you narrow it down to Meacher?" SSA Hanrahan asked. He had a lovely voice. Level but warm.

"We got the tip-off about Meacher yesterday afternoon at six-fifteen."

"You personally?" Hanrahan asked.

Danbridge pointed to her.

Mallory swallowed. "Erhm. It came into the office, and I picked up." *Gosh, really Mallory? You managed to answer a phone all by yourself?*

"You are?" Hanrahan asked.

"Special Agent Rooney, sir."

"I saw you on the news."

There was a huff of smothered laughter behind her. She held still when she wanted to turn around and glare. Hanrahan was watching her closely, knowledge alive in the depths of his blue eyes. *Damn.* She hated being the center of attention or an object of curiosity. That clear gaze told her he knew everything about her from her pedigree to her shoe size. She wanted to disappear into the floor. Unfortunately, her powers of invisibility failed her.

"On a normal day you'd probably have left the information to deal with the next day. Why didn't you?"

Because I have no life. "I started digging a little into Meacher's background and realized he was a perfect fit to the profile your unit provided, sir. So I took the information to SSA Danbridge"—her boss's eyes glowed with approval, because, *yes*, they both worked late almost every night and weekends and now everyone knew it—"and then we received a call from state police concerned that The Snatcher had claimed another victim."

Danbridge interrupted her. Thank God. "I took the information to the Special Agent in Charge and we moved immediately to act on the information we'd received."

Relief that a vicious killer was off the street was evident on every face.

"Where are you on identifying the anonymous tipster?" Danbridge asked her.

Crap. "Call was made using an untraceable cell and the voice was electronically enhanced. It's a dead end."

SSA Hanrahan met Mallory's gaze. If she'd given them anything useful she might have smiled, but she'd contributed nothing.

Danbridge's lips tightened. "Keep on it. Don't let those IT geeks drop the ball on this."

"Yes, ma'am." Mallory wanted to be involved in the Meacher investigation, not investigating an anonymous phone tip but she bit down on her frustration.

Danbridge moved on with the briefing. "We found photographic evidence of what appears to be Meacher torturing fifteen different women. Comparing those photographs to images of missing or murdered women using a preliminary facial analysis program the BAU brought in, we are almost positive at least ten of those victims' remains have been recovered." Which left five victims unaccounted for—presumably dead.

"We have teams of people collecting DNA from the farmhouse and tomorrow we're sending cadaver dogs to search out any possible bodies buried on the property. We'll enter the DNA samples into CODIS. The work will continue until we identify every woman featured in those photographs and videos." Her boss's knuckles whitened. "Meacher was forty-four years old and we believe he's been killing since his late teens, early twenties. Again—this is based on photographic evidence and the details need to be verified. We know he moved at least four times over the last two decades and we need to search each of those properties for potential evidence."

How to increase the property value of your home—not.

Danbridge was finishing off. "Although there's no criminal prosecution for Meacher we need to make sure the scene is processed carefully so that we can find his killer and gain closure for all the victims' families." The woman's eyes blazed. "We are treating Meacher's death as a homicide. Special Agent Randall will be case officer on that investigation."

Mallory's gaze shot to Lucas. He sent her a wink. Chances were the tipster and killer were related in some way, so hopefully that meant she'd get to help him out once she'd finished pissing off every IT technician she knew.

The meeting broke up and Mallory snuck out behind Lucas and went back to work. It was November and the anniversary of her sister's abduction loomed large, as did her mother's annual request to pose for photographs.

Not this year.

Payton was dead. She'd finally accepted it. Maybe it was

the twin thing, but for years after her abduction she'd sensed her sister was out there somewhere. Now there was nothing but a cold and empty void. Try explaining that phenomenon to her mother. *I don't think so.*

When she got back to her desk she had a message from Mike Tanner saying he'd managed to narrow the call down to the eastern seaboard of the United States—which was a real bonus given that millions of people lived there. She investigated different units that electronically disguised voices but couldn't pinpoint exactly what unit had been used, and according to Mike, neither could NASA.

Mallory leaned back in her chair. The shooter had hit the *exact* same bull's eye twice on a moving target. That was a hell of a shot. He'd also cleaned up after himself—no shell casings. It was almost like this guy was a professional hit man.

That was crazy, right?

She frowned and opened ViCAP. Entered "suspected killer" and "nine-millimeter" and got several thousand hits. She palmed her face. *Okay.* She typed in "suspected killer found dead." Still a lot of hits. She delved deeper into some of the files—it included suicide, accidental death. *Damn.* She rubbed her eyes. "Suspected death" "suspected killer found dead."

Still a lot of hits but manageable. She went over to the coffee machine and filled another mug. The office was buzzing, despite the fact most of the agents in this office had skipped bed last night. She smothered a yawn and trudged back to her computer and pulled out her notebook, going through each record, looking for similarities with Meacher.

Hmmm. Last April, a serial sexual offender had been found in his Tampa apartment with a matching pair of slugs rattling around in his brain. Cops had no idea who killed him, but they'd received an anonymous tip-off *after* he was dead suggesting he was a rapist they were hunting.

Bingo.

She trolled through thirty more cases where suspected criminals had OD'd on crystal meth or been killed by rival gangs. Not what she was after. Then she found another case similar to Meacher. Suspected pedophile. Nine millimeter between the eyes. Anonymous tip.

Mallory straightened.

Holy shit.

A yawn grabbed hold and contorted her face and she knew it was time to go home before she passed out from exhaustion. Okay, there was no solid evidence, and every case was just different enough not to create alarm bells ringing in the system, but…

"Agent Rooney." It was SSA Danbridge standing with her coat over her arm.

Mallory jerked. The office was dark except for her desk.

"You're making the rest of us look bad. Go home."

"Yes, ma'am." Eyes drooping, she typed in one last search term "vigilante" while she pulled on her coat and scarf. The file was huge so she forwarded the results to her email. "Night, boss."

She headed out the front door of the building and into the star-spangled night and found herself recalling the exact shade of Alex Parker's eyes as he'd asked her to go to dinner. Her lips tightened. She'd messed that one up.

Tears made the stars blur. "Sorry, Pay. I'm so damn sorry."

CHAPTER THREE

FOUR AM WAS a lonely time, the darkness had an empty feel to it. Trees cracked and creaked as the temperature dropped. The icy breeze scraped over exposed skin like pumice, raising a dull flush. A light dusting of snow made everything brighter, colder. Lonelier.

He pulled his ski-mask lower over his face, got out of his SUV, and checked that no one was around. He drew on gloves, blowing into the palms of his hands to heat cold flesh. Getting rid of a body was harder than most people would credit. He was physically fit and even he had trouble pulling a full-grown woman out of the back of his car and moving her dead weight any distance.

The body bag made it awkward to get a grip but with a little effort he managed to get it over his shoulder. He closed the door quietly, picked up his flashlight and headed into the bush.

There was a spot he remembered from a hike last summer, about three hundred yards off one of the official paths. She was unlikely to be found before spring, and it was close enough to the creek that critters were bound to come across the body sooner rather than later and help destroy any lingering evidence. And as careful as he'd been he wasn't naive enough to believe there was nothing left to link her to him.

He'd have buried her, but the ground was like concrete. This would have to do.

He ducked off the path, crunching through the detritus that littered the forest floor. He found the spot he'd earmarked and turned, scanning with his flashlight, looking for the best way to conceal the body. There was an eroded bank undercutting a huge sugar maple. He strode over, dumping the heavy bag on the ground, relieved to be rid of his burden, rolling his shoulders to ease the ache.

It took a moment to grasp the zipper with his gloved fingers, then he rolled her out like a broken toy. Except for the bruises, she was pale against the snow. He caught her wrists and pulled her up against the wall of the earthen bank. Her hair dragged through the dirt, leaves tangling in the black strands.

She'd been a mistake.

Her hair was the right shade, but her eyes were mud rather than whiskey. Jaw line too square. Hands too big. Mouth too vulgar and bitchy. By the end she'd repulsed him. He straightened her legs, moving her hands to cover her pubic hair. He'd burned her clothes; wiped her body down with Lysol.

There was a dull throb in his chest. A heaviness that affected his breathing. He'd thought she might be the right one, but she wasn't. He touched the initials carved above her heart, regret and loneliness slamming into him. His fists curled.

She shouldn't have died. He shouldn't have lost her. *It wasn't fair.*

His breath shuddered out of his chest and he wanted to smash his fist against something. He eyed the girl's swollen features and looked away. She'd been a mistake, but he couldn't stop searching until he'd found a replacement. He stood, kicked leaves over the body, covering it from prying eyes, removing it from his sight. In a few hours the snow would shroud her, and when spring came the creek bubbling lazily at his back would flood this spot and sweep her away like garbage. He picked up the body bag, quickly scanned the area for anything he might have left behind, and started back to his car. Fifteen minutes in and out.

Cold air burned his lungs and he shivered beneath his sheepskin jacket. He got in the SUV and started her up, blasting the heater. Taking someone so close to home posed a risk in some ways, but in others it was smart and might throw people off the scent. And he didn't need to keep killing…just until he found the right one. He hadn't realized it would be so hard.

You know where to find the right one…

He gripped one hand over his skull, knees automatically curling into his stomach as he fought to control the SUV.

He couldn't do that.

It made sense.

No, no!

But Mallory Rooney's features superimposed themselves over those of the last victim. How many other women had to die because of some stubborn misplaced loyalty to the family?

His gut churned. If he carried on like this eventually he'd get caught. His fingers tightened around the leather of the steering wheel and he straightened in his seat. No way in hell was he getting caught. No way in hell.

ALEX STOOD ON the top step of the Lincoln Memorial and watched people stream toward the WWII Memorial for the early morning Veterans' Day ceremony. He'd arrived back from North Carolina late last night. He should be sleeping but instead he was here.

The jingle of a police horse's harness rang across the wide open space. Elderly men, many using canes or wheelchairs, were helped by relatives and friends to attend the laying of wreaths at the monument at the far end of the Reflecting Pool.

He remembered being a small boy standing beside his grandfather—a man who'd flown bombers over Germany—not understanding why they were out on a cold November morning, dressed up in their Sunday best. He remembered slipping a hand into his grandfather's palm and the feeling of safety that had enveloped him in that moment.

Heat tingled in his palm. His fingers curled.

This was why he came to the ceremony every year. To honor the dead. To beg their forgiveness. As minutes marched onward there was a hum of respectful silence. An energy of fierce pride that was both emotionally charged and quietly stoic. It made him proud to be an American. Despite its idiosyncratic betrayal, he still loved his country.

"Reveille" echoed through the mist that clung to the smartly shorn grass and elegant marble edifices. The piercing notes of the bugle rang through his bones and made him quiver like a tine. His chin lifted, shoulders stiffened, fingers itched to form a salute. But he wasn't worthy.

Working in the shadows was a cold dark place.

His phone vibrated in his pocket.

Choice had been taken from him when he'd failed his last mission, and failed his country so he edged through the crowd, away from the dignified tribute to fallen comrades. Without the bargain he'd made he'd still be rotting in that North African jail with all the other vermin. He put his phone to his ear.

"I need to see you in your office." *Jane Sanders.* His boss's lackey.

He clicked off and hailed a cab. Ten minutes later he stood in front of the old brownstone in Woodley Park, which held a small brass plaque beside the front door with "Cramer, Parker & Gray. Security Consultants" etched in small block letters. It was quiet on the streets. Early morning on a national holiday. He hadn't been followed.

Jane got out of her car and came up the steps behind him. They didn't speak.

He unlocked the door and walked inside. The house had all the appearance of a normal business—reception counter, row of uncomfortable-looking chairs, low coffee table with glossy magazines laid neatly across the surface. Although they weren't exactly the usual nine-to-five operation, he and his partners—Haley Cramer and Dermot Gray—ran a legit security and crime prevention business that had made all three of them rich. They'd been best friends since MIT.

Haley and Dermot knew he hid stuff from them. They knew he'd been in jail in Morocco and had fought hard to get him released. But they sure as hell didn't know what he did for the government on a part-time basis. And that was the whole point of being a covert operative.

Welcome to the dark side.

He turned off the alarm system and unlocked his office door, indicating Jane should precede him inside. She flinched at the sound of the lock turning behind them. His office was soundproofed and swept for bugs before and after every appointment. Not that he handled many clients—just enough to make it look like he earned his pay the traditional way. Which didn't involve blood.

He turned on the signal jammer as a precaution he only used when the building was empty. Jane Sanders also had another job, but it was their work with The Gateway Project that brought them together.

"The Gateway Project" sounded so innocuous, like a community garden or construction company. Instead they did their best to show serial killers and pedophiles the Gateway to Hell. The Project involved some rich, very powerful people at the highest level of government. Dangerous people. Ruthless people. People who had a hell of a lot to lose should things go sideways. The work was more covert and deniable than any foreign assassination he'd ever carried out and, morally, he had less of a problem with his current targets than his former ones. The fact he had a problem at all was why there was a time limit on his commitment.

As always Jane found it impossible to hold his gaze for more than a fraction of a second. His being an assassin made her nervous, even though the only woman he'd ever shot had been decked out in a suicide vest. No direct orders necessary.

He didn't say anything. Just slumped in the chair behind the desk. Fading into the background was one of the things he did best and he'd be lying if he said he didn't enjoy needling this woman. They were about the same age and there the similarity ended. She was blond and pretty and put together like DC Barbie. If she had a mind of her own it was hidden under the thick agenda of their mutual task-master. She watched him from the corner of her eye the way you watched a supposedly tame lion—very, very carefully.

She stood in her tailored black suit, looking out through the window's old fashioned net curtains, so beautiful he wondered why he wasn't the least bit attracted to her.

One touch of Mallory Rooney's hand had electrified his skin, heart tripping like a teen on speed. Of course, *she* didn't know what he really did for the government and had blown him off anyway. Smart woman.

"Any trouble?" Jane asked.

Again he said nothing. She wasn't his superior and it pissed him off when she pretended she was. She was as complicit in the deaths of these people as he was, but she never got her hands dirty. They weren't pals. They weren't brothers-in-arms. He'd bet two fingers on his left hand she'd never even seen a dead body—why that irked him so much he didn't know.

"Did you find anything…?"

He waited for her to make full-on eye contact. Shook his head.

She cleared her throat. "I suppose you're angry because we cut it a little fine with the timing the other night."

He raised one brow. He'd had to call upon all of his magician skills to disappear without being seen at Meacher's house. Not that he'd really worried. The Bureau always followed procedure while the Agency did its best work by bending the rules. Not that Alex worked for the CIA anymore; and on paper he never had. But he expected this new operation to keep their end of the bargain, part of which was to supply critical intel and insider information on the exact movements of specific law enforcement personnel in a timely manner.

"My source said there were technical issues—"

"They fucked up." Accidentally or on purpose he didn't know. "If I go down I take everyone with me. Don't forget that." It was his only insurance from being screwed by these people. He'd learned his lessons the hard way.

Her hands fluttered over the hem of her jacket, the first physical sign of real nerves he'd seen in the woman. "They said there was some sort of dead zone." Her gaze flashed uneasily to his.

More silence, lengthening to discomfort. Hers.

"Who tipped off the cops?"

"I don't know—"

"Someone called it in *before* I'd done the job."

Her eyes went wide and frightened, and he felt a thousand years old.

Between the early tip-off regarding Meacher's identity and the delayed warning that the cops were on the way, the op had almost been compromised. Alex rubbed his hands over his face. He was exhausted and didn't want to deal with Jane's paranoia on top of his own. "Forget it. I'll figure it out."

Eager to be gone, she fumbled open a briefcase and pulled out a file. She almost handed it to him but changed her mind and slid it onto his cherry wood desk instead.

Scared was good.

Scared kept people at a distance and that's where he wanted them. For some reason Mallory Rooney popped into his head again, with her short hair as dark as a raven's feather and sparkling amber eyes. No point lying to himself—he wouldn't mind a little less distance between himself and that particular federal agent.

"They found another body," Jane Sanders said without preamble.

"Where?"

"In a remote wooded area in Virginia, near the West Virginia state line. A couple walking their dog. The killer took the trouble to hide the body." Excitement vibrated low in her voice. "I don't think he expected this one to be found until next spring."

Alex stood and opened the file. Looked down at the graphic color photographs of more pointless death. On top of eliminating serial killers they were also trying to solve one cold case. He picked up a photograph. Frowned. "The connection's a little thin, don't you think?"

Slim shoulders rose and fell with false confidence, as if she wasn't terrified to be in the same room with him. Because *he* was the scariest thing she knew. Pissed, he smiled. Maybe she was right. He was more dangerous than most of the monsters they hunted.

He studied the photograph. This particular killer generally dumped bodies out in the open in drainage ditches in remote areas. Why was this victim different? Or was it simply the first time law enforcement had found a body that he—or she—had hidden this way? Impossible to say for certain.

"Can we get access to the police and Medical Examiner's reports?" He wasn't a psychologist but he understood killers better than most. He didn't get the compulsion or the buzz, but he definitely had a handle on the mechanics, and the mechanics were usually what tripped these guys up. Like the FBI profile combined with Meacher's cell phone data had finally earned him his just rewards.

"Not immediately unless someone hacks them, but now the local PD has started searching ViCAP. It won't be long until they find a connection to the other bodies. The feds will be all over this very soon."

His eyes flicked over his wall map of the United States. Forensics took time. Finding a killer took time. "I have some other appointments that require more immediate attention—"

"The boss is most insistent—"

"It's a long shot at best."

"After all these years, *everything* is a long shot."

Alex hid his reaction by staring out of the window. It wasn't ghosts of the people he'd killed that kept him awake at night. It was the wreckage of families he'd left behind. He'd always followed orders. Right up to that last fateful mission when he'd been poised to break the neck of an international arms dealer. Then the man's twelve-year-old daughter had walked into the room and Alex had frozen. A better assassin would have killed them both, but he couldn't do it. He'd left them alive and walked away.

He'd had plenty of time to regret that decision.

What bothered him most was he still wouldn't be able to kill that arms dealer in front of his daughter. Even after the bastard had exacted some personal retribution in prison. Maybe Alex had deserved it.

Jane gathered her things, obviously in a hurry to get away from him. "There's something else," she lowered her voice to barely above a whisper. "Someone involved in the Meacher investigation started snooping."

It had only been a matter of time.

"We need to adjust some of our practices." A little more assisted suicide and a little less lethal force. "You need to inform the others."

Her slight gasp made him frown. Did she really think he didn't know about the two other assassins The Gateway

Project had recruited for this operation? He hoped they weren't as fucked up as he was. "Who's the person doing the snooping?" He'd tap their email and cell phones.

"I'm surprised you don't already know." There was a bite to Jane's tone that almost made him smile. "The boss wants you to keep a close personal eye on the situation." She paused again, but it would take more than a well-timed silence to crack him. "The person doing the digging is one Special Agent Mallory Rooney, FBI Charlotte Division." She walked out without another word as though she hadn't just smacked him in the face.

CHAPTER FOUR

MALLORY'S HAIR WAS wet from her rushed five minute shower and her ears burned from cold as she raced through the frosty morning into the building. She'd worked at home yesterday. Normal routine for a federal holiday, curled up in front of her fireplace. She took the stairs up to her floor, a bounce in her step that had been missing recently. Not only had she managed to get some decent sleep and run three miles this morning, she was also pretty damn certain there was a vigilante at large, targeting violent criminals. Maybe that was a good thing, but for the most part Mallory believed in the legal system—she had to.

She pushed through the door and saw a group of people hovering outside the boss's office. Wary glances shot to her and then darted quickly away. She frowned. She'd thought they'd be over the whole *Post* deal by now, although a new version had been rehashed and made the print edition. She rolled her eyes and walked to her desk, dumped her bags, and started to wander to Lucas's desk but he wasn't in yet. He was going to be the case officer in charge of this investigation, and if her theory was correct this could be special.

"Special Agent Rooney." SSA Danbridge's voice cracked like thunder from her doorway. "My office."

Mallory had thought they'd parted on good terms Monday

night. What had happened to destroy the truce? She closed the door behind her. "Ma'am?"

"You know I applied for that position at the BAU in Quantico?"

"You got the job?" Mallory smiled, cartwheels and fireworks going off in her head as her inner voice sang Hallelujah. "Congratulations!"

Danbridge's blue eyes glowed in narrow slits of rage. Mallory shifted back a step.

"No, I didn't get the job." The SSA thrust a piece of paper at her. "*You* did."

Mallory's mouth gaped. "What?" She took the paper and scanned it. She was being transferred to Quantico? She tried to hand the letter back but Danbridge wouldn't take it. "That can't be right. There must be some mistake."

Her boss gripped the edge of her desk as if to physically restrain herself. Her voice carried and Mallory could feel her colleagues' interest through the walls like darts in her flesh.

"There's been a mistake all right. There is no way you're the most qualified person who applied. You are nothing but a Harvard dropout—"

"No." Mallory corrected her. "I didn't drop out, ma'am." She hadn't done anything wrong and she could fix this. "I graduated with my law degree before I joined the Bureau."

"Well," Danbridge practically hissed, "we both know it isn't your law degree that got you a position at the BAU."

"There has to be some mistake. I didn't even—"

"There's no mistake! I called them to confirm. You got it. *You* got the best fucking job in the FBI." Danbridge leaned closer, her jaw muscles working frenetically. "You got it because your mother is a senator on Capitol Hill—"

"My mother has no pull within the Bureau." Mallory gritted her teeth. This had to be a clerical error.

"She shouldn't have that's for damn sure." Danbridge's lips curled, accentuated by blood-red lipstick. "Don't expect your mother to save your ass when you need back-up." Deep creases arrowed at the outer edge of her eyes. Her voice was low and mean. "I have a lot of friends in Quantico."

Was that a threat? Mallory turned on her heel and strode back to her desk. She called Quantico and got nothing but a terse change of orders spiel and a tight-lipped refusal to let her talk to anyone higher up the food chain. The transfer was with immediate effect. She texted Lucas that she needed to talk to him ASAP, but he didn't reply. A sense of failure wrapped around her like a cold, wet, shroud.

Filing the last of her reports and clearing her desk took most of the day. Two boxes and three plastic bags of belongings were all she had to show from her time in Charlotte. Plus, a few gangbangers safely behind bars and one dead serial killer, she reminded herself. She thought about Janelle Ebert as she hauled her possessions out the main door and past the frost battered trees. Maybe one day she'd look back at her time here and know she'd made a difference. She dumped her boxes in the trunk and slammed it shut. Right now she felt like a puppet on a string. The FBI played the tune, she just danced.

ALEX SWORE AS he drove past Mallory Rooney's small two-story home on the outskirts of Clanton Park. She didn't usually get back from work until late at night, but there she was struggling through the front door with a bunch of boxes.

Her change in routine screwed with his plans. Now he had to rethink.

He parked a couple of blocks over and approached from woods that edged the back of her property. He hoisted himself up a gnarled American oak grateful for the leather gloves he wore. Muscles burned from the strain until he was able to swing a leg over a branch about fifteen feet up, and straddle a bough that allowed him to look over her fence into the shadowed yard. There was a small shed and a rectangle of neatly mown grass. The neighbor's house on the south side was dark; those to the north appeared to be watching TV, images flickering through the drapes like flash photography. A light in Mallory's kitchen filtered outside. She came into sight as she rolled down the kitchen blind. Her features were pinched and tired. It made him wonder what sort of day she'd had, and what sort of woman chose to fight crime when she could afford to live in idle luxury.

The wind rustled the branches around him, the tree creaking and groaning in gentle protest at his weight. He needed to leave. The idea of breaking in while she slept didn't appeal. He didn't want to terrify her should she awaken, and if for any reason she saw his face, she could identify him. Then he'd be well and truly screwed.

Mallory Rooney represented a complication he didn't need. Since his conversation with Jane Sanders, he'd made it his business to learn everything there was to know about the special agent and the initial attraction had ramped up a notch. He liked smart women.

A light went on upstairs. He was about to swing down to the ground to head out when a shadow separated itself from the garden shed. Alex froze as the shadow took a crowbar and inserted it into the lock of the back door and jimmied the wood. The quiet crunch was barely audible from where Alex perched.

He hesitated as the figure slipped inside. *Fuck.* He stayed where he was. Going inside was a massive risk. He lived in a house of cards that could collapse with one wrong move.

His eyes tracked to the upstairs window. Had Mallory heard the guy break in? Did she have her weapon on her? Was she ready to take on the prick? Probably.

But what if she wasn't?

What if she'd removed her weapon and was listening to music or the TV? What if the guy caught her unaware in a blitz attack? Then what?

He dropped to the ground and pulled his ski mask low over his face. He vaulted the fence, sprinted across the grass before slipping silently into the house.

The first thing he noticed was the sound of water rushing through pipes. Mallory was either running a bath or in the shower. Vulnerable. Unaware.

He used all his senses to locate the intruder. Whoever it was knew there was woman in the house and had broken in anyway. The hair on his nape prickled beneath the wool of his cap. A stair creaked. Alex gave it a few seconds before following. He drew a knife from his boot and eased into the sitting room. He left the M1911 pistol he habitually carried in its holster. It was too loud and too deadly to solve this particular problem. He didn't want to be found here, especially armed. He didn't want to kill anyone unsanctioned by The Gateway Project. But he couldn't just abandon a woman to known danger.

Moving swiftly through the house and up the stairs, he

edged carefully around the doorway and peered into the master bedroom. Sure enough, the guy—tall, lean, dressed head to foot in black just like Alex—stood outside the bathroom door. No obvious sign of a weapon, although the pockets of the black jacket bulged with something and it was doubtful they were Girl Scout cookies. No sign of Mallory so she was presumably behind that bathroom door. *That* was a good thing. The only plus about the whole goddamned fiasco.

Now Alex had to get this asshole out of here without Mallory knowing she'd had uninvited guests. The intruder put his hand on the knob. That's when Alex noticed the surgical gloves. Hatred uncurled in his gut that this man meant to harm a woman, and had probably done it before. This guy was the sort of offender The Gateway Project was trying to eliminate, but it wasn't up to Alex to pick targets. He just carried out orders.

Moving swiftly, Alex got his knife to the would-be assailant's throat before the other man could open the door. The eyes behind the mask widened, then glittered. Alex used his left hand to indicate the guy head down the stairs.

It would have all worked fine if the guy hadn't decided to make a break for it. He slung his elbow high toward Alex's face. Alex dodged. He didn't intend to leave any DNA either. The guy had a slight size advantage and used it to try and swing around and capture Alex in a bear hug. Alex twisted out of his grip and danced on the balls of his feet out of the way of the other man, swiping the razor edge of his blade in an arc in front of him. They faced each other in a standoff.

The door clicked. There stood Mallory, wrapped in a blue towel, in a firing stance with a Glock 21 clutched in a two-handed grip. If she saw his face, his life was over. Alex palmed the knife. Before she could react, he twisted the pistol out of her hands. A shot went into the wall, the recoil punching both of their joined hands before he secured the weapon and pushed her away from him. Out of the corner of his eye, Alex watched the other asshole flee. Five seconds later, the front door crashed open and he was gone.

Dammit. The evening had not gone to plan. If he was caught here he'd be labeled a burglar, a Peeping Tom, maybe even a rapist. His company's reputation would be damaged, his friends would feel betrayed. This underlined all the reasons he insisted on seeing proof of a target's crimes before he took them out. Circumstantial evidence was not enough.

Her eyes were huge amber pools. There was fear there, but there was also anger, and frankly he didn't blame her. He backed toward the window and opened it wide, popping the screen with one hand and flinging it onto the bed.

"What do you think you're doing?" Her voice was raspy.

He didn't dare speak. Voices dug deep into peoples' subconscious and he wouldn't risk being identified. And no way in hell would he risk getting in a firefight with Special Agent Mallory Rooney. He pointed the gun at the floor and climbed over the window ledge.

She crossed her hands over her chest. Lips pinched. Eyes narrowed. "That's a second floor window." *Asshole* seemed implied.

He tossed her Glock behind him onto the lawn and lowered himself as far as he could before dropping the remaining ten feet to the grass. Her hands reached for him but she was too late. When he hit the ground, he rolled the same way he did for parachute jumps and sprang to his feet, no harm done. She yelled at him to stop, but he was already gone. Twenty seconds later he was deep in the heart of the woods, running like a greyhound as branches whipped his face. He ripped off the knit cap and black fleece to reveal a shirt and tie beneath. He stopped running when he hit the sidewalk and worked his way calmly back to his rental car. He got in, stuffed his clothes under the passenger seat, looking like just another ordinary Joe on his way home from work.

He did a quick drive along nearby streets and back alleys, searching for the intruder but saw no one. Calling it quits, he drove back to the airport where he knew a pilot who'd fly him wherever he needed to go with no questions and even less paperwork. He kept trying to shake the image of Mallory Rooney standing wrapped in a towel with her gun drawn, alone and valiant against the world, but he couldn't.

If she ever found out who he was, she'd be holding that gun on him for real. And he'd have to make a decision what to do about it.

THE BEHAVIORAL ANALYSIS Unit was no longer secreted in the dark depths of the basement, but instead set up in a smart spread of office space, complete with ubiquitous gray cubicles. Mallory headed toward the reception desk, feeling like a fraud. She'd packed the previous day while her backdoor was replaced by a sturdier model and an alarm system installed. Then she'd driven to DC. No word on the assailants, and local CSIs hadn't found any finger or palm prints to run through the system. B&E's were hardly rare occurrences in one of the fastest growing cities in the US, but what was more unusual—though not unheard of—was two perps wearing ski masks.

Because she was a federal agent the detectives and evidence techs had been thorough, but nothing had been stolen and, *Thank Christ*, the guy who'd jumped out of the window had left her gun behind. Her face still burned with humiliation at how easily he'd disarmed her.

She'd been about to get in the shower when she'd seen shadows moving under the door. Thankfully she'd still been wearing her backup because her primary weapon was downstairs in the drawer where she kept it. She didn't want to think about what would have happened if the men hadn't panicked and fled when confronted. She put it out of her mind. Training and situational awareness had kept her safe and it was no good worrying about might-have-beens.

A packing company was coming in and storing all her personal belongings. She'd just brought along the essentials for now—clothes, toiletries, computer, and her sister's files. She'd moved into her father's DC apartment until she figured out if this appointment was permanent. It was a forty-five minute commute, which was OK. Her dad spent most of his time as a federal judge in West Virginia and had bought the apartment when he and her mother had first separated, but were still pretending to be a couple. Now he kept it for retirement.

Mallory stood uncertainly in front of the reception desk in Quantico, noting the number of curious glances she was getting. She bit down on her lip and figured everyone here had pegged her body language as flat out terrified and she should just own it. She took a hesitant step toward a secretary's desk.

"Special Agent Rooney." The bark came from behind her and she whirled, clutching her messenger bag to her chest. Silver-haired SSA Hanrahan strode toward her, face stern and manner, frankly, not that welcoming. Her heart did a nosedive.

"Follow me."

She set off after him, trotting obediently like a dog brought to heel. Her mother had sworn inside out that she hadn't pulled any political strings to get her this job, but nothing else made sense. So she hadn't felt one iota of guilt when she'd refused to take part in this year's planned media stunt and even refused her mother's dinner invitation for this evening. If she felt bad for not being with her mother on this particular anniversary it was balanced by a dull rage that simmered just below her skin. She hated being manipulated.

She followed SSA Hanrahan down the impersonal corridor into his office. Hopefully she could convince him to change his mind and give this assignment to someone more deserving.

The office was crammed full of bookshelves, a big desk, two chairs and two computers with large monitors. The window overlooked the parking lot with the assault course that had brought her to her knees on more than one occasion, hidden in the nearby woods.

"Shut the door and take a seat."

She did, crossing her legs and uncrossing them, then crossing them again.

"Christ. Relax. You're making me dizzy." Hanrahan took his gaze off her legs, but it wasn't lust shining from his blue eyes, it was something akin to pity. "Your shiner's gone, I see. You certainly had a busy week."

She nodded. He'd obviously been checking up on her and that made her a little uneasy. "I don't know what I'm doing here," she admitted. "I never even applied for this position."

A smile made all the lines on his face deepen. "I know you

didn't."

"I don't want to be here just because my mother pulled some strings."

"Is that what you believe?" The intensity of his stare was unnerving.

"Yes."

He looked relieved. "And if I told you your mother had nothing to do with your appointment?"

She leaned forward. "Then I'd say you're either a very good liar or I don't understand."

"What if I told you I was so impressed by your performance at the briefing last Monday I decided I wanted you working here with me?"

"I'd say your reputation must be a fallacy or you've recently suffered a head injury." She shook her head. Maybe she could get herself fired by being honest. "I looked like a moron at that briefing."

"No, you didn't." He leaned back in his chair and sighed. "I'm not good at all this maneuvering and political bullshit."

Mallory closed her eyes and prayed the floor would just swallow her up. "I see."

"I don't think you do."

"Then tell me what is going on."

He pressed his lips together and stared at her like he was looking to find something wrong with her—the same way he'd stared at her during the briefing.

"Just *tell* me." She sounded exactly how she felt. Nervous and pissed.

"I didn't want to do this today…"

Mallory flinched. "Because today is my first day in a new office or because it's the anniversary of my sister's disappearance?"

Again he remained silent even as his eyes probed her. What the hell was going on?

Finally he spoke. "You were looking into vigilante killings on ViCAP."

Of all the things she'd expected him to say, that wasn't it. She nodded. "I think I've found several cases that have enough common features to warrant further investigation."

"What exactly did you find?"

She told him about several suspected killers, sex offenders and pedophiles being found dead under suspicious circumstances. "They were called in afterward as suspects by anonymous tipsters that couldn't be traced."

"Maybe nobody really tried?"

"Well *I* tried. And *Mike Tanner* tried." She stared at him. Everyone knew Mike Tanner was one of the best. Her arms crossed tight across her chest and then it struck her. "How do you know I was looking into vigilantes?"

"I have some flags setup for when people start searches using particular terms. *Vigilante* and *anonymous tip* are two of those phrases."

She didn't know what to say.

"Did you talk to anyone about your suspicions?"

God, she wished he wouldn't watch her like that, like he wanted to dissect her mind. This guy dealt with serial killers—did he really think she could hide anything from him? Or that she wanted to?

"I tried to contact Special Agent Lucas Randall who is leading the investigation into Meacher's death, but I couldn't reach him." She'd assumed he was pissed with her the same way everyone else was pissed with her. Landing a plum assignment by virtue of who she knew rather than how good she was at her job. But now she wasn't so sure her mother had been involved at all…

"No best friend, significant other?"

She shook her head. There was something in Hanrahan's gaze. Satisfaction? Relief? "Tell me what's going on."

"What do you think is going on?"

Her heart pounded with sudden anger. "You sound like my childhood shrink."

Sadness tugged at his mouth. "I am sorry about your sister, you know."

She nodded. What sane person wouldn't be sorry about something like that?

He was waiting for her to catch up, she realized. She was supposed to have figured something out already. "So you think there's a vigilante too?"

His mouth formed a thin straight line. "I do."

"Then why didn't you let me start an investigation in Charlotte?"

He drew in a deep breath through his nose. Even his breathing seemed controlled and patient.

The clues clicked into place.

"Because you think they'd find out." Mallory sat up straighter. "You think whoever the vigilante is, they have access to ViCAP? You think they have the same sort of flags in place that you do, in case someone starts searching?"

"I'm almost certain they have some sort of early warning system in place, but whoever it is hides their tracks better than my IT guy can uncover them, and he's the best the Bureau has."

"But in that case they already know I had suspicions about

vigilantism…”

He nodded. “When you fail to continue the search after your transfer here they’ll relax their guard and assume you’ve moved on to other cases.”

“And will I?”

“To all intents and purposes.”

“So you brought me here to…what? To protect me?”

His laugh was deeply amused. “You’re a federal agent. You get to protect yourself.” He leaned forward over his desk. “They appear to have access to all the same information we do, including criminal profiles.”

That was a scary thought. Mallory swallowed the knot in her throat because she suddenly knew what he was worried about. “You think they have a source inside the FBI?”

“Worse.” He held her gaze. “I think they have a mole in the BAU. Someone here has been compromised. If I open an investigation I risk sending that person to ground and we’ll never catch them, not to mention if this gets out it’ll damage the reputation of a great group of highly motivated individuals who dedicate their lives to catching bad guys.” He closed his eyes and pinched the bridge of his nose. “Every law enforcement agency in the US would hesitate to bring us in to consult. We can’t afford that. The people of this country can’t afford that.”

Mallory licked dry, cracked lips. “So you brought me here, to what? Spy on the others?” She didn’t like the idea of betraying the people she trusted with her life.

“I used the fact you have a powerful mother to get you on my team without anyone suspecting that we’re onto them. No one can know about it. Not your friends, not your family. It’s imperative this remains a secret.” His gaze drilled into hers. “I want you to go in there," he pointed to his door, "make friends, make mistakes, look like a non-threat and basically worm your way into their work and lives. It's going to take time—months, maybe years. You'll have to join the next training session when it starts, which will take more time, but it will gain you experience and contacts." His words hit her like hail, each one stinging just a little bit harder. "I'm putting you in a highly vulnerable position. Whether we catch this person or not, you're going to catch flak from all sides."

"Do I get a raise?"

From the narrowing of his eyes now wasn't the best time to joke. "I don't know if you realize how serious this is."

"Oh, I think I've figured it out." She felt sick inside. "When this is over, if we are wrong about our theory that there's a vigilante I'll be perceived as a blue flamer who got her position because her mother is a senator and will have zero credibility. If we do apprehend a mole, I'll be seen as someone not to trust because she rats on her colleagues." She was screwed either way, but she was also trapped.

A wry smile caught her off guard.

"If it's any consolation, I *was* impressed by your work in Charlotte."

She raised a dubious eyebrow at him. *Sure.* "Do you think this mole and vigilante are one and the same person?"

"No, I've been attempting to keep tabs on where agents from this office are when these deaths occur. They all have alibis, although alibis are rarely foolproof."

"Do you think they're dangerous?" she asked quietly.

"The person putting bullets in people is most assuredly a trained assassin—so I'd categorize them as dangerous. The people who work in this office—generally—" a bushy brow bobbed up and down at her, "have worked long and hard to get here." His lips pursed. "They aren't going to want to go to jail without a fight."

Fantastic.

"So, are you up for it?"

"Do I have a choice?"

"You can say no and I'll reassign you, but I don't think you will."

He was right. But probably not for the reasons he thought. Yes, she wanted to root out bad guys. But here, in the heart of the BAU, she had the opportunity to pick the brains of people who lived and breathed serial killers and child abduction.

Even though she hated the idea of spying on her colleagues, she'd never have a better chance to pursue her sister's investigation than this. She held out her hand and shook his. "I'm in."

Hanrahan smiled but she was overwhelmed by sudden loneliness. The search for answers was never ending. For the first time since she'd been accepted into the FBI academy, she found herself wondering if she'd made the right choice. Rather than chasing shadows, maybe a better tribute to her sister would have been to live a full and happy life. As Hanrahan led her out of his office and down the hall to her new office, she realized something else. She owed her mom a big fat apology.

CHAPTER FIVE

THE BAR WAS in an upscale DC hotel just a block from her father's apartment. She'd given herself permission to go out, get drunk and spend the weekend recovering, something she hadn't done since she finished law school. It was a Friday night in November and the place was dimly lit and packed by what looked like some weird engineering convention. Mallory grabbed an empty stool at the end of the bar. She slipped out of her coat and draped it over her knees, ordered a shot of McClelland's.

"Thanks."

She raised her glass in a toast to her sister and knocked back the drink. She'd put on make-up and changed into a black cocktail number so they'd think she was meeting someone for dinner and be less likely to throw her out before she hit her limit. She needed something to make her forget and sitting alone in her apartment with a bottle of scotch seemed even more pathetic than surrounding herself with strangers. She had friends in the city but she didn't want to see anyone—not tonight.

Eighteen years ago tonight, she'd gone to bed and by the time she'd woken up, her life, and that of many others, had been destroyed. Why had the bastard taken Payton and not her? Had she said or done something to put her sister at risk?

Was it her fault, or just blind luck?

Mallory had been a sleepwalker—had she been gone when the kidnapper arrived?—then climbed back into bed and slept on in childish oblivion? Had she unlocked the front door? Let someone into the house? She didn't know. Couldn't remember. The night was blocked from her memory. All she remembered was waking up and Payton being gone. She raised her finger to the barman who gave her a nod while he dealt with another customer.

Festive lights twinkled and Michael Bublé sang "Jingle Bells." If she'd had her weapon she'd have blasted the sound system into a thousand component parts.

She sipped the next drink and it scorched her throat. When that was finished, she switched to a white wine spritzer before the barman cut her off. She wanted to get drunk but she didn't want to be unconscious. Not yet anyway.

In the space of one week, her nice orderly progression through the ranks of the FBI had been turned on its head. She'd been burglarized, managed to upset her mother, and she was being sent into a new job for the express purpose of spying on her colleagues and figuring out if one of them was in league with a killer and therefore a potential candidate for Death Row.

Great.

It was not a way to make friends and Mallory was sadly lacking in friends these days. Someone brushed against her as they took the stool beside her. She set her teeth and narrowed her eyes as she stared into the bubbles in her wine. If someone tried to pick her up she was going to hurt them.

"I didn't expect to see you in DC, Special Agent Rooney."

Blinking in surprise, she turned to see Alex Parker sitting

beside her. Her heart gave a panicked little flutter. Not now. Not tonight.

But why not tonight? Everything else was messed up, why not this?

Screw it. She raised her glass in salute and took a big gulp. "My plans unexpectedly changed. Do you come here often, Mr. Parker?" There was a bitter edge to her tone. She was unaccountably glad to see him, but she didn't want company for tonight's meltdown. She just wanted mindless oblivion. No interested bystanders.

"Sometimes." He shrugged. He looked different today. Still gorgeous, but not in a businessman way. A black T-shirt molded well-defined muscles and well-worn jeans hugged the rest. Her eyes traveled over him as he ordered a beer. A tattoo peeked just beneath the edge of his sleeve. He looked like the soldier he'd once been rather than the security consultant he now was. He caught her eye, expression serious. "Do you mind if I sit here?"

She shook her head though she was torn. Fact was she wanted to get to know the guy—and wanted to spend time outside of her own head for a change. But talking wasn't nearly as satisfying as drowning her sorrows for a few hours or days.

"This doesn't violate your no-dating rule?"

Her mouth went dry. "Sitting beside me does not violate the no-dating rule."

His eyes darkened to charcoal. "How about talking? Would talking violate the no-dating rule?"

The wine cooled as it slid down her throat. But a warm glow spread through her stomach and her muscles started to unknot. The alcohol was finally doing its job. "Talking doesn't violate the no-dating rule either, but I don't have much to say right now. In fact I'm not very good company." She may as well be honest. He seemed like a nice guy and she didn't believe in stringing people along. Unfortunately she didn't have any choice at work for the foreseeable future. *Great.* She was being pathetic and she hated pathetic. She took another gulp of wine.

"I'm not much of a talker either." The edge of his lips curled and she felt a sexual ping down to her toes. The man had a sinful mouth. Full lips and a small cleft in his chin. And he smelled good too. Like sandalwood soap and clean male skin. "Any particular reason we're celebrating tonight?" He tipped a beer bottle to his lips and she watched the muscles in his throat work as he swallowed.

Then it struck her.

He didn't know.

He didn't know about her tragic past.

God.

Relief burst through her that someone in the universe didn't consider her an object of pity. She finished her wine and ordered another whiskey.

"Make that two." Alex told the barman.

They sat in silence, nursing their drinks, listening to Michael Bublé sing "All I Want for Christmas Is You." The melancholy of this time of year drifted over her like a cloud. The week before Thanksgiving marked her sister's abduction. Christmas itself marked a big fat void in her family's life. An empty seat at the table. Years of unopened presents.

Mallory wasn't in the mood for shots anymore. She had a nice buzz going and a different kind of energy was invading her cells. For some reason, the stupid sentimental Christmas song reminded her she hadn't had sex in over two years and that the guy sitting next to her was not only built, he'd actually asked her out. He wasn't some stranger pick-up; he was one of Lucas Randall's best friends, and Lucas didn't tolerate assholes. She caught herself leaning closer to him because he smelled so damn good. The biceps in his arms bunched under that tattoo every time he took a drink and she felt a funny little quiver just from looking at him. Her gaze ran over the hair cut short on the nape of his neck, the wide shoulders, and taut stomach. Even his boots were sexy. She turned away, only to catch his gaze in the mirror behind the bar. He smiled wryly. He'd seen her checking him out and the heat in those gray depths told their own story.

Desire coiled deep inside. She looked down into her glass but wasn't feeling thirsty anymore.

Her skin felt hypersensitive. Nipples beaded against the black silk of her dress making her arousal obvious. She felt his eyes on her. Felt the weight of interest. Heat flamed through her body. There was a quiver between her legs that had her squeezing her thighs together.

Anticipation. Want.

She licked her lips and he stopped watching her through the mirror and turned toward her instead. There was an alertness in his gaze. A gravity in the way he looked at her. The guy was incredibly sexy. Perfectly symmetrical face. Strong jaw. Bedroom eyes and that damn mouth of his. There were other ways to find oblivion…

She caught a drip of amber liquid down the outside of her glass with her fingertip and sucked it dry. She heard a low almost indiscernible growl and smiled. The idea of turning him on thrilled her. It was like she'd stepped into somebody else's skin. She never did this. She'd never picked up a guy in a bar in her life before, but to say she was going through a dry spell when it came to men was a massive understatement.

And, technically, sex wasn't dating.

She squirmed in her seat. Michael Bublé wasn't annoying her half as much as he had earlier. *Sorry, Michael. All is forgiven.* An image of Payton singing Christmas carols flashed through her brain, but with the reminder of her sister came the desperate need to forget what tonight was really all about.

She dropped her hand to his thigh. Felt his muscles tense to stone.

"Want to go somewhere quieter?"

His gaze held hers, his eyes almost black now. With desire? She didn't know. He took her hand from his thigh and squeezed her fingers. "That must break the no-dating rule."

"Only if we kiss," she said.

"What?" The word came out gruffly.

"I've been giving it some thought." *What if he said no?* She didn't want him to say no. "We only break the no-dating rule if I kiss you."

"If *you* kiss *me*?" Damn, she liked the color of his eyes when they went all smoky and dark.

"Correct." She nodded and held onto the bar. *Oops.* That first drink was catching up with her and it felt magical not to worry about every little thing. But she was a federal agent, she didn't want to fall over in public. She slipped money on the bar and slid off the stool. Her coat drifted to the floor. Alex picked it up and held it open while she slid it on. The brush of cold satin against her bare arms was delicious but it was the touch of his fingers that had her quivering.

"I'll walk you."

Did that mean he wasn't interested? Or was he being polite

and pretending she wasn't a sure thing?

They were out of the lobby and standing on the sidewalk. The frigid wind took her breath. Ice blasted her face and legs as she huddled into her coat. "Oh my God, why did I wear nylons?" Her teeth chattered despite the long wool coat and she stamped her feet in her stupid heels.

Alex looked down at her legs. "Why *did* you wear nylons? It's thirty degrees out here." But he was only wearing a light jacket and didn't look even remotely cold.

"Because..." She grabbed his arm as the lights started to whirl behind him "...these places let you drink more if you don't look like a bum."

They started walking along the wide sidewalk and she snuggled against him. The stars were bright in the frosty night though it was hard to see them through the DC glow. She'd forgotten how much she loved this city, and how good it felt to be with a man you were attracted to.

"And you wanted to drink more because...?"

Despite the buzz, that question hurt. God. She blinked away a sheen of moisture, pretended it was the vicious wind in her eyes. She needed another drink, or a kiss. She stopped him with a tug, whirled to face him and slid her hands up his chest. The man felt like he was carved out of granite and there was so much heat pouring off him she wanted to crawl inside his skin. How did men produce so much heat? It didn't seem fair. She slipped her arms around his neck and felt his hands settle low on her waist. Desire made her ache. Her breasts were pressed against his chest and she swore she could feel his heartbeat through the thick wool of her coat. He was watching her with a wary expression. She leaned forward to taste his lips but he reared back when she was just a whisper away.

His breath was warm on her face. "You forgot your no-dating rule."

"I did?" He was getting a little blurry around the edges, but the sense of safety he invoked wrapped around her like a cloak. She pulled back, then wagged her finger at him. "That's *right.*"

There was something she'd forgotten about that rule but it was so damn cold outside and the sooner they got to her apartment, the sooner she could find out if the muscles beneath that T-shirt looked as good as they felt. Her teeth chattered and he put his arm around her again.

"You're freezing." He tucked her close.

For years this night had been filled with nothing but painful memories. She wanted to blast that away. Wanted to erase all memory of those gut-churning uneaten dinners at her mother's table, and all the useless, endless grief.

What was her mother doing right now?

Guilt tried to cut in, tried to make her change her mind about Alex but the feel of him against her was so much better than the agony of reliving the worst day of her life. And then they were outside her apartment building—*magic.*

She delved for her wallet in her pocket but she couldn't pull it out.

"Let me." He slipped his hand inside her coat and they both jumped as his hand brushed the apex of her thigh. He froze, opened his mouth with what looked like an apology so she took his face in both hands and kissed him. *Who cared about the stupid rules?*

His lips were surprisingly soft, his mouth tasting of whiskey and beer and really hot man. Suddenly he took control of the kiss, diving deeper, tongue tangling with hers with a possession that made her insides turn molten. She found herself pressed up against the glass facade of the building, Alex's one hand still buried deep in her pocket, the other cupping the back of her head.

His body pressed tight to hers in a perfect fit. She didn't feel cold anymore. She felt like her skin was about to ignite. A groan reverberated in his chest though the hand trapped in her pocket remained frustratingly still and she desperately wanted him to touch her. She dragged her mouth from his on a gasp, suddenly aware they were in a public place.

"Let's go inside." Her voice came out all breathy and sultry.

He eased away from her and disengaged her wallet from her pocket and took out the keycard. Then he opened the lobby door for her. She headed inside, tugging his hand but he didn't budge.

"I can't, Mallory." The look in his eyes was tortured.

"What?" After that kiss there was absolutely no doubt he wanted her.

"I can't come up," he repeated.

"Why not? Are you married?" The disappointment in her voice would have made her wince on a normal day. Today had never been normal. Today was Groundhog Day with a twist. Well, she wasn't taking it anymore. If she had to strip naked in the street she was switching things up tonight and Alex Parker was just the man to help her.

"Not married or involved with anyone else right now, but…" He laughed but there was enough desperation in the sound to deny the humor. "You've had too much to drink. You're not thinking properly. I don't want to be something you regret in the morning."

Dismay bubbled up inside her. "I'm not that drunk."

He didn't look convinced.

"Really." *Please don't change your mind.* She bit her lip and watched his pupils flare and didn't think she was reading the signs wrong. *Okay.* She was going to have to seduce the guy. She frowned. How did you seduce a guy? If she'd ever known, she'd forgotten. He let go of her hand and she used the movement to slip out of her coat. It slid to the floor and, as Alex bent down to pick it up, the lobby door closed behind him. Grinning, she headed to the elevator, making sure she didn't wobble on her damn heels. So what if she was slightly tipsy? Was that illegal? No, sir, it damn well wasn't.

Holding the elevator door open she slipped out of her shoes and let them dangle from her fingers. He stood there looking edgy and uncertain, holding her keycard in one hand and coat in the other.

"I know what I'm doing, Mr. Parker."

At that, one side of his mouth curled up and his eyes gleamed. "I can see that."

She leaned against the side of the elevator and then let go of the button. He eyed the door behind him like an escape route and she thought he was going to just stand there as the doors closed between them. Then suddenly he was in the elevator and she didn't even see him move.

HE WATCHED THE drunken whore from the dark interior of his car. When the bastard pinned her to the wall outside her apartment block he wanted to pull his gun and put a bullet in them both. Today of all days he'd expected a little more respect for her sister's memory. Fury expanded through his body. She wasn't half the person Payton had been. She'd have been ashamed to see what her sister had become—a whore, a cheap cunt.

He checked his pistol. Gripped the door handle just as they went inside the building. *Shit.*

He watched for a moment. Waited for a light to come on somewhere in the apartment building, but it never happened. The image of them fucking seared his brain. Even though she wasn't Payton, watching them had been like seeing his beloved cheat on him and he couldn't stand the idea. His heartbeat sped up and he imagined taking his knife and carving her sister's name on her forehead. But she wasn't even worthy of that. His hands shook as he started the engine. He'd carve *slut* instead.

He checked his shoulder and pulled away, driving out of the city and heading for Route 66. His plans had gone awry. He'd expected to catch Mallory alone, maybe even waiting for him. A smile gripped his mouth. He was going to have to educate her on what he expected. Payton had never needed a lecture, not even a raised voice. She'd been perfect. Always happy to see him.

The highway was quiet even though it wasn't that late. He was working tomorrow so he needed to get back anyway. Just as well he hadn't taken her tonight. He needed to figure out a plan of exactly how to deal with this female who looked so like the woman he'd loved but acted like a hooker. An idea formed—he needed to remind her of her sister, needed to make her give a damn. He was pretty sure he knew how to do it.

His eyes snagged a lone figure on the side of the road. Female. Caucasian. Dark hair.

Don't do it. Temptation warred with common sense. *Keep driving.*

He indicated, slowed, and pulled over. *Dammit.* Rolled down the window. "Where you headed?"

The girl—late teens, early twenties—took a hesitant step forward. "Gainesville." Her eyes scanned the interior. Her teeth chattered as she huddled into her hoodie. It was well-below freezing with more snow on the way. "No offense but I only hitch with other women in the car."

He shrugged. "Fine by me, but good luck getting a woman to stop for you this time of night." He started to roll the window back up but with a quick glance at the quiet highway, she put her fingers on top of the glass.

"Wait!" Her smile was unsure. "Okay. I'd love a ride if you don't mind."

He smiled at her. She seemed like a nice kid, a hell of a lot more like Payton than Mallory was turning out to be. "Hop in."

She climbed in and braced her backpack on her lap. He pulled onto the road and for the first time in hours felt good. He shot a quick glance at the girl's profile. She had a sweet face. Brown eyes...

Maybe she was the one? Not Mallory, but this unknown girl?

He felt like he was being tested.

He sat straighter in his seat. He'd figure it out. It would take time and patience and determination. That was okay. He had all three and Mallory Rooney wasn't going anywhere he couldn't follow.

THIS WAS A mistake. A huge unmitigated fucking disaster. But he needed to know Mallory was safely inside her apartment and then he'd leave. Yeah, he was a real boy scout. Always helping old ladies across the road and nailing serial killers between the eyes.

But maybe he could make this work. A quick in and out—and not the sort his body craved.

If he got access to her laptop he could download software that let him monitor everything she did. He could also place the tiny camera he had in his pocket in her office or living room. He glanced at her across the elevator and resisted scrubbing his hand over his face.

Who the hell did he think he was kidding? He wanted her. But there was no way it was going to happen. She was drunk and hurting.

When he'd followed her into that bar earlier he'd known she was on the verge of some precipice. He understood the significance of the date and how it might screw up someone who was usually sensible and sober. He'd intervened when he had seen a couple of guys eyeing her like fresh meat. Figured he'd watch her get drunk, scare off anyone bigger and hairier than he was, carry her home and make sure she got safely to bed. Alone. Despite being a cold-blooded killer, the chivalry gene was alive and well in his DNA.

Go figure.

It was still a workable idea. As long as he didn't think about joining her. Because although his boss had ordered him to keep an eye on the special agent, it probably didn't include shoving his tongue down her throat and checking out her tonsils.

Mallory leaned against the metal walls of the elevator and

ran one stocking-clad foot up and down the back of her calf. She looked so damn sexy he wanted to stop the thing then and there, and kiss her until neither of them could stand.

Not happening.

Just a few nights ago he'd confronted her in her bedroom and scared her half to death. Now he was kissing her? Playing with fire, that was for damn sure. Tonight she looked fragile and in need of protection. She looked as if one tiny ding might make her shatter, which immediately made him think about watching her come and he shook his head. What the hell was wrong with him? What about this woman turned him inside out?

Prior to screwing up the Moroccan mission he'd dated plenty of beautiful women who meant nothing to him—he didn't even remember their names. Mallory was different. Everything about her was different; including the fact she was an FBI agent who'd nail his ass to the wall if she ever figured out what he really was.

It wasn't just her appearance that got to him, although those tilted eyes had an elfin look that did something to his insides. There was some inner glow that called to him. *Pussy.* He couldn't afford this sort of attachment. He couldn't afford to think about anything except fulfilling his commitment to The Gateway Project. Whatever people might think, he was an honorable man who paid his debts and kept his promises—five-hundred thirty-eight days and counting.

He stayed away from her during the elevator ride but the smell of her subtle flowery scent, the sound of her uneven breaths, dragged across his nerves like razor wire. They went up to the sixth floor and he followed her to her father's door, trying to keep his eyes off her body in that excuse for a dress.

"Is this your place?" he asked. Like he didn't know.

"My father's, but he lives in West Virginia."

He followed her inside. The lights were off but the drapes were open, revealing a magnificent view of the city lit up for the festive season. A crackle of awareness shot over his skin as the door clicked shut behind him. Okay, she was home safe. He draped her coat over the back of the couch and watched her walk away from him. Just the sight of her drove him crazy. He started backing up. He'd break in some other time to plant the bugs, when she wasn't standing there looking so totally fuckable. Time to get out.

"Would you like a drink?"

He spotted her laptop and hesitated. The chance of him gaining access to that was much lower because she took it almost everywhere with her and, as a fed, she had decent security from malware. He could do it, but it might leave tracks. "Sure."

The fact she'd been transferred to Quantico before she'd had time to do more than run a few searches on vigilantes was both a relief and a worry. The inside man—or woman—was keeping a close eye on her but with Lucas Randall being the case officer investigating the Meacher murder, there was a chance Mallory would at some point share her suspicions with his buddy. Alex needed to know if and when that happened.

He hated lying to his friend, hated lying to this woman who took her job seriously, but the alternative was much worse. The Gateway Project operated in stealth mode, however, this little wave of scrutiny had made everyone sink a little deeper into the shadows. Alex wasn't sure how far a clandestine government organization like this would go to keep its secrets, but given the potential consequences of what they were doing, he figured they wouldn't baulk at a few dead law enforcement officials along the way. No way would he let that happen.

He doubted Mallory was in any real danger from their operation, but right now he wasn't sure she was safe from herself.

"You realize you brought a virtual stranger into your home? What if I was some sick bastard?"

"You're not."

"How do you know?"

"Lucas is a good judge of character and he obviously likes you." She bent over to turn on the stereo, that skimpy dress rising high enough to give him a heart attack. Despite the alcohol she'd consumed—with the efficiency of a sailor on shore leave—she moved with the fluid grace of a dancer. "I wouldn't have brought just anyone home." She waggled her finger at him. "Plus, I have a gun"—she sure as hell wasn't armed right now because that dress wouldn't hide a quarter let alone a pistol—"and friends in the IRS. So if you *are* a sick bastard I'll make your life a living hell just as soon as I wake up Monday morning."

Despite her attempt at humor, something about the idea of Monday morning obviously depressed the shit out of her. What was that all about? BAU was a dream job for FBI agents, and she'd only been at Quantico for a day. She hadn't even had time to unpack her desk yet, much less piss anyone off.

She went over to her father's liquor cabinet and started poking through the bottles. She found the single malt, holding it up with a triumphant grin, poured them both a drink. He took the heavy crystal tumblers from her hands before she could take a sip.

"Slow down. You're going to make yourself ill." He put the drinks on the coffee table, trying to talk her out of self-destruct.

"I don't care." Tears welled up out of nowhere and her frantic blinking tore at a part of himself he'd long thought dead. "There's something I need to forget tonight, Alex. And trust me, I'm not even half drunk enough to do that yet."

"So you want to get hammered and fuck me blind so you don't have to remember?" He'd hoped the blunt words would snap her back to reality but instead he saw her soul drowning in her big amber eyes.

"Yes," she said simply.

CHAPTER SIX

THAT SINGLE WORD was like a kick in the gut. So he did another stupid thing. He kissed her, diving from about a thousand feet and landing with a silky glide of tongues. She tasted just as good as she had when they were outside on the sidewalk, like whiskey, rich, sophisticated and so damn hot it seared his flesh. His pulse pounded and he pulled back, breathing hard. He couldn't do this. He wasn't being honest. If she found out he'd lied to her after they had sex—tonight of all nights—she'd be furious. She deserved better than being fucked over by a lowlife like him.

He stroked her hair off her forehead and the touch made her quiver. "I have to go."

She pressed her lips together and pulled out of his arms. "Fine." Then she skirted around him, grabbed her coat off the couch and walked stiffly to the door.

"Where are you going?" But, shit, he already knew.

"Back to the bar." She was barefoot but didn't seem to notice as she struggled into her big wool coat. "I told you, I just want to forget for one night."

"Forget what?" His mouth went dry, choking on deception. Maybe he could keep her here by talking.

"*Everything.*"

Christ. Part of him wanted to shake her, make her appreciate the risks she was taking just by drinking too much, let alone seducing some stranger. But being lectured on life choices by an assassin was too hypocritical, even for him.

She held her head high but tears glittered in her eyes.

He'd made her feel bad. *Great.* Dread settled over him. Dread and an odd sense of defeat. The arousal of his body stretched his nerves taut. He could ignore his own needs; it was hers that crushed him. He eyed the liquor, picked up one glass and knocked it back, then picked up the other and did the same. *If you can't beat 'em...*

He understood the need to forget, to block out vast chunks of life—he'd give every last cent to eradicate certain parts of his memory—the death of his buddies in Afghanistan; the torture inflicted in Morocco; the faces of the men he'd eliminated in an effort to make the world a better place. Unfortunately there wasn't enough money in the world to obliterate some things.

She stood by the door, watching him. Sad and hurting.

This wasn't love or romance. This was sex. And he hadn't had sex in so long he could barely remember what it felt like. Now he wanted it—wanted her—with an intensity that should have scared him. He had too many secrets to get involved with anyone, least of all Special Agent Mallory Rooney, but it seemed that where she was concerned he made one bad decision after another.

A one night stand.

It might destroy what little was left of his soul but he had a terrible feeling it would be worth it.

He removed his jacket and pulled his T-shirt over his head, tossed it across the room. Her eyes flashed with shock as they locked onto his body and then his scars. There was the chance she'd be so repulsed she'd kick his ass out the door which would solve both their problems.

The light in her eyes wasn't repulsion. It was empathy. Compassion. Lust.

Okay then.

"Afghanistan?" she asked.

"Some." He couldn't tell her the truth, but lying would be equally impossible, even when she was drunk and hopefully wouldn't remember a word. That revelation startled the shit out of him.

Tonight she needed someone to help her forget and he was going to take one for the team like a good little soldier. What the hell harm could it do? He'd sate the need that raged through his veins and be gone in under an hour. She'd be home, safe and asleep and would have survived another heartbreaking anniversary.

Win-win.

He walked toward her and she watched him with keen awareness. She drew in a deep breath, those pert breasts of hers pressing against the black silk, making his fingers itch to touch. They both knew this was happening now. They were both onboard with where this was going. Because this wasn't about him. She just needed a warm body. *Any* body. He could do that. He could be anybody—he just couldn't be *somebody.*

He stopped in front of her and she dropped her coat to the floor. He traced a finger across the delicate jut of her collarbone. She held her breath. Her skin was soft as rose petals, far more erotic than black silk. His heart expanded in his chest. Something about touching her made him remember what it felt like to stand in front of a firing-squad. So scared his mouth turned to dust.

"Breathe," he reminded them both.

She sucked in a lungful of air and he couldn't resist spanning his hands beneath her breasts and then cupping each one in his palms. He brushed his thumbs over her nipples, once, twice, watching the peaks bead beneath the slippery fabric of her dress. Watched her eyes darken with arousal. Her head fell back against the wall, mouth open, eyes closed, and she was quite simply the most beautiful woman he'd ever seen. A moan came from her lips and he was instantly hard. He stood with his knee between hers and eased up that dress to get a view of mile-long legs encased in lace-edged stockings. Saliva pooled in his mouth. Touching the skin of her inner thigh was the most amazing thing he'd ever experienced.

He kissed her, those perfect pink lips so beautifully soft and giving he wanted to groan. Her tongue touched his in a sensuous sweep that made his heart punch like gunfire against his ribs. His lips found her neck, teeth scraping sweet alabaster skin. He made himself move slowly, sliding his hands over the curves of her breasts, the indent of her hips and the perfect roundness of her ass. Her fingers curled around his nape and up into his hair, pulling him closer. Slowly, so slowly the effort was killing him, he eased one finger inside her panties and slipped into the wet volcanic heat of her center. She went up on tiptoes, hands gripping his shoulders, eyes and mouth going wide in shock. Unable to resist her mouth, he kissed her again, desperate to taste every inch of her body but needing his mouth on hers. He withdrew and slid inside again, keeping up a steady rhythm until she writhed against his palm. She was tight and gasped as he thrust just a little bit deeper.

"Too much?" His voice sounded nothing like him. He'd heard this version before, in that prison in Morocco. His inner animal tearing loose, but this time it was from pleasure not pain.

She shook her head and her nails dug into his shoulders. “More,” she demanded. Then she kissed his neck, bit down hard enough to make him laugh.

She could put her mark on him anytime.

Her breath scorched his skin and he ached at the thought of her turning that pretty mouth on the rest of him the way he wanted to put his mouth on her. He smoothed wetness over her female folds and pressed his palm hard against the sensitive nerves of her clitoris. Her muscles spasmed in reaction. Legs shook. Or maybe that was him. He withdrew and lifted her higher, spreading her legs, making space for himself and rocking against her in a rhythm that made his pulse pound. Heat burst through his skin. Fire burned along his veins.

He kissed her, hungrily. She kissed him back, consumed him with mindless frenzy. Something snapped inside. Whatever measure of control he’d developed over the years broke. He didn’t want to stop. He didn’t want to be good or noble or let her come and leave. It was wrong but nothing mattered except burying himself hilt-deep inside this woman. He dug into his back pocket and pulled out his wallet. Digging one-handed into one of the compartments, cards and cash spilling, until he found the foil package and dropped the wallet to the floor. He let go of her mouth and tore into the package with his teeth. She tried to fumble with his zipper but he eased away, putting her feet gently on the floor as he covered himself and protected them both.

She reached for him but he grabbed her hand. “If you touch me it’s all over. I’ve never wanted to have sex with anyone as much I want to have sex with you right now."

"Good. Hurry." She looked at him with eyes the exact color as the whiskey they'd drunk.

He wanted to tear off her clothes, lay her on a bed and fuck her from top to toe. He also wanted to make love to her until she passed out. The bedroom was way too far away. He dragged her dress up to her waist. Breathing heavily against her ear, he gathered her silk panties in his fist. "Are you sure this is what you want, Mallory?"

She nodded and he ripped the panties clean off. Her fingernails bit into his biceps. He didn't care. She lifted one stocking-clad leg and wrapped it around his hip and he positioned himself at her core and, unable to hold back, thrust deep inside. The pleasure was instantaneous, as was the panic, because he was totally fucked.

"You're so tight." And he'd taken her against a wall. *Moron*. "Am I hurting you?" He went to withdraw but she clutched him tighter.

She shook her head, squirming to get closer. "More," she demanded and nibbled his jaw. Her nails scratched his back, digging into his skin with the sort of pain that aroused him more than he'd ever imagined possible. He wrapped his hand around her other leg and locked them both around his waist. And then every pulsing inch of him was embedded inside her, blasted by the velvet clench of wet heat.

"Okay?" he asked. *Okay* didn't even begin to describe what he was feeling. He was pretty sure the word for it hadn't been invented yet.

"Oh, yes."

Sweat broke out along his brow as he moved inside her. Trapped against the door by his body, her hips strained to meet his thrust for thrust. His brain started to implode. There was nothing but her heat and her eyes and the control she exerted over his entire being just by existing. He was sucked deeper and deeper into the vortex that was Mallory Rooney and he never wanted it to end. She started to come and every good thought or image he'd ever experienced coalesced in his brain and detonated like fireworks as she cried out, sobbing his name. Two more thrusts and her orgasm dragged him over the ledge. He came with an explosive crash that nearly brought him to his knees, a primeval shudder ripping through his frame, heart jack-hammering in his concrete chest.

His skin felt like he'd been electrified. His lungs felt like they'd never again catch a full breath. And then she started to cry.

THE WORLD STARTED spinning. At first Mallory thought it was the drink even though she was starting to sober up way too fast. She was in her bedroom. Alex was searching for the zipper in her dress and then slipping it from her shoulders, undressing her. She was surprised he hadn't run screaming from the apartment.

Seduced by the crazy lady. *Roll up, roll up.*

She squeezed her eyes against scalding hot tears that reduced her to an emotional mess when all she'd wanted was to forget. No matter what she did this day always ended in tears. The whole time she and Alex had been having sex she'd been able to ignore the date and what it represented. As soon as they'd finished, the guilt had smashed back into her like a wrecking ball.

He pulled away. Why wouldn't he? He must think she was a slutty lush with a screw loose. But she wasn't crying because Alex might think badly of her. She and Payton had shared a special connection. When she'd been taken, it had been like losing a limb. She missed her sister. She really missed her sister. And she'd been the lucky one.

Tears kept coming. Tears that drained her of energy and light. Shame washed over her. Not about sex. Sex wasn't important when you lined it up next to the loss or death of a young girl. She was ashamed she hadn't solved the mystery, that despite their almost psychic connection she'd never been able to find her twin. She wanted to crawl under the bedspread and stay there for the whole weekend, or just drown in a bottle—but that was more dangerous. She covered her eyes with her hands. "God, I'm so sorry."

"Shush." He pressed his hands to her shoulders and kissed her cheek. She leaned into that kiss. He unhooked her bra and then removed her stockings. She should have been embarrassed to stand there naked but she didn't care. It reminded her he'd made her forget everything earlier, and maybe he could make her forget again.

She ran her hands over his torso. He had the most amazing body and exploring it was a million times better than thinking about what some sick animal had done to a nine-year old girl, eighteen years ago.

She traced a scar. How had he gotten all these wounds?

He grabbed her hands. "Let me clean up and we'll talk." He went into the bathroom.

The last thing she wanted to do was to talk so she headed back into the living room for another drink. Alex caught her before she got there.

"Let me go." She tried to twist out of his embrace.

"Maybe I don't want to." His arms wrapped around her waist and pulled her tight against him.

"Then you're crazy."

"You and me both, babe. You and me both," he whispered into her hair.

"Will you stay?" She held her breath. She really wanted him not to leave.

She felt his sigh reverberate through her ribcage. "I can't."

Her fingers tightened their grip on his wrists as he nuzzled her neck from behind. He was hard again. She could feel him hot and heavy against her hip, but she wasn't going to beg. "I'm not ready to be alone yet."

He lifted her in his arms and carried her back to the bed, kicked off his boots and climbed in behind her. He held her tight, offering comfort in his warm embrace. It felt good to be held in strong male arms. Better than she remembered. But he was handling her like a fragile child, and she hadn't been a child in a very long time.

"I'm sorry about blubbing on you before." She expected a joke in response. Instead he flipped her on her back.

"Don't apologize," he said fiercely. "Don't you ever apologize to me."

He settled between her thighs like he belonged there and she tilted her pelvis to make the fit even better. A wary expression crossed his features. They both knew if he hadn't been wearing jeans he'd have been inside her again and that's exactly where she wanted him.

He had a tiny scar bisecting his right eyebrow. She hadn't noticed it before, but up close it looked like the sort of injury boxers got. She raised a finger to stroke it. The light in his eyes flickered. Then he closed his eyes and rested his forehead against hers. “I haven’t done a good job of making you forget whatever it is you need to forget.”

“Not true.” She rubbed her palm across the stubble of his jaw. “When you were inside me I forgot everything. I should thank you.”

He squeezed his eyes shut, looked almost in pain. “I should go.” His warm breath brushed her ear, and his hands gripped her shoulders so hard she was going to have bruises tomorrow. She didn’t care.

“Okay.” She licked his bottom lip because she wanted him to stay and despite the words coming out of his mouth he didn’t seem to be in any hurry to leave. She pressed her lips to his and kissed him deeper. Being with Alex took her away from reality and reality sucked.

She ran her hands over his strong back as he finally returned her kiss. His skin was smooth and hot, the muscles rippling in response to her touch.

He shifted, his mouth dipping to her breasts and she arched up off the bed as a fierce rush of pleasure pulsed through her. The scent of him made her hungry. The touch of his mouth and hands made her unable to hold a single thought in her head. Except sex. Sex. Right now. That driving primal urge. She went to work on his buttons and freed him from his pants.

“Condom,” he said between gritted teeth.

Crap.

She jerked open the bedside drawer, relieved to find a box. Alex scrambled out of his jeans, covered and buried himself deep. She locked her legs around his hips and then there were no thoughts, just sensation and pleasure and slick bodies, striving to get as close as possible, striving for that place where nothing else mattered.

Then just when she thought they were racing for the finish, Alex slowed everything down.

He brushed the hair off her forehead and pressed deep inside her, holding her gaze. He thrust again, leisurely, and each time a lick of wonder whipped through her. It felt amazing, one of those sensations you never wanted to end though you knew it couldn't last forever. She matched him, taking the movement deeper, making him blink even though he never dropped her gaze. She was climbing higher and higher, and he was letting her get there slowly, drawing it out, making it last. She clutched at him, gasping as she went flying, out of control and unable to care.

"Fuck, Mallory." And then he was pounding into her and groaning as he too reached that pinnacle where lightning burst along every nerve.

After a few moments they both stilled, skin damp, hearts thumping each other through hollow ribcages.

He started to withdraw. She gripped him tight. "Stay."

"I can't." But he didn't move away. He wrapped his arms around her and rolled them so she sprawled on top of him.

Sated and satisfied, she began to drift off to sleep. "You're a good man, Alex Parker."

He kissed the top of her head. "No. But you make me feel like I could be."

CHAPTER SEVEN

ALEX SLIPPED OUT of bed and dressed, careful not to make a sound. Mallory was finally resting. He'd lain awake for a good hour just holding her—making sure she was properly asleep. He rolled his eyes. He could never be anything but a cold-blooded killer and the sooner he reminded himself of that, the better.

Walking into her quiet living room he stood for a moment, trying to ignore the ache of loneliness. The room was decorated in neutral colors, attractive, plush, but with no real character. Unlike Mallory, who was so damn full of character she was impossible to ignore. He picked up her heels and grinned.

Damn shoes. Damn dress. Damn perfect body and tragic eyes.

He put the shoes down softly and reminded himself he had a job to do. Screwing Mallory was just a way of doing that more efficiently. *Sure, asshole.* He booted up her laptop and watched as it connected to the internet. Two minutes later he'd uploaded the software he needed to access not only her keyboard strokes, but also all ingoing and outgoing mail, plus the camera and mic. He deleted all evidence of the download from the system and closed down the computer. He picked up his jacket, which lay crumpled on the floor, checked the inner pocket for the camera and bug he'd brought with him. He'd initially followed her to the bar last night to get an indication of how long she'd be so he could break in and set up surveillance. Somehow he'd got caught in a honeytrap of his own making.

He bent down to retrieve his wallet and scattered belongings from near the door where they'd first had sex. He closed his eyes and counted to ten. If he carried on thinking about all the different ways they'd fucked, he'd end up crawling back into bed with her in the hopes of scoring one-last-time. And that wasn't going to happen ever again.

Regret clawed inside him.

There was no doubt he was highly attracted to Mallory and would love to see her again. But if she knew what he really was, and the illegal activities he carried out on behalf of people inside their government, she'd be disgusted. He didn't want her to want him under false pretenses, but there was no way he could confess the truth. So getting out of her hair before she woke up was the right thing to do.

So why the hell did it feel so wrong?

Added to the equation, his boss might not be too happy to know just how close he'd stuck to his target last night. Skin-on-skin probably wasn't what they'd had in mind when he'd received that order. Five-hundred and thirty-seven more days and he'd be out of this shit for good. For some reason the idea failed to bring its usual peace.

He removed the camera from his pocket and planted it beneath a table beside the front door. It gave a wide-angle view of the living room and a glimpse of the kitchen. The audio bug sat neatly inside a lamp on the far side of the room. There was a large blue box sitting on the dining table. Curious, he eased up the lid and saw a stack of files and newspaper cuttings about her sister's abduction. He clenched his jaw. How did it feel when someone you loved disappeared into the ether never to be heard of again? He didn't know but it reminded him of the importance of what he did.

He helped stop monsters.

Shrugging into his jacket he tried to ignore the guilt that ate at his conscience, telling himself he'd given Mallory what she needed—a few hours of mindless pleasure and a sound sleep.

Yeah, he was a real hero.

It had been a long time since he'd found comfort anywhere or in anything. It took every ounce of willpower not to return to the bedroom and climb back into her bed. Instead, he left soundlessly through the front door and started walking southwest. Maybe if he just kept going for long enough he'd escape all the mistakes he'd made with his life—another impossible dream. Although, like Mallory, he'd forgotten for just a little while last night.

Knowing he'd been out of touch for way too long he turned his phone on as he hit Dupont Circle. Swore as he read the messages. There'd been a major cyber attack on one of the big banks overnight—a bank that had originally consulted Cramer, Parker & Gray, Security Consultants, and then told them that their services were too costly and had gone with one of their less expensive competitors.

You got what you paid for, although you could never completely safeguard against attackers, you just had to be prepared to detect and defend once an attack occurred.

Alex was glad of the distraction. His colleagues had been running interference and damage control all night so now it was his turn. Better to think about code and strategy than to remember the dark head that had nestled against his heart while she slept.

Unable to stop himself, he texted her. "Emergency at work. Gotta go in. Enjoy rest of weekend." Even as he pressed send he shook his head and jammed the cell in his pocket. He'd obviously lost his fucking mind.

MALLORY HAD BEEN assigned to work with Supervisory Special Agent Frazer's team at BAU-4 which dealt with serial killings involving adults and other unusual crimes. The man didn't know about SSA Hanrahan's amendment to her normal duties. She sat in on her first team meeting at nine AM Monday morning. Despite knowing why she was really here, she was excited at the chance to be working with these people.

Expressions on her coworkers' faces were less than thrilled; they ranged from distracted, guarded, to openly hostile. One guy looked like he wanted to get in her pants. The last, Frazer's, was calculating. Despite his gleaming blond hair, he didn't remind her of a movie star today. He was stern and forbidding and brought to mind instead a powerful law enforcement officer who carried both a badge and a gun and took his duties very seriously. No way would he bend the rules and work with a vigilante—*right*?

"Special Agent Rooney has come to us from the Charlotte Division. She was heavily involved in the Meacher case." Frazer introduced her around. BAU-4 had finished assisting the Meacher investigation. All the video information had been copied and the originals stored in evidence. Victim identification was ongoing but that would be mainly up to the Charlotte field agents and forensics.

Mallory nodded and kept her mouth shut. She couldn't say she hadn't really done anything except answer the phone if she wanted to maintain an ounce of credibility here but she hated lying.

"Why isn't she doing the usual training course?" asked a woman with ink black hair and equally dark eyes.

Mallory shifted uncomfortably. Agents joining the BAU completed a sixteen week training course in the classroom before rotating through each of the Behavioral Analysis Units to gain a broad range of experience. It could take up to two years to complete. No wonder these people were suspicious and pissed.

"She is, but the next session doesn't start until late January so she's sitting in with us until that time."

The dark-haired agent sniffed.

"I know we all have active cases we're working on at this moment, but we have a new case that we've been asked to assist with and I want to make it a priority," Frazer continued. *Thank God,* because she was starting to sweat under the intense scrutiny. "Over the last year, there have been a series of murders of young women in their late teens to late thirties." He put up smiling photographs of six young women, all with brown-black hair. Below each one he placed a crime scene photograph of their bodies. Mallory winced. Their faces had been brutally beaten and it looked like they'd been strangled.

"Evidence suggests the women were all taken off the highways so we're working with Special Agent Tate from HSK—Highway Serial Killings Initiative—on this." He nodded to the guy who'd been staring at Mallory like she was his favorite flavor of ice cream.

She wasn't in the least bit attracted to the guy but was instantly reminded of Alex and what they'd done on Friday night. She swallowed hard. Waking up to find him gone had been both a relief and a disappointment. The fact he'd sent her a text had done funny things to her heart—things she couldn't afford. Friday night had been an anomaly. A one-off never to be repeated. The thought depressed the crap out of her.

She kept her expression neutral as she listened to Frazer. She took her work seriously, even if it seemed it didn't take her very seriously at the moment. There was no way in hell she'd hook up with a colleague, but—her stomach sank—it was probably a good angle to use in terms of her *other* investigation. Not hooking up, but maybe being friendlier than she really wanted. Although there was no way she could do anything that made her feel like she'd sold her soul. She needed to hang on to some shred of dignity.

"What's that on the victims' chests?" She leaned closer trying to get a better look at the images but she couldn't make it out. The women were naked, but posed almost childlike with their hands placed over their pubic region.

SSA Frazer pinched his lips together. "The killer carves something on the victim's left breast." Frazer pulled another picture from the case file and put it on the white board.

"Is that an AR or AK?" the HSK agent quizzed.

Frazer put up close-ups of all the mutilation and every cell in Mallory's body froze.

"The work in the first few victims is crude but eventually he refines his technique. We're pretty sure it represents the letters PR within a love heart."

Her heartbeat sped up. PR—Payton Rooney? Or something else?

Frazer held her gaze as if searching for a reaction. She refused to give him one.

"We don't know what the significance of the letters is yet."

"Ante- or postmortem?" The dark-haired woman asked.

Mallory braced herself and let out a sigh of relief when Frazer replied, "Post."

"Sexual assault?" asked one of the guys.

"Yes. Victims appear to have been kept alive for some time and subjected to repeated sexual assault."

"Any relation to the Meacher murders?" asked Mallory. There were similarities here, as well as obvious differences.

"Not that's been discovered so far. The latest victim was found two days after the Meacher takedown and the ME puts time of death after Meacher's demise. But these cases have occurred in the states of North Carolina, Virginia, West Virginia—Meacher's hunting grounds—so I'm not ready to rule out some connection. I want you to review the files with that in mind." He didn't look convinced, but good law enforcement officers kept open minds.

"So, unless Meacher had an accomplice, it's probably a different offender." Mallory mulled over the *accomplice-who'd-turned-against-his-partner* versus the *vigilante* angle. She needed to take a closer look at the cases and talk to Lucas back in Charlotte—she'd left him messages but so far no reply. It had been a blow to realize she couldn't share her vigilante theory with him anyway because Hanrahan had sworn her to secrecy. She hated this. Maybe the theory was the result of watching too many TV cop shows and listening to conspiracy theory crackpots.

"I heard you played a big part in the Meacher take down,

Rooney," a second female agent smirked. "Your old boss told me all about it."

Mallory exchanged a look with the slightly frumpy, lethally sharp, motherly-type and marked her as one of Danbridge's cronies.

Good to know.

"The fact this killer strangled his victims with his hands suggests this was personal." Frazer ignored the interruption. "As does the severe beating around the facial region." As if he were punishing them and trying to make them unrecognizable. "We've been asked to assist and provide a profile by State Police in Virginia and several sheriff's offices in West Virginia. I'm planning to visit local law enforcement next week and view the bodies. We all know due to budgetary restrictions some local police forces don't even report murders or abductions, so Rooney, I want you to start calling municipalities and sheriff's offices to see if there are any more victims out there that haven't been added to ViCAP—"

"I heard she was good on the phone," Danbridge's pal put in snidely.

Frazer said nothing, just watched the exchange carefully. "I should probably have introduced everyone. Rooney meet Special Agents Moira Henderson, Felicia Barton, Darsh Singh." He worked his way around the table. "Bradley Tate, Matt Lazlo, and last but not least, Jed Brennan."

Despite being in a meeting, Special Agent Brennan was clearly working on something else. Busted, he looked up and shot her a wry grin. "Nice to meet you, Agent Rooney."

"Agent Brennan is working on the Rainbow Murderer case." A particularly gruesome set of killings targeting young homosexual males. Frazer sent the man a quelling glance. "He gets a little obsessed by his work sometimes."

Brennan pulled a face at Mallory when Frazer wasn't looking, which made her lips twitch.

Frazer continued, "Sam Walker is another of our agents but he's on the road. He'll be back in a couple of days."

Mallory's heart sank. Until she or Hanrahan could prove otherwise they were all potential suspects.

Frazer's smile didn't quite reach his eyes. "Welcome to the team."

WINDING THROUGH THE remote hills, he drove home, dropping his SUV out front of his cabin—the one he'd inherited from his uncle. He went into his bedroom and changed, pulling on jeans, boots, a plaid shirt, wool hat. He picked up his ax from beside the front door and started into the woods. He'd always wondered if his parents had known about his uncle's deviancies, but they'd never mentioned it. He wished he'd killed him then, when he'd been the one suffering the abuse—he'd have got off with a self-defense plea and his life wouldn't have turned to shit.

He missed Payton so much he ached.

Her mother was a United States senator, her father a federal judge. He wished he could have explained to them that their daughter had been safe and well cared for. Except for that first couple of months, she hadn't suffered—and he'd made sure his uncle had paid for her initial pain. The damage to her mind hadn't fixed itself the way he'd hoped, otherwise he'd have let her go, swooping to her rescue like an avenging angel. But she'd never fully recovered from whatever his uncle had done to her. She'd been happy afterward though, and always so damned pleased to see him.

Emotion was like a fist gripping his esophagus. Grief and loneliness welled up at her loss. He wished he could explain to the Rooney family exactly how much he and Payton had loved one another. The image of her wearing a big white wedding dress and walking down the aisle on her father's arm was clear in his mind. The smile the man sent him as if he truly understood how staunchly he'd protected Payton. Hell, he'd killed for her.

He shook himself out of his reverie. They wouldn't have understood. That sort of fairytale wasn't for the likes of him and the only way to stop himself going mad with grief was to find someone to replace her, if only in body.

The hitchhiker—Kari—had turned out to be demure and sweet, but it might just be an act. He hadn't touched her yet so time would tell. And maybe the judge deserved one last Christmas with his other daughter. He'd already figured out how to remind her of her connection to her sister, but he didn't want to go too fast and slip up by doing something stupid. Planning took time. Nothing wrong with slow and careful.

About a quarter of a mile into the secluded forest, not far from the entrance of the chamber, he'd started a woodpile. It was surrounded to the north, east and west by briars that he'd let grow years ago. He propped the ax against the cut logs. Grass grew over the hatch and he slid back the iron bolt that formed the lock. He'd installed a proper wooden staircase since his uncle had first dug this pit. He put in TV and radio, and even a chemical toilet. There was a couch and double bed. He'd stocked up with water and food. It wasn't exactly a hovel.

You could last for months down here.

It did get chilly this time of year, but there was a compact propane heater for really cold nights, plus plenty of blankets. The soil held warmth better than above ground so no one was gonna freeze to death.

He closed the hatch behind him and picked up the flashlight he kept at the top of the stairs.

Kari lay on the bed. Her eyes were reddened from crying, mouth twisted. He'd handcuffed her to a long chain bolted to a cement block that sat under the bed. She could reach everything she needed, but she couldn't leave.

"Why are you doing this to me?" Her voice was croaky. Kind of cute.

He brought her a glass of water from the pitcher on the side. Handed it to her.

She held it with both hands and he sat beside her as she took a drink. He eased her hair out of her face where it had stuck to the tears on her cheeks.

"What do you think I want?"

Her eyes were huge, expressive. Scared. "I think you want to rape me."

"Do I look like the sort of guy who has to resort to rape to get a woman?"

Her eyes scanned his face desperately. "No, you're good looking, handsome even. If you don't want to rape me, what do you want? To hurt me?" She started to cower away from him but he hauled her back against his side. She fit nicely.

"I don't want to hurt you either." He shook his head. "Did it ever occur to you that maybe I just want someone to care about... to love?"

Her lips parted on a gasp of surprise. He held his breath.

The last two women had laughed and proved they weren't the ones. But she didn't laugh. She smiled at him tentatively and he touched his thumb to her bottom lip, liking the feel of its softness. Then he leaned forward and kissed her, parting her mouth beneath his. His heart seemed to stop for a long drawn out moment.

At first there was nothing and he felt disappointment, but then, finally, her tongue touched his. Maybe, just maybe, she was the one.

ALEX STOOD IN the shower with the water blasting down on him and tried to wake himself up. The cyber attack had taken days to shut down and sanitize. Two other clients had suffered similar intrusions. Securing data, changing password and email protocols between employees, plugging software holes, and figuring out who the hell was behind the infiltration was a painstaking process. North Korea seemed to be the location of the server but Alex doubted they had hackers or systems sophisticated enough to carry out this attack. North Korea felt like a decoy and Alex hated falling for the obvious. China was usually the main culprit, with state-sponsored hackers working out of a building in Shanghai, amongst other locations. But big corporations didn't want to name and shame China for fear of losing business with such an important trade partner. With intellectual property theft costing the US an estimated $300 billion a year, it was an interesting time to be in cyber security.

He'd sent people to business headquarters in New York and London, more to Silicon Valley and Hong Kong. Since his incarceration in Morocco, his team knew exactly how to operate without him and sometimes he felt more a figurehead than the boss. Still, it was good to be useful for something besides killing. Over the last few days he'd stolen a couple of combat naps and whatever spare time he'd found had been spent surreptitiously checking Mallory's cell phone and emails. He hadn't had the chance to look at video or audio feeds yet and was reluctant to cross that line. Stupid really. He'd done more than invade her privacy on Friday night but at least the pleasure had been genuine and mutual.

He turned off the hot tap and forced himself to stand still as cold water flashed across every inch of skin until his whole body tingled with numbness. *Yeah, asshole, no more thinking about Friday night.*

He got out of the shower and toweled himself dry and pulled on a pair of jeans. His apartment had a view of the Watergate building which always reminded him of the power of not just surveillance but also of ego, especially when dealing with politicians. He'd swept for bugs when he'd got in and now he grabbed a beer from the fridge and threw a sandwich together.

He wanted to fall into bed and sleep for a day straight, but first he needed to check that the camera and audio bug in Mallory's apartment actually worked. The idea he might need to go back and replace it was eating at him, like some hormonal teenager finding any excuse to talk to his high school crush. When both sound and vision came through crisp and clear as a satellite feed, he shook his head.

Watching her left a bitter taste in his mouth. He couldn't have her. Ever. She was beyond his reach in every way. He felt sleazy spying on her, like he was committing the worst kind of treachery. And he was. But the choice between him doing surveillance versus some other operative was a no-brainer. No one else was getting near this woman. She'd been hurt too many times for him to contemplate his organization hurting her again, however inadvertently.

He froze when he saw her sitting at the dining table, the blue box open in front of her. He flicked on his laptop and her laptop camera showed her biting her lip as she typed in a web search. She looked tired, no make-up, no gloss, but had one of the most exquisite faces he'd ever seen. Maybe because it wasn't painted on—her beauty came from within.

She spent all her downtime investigating her sister's abduction.

It was futile. The chance of anyone finding out what happened to Payton Rooney was almost zero unless the bad guy confessed. And the idea of Mallory wasting her life lay heavy on his shoulders. He sat up straighter when he saw exactly what she was searching. Newspaper articles on abductions throughout the US two years either side of Payton Rooney's abduction.

Good idea. Because crimes weren't always put into police databases.

But it was going to take her weeks if not months to sort through all that information. She yawned and rubbed her eyes and he was reminded how tired he felt. Somehow he doubted Mallory was any more rested.

An idea lit up the back of his brain, although he'd be foolish to interfere. She yawned again and he knew he was screwed. He was going to help her whether it was sensible or not. He had the tools to pare down all that information into useable bite-sized chunks.

His phone rang and he snatched it up. "Parker."

"Alex. It's Lucas Randall."

"What can I do for you, buddy?" Alex's mind switched back to wary. Lucas was investigating Meacher's murder, he had to tread carefully.

"FBI IT guys are having some trouble isolating cell phone data from the tower closest to Meacher's residence and I'm wondering if…"

Damn. "If I'll look at the information for you?" He didn't want to get involved in this investigation any more than he wanted to keep an eye on Mallory. Both involved betrayal and if there was something he understood it was just how much betrayal could hurt. "I doubt I can find anything that your guys can't."

"Will you just look for me?" Lucas lowered his voice. "I'm getting nowhere on this investigation and my boss is being such a bitch that pretty soon I'm going to kill her and dump her at the Body Farm. I don't think anyone will blame me."

Alex pressed the tips of his fingers hard into his temples. He'd known this guy since basic training and had fought side by side with him in Afghanistan. Self-condemnation tied his stomach in knots. He hated who he was and what he did. "Send me the files but I'm nose-deep in international fuck-ups and don't know when I'll be able to look at it." Not that there would be anything in the cell phone records. The signals on the phones he and Jane used to communicate were encrypted well beyond military standards. He'd created the electronic illusion of a burner cell. His laptop to which everything was forwarded, couldn't be traced either. If they tried they'd end up on a tiny island in the middle of the South Pacific. But he didn't like that he was so close to this investigation. Sure he could keep an eye on what they knew, but if he was being set-up…

Shit. He didn't like it. Didn't like traps. Didn't like manipulation. He flashed back to the prison. To his new boss standing before him in a suit so white it had hurt his eyes. He'd been filthy and bedraggled. He'd tried to keep active, but disease, lack of clean water, proper food had worn him down. Beatings had left him weak and emaciated. He'd known going in that no one would claim him if things went wrong. It was one thing to be told that, another to experience the brutal reality with each metal-edged punch. So much for service. So much for loyalty.

The Gateway Project had made him a proposition that had allowed him to escape that hellhole. He owed them. But he didn't kid himself things would be any different if he got caught on US soil.

"Send me the information, but I'm not promising anything." He took in a big breath. "I bumped into Mallory Rooney in DC."

"Mallory Rooney? *My* Mallory Rooney?"

Alex was surprised by the possessive edge to the man's tone. "Said she got transferred to Quantico."

"Yeah, she did." Lucas's tone morphed into protective older brother. "She's not the sort of girl to string along, Alex. Don't go sniffing at that door because if you break her heart I'll beat the crap out of you."

"We're not dating." He tried not to think about what they had done last Friday night and purposely looked away from his laptop so he couldn't see her falling asleep over her computer.

"She doesn't date," Lucas almost growled.

"So what the fuck are you worried about?" Alex bit out. As

her friend, Lucas should be encouraging her to have a social life not work every minute of every day.

The silence stretched for a taut moment. "Look, she's been through a lot. I just don't want to see her hurt, which reminds me, I need to call her."

The guy had feelings for her—why hadn't he seen that? Because he'd been dazzled himself, and trying to make sure he didn't end up under arrest for Murder One. "Send me the cell data, Lucas, but I'm not promising anything."

"Thanks buddy."

"Yeah, a buddy who's not good enough to date your so-called friend," he muttered.

"It's not like that—"

"You just keep telling yourself that." Alex disconnected. Three seconds later he watched Mallory pick up her cell phone. Her face lit up with a grin—Lucas. Jealousy smacked him in the head like a sledgehammer. Pissed with himself Alex turned off the laptop and headed out into the night. He didn't want to hear what Lucas Randall said about him on the phone, but this was exactly the sort of conversation he needed to monitor. He'd listen to it later, when his head was fixed on straight.

It took several hours and was well after midnight by the time he'd compiled all the information he needed. Wearing latex gloves to handle the paper and envelope, he printed out the information and used one of a series of false identities to have the package couriered to Mallory's work the next day. He might never be anything but a blurry memory to her, but maybe he could ease her burden just a little. He needed all the chances of redemption he could get.

CHAPTER EIGHT

BY FRIDAY AFTERNOON Mallory had spent most of the week reading case files and calling various police departments to talk to homicide detectives, sheriff deputies and medical examiners until her jaw ached. She'd doubled up on each phone call by asking about any unreported cases of child abduction fifteen to twenty years ago, never knowing when she might catch a break.

She didn't catch a break.

She looked up and realized she was all alone in the space she usually shared with eight other agents. They'd all gone to meetings and she was left whistling Dixie. She glanced around. It was empty. No one was here.

Her pulse pounded loudly in her ear.

The real reason for her being here flashed through her mind, followed by butterflies in the pit of her stomach that launched themselves into the air like vultures. The hum of the heating system and murmur of far-off voices drifted from a long way away. She climbed to her feet and eyed the desks closest to her. Moira Henderson or Felicia Barton? Henderson was Danbridge's crony so she tackled her first.

She went over and searched through the drawers. Handcuffs, ammo, staplers, post-it notes, a broken crucifix—nothing useful. There were photographs stuck to Henderson's cubicle walls—a family portrait with a couple of kids. Mallory checked her shoulder when she heard footsteps but they disappeared behind the bang of a door. There was a stack of file folders on the left-hand side of Henderson's desk. Mallory peeked in the first one and saw a photograph of herself and some of her personnel files. Holy crap, the woman had a file on her.

The fine hair on the nape of her neck stood taut as she heard another door being opened and closed out in the corridor. Quickly, she looked in the next file and saw background information on Edgar Meacher. Footsteps came closer and Mallory tiptoed back to her desk, heart drilling her ribcage as Special Agent Henderson walked in the room.

The woman's suspicious gaze flicked over her but Mallory could no more meet her eyes than she could juggle potted plants. Henderson went back to her desk and picked up the phone. Did she suspect the real reason Mallory had been reassigned? Why have a file on Meacher?

Of course, Meacher was the sort of killer she investigated on a daily basis, so why wouldn't she have a file on Meacher?

Paranoid much?

Dark-haired Agent Barton wandered in carrying a Fed-ex box. "It's for you, Rooney. Mailroom checked it for suspicious substances but said it was clean. No one is trying to kill you—yet." The other agent handed it over with a smirk. Mallory sent her a smile of thanks, but it was rejected. The woman stared at her thoughtfully. Henderson said something and Barton moved on. Mallory shuddered. And these people were supposed to be on her side?

Thanks, SSA Hanrahan.

The box was about three-inches deep and when she

opened it what she saw shocked her. Printouts of old newspaper articles about child abductions in West Virginia, Ohio, Pennsylvania, Virginia and Kentucky, dating back twenty-five years.

Who the hell knew she was looking into this stuff?

Agent Frazer had given her the idea at Monday morning's meeting, but she hadn't told anyone...except every law enforcement office she'd spoken to over the last five days. Plus anyone in the office could have overheard her inquiries. She scratched her head. Someone had done her a huge favor, she just wished she knew who it was, and their motive. She looked for return information, saw an address in DC. She'd see if she could track down a name.

She put the box on the floor to take home tonight. Her whole weekend had just been shaped by some unnamed source and she wasn't sure she liked it. Leaning back in her chair she gazed at the map she'd pinned to her cubicle wall. It showed the locations where the young women were believed to have been snatched and where their bodies were found. Her gaze was drawn back to the home state where she'd spent the first ten years of her life. Her father's family estate, Eastborne, in Colby, West Virginia.

After Payton's abduction she'd been forced to attend boarding school in DC, but she'd spent several of her summers back there, missing Payton, hanging out with Lucas and his sisters who lived nearby. She hadn't been back much since college. Virginia Tech, then Harvard Law School. For the last two years her career had been her top priority and time off was scarce. What little vacation time she did get, she spent in DC seeing both her parents at the same time. Despite the divorce they got on well. In fact, her father wanted them all to go up to

Eastborne for Christmas one last time and then he was putting the place on the market.

The idea saddened her even though she never wanted to live there. The ties that bound her to that beautiful old house were deep as mine shafts and strong as steel, but it was a shame for such a gorgeous house to remain empty except for the housekeeper most of the year around.

Her eyes flickered over the map. One of the latest serial killer's victims was from Greenville, only fifteen miles from Colby.

Her phone beeped with a text from her mother about dinner over the weekend. She sent her a quick reply to say she'd think about it, then stared at the screen on her phone. The fact she'd saved Alex's text from last Friday night showed how truly pathetic she was. For the hundredth time, her finger hovered over the keypad to ask him if his crisis was sorted. The urge had her shaking her head with frustration. She put the phone in her pocket. She didn't have time for a relationship even though she really wanted to see him again.

"Problem?"

She jumped an inch off her chair and her heart did a triple salchow. "No, sir."

Frazer stared at her the way an eagle eyed a mouse, wondering if it was worth the bother. The guy still looked pristine whereas she'd managed to spill coffee on her white shirt and whatever make-up she'd applied that morning was long gone. From his expression, she was beginning to suspect the spinach salad she'd had for lunch might be stuck between her front teeth. She swept her tongue around her mouth but didn't feel anything except enamel.

A small smile touched the corner of his mouth and she

narrowed her gaze.

Oh, he was definitely psyching her out.

Special Agents Barton and Henderson came across to her desk to heckle.

"Any luck with other law enforcement agencies?"

"Not yet, but I've still got a lot of calls in and I started on some of the adjoining states."

He nodded sharply. "Good. What do you make of the geographic profile?" He pointed at the map that she'd pinned to her wall.

Mallory frowned. "There's a pretty wide spread area, but a heavy concentration in Virginia suggests that's his comfort zone." She indicated the middle zone of the dots.

"You remember that from the academy, Rooney?" Barton asked.

"Considering she's barely out of it, she should." Henderson didn't bother to hide her contempt but Frazer didn't try to defend her.

Mallory squared her shoulders. Before she could open her mouth, Frazer interrupted. "I'm taking that drive up to Greenville, West Virginia, on Monday. That's near where you grew up, correct, Rooney?"

She nodded.

"I want you to accompany me"—Mallory's mouth dropped open in shock—"I should warn you we will also be visiting the Medical Examiner's Office in Manassas to view bodies of three of the victims before they're released for burial."

"I've witnessed a few autopsies, but thank you for the heads-up—"

"I thought I was going with you for that." Henderson cut

in. Her expression was tight. Appalled.

The excitement at the idea of a road-trip plummeted.

"You've made me all too aware of how under-qualified Agent Rooney is, Agent Henderson. So she can accompany me as a second pair of eyes and gain experience." He kept a straight face but Mallory had no doubt he was putting the other agent in her place for being such a bitch. It didn't mean he liked her any more than Henderson did but it sure as heck made Mallory feel better. "Plus, Agent Rooney has personal experience of West Virginia that you don't have." He cocked a brow. "Correct?"

Chastened, the other agent nodded.

"We leave here at eight AM sharp, don't be late." He gave Mallory a stiff nod and walked away.

She watched Henderson inhale so massively she thought the woman's lungs might burst. Then she turned on her heel and strode away. Barton watched her with an odd light in her eyes, like she'd just had a few of her fundamental ideals flipped on their heads. *Welcome to the club.* Then she also turned and walked away.

Mallory refrained from fist pumping and instead got everything together she might need for the weekend. This was fantastic. She'd hopefully be able to add something concrete to the investigation, even if it was only breaking the ice with local law enforcement personnel who'd be happier dealing with one of their own than an "outsider" from Virginia. It probably made her sick to be excited by this latest killer carving "PR" into his victims but it was the closest thing she'd had to a lead in her sister's case in years. And it was still spider web thin. She grabbed her laptop, coat, mysterious box, and headed into the frigid night toward the parking lot. It was dark. Theoretically the traffic shouldn't be too heavy as she did the opposite commute to most of drivers in the DC area; somehow theory never made it into practice.

She strode past row-upon-row of cars and eventually found hers where she'd left it near the edge of the forest. She opened the passenger door and dumped her belongings on the front seat. Then she strode around the trunk, noticing the car sat at an odd angle.

She had not just one flat tire, but two. *Dammit.* Frustration made her want to howl but that never looked good. She stiffened as Special Agent Henderson rolled slowly by in her SUV. The woman lowered her window. "Problem?" she asked.

Mal put her hands on her hips. "No problem."

With a smirk the other woman drove away. Had Henderson done this to her car? FBI agents were notorious for playing pranks on one another but this held malice rather than fun. A shiver of unease swept over her shoulder blades and she glanced toward the forest.

Don't be stupid, Mal, you're surrounded by the US Marine Corps. Like she needed to invent imaginary foes when she had a whole rack of real ones to choose from.

Mallory pulled out her cell phone and dialed her recovery company. After she hung up she stood there staring at Alex's text message.

She typed, "Hope emergency all sorted. Thanks for Friday night." It seemed trite and insufficient but she was hardly gonna type "thanks for letting me screw your brains out." *Christ.* Her fingers hovered between send and delete for a full thirty seconds before she finally pressed the send button. *Shoot.* Just because *she'd* been thinking about *him* constantly didn't mean he'd given her another thought. She bit her lip.

Didn't matter now.

She glanced at the forest and shivered. She didn't know what scared her most—getting attacked by some unknown boogeyman, or falling for Alex Parker.

HIS PHONE PINGED. A text from Mallory. His pulse raced. So much for being the cool, dispassionate operator. Although he'd lost that title when he'd faced that young girl with his arm wrapped around her father's neck and chickened out of killing the motherfucker.

"Hope emergency all sorted. Thanks for Friday night."

He grinned. It was so un-Mallory-like and he'd bet she'd spent an age figuring out exactly what to say.

He checked his phone tracking data. She was still at Quantico. Not in the building itself, but in the parking lot. He was only ten minutes away, driving home on the 95, which was snarled with the usual rush hour traffic, after a meeting in Fredericksburg. She must be on her way home.

He got another ding on his computer telling him Mallory had made more phone calls. He set his teeth as he listened, the sound of her voice reminding him of her lips and the memory of her lips reminding him of how hot her kisses were, and how sad her eyes, and how massively he'd betrayed her trust.

Then he listened to the words. Two flat tires? He glanced at the tracking data and sure enough she was still in the Quantico parking lot. *Fuck.* He checked his wristwatch and heard the recovery company say they'd be there ASAP—which would be at least another hour. He didn't like it. He dialed her number.

"Hello?"

"It's Alex. The answer to your question is yes."

"My question?" Her voice was hesitant.

"My emergency is more or less sorted out. And as for the second part of your message, the pleasure was all mine."

She snorted but he could hear a frisson of tension in her voice as he maneuvered his Audi around traffic. "It wasn't *all* yours."

"Don't argue with a hungry man. What're you doing?" He needed to keep hearing her voice because he was worried that even though she was surrounded by feds and Marines, she was vulnerable. It was crazy. It was obsessive. But two flat tires were unusual.

"I'm working late." She didn't want to tell him.

"You want to go out for supper?" He overtook a lumbering tractor and sped along the highway toward Quantico and DC. "Or does anything involving food violate the no-dating rule?"

"I think my no-dating rule needs a few tweaks."

He could hear the grin in her voice, wished he could see it. His foot was pressed to the floor and he'd be lucky not to get pulled over by the highway patrol, but the urge to get to her was strong so he didn't ease up. "Hell, no."

"That's because I jumped your bones—"

"Damn straight."

She sighed. "But regardless, I'm stuck at work for at least another hour. My car has two flat tires and I'm waiting for the recovery guy to come and fix them."

"Two flat tires? Were they slashed? Where are you, are you safe?" He wanted as much information as possible.

"I'm at Quantico, heavily armed in my car, so I think I'm

safe. The tires weren't slashed, someone just let the air out."

"What the hell?"

"Let's just say it appears I haven't made such a great first impression on some of my new colleagues."

"I'm five minutes away, leave the keys for the recovery guys and I'll give you a ride home." She went quiet. Too quiet. He could feel her slipping away. "I'm not expecting a repeat of last Friday night, Mallory, I'm just making sure you get home safe." Although, really, why should she trust him?

"I want to say yes, Alex, you have no idea how much. But I have to say no. I'm just not in a place to start a relationship right now…" He thought he might hear tears in her voice but that had to be his imagination. "I want to say yes, but I can't."

He took a left into the FBI portion of the Quantico grounds and pulled up at a checkpoint. "If you don't accept a ride from me, I'm going to look like a damn fool in front of all these jarheads."

"You're already here?" She hung up and he showed his ID to the guard. The fact they let him through suggested she'd taken pity on him by calling ahead to vouch for him.

He turned into the parking lot and saw Mallory standing beside her car, pulling out a box he recognized, followed by her laptop and purse. She opened his trunk and ditched her stuff and he used the time to silence his cell phone and tuck it into his pocket. She opened the door, her expression stern, eyes twinkling.

"Mr. Parker."

"Special Agent Rooney." He nodded solemnly back. The sight and scent of her drew him in. She smelled like mint.

"We need to stop meeting like this." She climbed in.

His gaze swept over her. Every time he saw her she affected him more, and he didn't know why. "Are there laws against meeting like this?" he asked carefully.

"Only if we start doing what we did last Friday night right here in the FBI Training Academy parking lot."

"You had to say that out loud?" He pulled away as soon as she'd done up her seatbelt. "You couldn't pretend I hadn't seen you naked?"

"I'm not the pretending type." Her expression darkened for a moment. "At least not most of the time." *What did that mean?* "But I'm not trying to lead you on. I really don't have time for a relationship—"

"Who said I was looking for a relationship?" Because he wasn't. He really wasn't.

She tilted her head to one side and bit her lip. "Maybe I keep saying it in the hopes I'll convince myself as much as I'm trying to convince you."

"You like to get it all out there on the table, huh?"

"I like honesty," she agreed.

His mouth parched. "How about we just relax and get to know each other?" Christ, where did that come from? He just wanted her home safe. Nothing more. No "getting to know one another." *Frickin' idiot.*

"Tell me about your family," she prompted.

"Not much to tell."

She raised one arched brow at him as he turned back onto the main highway.

"My mother's dead." He never spoke of her. "She died of cancer when I was fourteen. I don't have anyone else."

"I'm sorry." The pain in her voice was obvious.

"It was a long time ago." His fingers tightened on the steering wheel. There had been times when he was sure his mother's spirit had visited him in that rancid filthy jail—those were the good times. "She would have liked you."

She let out a big sigh. "You've only seen the good parts and they were clouded by alcohol consumption."

"They were naked which is always good in my book. But that's not why she'd have liked you." They passed a tow truck with flashing yellow lights which must have made record time. "I remember her telling me before she died to make sure I did something worthwhile with my life. I'm not sure I've done that, but you have. You should be very proud."

She eyed him wryly. "Maybe one day I'll get there." She looked away as if the conversation was too intimate. It probably was.

So he lightened it up. "My dad was a professional gambler from Reno."

She looked back. "No kidding. He made a living at it?"

"Fuck, no."

She laughed.

"He used to travel between cities on the Greyhound bus, which is not the mark of a successful businessman. When he occasionally showed up for visits it was usually because he had nowhere else to go. Mom let him stay. I don't think she loved him, she just felt sorry for him. He was an addict and gambling was his drug."

"What happened to him?"

"He struck lucky one day in Carson City and won a hundred grand."

"From your tone this doesn't have a happy ending."

"He was knifed in a back alley. Probably trying to score enough speed to keep him awake long enough to lose his winnings." He shrugged. Talking about his father didn't hurt the way talking about his mother did. They'd had no connection beyond DNA.

They passed another tow truck. "Wow, it looks like I'm not the only one in trouble tonight."

"You didn't leave an apartment key or your address in your car did you?"

"No. The company has my address on file but agreed to tow it to the garage I use." She shot him a look under her brow. "I'm not an idiot, Alex."

He nodded but something about this whole thing teased his senses. It didn't feel right, but maybe it didn't matter because Mallory was sitting safe beside him and he wouldn't let anyone hurt her.

"Lucas said you were consulting on the Meacher investigation?" she said.

And just like that the atmosphere chilled. "He sent me some cell tower data but there's nothing in it of value."

"Maybe whoever shot Meacher didn't carry a cell phone?"

"Maybe. You have any idea who did it?" He tried to sound nonchalant.

"I'm not on it anymore and Lucas didn't say." She shrugged but sat up a bit taller as if her brain had switched on and it reminded him she'd been the only agent to suspect a professional hit man. She had good instincts. He needed to be careful. "He sure as heck didn't sound like he'd gotten anywhere when I spoke to him last night. With Danbridge breathing down his neck he's getting desperate."

"You guys are close?"

She flashed him a look. "Friends, nothing more. Don't go thinking we've stepped out on a buddy because it isn't true. Lucas's like an overprotective older brother to me. The idea of kissing him—*ugh.*" She shivered with apparent revulsion which was fine with him. Hopefully Lucas Randall felt the same way.

They sat in silence for the rest of the journey. He could have peppered her with questions but he could tell by the tightness of her lips and set of her shoulders that she was exhausted, and he knew exactly how late she stayed up every night. She fell asleep near Dale City and he felt content just to share her space. Something about Mallory Rooney soothed him. Maybe her ongoing dedication to her sister. Maybe her lack of guile in a world full of dangerous secrets. Or maybe it was his masochistic streak. When he pulled up outside her building he waited for a moment, just watching how the light molded her profile. *Fool.* Very gently he stroked her cheek.

"We're here, Special Agent Rooney."

She blinked herself awake, then grimaced. "Sorry. I hope I didn't snore or drool." She unclipped her belt and leaned toward him and pressed a chaste kiss on his lips. Mint laced her breath, and she smelled so sweet he wanted to eat her up. Every cell in his body begged him to take it deeper but he hung onto his good intentions by the thinnest of margins.

Pale fingers curled over his much larger, darker hand. "Thanks for the ride."

The sight of her skin against his snapped something inside him. He took her face in his hands and kissed her hard, tasting the passion she kept hidden beneath the hardworking persona. He dragged her towards him, and she was kissing him back, inhaling him as her tongue curled around his in a fiery dance. He jerked her blouse out of her pants and her lace-clad breast was filling his palm as she pressed closer and closer. It wasn't close enough. He found her nipple and rolled it until she almost climbed on top of him. The damn car wasn't meant for necking—he needed a new car, with a bench seat. He was burning up with arousal, as if he'd been doused in gasoline and someone had struck a match.

A rap on the glass had them jerking apart. Shit, a traffic cop was giving them the stink-eye through the glass. Mallory seemed to realize what was going on before his brain reengaged. Of course she only had one head to deal with.

She rolled down the window.

"Sorry Officer, we weren't thinking."

He snorted, "No kidding. Move it."

"I'm an FBI agent. I live here and I'm getting out now."

"This town is full of feds, politicians and diplomats. You've got thirty seconds before I pull you both in for public indecency."

"Thank you, Officer."

The guy turned away to go back to his motorcycle.

Mallory's lips murmured urgently against his, "I have to go. You don't know how desperately I want to invite you inside."

From the straining erection in his pants he had a damn good idea. "Go. Before this guy gets pissed." He should be thanking the cop for stopping them because he sure as hell hadn't been going to. She opened the car door, blouse half-in, half-out of her pants, short hair sticking wildly in all directions.

He grabbed her hand at the last moment. "If you ever need me"—her amber eyes widened—"you know where to find me."

She swallowed and gave him a slight smile. "Don't wait for me, Alex."

He felt like he'd already waited a lifetime. It didn't make

any sense. She grabbed her stuff out of the trunk and waved to the traffic cop who just shook his head and cracked some smart ass remark that made her laugh.

Once she was safely inside her building, he drove home. And dreamed of two little girls being chased by bad guys. He was the bad guy.

FURY MADE HIS vision tunnel. How'd she escape him again? All that planning? An entire day wasted setting up an ambush? The risk involved in letting the air out of her tires? He debated taking her car and dumping it in the bush out of sheer spite but didn't want to raise suspicion. Instead he turned around and told the guard he'd made a mistake with his pick up location and left. No harm, no foul.

She was like a cat with nine lives.

He had no fucking clue who the other guy had been when he'd broken into her home in Charlotte. Damn near gave him a stroke when the man had held that knife to his throat.

He trundled home through the darkness, not wanting to get pulled over or catch anyone's attention. A lone figure at the side of the road stuck her thumb out, tempting him until a cold rage flashed over his flesh. He blasted the horn at her and she gave him the finger. Bitch. What the fuck did she think would happen out on the streets like this? Christ, some women were so fucking stupid.

Payton had been smart, right up until his uncle had smacked her head against the floor. He'd damaged her brain. He knew that. His uncle had been a sick, vicious bastard who shouldn't have been allowed within a mile of a kid. A lump clogged in his throat. If he could go back and change the night they took her he would, but Payton was dead and wasn't ever coming back.

Taking a deep breath he remembered what was waiting for him back home and felt lighter as a rush of anticipation hit him. It was possible the hitchhiker might just be the one. He was still going to get Mallory. She'd pissed him off now and the idea of keeping two women at once had curled inside him and taken root. He smiled as he turned on the radio and Aerosmith started singing. Life was good. Mallory Rooney had earned herself another weekend of freedom but it wouldn't be long now. He had a good idea where he'd keep her. Not the bunker. There was an old mine shaft not far away that had a storage shed inside it. He'd reinforce the thing and keep her chained up there. Decide what to do with her after he'd looked her in the eye and told her who he was. See if there was anything of her sweet sister inside that sophisticated exterior. He was looking forward to making her beg for mercy; even the idea had him aroused. He pressed his foot on the accelerator eager to get home.

CHAPTER NINE

MONDAY MORNING SHE'D given herself an extra thirty minutes to make the forty-five minute drive, but an accident on 95 meant she had to run from the parking lot to the office to make sure she wasn't late for her appointment with Supervisory Special Agent Frazer.

She'd spent the weekend immersed in internet searches on some old news stories and when she hadn't been thinking about the viciousness humans could inflict on one another, she'd been thinking of the searing kiss she'd shared with Alex Parker. She didn't know the last time she'd been so attracted to anyone, or so conflicted about a personal decision.

Her footsteps were brisk against the gray linoleum of the corridor. Heads looked up and then turned away. No smiley hellos, no casual waves. This situation at work was making her increasingly queasy. She passed Hanrahan's open door and stopped. He raised his hand in acknowledgment and sent her a wry smile. She opened her mouth to say something but he shook his head. *Fine.* She almost plowed into Frazer as he came out of his office.

"Good. You're not late." He locked his door. "Let's go."

She barely had time to suck in a breath as she turned on her heel and started walking back the way she'd come.

Frazer was sharply dressed in a pale gray pin-striped suit,

hair combed and shiny, chin shaved to granite-like perfection. Weird that he didn't even give her a tingle of attraction, even though he was a classic blue-eyed Viking. Not that she went around being attracted to guys left, right and center. If it wasn't for the spark she'd experienced with Alex, she'd have forgotten there was a sexual side to her nature. It made her wonder again if she wasn't making a huge mistake blowing Alex off. How many times in life did you really connect with someone that way?

"You reviewed the case files?"

She snapped back from pondering her love life. She had work to do. "Yes, sir."

He held the door for her and she met that cold assessing gaze. Could Frazer be in league with vigilantes?

He said nothing more until he was behind the wheel of a big black Lexus—his Bureau vehicle—which meant he was well connected in all the places that mattered. She strapped herself in. There was a time when this sort of luxury had been a constant in her life. After she'd switched career tracks from law to law enforcement her parents had cut off her allowance, aiming to prove a point. It had backfired because she hadn't known how great it would feel to be financially independent. And sure, she had the cushion of enough money for down payments on furniture and a mortgage, but she hadn't gone running back to them for help. She'd learned to economize and live within her means. She got a ridiculous amount of satisfaction from achieving that small measure of independence.

"What can you tell me about the cases?"

This was a test and she wanted to prove herself not to be completely incompetent. Mallory cleared her throat. "Over the last twelve months this killer has abducted young Caucasian females with long dark hair. He rapes them, beats and strangles them, and dumps the victims in remote locations where he knows the bodies will eventually be discovered, but not immediately. He gives himself time to get away from the scene."

She mulled over her thoughts. "Except Lindsey Keeble was dumped in a place where it was unlikely she'd have been found until spring. We got lucky. She's probably our best chance of catching this guy."

"She might not be an exception—we have no idea how many women he's killed and disposed of in really remote locations. Lindsey might be the only one we have found."

"True." Which was a sickening notion because who knew how many undiscovered bodies were out in the wilds. She forced the thoughts away and carried on because he seemed to expect it. "The cars of the victims who were driving have sometimes been found in remote areas, generally off-road, in the bush. Some of the women were believed abducted while hitchhiking. No one saw anything suspicious."

"Which suggests what?"

Mallory frowned. "He has a vehicle. Spends a lot of time on the back roads. He could maybe be playing the role of Good Samaritan if they break down. Or disabling the cars so he knows they'll break down at some point, being there to offer assistance when they did." She thought about last night's flat tires and grimaced. She'd rather have Henderson on her ass than some serial killer.

"Or he could be posing as someone who needs assistance himself," Frazer added. He seemed to be taking her input as valid even though she was so under-qualified it was laughable.

She had studied criminology and criminal psychology in college and the academy, and had read about endless cases looking for clues about Payton's abduction. Still.

Frazer pulled over to buy coffee and she could sorely use a caffeine hit about now. She dug for change in her wallet as Frazer handed her a steaming cup of black coffee.

"I'll get this one." Frazer said.

"Thanks." She took the coffee and savored the warmth against the chill in the air. Frazer didn't believe in cranking the heat and it was another dull, dank November day. She shivered.

"Time of death?"

"It's hard to judge TOD accurately. Most of the bodies were too decomposed. But the last victim, Lindsey Keeble, was killed within twelve hours of her body being found. She was abducted Friday night and her body was discovered on Sunday morning. So he kept her alive for about a day before he killed her."

"So he has a vehicle or place where he can take his victims and do what he wants to them. Somewhere secluded enough he isn't worried about being discovered." She flashed back to Meacher's farmhouse on the outskirts of Fleet. They were passing houses like it, dotted across the countryside as they headed north. The moisture in her mouth evaporated.

The idea of spending that amount of time at the hands of evil filled her stomach with oily disgust. What made them think they had the right to do that to another human being? How long had Payton suffered? She stuffed her knuckles in her mouth, holding the coffee carefully in the other hand. *Don't fall apart, Mal. Do your job.*

"Cause and manner of death?"

She took a swallow of coffee to try and ease the soreness in her throat. "The beatings were severe enough to disfigure but didn't kill the victims. COD was asphyxia resulting from manual strangulation. They haven't found any fingerprints on the bodies, nor DNA. Decomp was generally too advanced. He—or she"—not likely but not yet one-hundred percent ruled out—"also wipes the victims down with a mild bleach solution before he dumps them. The ME took samples from Lindsey Keeble that might provide viable DNA samples."

"Which is all well and good if he's in the database or we have a suspect."

But ineffectual in stopping the guy otherwise.

"Signature?"

"The whole cause and manner of death seem part of his signature. But the carving of PR on the victims' chests seems peculiar to this particular offender."

"You've been studying. To look into your sister's abduction?" he asked.

She set her jaw. "It's what made me join the FBI. So, yes, I have."

"Is that why your mother pulled strings to get you into the BAU? In the hopes you might somehow mysteriously solve a case that we have been looking at for years?"

Mallory froze in the act of taking a sip of her coffee. He'd ambushed her. She decided to go with honesty. "Frankly, I have no idea how I ended up at the BAU."

"You applied didn't you?" It was said in such a derisive tone she didn't bother to contradict him. It wasn't as if she could tell him the truth.

"Obviously it's a dream of mine to work with the agents in the BAU." Surely, Hanrahan couldn't suspect the agent he worked most closely with, but if that were true why the hell hadn't he confided in the man? "You guys deal with the most interesting cases, and yes, I know they are often the most horrific."

"Think you'll be able to handle it?" His gaze was laser sharp.

She forced herself to hold that piercing gaze. "I don't know, Supervisory Special Agent Frazer. I hope so, but right now, I'm just following orders."

There was a reluctant softening of his expression and he turned back to the road. "I don't think any of us really know, Agent Rooney. Not even after years of practice. Some cases hit us unexpectedly."

They were quiet for a few minutes, the Lexus eating up the drive to Manassas.

"Your sister's case," he began.

She pushed back in her seat. "What about it?"

"Do you think that the initials this killer is carving on the women's chests are in any way related to your sister's disappearance?"

"No." Was he looking for a reason to get her thrown off the team? If so, why? Because he thought she was incompetent, or because he knew that she'd started investigating vigilantes and then been transferred to his office?

There was a slight smile on that good looking face that she didn't trust.

"What?" he asked.

She frowned. Obviously he was a man used to getting his own way. Still she'd grown up surrounded by powerful, manipulative people. She looked away. "Nothing. I'm just cold."

He adjusted the heating which was something. But it reminded her of old-fashioned interrogator techniques. *Offer them a kindness. Show them that you are the one in control.*

"It was a sophisticated abduction. It took a lot of planning. Do you have any memories from that night?" he asked.

She bit her lip and felt her eyebrows bunch together. What about the dreams she'd been having lately? Were they memories? Or founded on fear and guilt? She shook her head. "I don't remember."

"Have you tried hypnosis?"

Her mother had tried to force her but her father had refused. "No."

"Want me to set it up for you?"

She put her coffee cup in the holder and swung around to face him. "Why the sudden interest?"

A sardonic smile twisted his lips. "I helped out on that case." He shrugged. "It bothers me."

"What?" She sat up straighter. She hadn't seen his name on any of the reports.

"I was twenty-five. After college, I did a couple years with the State Police back in Wisconsin and joined the Bureau in '95." The year Payton had gone missing. That made him in his early forties. She hadn't realized he was so much older than she was. "I was a field agent in the Pittsburgh division. Your sister's abduction was one of my first cases." His lips tightened. "I actually remember seeing you as a little girl at the vigil."

That felt like a slap. "You were at the vigil?" Why that shocked her so much she didn't know. She felt exposed. Vulnerable. She'd been feeling that way for years now. Maybe that was the real reason she'd joined the Bureau. To take back control. Her plan wasn't working out so well.

"I was told to blend in with the locals. See if there was anyone attending who looked off."

"Did you see anyone?"

"No one who checked out." He was looking at her again and Mallory resisted squirming. "It was pretty freaky to see a little girl who looked so much like the one we were searching for, just standing there like a ghost."

People had whispered the same thing for years. Pity they hadn't whispered it quieter. "The Bureau never found a viable suspect," it came out of her mouth like an accusation.

"It was a sophisticated and well planned abduction with no sign of forced entry, but there was never any ransom demand."

"The cops kept wavering between it being someone who knew the family, or a random act perpetrated by someone passing through the town. When no note arrived they assumed Payton had been stolen by a pedophile." Arctic cold swept over her flesh.

He pressed his lips together and shook his head. "The thing I find hard to believe about it being a pedophile is they'd have grabbed both of you. Identical twin girls? Once the guy was finished with his fantasy, he could have sold you off for hundreds of thousands of dollars—"

"Pull over!" She put one hand over her mouth and braced against the dash with the other. She gagged, but thankfully was able to make it outside to the verge before she was sick.

SSA Frazer got out and watched her over the top of the car. "You okay?"

She spat and nodded.

"I'll em…maybe take a look at the bodies alone."

"No." She took her coffee from the cup-holder and swilled

out her mouth and spat again. She tossed the rest of the liquid on the brown grass at the side of the road and crumpled the cup in her fist. "I'll be fine. Just maybe we shouldn't talk about the possible rape and murder of my nine-year-old sister while we're in a moving vehicle."

He nodded and his expression remained blank, but she couldn't help but wonder if this hadn't been his intention all along. Shake her up and see what rattled.

Best job in the Bureau.

THE MORGUE WAS situated near the Prince William Campus of George Mason University. In a viewing room off the main autopsy suite, three gurneys had been pulled out and the victims' bodies were covered by white cloths to preserve some shred of dignity. The room was refrigerator cold and Mallory's fingers curled into her jacket cuffs trying to eke out a measure of warmth. The strong odor of chemicals clung to her nose as well as something that smelled suspiciously like spoiled meat.

Thankfully her stomach had settled and Frazer had made no more comment.

The Medical Examiner was a tall man who probably weighed two-hundred fifty pounds. When he walked into the room Mallory couldn't hide her surprise that someone so big managed such delicate work.

"Agent Frazer, Agent Rooney? I'm Dr. Ross Avery." He shook hands with them both, his skin almost burning hot against the chill of the room. "This is the first woman we examined. Lucy Fairfax, found near Woodstock. They brought her in last May but we only recently identified her when her parents uploaded DNA to the National Database." Mallory looked down at the long dark hair of the victim. Her face was unrecognizable, skin black and swollen from decomp. Animals had predated the body before she'd been discovered.

"We didn't get an awful lot from Lucy until we brought in the next victim." He moved onto the second gurney and pulled back the sheet. "And saw similarities between them. Then I went back and did some comparisons. Kendra McCloud was found July 11th; she went missing at the end of June. They were very alike physically—both five-eight, slim frame, dark-eyed brunettes. Both had been sexually assaulted, both had severe facial trauma, and they'd died from manual asphyxia. This is a very hands-on killer."

"Toxicology?" Frazer asked, arms crossed over his chest.

"Nothing out of the ordinary. No alcohol, no drugs were obvious in the tissues but the timeframe wasn't conducive to those kinds of tests. We do know he wipes them down with some sort of disinfectant solution that contains bleach." Dr. Avery looked up from where he bent over the table. Blue eyes pained. "When Lindsey Keeble arrived I put a rush on her tox panel but it was the same thing. He didn't subdue them chemically, or if he did it was using something so fast acting there was no trace left in the blood or tissue. But Lindsey did tell me a couple of interesting things that the other victims weren't able to." He pulled the sheet back to reveal her feet.

Mallory didn't know why the sight of silver-painted toenails shocked her so much, but in that moment Lindsey Keeble became a real person. She was a woman who'd sat down one day not long ago and taken the time to make her toes pretty. The knowledge hit her in the throat.

"See the marks on her left ankle?"

She and Frazer both leaned close. There was a series of red abrasions on her lower leg.

"She was shackled?" Frazer asked.

Dr. Ross nodded. "That's what I'm guessing. Some kind of metal cuff."

A shudder ran through Mallory. Being chained like an animal. How would that feel? Anger grew. She flashed back to the intruder in her house. It could have been her lying here with her painted toenails on display.

"Any idea how he's subduing them if he's not drugging them?" Frazer asked.

The ME nodded. "I missed it at first, but I think I've figured it out." He pushed the sheet up onto Lindsey's torso and revealed her left side. "See this faint mark?"

Mallory squinted, not really able to see anything against the mottled purple of the body. "Not really."

"It's hard to see because of the lividity—the color is indicative of asphyxia—but there are a couple of tiny burn marks hidden there. Image analysis confirms it."

"Taser," she said quietly.

Frazer nodded as if it confirmed what he'd already been thinking. Must be nice to be infallible. "Thank you, Doctor. You've been very helpful."

"I can release the bodies to the families?"

Frazer's expression remained as impassive as a mask. "As long as you've documented everything you told us today you can release the bodies. The families have waited long enough."

ALEX SAT ON a bench looking at the Giant Pandas. The zoo

was only a short distance from his office and this was where he came when he needed to think. He'd spent the weekend watching Mallory work sixteen hour days searching and researching cases similar to her sister's abduction. It depressed the fuck out of him to see her so driven.

Even if he wasn't spying on her he wouldn't have been able to get her out of his damn mind. Friday night's kiss kept replaying itself in his head. The feeling of anticipation, of gigantic need to finish what they'd started, was like an itch on the inside of his skin. One he didn't dare scratch. It was driving him crazy wanting her again. He didn't want to deceive her, or mess with her head, but *Christ*, the need to be with her, to call her and just frickin' *talk*, was almost irresistible. He could help her…

Yeah, she's suffered enough.

The bench creaked as Jane Sanders sat next to him, wearing a suit that probably cost enough to keep pandas in bamboo for a year. The sun was so bright it blinded him. He squeezed his eyes closed, enjoying the cold sunshine on his face, wishing for the millionth time he could reverse some of the pivotal decisions he'd made in his life. Decisions such as working for the CIA as a private contractor in the naive belief he was saving his fellow Americans.

"The boss is not very pleased with you."

He opened his eyes. Jane's hair was loose around her shoulders. Almost white-blonde. For some reason he didn't hold her in quite so much contempt as he used to. He was getting mellow in his old age. Or getting laid made him less of a bastard. One or the other.

She handed him a photograph. Gerry Rodman, a man he'd been ordered to terminate on Saturday night, raping a boy of about eight years old. He'd refused because he didn't trust the FBI's inside man and he didn't trust her. This little boy had paid the price.

Nausea unfolded in his stomach.

"On the positive side," Jane spoke lightly, "the cops got an anonymous tip and busted him for supplying drugs to minors and child pornography on his laptop—so he'll do time. They found a considerable amount of methamphetamine, weapons and cash in his apartment too." Her smile was cold as a Norwegian fjord. "When these photos are circulated among certain sectors of the prison population…well, the job will get done and no more kids will get hurt."

He held her gaze as he handed the picture back. Perhaps it was for the best. Prison justice could be more brutal than anything he ever dealt.

"Who called the cops?"

Jane shrugged. She kept her distance on the bench. Although she'd warmed a fraction, she still seemed cold and unreachable, a lot like him. That's why he was so attracted to Mallory—she wasn't anything like him. She was vivacious and warm, and holding her in his arms felt like trying to hold on to sunshine.

"I traced the anonymous tipster in the Meacher investigation," he told her.

She stretched out her toes in her fancy open-toe heels. "Who was it?"

"It came from your phone."

"What?" Her eyes flashed electric blue, blood drained from her face. "What did you say?"

"The anonymous tip came from your phone."

She shook her head. "That's not possible."

He assessed her lazily. Would she betray the organization? Maybe. For the right price. “So you’re saying it wasn’t you?”

Her features were stark, etched with fear. “I know what happens if you get caught. I don’t want to go to jail.”

“Jail is the least of your worries.” She took it as a threat and her whole body quivered. Alex didn’t like being the monster but that was his role in this nightmare. “Was your phone out of your sight at all that evening?”

She started to shake her head but stopped. “I leave it on my desk when I use the ladies’ room.”

“Because?”

The pale column of her throat rippled with a swallow. “I’m worried you’ll spy on me.”

“I’m not a pervert.”

Her eyes flashed. “And I’m not an exhibitionist.”

“I don’t go around spying on women unless I am instructed to do so by our boss. Don’t leave your phone unattended else we’re both going to end up regretting it.” The powers-that-be wouldn’t give him or Jane the chance to turn State’s evidence. She’d be lucky to last twenty-four hours in jail.

Thankfully he had a pretty good idea who’d made the call and why. Maybe this whole mess wasn’t so much sabotage as bad timing and piss poor judgment.

“Whoever your inside guy is at the FBI they need to take more care with communications. One fuck-up is acceptable, but another…he’ll answer to me.” He felt beyond tired. Hell, maybe he just needed a vacation—a couple of weeks of peace, quiet, hot sand and cold surf. A man could dream. What he really needed was to quit, but he’d made a commitment. Five hundred and twenty-eight days left. No chance of parole.

She cleared her throat. “The boss was wondering if there

had been any developments regarding that other matter with certain federal interests?"

Alex flashed to lace-edged stockings and sex against a door. "It's under control."

They sat quietly for another moment. A little girl ran past, the mother or nanny in hot pursuit. Jane flinched. Alex pretended not to notice. "Does this mean you're going back to work or are you still on hiatus?"

His instincts were telling him something didn't feel right. "I think we need to cool things down for a little while," he said. "Change things up a bit."

"Are you breaking up with me, Mr. Parker?" She managed to hold his gaze.

"No, but we should spend some time apart and enjoy other people's company for a few weeks. Unless something urgent comes up." By urgent he meant irrefutable proof of the identity of a serial killer who was an imminent threat to life.

She played with the bottom hem of her skirt which rested across her knees. "Actually the boss wants me to," she pursed her lips for a moment before continuing, "*persuade* a friend of yours to go on a date."

"A friend of mine?" Then he swore. "You are not messing with Lucas Randall's head."

"He might be our best way of accessing information on the Meacher inquiry."

"Are you supposed to fuck him too?"

She blinked like an owl. "I hardly think you're in any position to lecture me, Alex."

He raised his brow at the fact she'd finally had the balls to address him by name. Did she know about his night with Mallory or was she referring to his general duties for the organization? He didn't know and didn't care. He did care about his friends though. And he cared about Mallory and that was why he wouldn't call her again no matter how much he wanted to.

He leaned close to Jane's ear, watching the pulse at the bottom of her throat jump in response to his proximity.

"Right now the Meacher investigation is going nowhere. But if you hurt Lucas Randall, in any way, I will turn on you and this organization faster than you can say Senate Inquiry." He held her wide, blue gaze. "Do we understand one another?"

She nodded and he kissed her. A man saying goodbye to a former lover. Her lips were cold and he was unmoved.

"Watch out, Alex," she called out as he walked away. "Things aren't always what they seem."

CHAPTER TEN

MALLORY AND FRAZER got to Greenville just after lunch. Viewing the bodies hadn't upset her stomach as much as Frazer's earlier insensitivity. Given who he was and what he did, she had a hard time thinking he hadn't planned that attack to judge her reaction and put her off her game.

Not that she had much game.

The town was familiar to her. When she'd been a little girl, coming to Greenville had been a major adventure. They'd come for Fourth of July parades and ice cream sodas. The local sheriff's office was situated on Main Street opposite an old-fashioned cinema that she and Payton had occasionally visited. The smell of popcorn wafting across the street brought with it vivid memories, and she could almost hear her sister's unrestrained giggles. Sadness filtered through her but she ignored the onslaught. She was here to work, not reminisce. She followed Frazer into the atrium of the sheriff's office, aware of several pairs of eyes watching her closely.

"I'm Supervisory Special Agent Frazer and this is Special Agent Rooney, we're here to see Sheriff Williams," Frazer told the deputy at the desk.

"You with the FBI?" The accent was pure sweet West Virginia and sent a little quiver of home right down to Mallory's toes.

"Yes, ma'am." Frazer used his charm on the deputy.

It sure as hell would be lost on her from now on. She'd figured out over the last few hours that the reason he'd asked her to accompany him was so he'd be able to interrogate her in private for the duration of the journey. His suspicion of her had raised her suspicions of him, although it would take more than a few hours in a car to trip up a man as intelligent as Frazer.

Heck, she didn't even know his first name.

Sheriff Williams came out of his office and sized them up before coming over to meet them. A deputy interrupted just as they were shaking hands. "Road Traffic Accident out on Highway 3 involving a school bus, Sheriff. No passengers at the time. Both drivers have minor injuries."

The sheriff's mustache bristled over a full top lip. "Ray James the bus driver?"

"Yeah." The deputy was tall with almost military bearing. His glance kept sliding toward her like she was some kind of curiosity. It was natural that people here recognized her, from both the recent article in *The Post* and her mother's yearly TV campaign. She feigned ignorance and stared at the wanted posters on the wall.

"Make sure you get a blood sample from them both, Deputy Chance. If that sonofagun James has been drinking on the job I want to know it. The safety of the children in this county are my priority, I don't care who the man's uncle is."

"Yes, sir." The deputy strode away.

Mallory jerked her gaze back to the sheriff who was watching her carefully. He nodded stiffly and then led them to a conference room at the back of the building.

Her phone rang. She checked the number and saw Lucas

Randall was calling her. She let it go to voice mail.

The sheriff planted himself at the head of the table and indicated they take a seat. "If you don't mind me saying, Agent Rooney, it's good to see you again after all these years. I remember you as a little girl."

Apparently it was going to be a day of reminiscence after all. She nodded, conscious of Frazer staring at her with that dissecting gaze of his, waiting for her to screw up.

"The law enforcement community in Greenville was always very good to me and my family, Sheriff. I appreciate everything you did." Her mother still harbored a great deal of resentment toward law enforcement for not solving the case but she wasn't about to bring that up.

He blinked back a tear. "Well, we were all shaken up by what happened to your sister. Nothing like that ever happened since that we know of. Closest we've come is this poor girl, Lindsey Keeble. The cases aren't even remotely similar, but we're seeing the same kind of panic within the community. Not that I blame folk."

What if it was *the same guy?*

The idea tugged at her mind.

"What can you tell us about the victim, Sheriff? Did she have a boyfriend?" Frazer led the questioning.

"No boyfriend. All her classmates say she was determined to make something of herself and didn't have time for dating. She was a good kid. Smart, worked hard, earning money to pay her way through college."

"How long had she been working at the gas station?"

"She started there in the fall. Her dad said it was the only thing she could find that still let her go to school but didn't involve a bar."

"She objected to alcohol?"

"Her mother was a drunk who spent most of Lindsey's young life inside the local taverns." The sheriff's face pinched. "She died a few years back. Exposure. Got caught in a blizzard too drunk to find her way home." He looked up. "I think it was a blessing for the rest of the family."

"Now there's just the father?"

The sheriff nodded. "Bryce Keeble."

Mallory's eyes widened and the sheriff caught her expression. "Remember him?"

"Vaguely." She nodded.

"He worked as a handyman on your parents' estate."

"He was questioned and cleared of any wrongdoing in regards to Payton Rooney, correct?" said Frazer.

The sheriff nodded and looked uncomfortable as he spoke to her. "Your mother sacked him anyway. I know losing his job hit the Keeble family hard because it was around the same time Lindsey was born and he struggled to find work."

Oh, Mom. Mallory splayed her fingers on top of the desk. "Payton's disappearance hit us all hard, Sheriff, but particularly my mother. She didn't always make rational choices." Something her political enemies would love to use against her.

"Anyone with kids can understand her reaction, but…"

"What is it?" asked Frazer.

"You going to see Bryce next?"

Frazer nodded. A feeling of dread squeezed Mallory's insides.

"Bear in mind he's the one who lost a child this time. He might not make rational choices either."

Frazer filled him in on the few details they knew about the cases. It wasn't much. "As soon as we have a profile we'll send it to you and assist your department in any way we can." They stood to go.

At the door to the conference room, the sheriff stopped her for a moment while Frazer went ahead. "Good to see you doing so well, Agent Rooney." He squinted. "You must be one of the youngest agents in BAU history."

Mallory forced a smile. "I do believe I may have that honor, Sheriff. For now anyway," she added quietly.

Outside in the main atrium of the sheriff's office she caught the eye of another deputy staring at her intently. She frowned and stopped walking. Pointed her finger at him. "I remember you."

He gave her a shy smile and stepped forward and held out his hand. "We used to play together as kids. I can't believe you recognized me. You'd remember me as Seany Kennedy." He pulled an embarrassed face. "Deputy Sean Kennedy, nowadays."

"We used to go swimming in the quarry during the summer."

"Now, ma'am, I wasn't about to say that I'd seen you naked but since you brought it up."

She laughed. "I think we were, what? Five?"

"I do believe I might even have been six or seven, Miss Mallory."

She pointed self-consciously to her shield. "*Agent* Rooney nowadays, *Deputy* Kennedy. Just call me Mallory." She remembered Sean as a chubby kid with a soft heart. He'd slimmed out some.

"I thought you were going to be a lawyer?" He settled back against his desk.

"So did my parents."

"I bet that went down well." He tucked his arms over a broad chest. "At least some good came out of what happened to Payton." The fact he'd said her sister's name out loud, the fact that he'd *known* her, was incredibly moving. Some days it was like Payton was nothing but a photograph on a police report. But that wasn't the real Payton. The real Payton had been sweet and generous and had loved *Scooby Doo,* swimming, Disney movies and ice cream. Not many people remembered that.

"You joined the FBI, and I joined the sheriff's office. Fighting bad guys as best we can."

"Always plenty of bad guys to fight."

"Ain't that the truth?"

Frazer was eyeing her from the doorway with irritation. She needed to go.

Sean noticed the direction of her gaze and stood. "It sure is nice seeing you again after all these years. Does a heart good to know life can go on after tragedy."

"It was good to see you too." She choked up as she shook his hand. Actually wanted to hug the guy, but managed to hold herself back. Her mother wouldn't have approved of such uncontrolled displays of emotion and neither would her supervisor. "We should catch up sometime. Dad wants us all to come out here for Christmas—one last family get together before he sells Eastborne."

"I didn't know he was selling up. It's a shame, but I guess I'm not surprised." He pressed his lips together and gave her a sad nod. "I'd like to catch up at Christmastime, *Agent* Mallory."

She laughed, gave him her card and walked briskly to find Frazer. She hadn't realized just how deeply her sister's disappearance had affected this entire community and all the people who'd worked on the case, including the icy cool SSA Frazer. She should have come and talked to these people years ago; maybe then she'd remember exactly what happened that night.

THE KEEBLES LIVED in a rundown house on the edge of Greenville, within a stone's throw of the railway tracks. It needed a fresh coat of paint, the front porch sagged slightly at the northwest corner, but the grounds were neat with no trash lying around. A wreath decorated the front door, and Mallory would bet everything she owned that she knew who put it there. A dog—half pit bull, half coon hound—snoozed in the dirt. He stirred himself enough to start barking when they pulled up and got out of the car.

Mallory eyed the dog warily. A yell from inside the house had the dog giving a disgruntled snarl and curling back into the dirt. She liked dogs but didn't trust the malevolent glint in the old dog's opaque eyes. Frazer surprised her by dropping to his haunches and giving the mutt's head a scratch. The dog stretched out his neck for better access.

Great.

A man came to the door. Their eyes connected and he gave a start as recognition hit. She remembered him vividly now that she'd seen him again. He'd given her and Payton piggyback rides, taken them for jaunts on the back of his dirt bike and generally joked and teased them.

His face was older, broader, coarser than it'd been eighteen years ago. She and Payton had thought him handsome back then. Not today. The whites of his eyes were crimson, irises black, face a splotchy, unhealthy red. His hair had been shiny blue-black but was now streaked salt-and-pepper gray.

"Mr. Keeble?" Frazer approached the man with his hand outstretched. "Supervisory Special Agent Frazer. This is Special Agent Rooney."

Bryce Keeble shook Frazer's hand without dropping Mallory's gaze. "What are you doing here?"

"We're investigating your daughter's murder. We need to ask you a few questions."

"Feds?" His gaze ping-ponged between them. "Do you know who did it yet?"

Frazer shook his head. "We don't have a clear suspect at this time."

Bryce Keeble's head bobbed as he raised his chin. "You come to pin it on me? Come to make a grieving man suffer?" He gave a hollow laugh and opened his front door and waved them inside. "Not that I give a shit."

There was no doubt this man was hurting, that his whole world had been ripped away. It didn't mean he didn't do it, but he wasn't high on her suspect list.

Frazer stood in the living room looking out of place and overdressed. There were pictures of Lindsey everywhere. The place was clean but messy. Empty mugs littered the surface. Cigarette smoke hung heavy in the air.

"Never let me smoke in the house—Lindsey." His voice caught and broke. "She wouldn't let me smoke anywhere but outside and busted my ass even when she caught me doing that."

"She was a smart girl." Mallory eyed the overflowing ashtrays. "I'm very sorry for your loss, Mr. Keeble."

He glared at her for a moment, nostrils flaring, eyes watering with a sudden onslaught of tears. "People keep saying that to me." He lit a cigarette from the box beside an old worn-out recliner, inhaling the smoke like it was oxygen. He blew out a thick curling stream that made her cough. "*I'm sorry for your loss*? What do I say to that? 'That's okay'? 'Thank you'? I mean what the fuck do you do when people say that to you?" His eyes drilled into her, wanting an answer. Wanting a way of dealing with the awful reality of having lost the only thing that truly mattered.

A dark truth escaped from somewhere deep inside as she held his gaze. "People aren't saying it for your benefit. Not really. They mean well but the words let them acknowledge the tragedy and move on. People like you and I, we can't move on, not at first." Emotion made her voice rough. "Losing someone to violent crime isn't like normal loss. We grieve differently than other people. We *hate* differently."

His eyes locked on hers because now he knew she understood him completely.

"That hatred can either swallow us up, or we learn to let it go." Which path had she chosen? She didn't know yet. "Nothing makes grief better except time."

His eyes burned, fiery red. "I suppose you heard it often enough."

Way too many times to count.

"I'd like to see Lindsey's room if I may?" SSA Frazer cut in. He'd catalogued the exchange like the profiler he was. Had probably learned more about her than Bryce Keeble.

"Help yourself but don't take nothing without asking."

"I won't." He looked at Mallory pointedly. "Agent Rooney can make you some tea or coffee."

She felt her eyes widen but nodded. That she could do. She walked into the kitchen and tried not to wince. Although it wasn't filthy there was a strong smell from the garbage and piles of dirty dishes in the sink.

There was no coffeepot so she filled the tea kettle on the electric stove and opened the dishwasher and gingerly started stacking it. She may as well help on a practical level because she'd gotten a clear 'get lost' signal from Frazer. She felt eyes on her from the doorway. Bryce Keeble had followed her.

"I take it Lindsey was the housekeeper of the pair of you?"

A look of shame swept his features and he stopped slouching against the doorframe. "I'm not usually a slob, I just…find it hard to care."

The heartbreak in his eyes undid her. "She wouldn't want this to destroy you, Mr. Keeble. She loved you. From what I've heard Lindsey was a tough and determined young woman." She tried not to picture her corpse under that white sheet.

Tears streamed down his face and he wiped them on his shoulder. "She was tough and determined. After her mother let her down she learned to take control of her own destiny… Someone ripped that away from her." He swallowed repeatedly. "She'd have fought him and he'd have hurt her more because of it. And she'd have been waiting for me to save her." A sob ripped free. God, she understood that sort of guilt. "The way I was supposed to save her." His breath was a raw choking rasp. "I want to find the person who did this and rip them apart with my bare hands." His fists were doing just that.

"Vengeance isn't the way to deal with this," she tried to calm him. "Don't betray your daughter's memory by ending up in prison. Let us do our jobs."

"Like the cops did for your sister, you mean?" His expression turned scathing and bitter. "They thought it was me, did you know that?" He took a step toward her. Too close in the tiny kitchen. After her encounter with those intruders in her home she was jumpier than she used to be. It pissed her off. "When they figured it wasn't me, your bitch mother fired me anyway because someone told her I used to take you girls on the back of my bike. 'It's too dangerous'." He mimicked her mother. "Well, I never hurt anyone, but the cops never did me a blind bit of good." His voice rose, his body language was getting increasingly aggressive. She forced herself not to put her hand on her weapon because she knew how much he was hurting.

The anger in his face dissolved to be replaced by misery. "I just realized something else. If someone as high and mighty as your bitch of a mother can't get justice, someone like me doesn't stand a chance."

"The law doesn't come with a price tag."

Bryce sneered. "You keep on believing that." He whirled, strode to a corkboard near the backdoor and ripped down an old newspaper clipping. He thrust it toward her face and she stopped it with her hand, prepared to take him down if he got any closer. He didn't. He stepped away. She looked at the piece of paper he'd given her. It was a cutting of one of the first pieces written about Payton's disappearance and featured a picture of them both on the lawn of Eastborne with their dog lying between them. "I kept it to remind myself never to stop looking for your sister, but she's dead, just like my Lindsey's dead and we'll never figure out what happened to either of them." The disgust in his eyes made her breath stop.

"I don't know whether to envy your parents or pity them." His gaze raked her from head to toe, "On one hand they still have a kid who looks exactly like the one they lost. On the other, the constant reminder must have torn them inside out every single day."

She'd witnessed that pain in their eyes. Raw emotion rose up and wanted to swamp her but that wasn't her fault any more than his daughter's murder had been. "I'm not my sister, Mr. Keeble. We just looked alike."

Frazer appeared in the doorway as the kettle started to whistle. "Everything all right?"

Bryce Keeble shuffled over to the stove to turn it off. "Fine. I've got it." To her relief, he started filling the sink with hot water and dish soap. Maybe he'd make it through this mess. Maybe.

"We'll be in touch, Mr. Keeble," said Frazer.

On the front step he turned, hands on hips. "What the hell was that?"

She pressed her lips tight together and ignored him. She couldn't speak. The dog wagged his tail at Frazer but eyed her with suspicion. She ignored the mutt and got in the Lexus. She'd stopped caring about whether or not she impressed SSA Frazer. She smoothed out the newspaper cutting and laid it over her knees, staring at the fragile yellowed paper. Keeble was right. It *had* been hard for her parents since Payton was taken. They'd never found justice. Never got closure. Her sister had been taken and no one had ever known why. She wanted to prove Keeble wrong about cops. She wanted to believe in the system. She wanted to find justice for Lindsey and her grieving father. Then, maybe, there was still a glimmer of hope she'd get justice for her family. They all deserved that.

HE CAME DOWN the steps whistling. It was almost Thanksgiving and he had a lot to be thankful for. He'd sent Mallory Rooney a little gift in the mail this morning and felt better than he had in months. The girl sat up on the bed.

"How you feeling today?"

She smiled nervously. "O-okay. Sore, I guess."

They'd had sex twice. Nothing adventurous. Nothing rough. Nice and slow and easy; he'd been a considerate lover. He'd used a condom—he wasn't ready to commit to any other level of trust just yet, but he was considering the idea of starting a family. He glanced around at the space. There was no way they could raise a child here but he'd given it some thought. That was his biggest regret with Payton. Not having a baby with her.

"I brought you some clothes." He held out the garments he'd picked up in a big box store over in the next county when he'd arranged to send his package.

She reached for them. "Thank you."

Her nails were dirty. She could probably use a bath. "Want me to heat some water to wash with before you put on your new things?"

She cleared her throat. "That would be nice, thank you."

Well brought up and good manners. His mother would have approved.

He put a pan of water on the propane stove on the counter top. When he turned around she was still sitting on the bed. He was amused by her coyness. "You'll need to get undressed."

Her hands gripped the new clothes tighter. He frowned. It was natural to be uneasy around men but surely he'd proved he wasn't going to hurt her? He'd gone out of his way to make sure she'd enjoyed it too.

"Don't be shy." The sharpness of his tone startled her into action and she started undoing the buttons of her shirt. She folded it and placed her bra neatly on top. She pulled off her jeans and socks, one leg catching on the chain around her leg. He knelt down and undid the shackle so she could properly change. One day they wouldn't need the chain.

She stood before him, naked, head bent in submission.

"That's better."

He dipped the washcloth in the warm water and tipped up her chin. Washed the dirt and grime from around her mouth and cheeks. Her lips were a deep natural red. Hair fine and almost black. He did sweeps down her neck, holding her long tresses up out of the way while he worked. She shivered, nipples turgid red peaks against milk pale skin. She was slim to the point of scrawny, except for full breasts, which were bigger than Payton's had been but he had to admit he liked them anyway. Blue veins were visible under the translucent skin. He felt himself growing hard but forced himself to wash all of her because he'd promised. Along her arms, hands, each finger, her nails. "Turn around." He rinsed out the cloth and washed her back, her buttocks, her legs, feet. By the time he made her turn around again he was almost bursting out of the top of his jeans. "Open." He pointed to her legs and she obeyed without hesitation. From his knees he looked up at her face but she avoided his gaze. He liked the way she did what she was told even though she was inexperienced.

He ran the warm cloth up one delicate ankle, up the inside of one leg, and then the other. The shackle had rubbed her ankle and he made a mental note to bring longer socks.

When she was clean, he leaned forward and kissed her stomach. She went to take a step back. "Don't. Move," he warned her. He met her gaze, eyes so dark he couldn't have said what color her irises were if he hadn't already known. "Lie down on the bed."

She did and he smiled as she lay there shivering with her legs pressed tight together. She might not be Payton, but she did what she was told. Maybe one day she'd try to please him the same way Payton had pleased him. One day.

"Spread your legs for me."

She parted them just a little bit.

"Wider," he bit out impatiently.

She did so immediately.

"That's better, sweetheart." She needed to know who was boss. But he needed to remember she was unsure and nervous and to give her time. She wasn't like those others. Or like Payton's slutty sister. "You keep pleasing me the way you've been doing and everything is going to turn out just fine. I'll take care of you. I promise."

CHAPTER ELEVEN

PINK'S "BLOW ME" was playing on her iPod as she drove home, and she too had had a shit day. Actually her second full week at the BAU had been so bad that the stress headache pounding her temples was preferable to being at work. She'd worked straight-through Thanksgiving with the promise to her parents she'd make it up to them at Christmas. The joys of public service.

She wanted to crawl under her duvet and sleep for two days straight.

There had been no additional cases of abductions reported or bodies found with PR carved into the skin—which was good news. They hadn't got the results back from the possible DNA samples the ME sent to the lab yet, so there was still hope the killer might have screwed up and be in the system.

She'd sensed a tiny thaw in her relations with a couple of members on the BAU team—the secretary and the janitor. Yesterday, on Thanksgiving, she'd managed to search Barton and Singh's desks and found exactly nothing. Hanrahan hadn't been blown away by her results so far but he'd stressed patience and stealth. People this smart wouldn't leave incriminating evidence in plain sight.

Moira Henderson had restrained herself from letting down any more tires or being quite so openly hostile. So far

Mallory hadn't seen anything to make her doubt the integrity of her colleagues. They worked their asses off hunting monsters.

The scary thing was deep down she understood the vigilante. Over the years she'd often fantasized about what would happen if she ever found the man who took her sister. In her mind she put a gun to his head and demanded he tell her where Payton's remains were. But after he told her it became a blur. Would she pull the trigger? Or would she read him his rights and arrest him?

She didn't know, and hated herself for the weakness.

Lindsey Keeble's case haunted her. Her father's grief was so raw, so negative, and her family had added to his burden. She remembered the devil-may-care young man who'd carted them around the swimming pool on his dirt bike, and the infectious grin he'd once sported. The grin was gone now. She didn't think he'd ever get it back.

He could have taken Payton... Or he could be yet another victim of the whole sad episode. He'd obviously loved his daughter.

Traffic was heavy. She inched her little sedan through a busy intersection. Another Friday night with DC all dressed up in its pretty festive dazzle. She pushed thoughts of Alex Parker out of her mind. Tonight she planned to stay in and do nothing. Not a goddamn thing. Definitely not call the guy for a repeat performance no matter how tempting it was just to hear his voice.

She'd volunteered to go to Lindsey Keeble's funeral next week even though she hated funerals—probably because her sister had never had one. There was no headstone to place flowers. No grave to tend. But she owed Bryce Keeble, both because of her family's treatment of him, and as a law enforcement officer investigating his daughter's death.

Frazer had leapt on the suggestion and by the end of the conversation he seemed to have persuaded himself it was his idea. *Men.* She rolled her eyes as she turned into her parking garage. She pulled into her space, switched off the engine and relaxed.

She closed her eyes and sagged in her seat.

Silence. Blessed silence.

This time two weeks ago, all she'd wanted to do was forget. Now, it seemed imperative that she try to remember. There were so many things she didn't recall from that period of her life. Going to Greenville, meeting Bryce Keeble and that deputy, Sean Kennedy, had made her realize she needed to dig deeper into the past because maybe, just maybe, the answers were still there waiting for her.

She thought of Alex, and how she'd blown him off and how desperately she wished she hadn't. "Damn you, Pay. Why'd you have to go and leave me?"

The headache ratcheted up a notch, relentlessly grinding her temples as she climbed out of her little silver sedan and hauled her laptop out of the passenger seat to the elevator. It weighed a thousand tons. Maybe she'd take the night off. Reboot her brain. Visit her poor neglected mother like she kept promising. She stopped to check for mail and found a slightly battered looking parcel from Amazon. Her mother and father often ordered her things off the web, maybe compensating for their general lack of family togetherness. She put it under her arm and headed up to her father's apartment. In the elevator she kept flashing back to that Friday night and the man who'd rocked her world. Her toes curled remembering the feel of his hands on her skin. Her pulse sped up.

But there was a limit to how many times you could push someone away without them actually going. Tears wanted to form in her eyes but she refused to let them. She wasn't that weak. She didn't need a man in her life right now, it was too complicated.

She managed to unlock the door and stumble inside the apartment. It was cold and quiet. She boosted the heat and dumped all her possessions by the front door. She kicked off her boots, hung her jacket in the closet. Put her Glock and its holster in the drawer beside the door. She put the parcel on the coffee table and poured herself a large glass of water and found headache tablets in the medicine cabinet in the bathroom. She wandered aimlessly through the kitchen. She was going to have to go grocery shopping soon or face starvation.

Back in the living room, she turned the package, squeezed it. Whatever was inside was light, and soft. A T-shirt maybe? Her father had a wicked sense of humor and often sent her shirts he couldn't wear himself. She slowly peeled back the flap, enjoying the element of surprise. She pulled out the contents and frowned down at them, not understanding for a whole three seconds. Then her heart pounded like a pile-driver and she dropped the plastic wrapped clothing as if it had stung her. She groped for her cell, hit redial. Shock made her brain stop working.

"Mallory?"

She blinked, confused. She thought she'd dialed work, but as soon as Alex answered she needed him. "Something happened. Will you come? I'm at the apartment."

"I'll be there in five minutes."

No questions. No drama.

She covered her mouth with her hand as she stared down at the children's pajamas someone had sent her. She leaned over the package, knowing she mustn't touch the wrapper again with her bare hands, but searching for clues as to its authenticity. The garments had purple horses on a white background, solid purple cuffs. They were exactly the right type of clothing they'd both been wearing the night of the abduction, but were they Payton's? She examined them inch by inch and finally found the answer in the hand-stitched repair job on the left cuff. Her mother had used blue cotton because she couldn't find purple. Mallory fell back on the floor, away from the clothing, away from the evidence that they'd been searching for all these years. Evidence that someone somewhere knew exactly what had happened to her sister.

There was a pounding on her door. She scrambled to her feet and ran to the entrance, checking the peephole before unlocking it and throwing herself into Alex's arms. They closed around her like a vise. He radiated strength, safety, security. He'd obviously been out running when she'd called him. He was damp from sweat and his heart beat strongly against her ear and calmed her racing pulse. He maneuvered her inside, closed the door with his heel and herded her to the couch where he pulled her onto his lap and rocked her. She held on, so shaken, so torn between despair and hope she couldn't speak. She gripped his T-shirt tight in her fist. She could feel the heat of his skin through the fabric and the effect curled through her and offered such comfort that for a moment she couldn't breathe. He smelled wonderful. Strong clean male sweat with that hint of sandalwood that seemed to be an integral part of his being.

Eventually he spoke into her hair. "What happened?"

She released a deep breath. She wasn't usually this emotional but events lately had been turning her inside out. "I received a present in the mail."

He shifted her so he could lean forward. She tried to escape his arms because she was a federal agent, not a weakling girl, but he wouldn't let her go and he was a damn sight stronger than she'd realized.

"Hush." He held her tighter. "You scared the crap out of me on the phone. Just give me a minute."

She closed her eyes and squeezed her arms around him.

He peered at the envelope and plastic wrapped clothes. "What is this?"

She told him quickly about her sister's abduction. "They were Payton's." Then she let him go. And pushed away. This time he let her.

He looked at her sharply. "Are you saying these are the actual clothes your sister was wearing when she was taken?"

She nodded, her throat too raw to speak.

"And they sent it to you? Here? To your home?"

She nodded.

His face hardened. "You can't stay here alone, Mallory."

She just looked at him. She hadn't even thought of those implications.

"What if he comes after you?"

She couldn't stop the tear that rolled down her cheek. "Then I finally get to find out what happened to my sister."

"Even if it costs you your life?" His voice was soft.

"I have to know, Alex. Not knowing is killing me." She crossed her arms over her chest. "Anyway, I'm not a little girl. I'm ready for the bastard if he tries anything."

He nodded slowly like he'd made some sort of decision. "Okay. Find something to package this up in and I'll drive you to Quantico with it right now."

That made sense.

"And then we'll swing by my apartment and I'll pick up some stuff—"

"Wait. What?"

His jaw firmed. "I'm not leaving you alone. Not until I know you're safe. Not until this sick sonofabitch is either locked up, or dead."

"That could take months, years even…"

"We'll figure something out, but in the meantime if you're staying here, you're stuck with me."

She couldn't believe he was doing this for her, but he was a security consultant. Maybe she'd known exactly how he'd handle the situation. That made her a coward because she wanted him here and hadn't had the courage to follow through by simply asking him. Her hands clasped one another. She felt small and petty and confused. "I'm sorry I didn't reply to your texts."

He laughed and climbed to his feet. He was dressed in black running shorts and a blue/black work-out T-shirt that make his eyes look smoky and dark. He caught her hand and rubbed her knuckles with his thumb. "I don't care whether or not you texted me. I'm not a teenager. You told me from the start you didn't want a relationship, but you called when you needed me. Thank you." He brushed her bangs aside. "Whatever happens in the future, no matter what happens between us…you need to know I'll always be there for you if you need me. Always."

A shiver rippled over her. The last time she'd felt this sort of connection with anyone, they'd shared the exact same DNA. What she and Alex felt for one another was more intense than it should be, and she knew he felt it too. "I don't want to drag you down to my level of crazy."

The smile on his face was beautiful. "I am *way* beyond your level of crazy, sweetheart. Truth is, you might be the most normal thing there is about me."

IT WAS CLOSE to midnight when they got back to Mallory's apartment. He'd run by his place and grabbed more stuff and his weapon. Not the one he used for missions, this one he legally owned and was allowed to carry concealed.

He'd waited outside at Quantico. It was easier all around rather than trying to sort out a visitor pass this late at night, and he figured she'd be safe enough on base. She'd handed the evidence to her boss, who'd met her there. SSA Frazer had sent the clothes and envelope straight to the crime lab and taken her statement.

Now, standing in her apartment, Mallory was so pale Alex was scared she was going to pass out. She hadn't eaten anything. He touched her cheek. "Go to bed. You're safe. I'll sleep on the couch."

She shook her head and pulled him with her to the darkened bedroom. "Sleep with me." She let go of his hand and stripped without a measure of seduction or self-consciousness. Pulled on a nightshirt. He watched her, making sure none of the thoughts he was thinking leaked through.

He wanted her.

Even though she was tired and upset. He wanted her. And

he wasn't about to let her know what sort of a guy he really was.

She slipped under the covers. He sat on the edge of the bed, stroking her hair. She caught his hand as her eyes drifted shut, already asleep. The trust factor was immense and it floored him.

She was a federal agent who lived to uphold the law.

He was a killer who'd die to keep her safe.

He blew out a sigh. Hell, his hands were shaking. It had been his idea to stay but he hadn't slept with another person in the same room for a long time—except prison where the cell had been packed ten deep with innocent and guilty alike.

He didn't know if he *could* sleep with anyone. But he couldn't leave her vulnerable with this asshole on the loose, taunting her about her sister. She needed some measure of comfort and he needed reassurance that she was indeed safe. *Shit.* He pulled off his shirt and tossed it on a chair. There was no way he was going to get out of this situation unscathed, but after weeks obsessing about the woman maybe it didn't matter. Maybe her safety was the only thing that truly mattered.

And maybe he was viewing this situation all wrong. What better way to keep his eye on what the FBI might know than by sticking close to this woman as he kept her safe? The idea felt like a betrayal, but it was justification enough. He needed to protect her, he needed to fulfill his commitment to The Gateway Project. So being here was a win-win situation. Get over it.

They didn't even have to have sex. She might not want sex. She just wanted comfort and the feeling of security you got when someone you trusted watched your back. And she could trust him. He wouldn't let anyone hurt her.

He kicked off his shoes and socks and removed his pants, but kept his boxers on. Then he lay on top of the bed staring at the ceiling. He was royally fucked.

Twice, he got up to leave and found himself unable to go further than the bedroom door. He didn't want her waking up thinking she was alone. Or that he could only be with her for sex.

Mallory shivered in her sleep and he adjusted the duvet higher over her shoulders, his fingers lingering on the soft skin of her upper arm. He'd made an error in judgment being with her before because now she was in his system like liquid heroin and he was hooked.

He was a professional liar, but he didn't bullshit himself. He was actually glad the bastard had mailed her those clothes, because now he had an excuse to stick close.

Fuck.

That was sick.

He really should leave before she woke. Go sleep on the couch and pretend to be a decent human being. That's what he told himself, but his limbs were welded to the bed and his body stubbornly refused to budge. It felt like his head had been cracked open and his conscience was being laid bare and he didn't know how to handle it.

Something inside him was shifting.

Years of telling lies and keeping secrets from the people who mattered had eroded the man he used to be. The stint in the Moroccan jail had finished him off—or so he'd believed. The beatings, the abandonment by his country, his own pathetic failure had made him wish he was dead. By the time The Gateway Project had intervened he'd thought himself past saving, but the human spirit was an incredible thing. The will to survive overrode all other considerations. So he'd agreed to their offer. Agreed to once again work for the people who'd left him in that hellhole to rot.

Somehow, something about Mallory affected him in a way no one else ever had. She made him want to find out if there was anything left of the old Alex Parker. Anything left of the boy who'd held his grandfather's hand at that cold Veteran's Day ceremony all those years ago. Anything left of the soldier who'd been recruited by the CIA after his friends had been killed when betrayed by someone who was supposed to be on their side. And for years he'd made a difference. He had to believe that. He hadn't just been killing in cold blood. He'd been neutralizing threats to US concerns around the world.

So why did he feel like nothing but a cold-blooded killer? And if he was just following orders why hadn't he killed the arms dealer? Or Gerry Rodman? And if he wasn't following orders what the hell was he doing? Picking and choosing who deserved to live and die the same way a serial killer might? The idea made him sweat.

Mallory turned over and draped her arm across his chest. It should have made him feel hemmed in or claustrophobic. It didn't. It calmed him. He wrapped his fingers around hers.

He must have drifted off because he awoke with a start. It was dark but he instantly recognized Mallory's scent, warm and intoxicating. Gentle lips traced a scar on his right side—courtesy of a knife and that fucker whose neck he should have snapped.

He let her play, watching her kiss him as his eyes grew accustomed to the shadows. Teeth scraped feverishly hot skin, nerves short-circuited by lust. She had no idea that no one else had touched him since his incarceration.

Christ.

She had the power to destroy him. And if she ever found out who and what he was, she would have no hesitation in doing just that. Somehow, Mallory Rooney had complete and utter control over him. All because her sister had been stolen and she'd looked at him with those big amber eyes and had *seen* him. Not the assassin, not the businessman, but the essence of a man no one else seemed to see anymore.

Tender kisses teased his body and stirred his flesh. He felt like he was being burned alive from the inside out and liberated all at the same time. The feelings she evoked terrified him and he was actually shaking.

He wasn't in love. He wasn't the sort of man who could afford to love. Too many secrets. Too much death.

City lights shone beyond the drapes, coating the room with soft light. A tongue licked the ugly line from his hipbone to halfway down his thigh. He groaned at the sensual slide of wet flesh against taut skin. Then she wrapped her fingers around him and he squeezed his eyes shut as her mouth closed over him.

"Mallory," he groaned, desperate for something he couldn't even name. "You don't have to do that."

"Maybe I want to." Her smile had fiery lust snaking through him. Watching her go down on him was the most erotic thing he'd ever experienced. Every muscle clenched against the pleasure she wrought on him. He felt helpless. Her fingers gripped him tighter around the base and her lips milked him.

He was a ruthless killer and she held him literally in the palm of her hand.

It was impossible not to just take everything she was offering. The suction of her mouth grew stronger, the pressure building at the base of his spine coiling like a spring. He was seconds from losing it when that lone brain cell kicked in and he pulled her gently off him.

"But..."

He pressed his finger to her swollen lips. "Not yet."

She nipped his finger.

He stripped the nightshirt over her head and lay beside her on the bed, tracing the rosy circle of her nipples. "What do you like, Mallory?"

Her gaze turned curious. "What do you mean?"

"Obviously you know what works for me." Her in the same room seemed to be enough to get him hard. "What works for you?" He nuzzled her ear.

"I don't think anyone has ever asked me that before. The usual—you inside me." She laughed and the sparkle of it punched him in the gut. She traced his scarred eyebrow with her index finger. "Believe it or not, I'm not that experienced at sexual encounters."

The temperature shot up twenty degrees. He kissed her slowly, teasing nibbles until she relaxed beneath him. His tongue traced the lobe of her ear. "Anything you'd like to try?"

Her eyes went wide. "I don't even know. I don't think I'm into kink if that's your thing. The idea of pain and bondage really doesn't do it for me." She glanced at his scars just visible in the dawn light.

"I didn't get these from sex games, Mallory." It was the first time he'd been amused by his scars.

"You said you got some of them in Afghanistan." She hesitated. "How?"

"I was tortured." *Christ.* "I don't want to talk about it."

Because, all she had to do was ask him the right question and he may as well go home and blow his brains out.

His heart gave a little tumble at the sadness he saw on her face, sadness for him. No one had cared in a long time. Unable to resist he kissed her deeper, holding her chin. He wanted to touch every part of her, to give her pleasure and make her forget the world. He palmed her breast, flicked a calloused thumb over the hard pink tip until she arched against him.

"You like that? Tell me what else you like."

Her fingers sank into his hair. "Only if you do the same."

The thought of Mallory trying to please him made him feel humble and unworthy and as aroused as hell. "You first," he said gruffly.

"Let's stay in bed all weekend having sex."

A weekend to explore Mallory's sexual boundaries—although he already knew she'd teach him more than he'd ever teach her. Sure he could show her new positions, but she'd already taught him how to feel again. *That* should have been impossible—like a man with a severed spine relearning how to walk.

"You're trying to kill me." He drew one nipple into his mouth, using his tongue on her sensitive skin until she gripped the sheets tightly in her hands.

"It would be a hell of a way to go."

He reared back and smiled into her eyes. "I'm not even any good," he warned. "Last time you were too drunk to notice but you didn't even come—"

"Liar." She gripped his face in her hands and pulled him down for a kiss. "I wasn't that drunk, and if you're that bothered by your performance you can make it up to me now." The laughter in her amber eyes sucker-punched his heart.

"You don't even know me." His voice was an ugly rasp.

She touched his cheek. "I want to know you."

He slid over her and into her, freezing against the fierce pleasure of skin on skin contact. Christ, she was so wet and ready for him he wanted to just pound home.

He withdrew and grabbed a condom from the drawer. "You make me forget. Everything." He couldn't afford to let his guard down but surely one weekend with Mallory wouldn't hurt? It would give the feds time to process the evidence and maybe find the bastard who was taunting her. She sure as hell needed the escape more than he did.

He covered himself and slid deep into her heat. He captured both hands and held them above her head as he thrust into her hot willing body. He never let go of those hands or those pretty eyes as he ground against her harder and she groaned and moved with him, taking him as deep as he could get.

And it was in that exact moment that he knew he was completely fucked. Having sex with this woman unmade him. Mallory ripped him apart, gutted, stripped him to bones and blood. Made him think he could be anything he wanted to be.

Maybe he was having a breakdown. Maybe he was going insane. All he knew for sure was she'd completely destroyed whoever the hell Alex Parker was supposed to be. All the new Alex Parker cared about was *her* pleasure, *her* well-being. Everyone else on the planet, including himself, could go to hell.

MALLORY AWOKE WITH a start. She'd had the dream again. She was trapped in a small space, terrified someone was searching for her, but unable to move and confront them and unable to run away. Sweat beaded on her upper lip though the room was cool. Her heart thumped loudly in her ears as she tried to control her breathing.

Realizing she wasn't alone in bed she looked over to where Alex lay sleeping. His face was relaxed and younger-looking than when he was awake and aware. After spending most of the night driving her insane, he had to be exhausted. A warm feeling replaced the terror of the dream. Something about him really got to her and she didn't know what it was. Maybe it was because she'd had to work so hard to get him into bed or the fact he was so damn thorough once he got there.

Actually sex was a bonus.

He treated her like she mattered. Like what she thought mattered. After years of people assuming they knew her because of what had happened to her family, it was great to have someone pay attention to what she said and thought.

Mallory slipped quietly out of the covers and grabbed her robe. She got herself a glass of water, and checked her laptop, which was set up in a corner of the living room. Nothing from Frazer. She knew she needed to tell her parents about this development with the pajamas but Frazer had suggested waiting to see if the lab found anything before raising their hopes.

He was right. They'd been through enough hell.

She pulled out the files on her sister's case. To anyone else the photograph on the first page looked like a young Mallory, but the nose was too straight, the eyes slightly too large. She touched the old image; a school portrait where they'd both been forced to wear identical blue dresses, hair in matching pigtails at their mother's insistence. But Mallory had rebelled at school and by the time the photographer got hold of her, her hair had grass in it and was down around her shoulders.

Payton had been the good girl. The obedient child. Mallory had been the troublemaker, the imp, the pain in the ass. Some things hadn't changed.

A lump expanded in her throat. No matter how she tried to be objective about her sister's case it was impossible. What the hell good could she do if she couldn't even get past the first page without weeping?

"Hey."

The papers went flying. "Oh, God. You startled me," she told Alex.

"Not used to having strange men in your apartment?" His eyes twinkled. He'd pulled on jeans and a T-shirt but his feet were bare. Sexy feet.

"Not used to having anyone in my space, period."

A slight smile touched that gorgeous mouth. "Me either." He squatted down to the floor while her heart did somersaults in her chest. One look at that smile and she knew she'd fallen for him. This wasn't good.

"What are these?" He frowned at the photograph and papers. Rubbed a thumb over the image. "Your sister's case file?" He looked up.

"A copy." She nodded. Too upset with herself to speak.

He read some of the file. "So the thing you wanted to forget the other week was the anniversary of her disappearance?"

"Eighteen years." Her throat was raw with suppressed emotion.

He straightened the pages and put them neatly back in the file. "Is she the reason you became a fed?"

How many times had she answered that question recently? And every time it made her feel like more and more of a failure. She took the file from his hands and laid it on the desk. "I've been looking into Payton's disappearance on my days off, but I haven't gotten any further than the officials did back then."

He took her hands in his. The warmth of his skin seeped into her fingers. She hadn't realized how cold she was until she touched him. There was something in his eyes that made her want to tell him everything.

"Is she the reason you don't date?" Those eyes of his bore into hers, demanding answers.

"No." Except the word felt like a lie. "Maybe," she finally admitted. "I don't have time to date. I spend all my spare time trying to figure out what happened."

"She wouldn't have wanted you to give up your life for her."

Was that what she'd done? Given up her life? It didn't feel like it but maybe Alex was right. But how could she carry on as normal when her twin had been kidnapped? How could she move on as though it never happened?

She shook her head. "I can't get over the guilt of not saving her…" Dark, brooding thoughts pressed down on her from all sides. She tried to pull away but he wouldn't let her.

"You were a child. There was nothing you could do."

Her eyes moistened and she had to clamp down on the emotion that wanted to drive her to her knees. "She was nine years old, Alex. She was my sister. My best friend—" Her voice cracked. Too much heartbreak. Too much pain.

Alex pulled her to him, spoke into her hair. “You can’t change what happened. And you can’t let that asshole ruin your life too.”

But she wanted so badly to catch this guy. She couldn’t let it go, especially now, with new clues turning up. She leaned back in his arms and looked into his eyes. “My life isn’t going to be normal until this killer is either dead or in jail. It might not be healthy or sane but I can’t just flip a switch and pretend it never happened. I don’t have a lot of time for dinners and movies so you might do better looking for a nice normal woman to date.”

“What would I do with a normal woman?” He kissed her brow, making her feel like he understood her down to her bones. “Anyway, I already told you, your no dating rules work for me.”

“Funny.”

“Sexy,” he corrected.

Laughter bubbled through her, bursting the melancholy. “You made me fall off the wagon.”

“Glad to be of service.” He held her gaze. He still smelled great, but combined with bed-head the whole package made her want to spend the weekend under the covers wearing him out. And that’s what she’d promised him last night. But knowing her sister’s killer was out there somewhere drove her crazy. The idea that she was having fun while Payton was dead made the guilt pile higher…but Payton would still be dead if Mallory was miserable and that was just as hard to deal with.

“Mallory.” His voice was patient. More patient than she deserved. “I can see you backing away and having a million regrets, but I’m not going anywhere until this guy is caught. We don’t have to fuck each other’s brains out”—the look in his eyes made her shiver—"but I meant what I said last night. You're in possible danger staying here alone. This guy knows where you live. As a security expert you have to trust me on this."

She squeezed his fingers. "Thanks for being there for me last night."

The light in his eyes changed and he looked away. "I'll always be there for you, Mallory, but I need you to know something else. I'm not good at relationships. I fuck them up. I let people down. And I don't want to hurt you."

A twinge of regret shot through her chest, but it was tempered by experience. She didn't need worthless promises. She'd rather have unstable truth. No one knew what the future held and only money was bankable and even that could get stolen. She looked at her sister's file. "We all let people down." An idea struck her. "Hey, maybe I should hire your company."

"What for?"

"Finding out information. Your company must use hackers."

He tilted his head. "Nothing illegal unless the government asks us to break in."

"They ask you to break in?"

"It's usually a choice between us and the Chinese, so yeah, they ask us. Pay us for the privilege even—double when we breach their security undetected." His grin suggested his firm had done it more than once.

"Then digging up phone records from eighteen years ago should be a piece of cake?"

He backed away a step and she didn't blame him. "Except it's illegal and you work for the FBI."

Mallory bit her lip. "I know. But all legal avenues have

been exhausted. Now the only things I have left are invading people's privacy." Except for those old news articles about stolen children. It hadn't escaped her mind that the box of printouts might have come from the same person who'd sent the pajamas. But that had been addressed to her work, not her home, and none of the stories had thrown up any definite links yet. Anyway, she'd handled the information repeatedly and it was probably useless forensically. "I'm hitting brick wall after brick wall."

"Is this *all* you do with your time off?"

She looked up and met those smoky eyes. "Pretty much." One side of her mouth pulled back. "Exciting, huh?"

"When was the last time you took a day for yourself?"

Her fingers gripped the file hard enough to bend the cardboard. "When I go on vacation I can't stop thinking about her. About what might have happened to her."

He closed her laptop, grabbed her hand. "You need to step away from this before it completely takes over your life."

"I think that horse already bolted. I wouldn't know what else to do with myself—"

He kissed her. Hard. Deep. When he released her mouth she was trembling.

"Didn't you say you wanted to spend the weekend with me?"

"I did—I do." She glanced at her sister's file and the familiar guilt crept into her brain.

"Good." Tugging on her arm he dragged her to the bathroom and turned on the shower. "We're both going to take one weekend and pretend to be normal people." He slipped the robe down her shoulders.

"But—"

He gripped her robe tight around her upper arms, trapping her, and kissed her again. Hunger for him rose up inside her and her lips followed his when he pulled back.

"Your sister wouldn't resent you one weekend of living your life, Mal. If she was anything like you she'd want you to be happy."

He stripped off his shirt, shucked his jeans and lifted her into the tub like she weighed nothing at all. When she was wet all over and begging him to take her, a tiny portion of her brain finally realized it was okay to just forget for a little while.

CHAPTER TWELVE

TWENTY-FOUR HOURS LATER, Alex gripped Mallory's hand as he pulled her toward her front door. "We're going even if I have to drag you all the way there." The irony didn't escape him. He preferred his own company and was a workaholic, but he'd rather spend the afternoon strolling around DC with Mallory than anything else he could think of.

Since he'd got out of jail he'd found a new appreciation for fresh air and walking. After nearly thirty-six hours of being cooped up he needed to be outside, to get Mallory out of the apartment and into the real world again. Maybe he could be good for her, short term.

"Fine." She rolled her eyes, but she laughed too. The sound went straight to his heart. He didn't know the last time he'd enjoyed being with another person; of connecting with someone and taking pleasure in their company. He was setting himself up for disaster but the more time he spent with her, the more he was determined to do his damnedest to coax her away from the obsession with her sister's case. Catching the bastard would be the most effective scenario. He hoped the FBI lab had found something useful on that new evidence.

"We'll grab you some groceries on the way home." Her cupboards were empty except for ketchup, some tins of soup and a box of stale crackers. "Even the mice moved out in disgust."

"Watch out, Mr. Parker. I'll start to think you care."

"I do care." That admission felt foreign on his lips but like he told her yesterday, it was true. He pulled her to him and kissed her deep and turned it into something light. "I need to keep up my strength around you."

She pressed against him and he couldn't believe he was growing hard again. She'd turned him into a walking hard-on and frankly his lack of control was starting to piss him off. He wasn't a randy teenager. He was thirty-four and she was driving him crazy.

"We could order pizza," she whispered against his lips.

"We're going out to get some fresh air, otherwise I'll start to think you're ashamed to be seen in public with me." A thick wedge of emotion lodged at the back of his throat.

One side of her mouth kicked up and she said with perfect seriousness. "Alex, you're built, gorgeous, and wealthy—the perfect man—and no one has ever taken care of me the way you have. Why would anyone ever be ashamed of you?"

Because I kill people? Because he took out human targets the same way most people swatted a fly? He looked away. The truth was dark and repulsive and unfortunately real. Well, she wasn't going to know the truth. It would hurt her and then she'd bust his ass. Not going to happen. He was being as honest as any covert operative could afford to be.

He couldn't take a weapon where they were headed but he didn't think this asshole would go for a direct confrontation when Mallory had company. Alex was pretty sure, between the two of them, he and Mallory could handle most threats. He opened the door and stopped dead. *Except this one.*

The shock on the woman's face made it almost worthwhile

being discovered. Until she turned that disappointed gaze on Mallory.

"Mom," said Mallory.

Dressed in the usual politician's attire of thick wool suit with perfect hair and nails, Senator Margret Tremont looked every inch the power-broker. The woman's gaze raked him from top to bottom and found him wanting.

"What's going on here?" she demanded.

"Mom meet Alex Parker. Alex Parker meet my mother, Senator Margret Tremont."

The air around them vibrated with tension. He wondered if Mallory felt it too.

He held out his free hand. "I've heard a lot about you, Senator."

"Is this why you didn't come for Thanksgiving?" She pointedly ignored his handshake and he moved his lips into a cold smile. *Not good enough for her daughter—check.* Not that he didn't already know that.

"No, Mom. I told you. I was working."

"Mallory," the senator's West Virginia accent was just noticeable beneath the steel, "I need to speak to you alone, please."

Mallory's gaze flicked to him and then back to her mother. The tight look was back around her eyes. All laughter gone. "Mom, I'm busy. Can't it wait?"

"It's about your sister's disappearance." Her eyes were as hard as glass beads.

"I was just going to the Smithsonian with Alex." Mallory sounded defensive and angry. She'd decided not to tell her parents about the pajamas until after the crime lab techs had gone over them. The price of deceit was measured in guilt and

Mallory already shouldered enough misplaced guilt to last a lifetime. "Can't it wait a few hours?"

"Maybe Mr. Parker could leave us for a few minutes while we discuss this private family matter." The senator's voice sliced the air like a knife.

He'd spent a lifetime obeying orders and all it had earned him was contempt and fear. But it was obvious to anyone with half a brain he'd just spent the night with Mallory and that was never popular with parents. She had every right to be pissed.

Common courtesy demanded he give them some privacy, but as he tried to move away, Mallory's hold on his fingers tightened and she refused to let go of his hand. He squeezed her back, trying to offer reassurance. Whatever it was he felt for her was morphing into a protective urge that included keeping her safe from her own mother.

The senator's disdain for him was obvious.

"Just come on in, Mom. Alex isn't going anywhere."

The words both thrilled and terrified him. He was playing a foolish game. His feelings for this woman kept growing stronger, more intense. It wasn't just sex. And he didn't want to hurt someone who'd already suffered so much.

The senator stepped inside the door and glanced uneasily around obviously worried she'd find physical evidence of their orgy. He let go of Mallory's hand. "How about I get everyone a drink while you guys talk?"

The senator pinched her lips. "Don't bother, Mr. Parker. Stay and hear all about the family skeletons. You'll find out soon enough anyway."

With that ominous statement she went over to the couch and perched on the edge. For the first time he noted the strain etched around her eyes and mouth. It reminded him that while she was a politician, she was also a mother who'd lost a child.

"Do you still have the signet ring Daddy gave you when you were little?" she asked her daughter.

Mallory frowned and then turned on her heel. She came back a few moments later with a wooden jewelry box he'd spotted on the top of her dresser. She raised the lid and removed a small silver ring and held it up.

The senator opened her briefcase and handed her a piece of paper. "This was just sent to the editor of *The Washington Mail*. He graciously sent me a photograph." Her tone dripped venom.

Mallory put a hand over her mouth and sank to the sofa beside her mother. "Oh, God."

Alex stepped forward and peered at the image. It was a photograph of a signet ring with the initials PR engraved in the middle of a heart-shape. His blood chilled as he looked at the ring in detail. *Shit.* The coincidence in the timing—the emergence of a killer who carved the letters PR inside a love heart on the chest of young women with long dark hair, and all this new evidence turning up in the Payton Rooney case after eighteen years? Worst case scenario had just become the most likely reality.

"This *just* turned up?" he asked.

"The editor received it in the mail Friday. His researchers at first linked it to a new serial killer, but it's so small they knew the ring must belong to a child. Then he remembered Payton and called me to see if I recognized it."

"You think it's the real deal, not an elaborate hoax?"

"It's the real thing." She pointed to an image showing the hallmark. "It's made of platinum, not silver. Unless he had access to the jeweler's records he wouldn't know that. The police always described it as silver but it was platinum." She folded her hands back into her lap.

An uneasy feeling slipped through him. He took the photograph from Mallory and examined it closer. When he met her gaze the shadows under her eyes were dark as bruises.

"Who has the ring now?" Mallory asked.

"The editor sent it to your colleagues in the FBI." The senator was shaking with suppressed emotion. Mainly anger but grief too.

"Good," she said. So much for one weekend of normal. "The techs will find something to catch this guy. Finally."

"There's more." The senator pulled a folded newspaper from her bag and put it on Mallory's lap.

Ah, shit.

Mallory blinked rapidly. "They ran the story already?"

"I suppose they didn't want to give me the chance to sic my lawyers on them." Her tone was sharp, but for her this might be good news. After all, someone out there knew something about Payton Rooney's abduction and was taunting law enforcement with crumbs of information. The attention of the press could fuel that monstrous ego and force him into making a mistake.

Mallory unfolded the front page and groaned. Alex cursed. There was a big photograph of Mallory in her FBI guise, beside another one of her and her sister as little girls. He didn't like the way the media was focusing in on Mallory like this. He examined the senator and could tell she didn't like it either. The fact she'd been the one to constantly thrust Mallory into the limelight didn't seem to register.

Alex had no doubt the person taunting the Rooneys was

the same person killing these young women and probably the same person who'd stolen their little girl all those years ago. The motif of those initials in that heart-shaped ring was too precise to be a coincidence, the use of the press to garner attention? It all screamed classic serial killer on a mission.

Had he confronted her sister's killer in Mallory's house in Charlotte that day? It seemed a little too coincidental to have a random break-in when all this other shit was going down. If he'd been less bothered about his own skin could he already have eliminated this problem?

"I've got something to tell you, Mom." Mallory took her mother's hand. "I didn't tell you before because the FBI wanted to be sure first, but I think this seals it." Mallory told her mother about the pajamas. He could feel the senator's anger. Fury that her daughter hadn't told her the instant she'd found out. "Don't be mad."

The senator forced a smile and climbed to her feet, brushing off her skirt. "Maybe we'll finally get some answers about where Payton is. I have to go. I have a brunch appointment with a Supreme Court judge." She paused. "I know you think I was the one who got you this new position in Quantico, Mallory, even though I told you I didn't." Alex saw Mallory flinch probably because he was here. She'd insisted and her mother was punishing her for it. "However, I hope regardless of your feelings, you take full advantage of this opportunity to make the FBI step up their efforts to find Payton."

"I'll do what I can, Mom, but I can't promise anything." Mallory sounded despondent as she hugged her mother.

Margret Tremont narrowed her eyes at him over Mallory's shoulder. "Look after my daughter, Mr. Parker. She's all I've got." Then she surprised him by shaking his hand before she left.

The phone rang. Mallory checked the number and looked up at him. "It's work."

He nodded. "You should probably answer it."

A dimple quivered in her cheek. "So much for our first date."

"We don't date, remember?" He took her face in his hands and kissed her. "The Smithsonian will still be there next week." He could almost see what she was thinking in those large expressive eyes. "You'll be here too, Mallory. I'm not going to let anyone hurt you." But his words couldn't dispel the cloud of doubt. For the last eighteen years this shadowy figure had haunted her family. Now he was killing women who resembled Mallory and Payton Rooney. Alex was going to make it his mission to catch the sonofabitch and make sure she didn't disappear the same way her sister had. When he found the bastard, regardless of what The Gateway Project sanctioned, he was going to make sure he never hurt anyone ever again.

MALLORY SAT AT the conference table surrounded by the same colleagues she'd met not so long ago. The only difference was they now eyed her like a witness rather than a fellow agent, and looked a damn sight happier about it.

"You really think the person killing these women is the same person who took Payton?" she asked again. This was a hell of a way to spend a Sunday afternoon.

"The MO has changed," Barton conceded.

"He's been inactive for eighteen years."

"Not necessarily." SSA Frazer raised a finger at her and she wanted to raise one back, a different one.

"There's a gap in what we know about him, it doesn't mean he wasn't killing."

A chill moved through her body but Mal refused to acknowledge it. She needed to be professional enough to discuss this.

Frazer continued. "For some reason about a year ago something happened to trigger a rash of murders in this area, all with the same signature. And now I think they are related to the Payton Rooney case."

"Who's probably been dead for eighteen years," Henderson put in.

Most children who were abducted were killed in the first couple of hours.

Mallory crossed her arms over her chest, wanting to hide what she was thinking because it would sound so out there, but she couldn't. "I think he kept her alive."

Frazer stared hard. "Why do you think that?"

She pursed her lips but these guys already thought she was an idiot so who cared. "Because I could *feel* her."

"Are you telling us you're psychic now?" Henderson's skeptical brows disappeared under her frumpy bangs.

"Not psychic. It's a twin thing. I can't really explain it," Mallory surveyed the faces of her colleagues. Outside, snow had started to fall. Alex was in the car waiting for her. It gave her the impetus to go on. To get this over with. "Our whole childhood we shared a connection. I knew where she was in the house, I knew when she was hungry and even what she was hungry for. I knew when she was sad and when she was hiding a secret." She dug her nails hard into the palms of her hands. "I can't explain it, but it was like *we* were hungry and *we* had a secret. I didn't even know that wasn't normal until I was older." She licked her lips. "When she disappeared I still felt her even years afterward though it wasn't as strong. That connection ended sometime around last October. I woke up one morning and she was just...gone."

Henderson leaned forward across the desk and jabbed her pen toward Frazer. "This is why she shouldn't be here. She's going to affect how we view the case."

"She might be the reason we finally crack it," Frazer argued. He stared at her for another long moment then looked away. "This is the first year you didn't appear on TV talking about your sister's abduction, correct?"

She nodded.

"I think the killer was pissed and wanted to get your attention." Frazer spoke to his team but never took his eyes off hers. "That's why he sent you those clothes and the media that ring. He wants you to know he's out there. He wants you to know he took Payton and killed those other women so you don't forget him."

"The cases are so different though—"

"Maybe." He pressed his lips together. "But not necessarily. *If* you're right and your sister was alive all these years, then maybe he had whatever it was he needed to curb that killing urge."

The idea her sister might have been alive all this time made her stomach spasm. And if her theory about Payton being alive was correct should she have told the FBI about it years ago? Should she have explored it more? Pushed the authorities even though she knew they'd already exhausted every lead?

Mallory's hands were shaking so she hid them under the

table. So much for being in control. Barton watched her with a hint of pity but Henderson looked like she was getting ready to deliver a killing blow.

Mallory lifted her gaze to Frazer's. "Each of the women he kills is his attempt to fill the void created by Payton's death?"

Frazer looked uncomfortable. "It's a theory."

"He's looking for a replacement," Barton stated.

"In that case, there's an obvious factor you aren't stating out loud, SSA Frazer." Henderson's voice was sharp.

He flicked a scowl in her direction but Mallory spoke up. "It's okay. I think I've already figured that the perfect replacement for my identical twin sister would be—in theory—me."

"Why only in theory?" Frazer asked intently.

"Because we have—had—very different personalities. Pay was a rule follower. Always polite, never argued. She was really sweet." She caught Henderson's eye. "I'm not that way."

"I suggest that if this person ever gets hold of you, you play along with being exactly what he's looking for," Henderson said. "Otherwise he's gonna beat the crap out of you and then strangle you with his bare hands, the way he killed those other girls."

"I can take care of myself." She thought of Alex, so determined to look after her that he was camped out in his car in the parking lot. She was going to have to figure out a way to persuade him she didn't need a 24/7 bodyguard, except…she liked being with him. But she needed to stand up for herself and do her job. This person had taken enough from her already.

"Let's hope it doesn't come to that." Frazer cleared his throat. "It's possible he's already inserted himself into your life at some point. Is there anyone you've become close to recently?"

Her throat closed. "You've got to be kidding."

"I'll take that as a yes. Name?"

She glared at him. "It isn't him."

"Then it will do no harm to run a background check. Name?"

She gathered her papers and tablet into her bag. "Alex Parker."

Barton's eyes widened a fraction as if she recognized the name.

"He's a security consultant. He consults for the government, including the FBI."

Frazer gave her a tight-lipped smile. "Handy. We should have a file on him then. Any other things happening in your life lately that might be considered suspicious?"

Damn, what wasn't suspect about her life right now? "There was a break-in at my house in Charlotte just before I transferred—I assumed it was just a normal attempted robbery." Her skin went cold. "But there were two men involved so it was probably just a coincidence."

"Unless there are two killers working together?" Barton suggested.

Frazer swore and made some notes. "I'll talk to the detective on the case. Anything else?"

She frowned as she thought about the flat tires in the parking lot. But Henderson would no more admit to that prank than the UNSUB would give himself up. It would probably be a massive waste of time. "Nothing." Disgusted, she pushed her chair back.

"One last thing," Frazer pointed the pen at her. "We discussed it on the way to West Virginia."

Before or after I puked?

"I want you to submit to hypnosis." She flinched. "There's a wealth of information untapped in your brain. I want it."

She rose to her feet. "Fine. Whatever," she snapped. She'd stopped caring about making a good impression with these people. The idea she'd figure out who—if anyone—was in league with a vigilante was becoming more and more ridiculous. "When?"

Frazer smiled and she felt like she'd fallen into a trap. "How about right now?"

ALEX SAT IN the passenger side of his Audi working on his laptop. He was figuring out the most efficient way to run searches on cell tower information near where each of the PR-killer's victims were believed to have been snatched, and comparing them to cell phone data from near where the bodies were found. He also wanted to access information about the victims' phones too. Positional data. It sounded easier than it was because first he needed to hack into all the major phone companies involved and cross-reference. If he found a pattern or a connection with a specific person he'd suggest the FBI gain warrants so they could use it in court if it ever came to that.

He didn't need court-worthy evidence. Just enough to convince The Gateway Project he'd found the right person. Trouble was, he was finding it harder and harder to believe The Gateway Project had a better way of dealing with criminals than the traditional justice system.

Do what Uncle Sam tells you. Obey orders and your conscience is clean, like any good soldier. But being a soldier on US soil, taking up arms against fellow Americans wasn't legal. In a court *he'd* be the one convicted of murder—hell, he was *guilty* of murder. The legitimacy of the shadowy organization was starting to bother him. Not just because he knew who'd pay the price should their activities come to light, he didn't like the realization he might not be any better than the monsters he hunted.

Out of the corner of his eye he saw a woman approaching his car. He closed the laptop, rolled down the window.

"Alex Parker?"

"Yes, ma'am."

From the sharp lines at the side of her eyes when she smiled she was probably early forties. Black hair, black eyes. Trim. Compact. Was she the one who'd let down Mallory's tires? He'd done a little digging but he hadn't had much time to run thorough background checks yet. "I'm Special Agent Felicia Barton. Agent Rooney is going to be longer than expected—"

"She all right?" he interrupted.

Her smile tightened and he could see he'd given himself away.

"She's fine, Mr. Parker. She mentioned you were out here. I thought you might want to come inside. I see you have some security clearance so it's not a problem," she added.

"That's real nice of you." He kept his expression blank. A good old American boy believing in altruism. He placed the laptop in its case and opened the door as she stood back. He was in jeans, a black sweater and combat boots. He could hear marines being drilled in the distance. The sound reminded him of his days in uniform. The good old days.

He closed the door, locked the car with the fob.

"Nice car." The fed admired with a low whistle. "Public service doesn't pay quite so well."

"But we appreciate you all the same." He gave her a smile.

"As I appreciate your service as a veteran." They started walking back to the main building. Doing the dance. Each knowing what to say. What not to say. "You served in Afghanistan?"

"And Iraq."

"You were awarded a Distinguished Service Cross. That's pretty impressive stuff."

"You seem to know a lot about me, Agent Barton."

A quick smile flashed over her features. "It's my job, Mr. Parker. Don't take it personally."

"My ego isn't that inflated, ma'am."

He followed her through the building, up in the elevator. When they got off he looked for Mallory but didn't see her. Barton brought him into a large space filled with cubicles and desks. There was an empty desk by a window beside a photocopier. "It's not much but it beats sitting in a car all day."

"Thanks."

She hesitated, clearly nowhere near done with him yet and looking for an angle to wheedle out more information. "I lost a brother in Operation Desert Storm."

He couldn't tell from her eyes whether or not she was telling the truth. Maybe he was losing his touch. "I'm sorry to hear that."

"I have another brother who joined up after Phil died." She swallowed and looked uncomfortably close to tears. "The whole time he was over there I was terrified he was going to get himself killed because of some misplaced survivor's guilt."

His mouth went dry. "Survivor's guilt is a strong motivator."

"Did you ever suffer from it? When the men in your unit died?"

"That was sloppy, Agent Barton. I'd expect a better segue from an agent of your caliber." He straightened to his full height so he was staring down at her. Not that she appeared intimidated. "If you want to interrogate me why don't we do it the old-fashioned way," he suggested.

"Rubber hoses?" she grinned.

"I was thinking a room with a tape recorder."

"Oh, you're no fun." She laughed and crooked her finger. "Follow me. I'm going to take you up on your offer, because when Agent Rooney finds out I'm questioning her boyfriend, she'll probably find a way to get me fired—"

The term "boyfriend" gave him a juvenile thrill even though it was ridiculous. He didn't allow it to distract him. "You don't like Mallory?"

"I like her just fine. But I don't like people getting where they are because of the people they know."

"You think that's what she's done?"

Special Agent Barton eyed him over her shoulder. She was shrewd, but he wasn't sure how shrewd. For all he knew, Special Agent Barton could be The Gateway Project's inside person seeing if he'd turn on them under pressure. He already knew the answer to that. If they betrayed him he'd have no compunction about taking them down. If they kept their promises their secrets would go to his grave.

He followed her. This was a good opportunity to see how this woman ticked. The main thing right now was keeping Mallory safe from anyone who wanted to do her harm. And that included her coworkers at the BAU.

CHAPTER THIRTEEN

MALLORY WENT INTO Frazer's office feeling as relaxed as a rattlesnake being poked with a sharp stick. There was a couch in the corner where her superior obviously slept sometimes, judging from the pillow and blanket folded neatly beneath. Plants and books dominated the shelves. The space was crammed tight but it wasn't cluttered with knickknacks. His desk was clear except for a single glossy white file folder with the FBI crest embossed on the front.

"Where do you want me?" she sounded like she felt. Bitchy. Defensive.

He turned from where he was closing the blinds. "I can hypnotize you without you being relaxed, but considering we have to work together it might go better if you try to trust me."

She raised a brow.

He held up his hands, palm out. "Fine, I'm not cute and cuddly like SSA Hanrahan but I'm a good agent. We're on the same team and I've done this a million times with a lot of success."

Mallory released a pent up sigh. "We may as well get it over with."

"That's the spirit." His dry humor actually made her smile. He put on some background music. Birdsong, and the sound of the wind in the trees. A cold shiver stole over her.

"Lie down on the couch and close your eyes. I promise I won't make you quack like a duck and post it on Youtube."

"Been there, done that, after I graduated Harvard." She toed off her shoes and lay with her head on a green velvet cushion and stared at the ceiling.

"I want to take you back to a happy memory."

She thought about Alex and smiled.

"Yeah, not that sort of memory."

"Ha." She closed her eyes. "When this is over I get to quiz you about your private life, Supervisory Special Agent Frazer."

"Nothing to know. My work is my life. Got an ex-wife to prove it."

Not a lot she could say to that. Divorce was common in law enforcement. Another reason to enjoy what she and Alex had found—while it lasted. Barton had offered to go get him from the parking lot and set him up in her office. Mallory knew she was going to pump him for information but there was no way she was sleeping with a monster. "He has a Distinguished Service Cross."

"What?"

"My..." Boyfriend? Lover? "Alex has a medal for heroism. He went to war. So unless there is more than one kidnapper, assuming Payton *was* kept alive all these years and wasn't a willing participant, there's no way he's the guy we're looking for because he couldn't have left Payton alone for that amount of time when he was serving our country." The words came out in a rush and a wave of relief hit her. Not that she'd thought it was Alex but she liked proof.

"I hope you're right."

She opened her eyes and looked at him. He'd pulled a chair over, just a few feet from where she lay down on his couch. He held up a voice recorder. "May I?"

"Sure." Her lips tightened. She felt stupid.

"Okay. I promise this isn't going to hurt. During this session *you* are my priority and I will make sure nothing can harm you. Take a deep breath. And let it out slowly." They repeated some breathing exercises together. She felt like a fool but he did them too and slowly the tension leached out of her muscles. A heaviness in her limbs crept over her. She hadn't had much sleep for a few days.

"You're in a happy place, a safe place where no one can hurt you." Frazer's voice deepened as he started asking her questions. It sounded like he was a long way away. "Did you have a pet when you were growing up?"

That brought back a happy memory. She wanted to smile but her lips wouldn't cooperate. Too tired. "We had a spaniel called Taffy. She was always getting into trouble with Mama for sleeping in our beds. Mama started locking her in the mudroom at night."

"That's a shame. Taffy might have made enough noise to gain someone's attention if she'd been there."

A giant wave of sadness crashed over her but before it dragged her too deep Frazer said, "Do you remember the color of your bedroom walls when you were a child?"

"Blue, pale blue. The window trims were painted white and we had yellow drapes. Yellow was Payton's favorite color." The image of those drapes was blinding. Bright and cheerful like sunshine.

"You shared a bedroom with your sister?"

"Yes. We didn't like to sleep apart." Her sister's laughter teased the edge of her mind. She wanted to reach out and grab her, but there was something lurking in the darkness and she was scared. "I sleepwalk." She clapped her hand over her mouth like she'd told him a big secret.

She heard a rustling sound as Frazer shifted in his seat. "I used to sleepwalk too. Ended up on the main road once. Almost scared my mother half to death," Frazer told her. "Did you sleepwalk the night Payton went missing?"

"No." She shook her head. An image flickered through her mind. Gone so fast she couldn't grab a hold of it or figure out what it meant.

"The night she went missing. Did you see anyone come into your bedroom, Mallory?" His words sounded like he was standing far, far away and she could barely hear him over the sound of leaves rustling in the trees.

She nodded and felt his excitement.

"Was it a man or a woman?"

"A man."

"Do you know who it was?"

"No." She shook her head.

"Can you describe him?"

She searched lazily around her mind for some clue but it was all cloudy and vague. "Feet."

"What do you mean 'feet'? You saw his feet?"

"Yes."

"Can you describe his feet?"

"Green converse trainers. He has big feet."

His voice changed. She registered it on some other plane. "Are you *under* the bed, Mallory?"

She nodded. "I sleep under the bed a lot." She hadn't remembered that until now. *That's* why he hadn't taken her.

"Why do you sleep under the bed?"

Her pulse jumped. Even in this relaxed state she felt her

blood pound. "Because I'm scared of monsters."

There was a long silence. "Did the man speak? Was he looking for you too?"

She frowned again. "I don't know. I woke up when he was standing by Pay's bed. I closed my eyes because I was scared. When I opened them again he was gone." Tears scalded her eyes. "I didn't know he'd taken her with him. I didn't know he'd stolen her. I just went back to sleep." Agitation swirled inside, pushing against the lethargy.

"It wasn't your fault, Mallory. You're doing really well remembering so much." His voice soothed and calmed. "Where were you when your parents discovered Payton was missing?"

"I was the one who told them she was gone when I woke up in the morning. They were in bed."

"Together?"

"Yes. They always slept together."

"Did anyone ever show special interest in Payton?"

"Everyone loved Payton. She was nice to everyone, even people who weren't nice to her."

"Who wasn't nice to her?"

She bit her lip. "I wasn't always nice to her. Once I sat on her back and pulled her pigtails. She didn't tell Mama or Daddy because she didn't want to get me into trouble."

"It's normal for siblings to fight. It wasn't your fault she was taken, Mallory."

Her eyes watered but she didn't have the energy to wipe them.

"Was there anyone else who used to follow her around? Or maybe watch her?"

"Maybe..." She flashed to an image of a man and a boy

standing at the edge of the woods beside their property, but it was gone. She tried to pull the image back, saw only vague shapes in the distance. "I don't remember." The weight of not knowing felt like it was crushing her chest and her breath got hoarse. She struggled to pull in a lungful of air.

"One last question." His voice pulled her away from her struggle to breathe. "You're not going to remember this question when I wake you up." She stilled even as the pressure in her lungs built. "Why are you working here at the BAU?"

Warning sounds pierced her brain, which shook itself awake like a wet dog climbing out of a lake. Finally she drew in a long clean breath, opened her eyes and stared right into his. "I'm looking for justice. Why are you here?"

ALEX SAT OPPOSITE Special Agent Felicia Barton in a conference room with a massive window, affording a magnificent view of the surrounding Virginia countryside. He liked Virginia. The history. The quiet leafy greenness of the state. Loved the changing seasons. Even late fall held its own subdued, fading beauty.

"I don't know why you're interviewing me," he said carefully.

"I just have a few questions to ask you."

She pulled a recording device from her pocket, and took down a couple of details like his name and date of birth.

"I'm curious about how you got your Distinguished Service Cross, Mr. Parker?"

That day had been a turning point in his life he didn't talk about. Five of his best friends had died in combat, two more damaged beyond repair, and he hadn't suffered a scratch.

He tapped his fingers on the desk. Survivor's guilt. He knew all about it. "Did you request the file from the military?"

"I've sent in a request but it'll take time. You're here now, this would save me some trouble."

He ran a hand through his short hair. "Most of it is still classified."

"Why?"

Because the CIA fucked up. When he'd challenged them they'd thrown it back at him and offered him a job to see if he could do any better. And he had done better, right up until that arms dealer. "National Security."

Her focus honed in on him. "I think you can assume I have appropriate security clearance."

"In which case they'll send you the file." He narrowed his gaze. "As the person at risk of prosecution for revealing my country's secrets should you be lying, Agent Barton, I will respectfully decline your request for information about that mission." Because he sure as hell didn't want to talk about it.

The muscles around her mouth flexed visibly beneath the skin. "When did you get back in country?"

"I left the army in '05. Two friends and I set up a security company—"

"What type of security?"

"Everything. Personal protection with bodyguards, alarm and monitoring systems; advice about protecting major facilities in terms of infrastructure; and cyber security."

"That's your gig, right?"

He nodded. Tapped his fingers some more. "The guys who work for me are the real brains of the operation. I just get to look good."

"And drive the fancy car."

"One of my employees drives a Maserati. Need a job, Agent Barton? Or just a new car. I'm pretty sure I can set you up."

A flicker of fire lit her eyes. "Remember what I said about people getting jobs because of the people they know?"

He smiled.

"So, not so much, but thanks." Her expression was icy now.

"Let me know if you change your mind."

The look on her face said when Hell froze over. She took a moment to calm herself as if she'd just realized he'd hijacked her interview. "So, you won't tell me how you became a decorated soldier, and you're a little vague about the exact nature of your work—"

"Not true." He leaned forward. "I can tell you in excruciating detail but you're not going to understand it."

Her nostrils flared. She didn't like being told she wasn't smart enough. The woman had a lot of buttons he could push.

"Can you tell me how you met Special Agent Rooney?"

"Sure. I was asked to address a Counterintelligence Awareness Group briefing at the FBI Charlotte's division by an old army buddy of mine. Special Agent Lucas Randall." He peered at her notes. "Two 'l's in Randall."

She audibly ground her teeth.

"Randall introduced me to Mallory who worked with him there and whom he'd known since she was a kid."

"Did you know Randall or Rooney when you were a child?"

"No." He frowned. This line of questioning was starting to make sense. It wasn't about his vigilante activities but it could still trip him up if he wasn't careful. He was foolish not to have expected it. "I grew up in the mid-west. Met Randall when we deployed to Afghanistan. I just told you when and how I met Mallory."

"You're thirty-four, Mr. Parker?"

"Yes, ma'am."

"So you'd have been, what, sixteen, in nineteen ninety-five?"

"Ninety-five? Christ, I can barely remember where I was in ninety-five. High school, I guess. Where are you going with this?"

Black eyes latched onto his. "Ever been to West Virginia, Mr. Parker?"

"Can't say I have." He knew exactly where she was going with this but he had no intention of making this easy for her.

"You got any family?"

His mouth went dry. He didn't care about his own reputation but he sure as hell wasn't having anyone sully theirs. "My mom died when I was fourteen. My grandfather died a year later. After that I was a subject of the state until I went off to college." He leaned forward, held her gaze. "Neither my mother nor grandfather were ever in West Virginia, and neither of them abducted Payton Rooney."

Her expression became relaxed and exasperated all at the same time. "You have to understand that now it's obvious Mallory has been targeted by someone 'involved'"—she rolled the word around her mouth—"in Payton Rooney's abduction, we need to check out all her close relationships. Especially those that began recently."

"I don't have to understand anything if you plan to implicate my family. Maybe I should call my attorney?"

Her eyes widened, maybe realizing he wasn't quite the pushover she'd anticipated. "Fine, let's clear this all up right now. Where were you Sunday, November 9th?"

The night Lindsey Keeble had been abducted. The same night he'd shot Meacher. "How does that clear things up?" He wasn't supposed to know the PR-killer's itinerary.

"Just answer the question, Mr. Parker."

"I was in DC. I went to dinner with a friend. Left at four AM the next morning to drive to Charlotte for that meeting." His GPS and cell phone data would confirm every word, which went to show if you knew what you were doing you could be in two places at once.

"Girlfriend?"

He said nothing. Theoretically he and Jane had a casual dating relationship as a cover for their meetings.

She waited impatiently. "A name and address would be helpful."

Fuck. He wrote Jane Sanders' name, address and phone number on a piece of paper. He didn't want Mallory to know about this. The room felt suddenly too hot. Things were getting complicated. He raised his gaze to the door, and there stood Mallory looking furious on his behalf.

Barton checked her shoulder. "I'll need to confirm your alibi, Mr. Parker. Don't take it personally."

"Why would I?" He didn't take his gaze off Mallory's. "You're just doing your job, right?"

"Let's go, Alex. I'm sorry you had to go through this," said Mallory.

He pushed his chair back and ignored Barton. "The only thing I care about is you and making sure this asshole gets caught." At the doorway he looked back at Barton where she was still scribbling away. “As long as your colleagues are all on the same page, we’re good.”

The quirk of Mallory’s brows told their own story. She touched his arm and leaned close to his ear. “If it came down to a contest about who I trusted more…you or them.” Her lips brushed his ear and sent a bolt of sensation straight through him. “I’m pretty sure you’d have the edge.”

Barton watched them as they left and he knew she was going to keep digging. Whatever his misgivings about Jane and Mallory, he better make damn sure his alibi stuck.

CHAPTER FOURTEEN

HE'D HAD HER for a couple of weeks now. She'd passed the tests and lasted a hell of a lot longer than the others and he was starting to think she really might be the one. He'd showered, put on cologne, pulled on a wool hat and his sheepskin jacket, picked up the flowers he'd bought.

Work had been flat out for the last few days and he hadn't been able to check on her. She had food and water but if she got sick the way Payton had gotten sick…

His boots crunched through the dead leaves in the woods, faster now. It was dark but he knew the route so well he didn't even need a flashlight as long as the moon shone.

He'd been the officer to find Lindsey Keeble's car, which had earned him a lot of kudos within the department. He figured it was only a matter of time before someone saw it and may as well use his problems to his advantage. Lindsey had been a bitch with a mouth that could blister paint. Man, he wished he hadn't grabbed her. Too much trouble. Too close to home. But maybe she'd been fated for another reason because Mallory Rooney was coming to her funeral tomorrow.

Should he take her?

The idea of having two women at the same time haunted his fantasies now. Nothing unusual in a man wanting to screw two females at the same time, but this was riskier. He'd need to keep Mallory under control, physically and mentally. Maybe get her hooked on heroin and dependent on him for a fix. That might keep her malleable.

He liked the sound of that.

He'd never have contemplated keeping two women when Payton was alive, but he had to find a way to get through the remainder of his life without descending into madness.

He tripped over a stick. "Shit!" That's what he got for not paying attention. Maybe he'd just kill Mallory. The idea of her not respecting her sister's memory made him fume. But he couldn't kill her without at least giving her a chance to redeem herself, because Payton had loved her so much. And maybe she was like Kari and just needed a bit of coaching.

He'd drilled a metal ring into the wall of the abandoned mine. He had chain to keep her locked up but still needed to reinforce the door to the storage shed. As long as he didn't show Mallory his face he could risk holding her somewhere like that. Kari was going to have to stay in the chamber though. If she ever escaped she could identify him and he wouldn't risk losing his freedom.

Kari was sweet. She didn't seem to mind the basic accommodations too much and he could try and spruce up the place. If she had a baby he'd figure out a new plan. Maybe move somewhere remote where he could build some sort of compound…or join one of those militia groups with Kari as his wife?

Yup. Starting tonight, he was going to see if he could get her pregnant. No point in waiting any longer.

The idea had him so hard his dick throbbed.

He got to the woodpile and stood around for a moment to make sure no one was nearby. He hadn't remained undetected all these years by being careless.

The forest was unusually silent tonight, the first severe frost of winter starting to really bite. Sliding back the bolt he lifted the hatch and reached for the flashlight that rested just inside. He flicked the switch, but nothing happened. The bulb had probably blown. He gave it a shake and something rattled inside the plastic casing. Piece of shit.

It was dark in the chamber. Pitch black. *What the hell?* Had the paraffin lamp run out of fuel?

"You all right down there?" He descended the stairs carefully in the darkness. The silence had him panicking. Shit, was she okay? He reached for another flashlight that he kept on one of the shelves that lined one wall. Groped around, knocking off books and a mug. Where the fuck was that thing? Why wasn't she answering?

Something slammed into his temple and a knee connected with his balls, white hot agony slicing his body in half. The flowers fell from his fingers as he went down like a slab of concrete and hit his head on the edge of the bed. He curled into a fetal ball. Holy *shit*. The pain was excruciating, sweat broke out over his body and he dry heaved.

Feet scrambled behind him, the noise of the chain curiously absent. *Shit.* She'd gotten loose. She'd ambushed him. Little fucking bitch. If he didn't move his ass she was going to trap him down here and then go running to the cops like the sniveling bitch she really was.

He dragged himself to his feet as she scrambled up the ladder. He jammed his shoulder through the opening just as she tried to slam the wooden hatch closed.

"Get back here!" He sounded like he'd been strangled. Shit. His balls ached.

He lunged for her ankle but she jumped away. Her gasp of fear made him yell out loud. Then he could hear her running away. Lying, fucking deceitful whore. He threw himself up the ladder and closed the hatch behind him and started after her. Forcing himself not to run, forcing himself to take deep calm breaths even as his anger rose up and engulfed him.

He'd been a fool. She'd tricked him into trusting her when he knew he shouldn't have.

She cried out in the darkness, making enough noise for a blind man to follow. She was heading northwest. He caught a glimpse of pale skin in the darkness and started to jog.

He'd grown up in these woods. Knew every inch, in every season. She didn't stand a chance.

He was gaining on her but decided to circle around so he got in front of her. He ran ahead and waited behind a tree in the darkness. But the sounds of her movement had veered east and she suddenly sounded further away. *Hell.* She must have seen the light from the McCafferty property that skirted the edge of the forest. He started running fast, uncaring of the uneven ground and branches that tore up his face.

His foot went down a hole and he hit the ground hard. His chin slammed off the dirt and white light burst through his brain. His heart was pounding. *Christ Almighty*. Fear crowded his mind, crushing his carefully laid plans to dust.

Sonofabitch.

Son of a fucking bitch!

He stood. Tested his ankle which hurt but wasn't broken. He started walking fast. Limping, but so angry he didn't feel the pain. Fury burned through him in a red hot wave that fueled him.

There was a pounding sound. A desperate beating of fist

against wood.

"Help! Help me!"

Don't be in. Don't be in. Don't be in. He was about fifteen feet from the cottage when the door opened. Kari turned toward him and he saw her desperate frightened eyes find him in the darkness. He never stopped moving. She squeezed past Mrs. McCafferty and tried to shut the door behind them but the old woman fought her.

"Help me. Help me! He took me and raped me. Please help!"

"Who are you? Get out of my house."

And then he was there and he walked straight inside the simple log cabin. "It's okay, Mrs. Mac. You're safe. I'll take her back into custody now."

"He's lying!" Kari's eyes were huge as she ran from him and grabbed thc phone off the wall.

"Thank goodness you're here." The old lady clutched her throat. "Is she a fugitive? She looks dangerous."

"Don't you worry none." He swiped the telephone from Kari's hand and she cowered away from him, trembling with cold and terror. She opened her mouth as if to plead for help but no sound came out.

"Is Mr. Mac home? I sure could use his help with this one."

"He's gone into town. Decided to go to the tavern for that live bluegrass band that's playing tonight. I had a headache so I told him to go alone. Who is she?" Mrs. McCafferty nodded toward Kari who was staring at him with a stricken expression. "Vagrant?" The old woman's tone was distasteful which he found ironic given how pious she was in church every week.

He eyed the knife block and pulled one out, testing the

sharp edge on his thumb. "She's a dangerous criminal but you don't need to worry."

"Oh my—"

He pushed the knife into Mrs. McCafferty's abdomen and angled it sharply upward. He held her as she sagged against him, feebly grabbing onto his clothes as she twitched and spasmed in his grasp. Hot blood soaked through his shirt, his jeans, touched his skin. This was why he didn't like knives. Too messy. Too much trace evidence.

"See what you've done?" he snarled at Kari. "I've known this woman since I was a kid and because of you, she's dead."

She stood in the kitchen staring open-mouthed at him as Mrs. McCafferty bled to death in his arms. *Stupid bitch.*

"And when the cops find her." He let Mrs. McCafferty's body slide gently to the floor. "They're gonna blame you." He washed his hands, then wiped his prints and DNA from the faucets and phone.

He turned toward her, disappointed. She'd ruined everything. The bitch started shaking her head and moving away from him, but there was nowhere to go in the small kitchen. He walked up to her and smashed the handle of the knife into her temple and she crashed to the floor in a heap. Rifling through the drawer, careful not to leave prints, he found duct tape and tied her wrists behind her back. He pulled her head back using her hair and looked at her eyes. She was out cold.

He wrapped tape around her mouth. He wasn't done with her yet, he was going to teach her a lesson about the cost of betrayal. But he needed to wait. Needed to make sure the next twenty-four hours went exactly to plan because he would not go down for murder. He would rather die right here and now than be locked up with filth.

He latched the kitchen door, turned off all the lights and removed the light bulb from the hallway fitting. In the meantime he ransacked the house the way a thief would, looking for cash and easily fencible goods that he'd dump as soon as he got the opportunity. It was thirty minutes before he heard a car in the driveway. The blood had dried and crusted on his skin and itched unmercifully.

Old Mr. McCafferty ambled through the door, a little worse for drink—not that he should have been driving—but hopefully it would make what was about to happen less painful. As the old man tried to ease out of his heavy winter jacket, he grabbed his hair and pulled his head back. "Sorry," he murmured. Then he sliced the knife deep across the man's throat.

A hot spurt of blood hit his cheek and slid down his neck. The old man was dead before he hit the floor.

He closed the front door, then rifled through the old guy's pockets, taking his wallet. The sight of the body made his stomach clench. Using paper towels he wiped the knife clean and then pressed the pads of Kari's fingers onto the handle before dropping it beside Mr. McCafferty's body. The paper towels went in his pocket as he walked to the kitchen, trying to avoid stepping in the large pools of blood. His footprints were visible but attempting to clean this up would make it look less like a random attack. He'd dump the shoes along with the clothes. Burn them to ashes somewhere other than these woods. He let out a sigh. He'd known these people his whole life and they'd built this cottage just a few years ago for their retirement. They were good people. It was a damned shame.

He was going to have to make sure the chamber was well and truly hidden in case cops started searching the woods, although he'd try and divert them. He went back into the kitchen and hoisted Kari over his shoulder. She was limp. He hoped to hell he hadn't killed her because he intended to make her wish she'd never tried to get away from him. By the time he was finished with her she'd wish she was dead.

And then, if she was lucky, he'd kill her.

FOUR DAYS AFTER Thanksgiving was not a time a parent wanted to bury a child. But there was never a good time.

The church belonged to the Methodists, with a steepled bell tower and green tin roof. The portico on the front was supported by four white columns. Bare limbs of three maples enfolded it in a protective embrace.

The graveyard was at the back of the church. Row upon row of old family plots marked with simple white crosses.

Bryce Keeble stood beside Lindsey's white coffin, hunched over like an old man. The whites of his eyes were still red from crying. Skin gray. Grief etched on his features like lines of graffiti. Some truths were too immense to leave you physically unchanged.

He ignored everything except his beloved daughter.

The pastor was saying prayers for Lindsey's soul but Mallory doubted her soul was in any danger. She'd been a good kid. A young woman on the cusp of a bigger, better life. No one had the right to steal that from her. No one had the right to destroy something priceless and precious.

Looking at that coffin made Mallory face some hard realities of her own. As painful as this funeral was, as awful as it was to bury someone you loved, it was worse not to bury them.

For them to just disappear like smoke in the rain and to never know what became of them. The thought of Payton's remains being abandoned somewhere—it was like an ulcerous sore inside her gut.

Not that she was going to share those thoughts with anyone else, especially not today. This was about *their* grief. *Their* loss. Hers was old and ingrained. Theirs was a fresh bloody wound.

She stood at the back of a crowd of mourners, shivering despite her thick woolen coat. Her leather boots crunched the grass beneath her feet. Winter was nipping hard at the Mountain State. She wouldn't let it hamper their investigation, but it might slow down this serial killer.

And maybe she was grasping at straws.

She'd arrived early and taken photographs from the privacy of her car as people had arrived for the service. She didn't recognize any of the mourners except for some of the cops she'd met last week. She'd go talk to them after the service. See if they'd come up with anything new.

Alex stood beside her, offering silent support as if he'd been part of her life forever. He'd vetoed objections that she was working and offered to ride along so he could advise her on where her personal security weaknesses lay. It was actually a good idea, not that she'd told her colleagues in Quantico about it.

She wasn't sure where "they" as a couple were going, but right now she was willing to take a chance on something, anything, that gave her a moment's respite from the tangled mess of past and present her life had become. She didn't know how Alex felt about her, she just knew that after being grilled by Barton yesterday he hadn't left in a huff, or bitched like a teenage girl.

He'd stuck.

She was pretty sure she was falling in love and this had never happened to her before. Sure, she'd dated in college and had boyfriends, but she'd never felt like she'd jumped off a cliff onto an emotional rollercoaster.

It scared the crap out of her.

Part of her wanted to hang on tight and see where it led. The other part wanted time and space to try and figure out exactly what was happening. But if she'd learned anything over the years it was time and space didn't always provide answers.

All she knew for sure was Alex was gorgeous, sexy, great in bed, and just plain *nice*—basically too good to be true. Like she'd told him the other day, he had a hell of a lot going for him and she'd decided that, in spite of her responsibility toward her sister, she'd be a fool not to give the spark between them a chance because life didn't give you many chances like this.

Not that she could shake him right now even if she'd wanted to. Mallory doubted this killer would actually attempt to kidnap a federal agent in broad daylight. Considering she had some martial arts training and carried a Taser, two Glocks as well as her FBI shield, she felt a little bit of a fraud letting him accompany her at all. But as she didn't know which of her FBI colleagues to trust it was nice to have someone watch her back. That this psycho was out there gave her the creeps, but it was also an opportunity.

Bryce Keeble sobbed loudly as Lindsey's coffin was lowered into the ground. Hidden in the folds of their heavy coats Alex's fingers once again found hers, offering silent support. She blinked away the sudden onslaught of tears. She was here as a professional and no matter how difficult it was, she wanted to do her best by Lindsey and the other women this UNSUB had killed.

She felt eyes on her and looked over toward Sheriff Williams and a couple of his deputies who stood with their heads bowed. Sean Kennedy caught her eye and she nodded a greeting. He nodded back but there was an impatience in his stance, a tension in his face that suggested something had happened, something beyond burying a victim of cold-blooded murder.

Excitement shifted along her skin. Maybe they'd brought someone in for questioning or identified a suspect?

The pastor started winding things up and she shifted her weight from one foot to the other. Alex released her hand and she slipped it into her pocket, immediately missing his warmth.

As mourners began to drift away she hung back, then made her way across to Sheriff Williams who waited for her.

"Special Agent Rooney. Good of you to come all this way," he said it with a smile but he knew it was standard procedure to take a close look at the mourners at the funeral of any unsolved murder victim. They'd be doing the same.

"Sheriff. Deputy Kennedy. Deputy Chance." She nodded to deputies she recognized from her visit last week and introduced Alex as an FBI consultant, but didn't elaborate on his role. "Any developments?"

"There's been an incident but I don't know yet if it has anything to do with Lindsey Keeble's murder. You heard we found her car?"

Mallory shook her head. "Did the crime lab find any prints?"

"Still processing the sucker. It'll be a few days before they get back to us."

How was the killer luring them out of their cars?

"What was the incident you mentioned?" Alex asked from beside her.

The sheriff looked him up and down, and then back at her. "Double homicide."

"You don't think it's connected?" Alex spoke with the same cool authority Frazer had mastered. Must be a gene for it.

"Too early to tell for sure but totally different type of crime. Looks like a robbery gone bad. No sign of sexual assault. Two seniors knifed to death. Niece found them this morning."

"Can I view the scene?" asked Mallory.

"Sure, I've got to head back there right now." His radio went off and he turned the volume down. "Pretty horrific. You need to brace yourself. Hell of a lot of blood everywhere."

Mallory nodded even as her stomach roiled. This was the job.

"We got prints on the murder weapon. Running them as we speak."

"Hopefully they're in the system." She added, "We'll follow you over there."

The mourners were long gone and the grave diggers were starting to throw soil on top of Lindsey's coffin. The sound of it hitting was a dull thump that echoed through Mallory's chest. Death was so final. The audacity of the killer hit her with renewed force.

She and Alex got in her car and followed the sheriff down country roads she'd never traveled before. Alex didn't make small talk and she appreciated the silence. Leafless trees and hills surrounded her, the Alleghenies preparing for winter. There were houses set back in the trees, but scattered far apart. If a killer wanted to hide in this sparsely populated state it wouldn't be difficult. Her sister's laughter teased the edges of her mind.

The pajamas and ring that the killer had sent had traces of Payton's DNA—Mallory's DNA—but nothing else. The labs were pulling out all the stops testing for touch DNA transferred to the plastic wrapping and envelopes. It wasn't much to hold onto, but it was better than nothing.

She drove down another quiet road and then the sheriff took a left and parked the car along the verge. She followed suit.

She unclipped her seatbelt. "You better stay here."

Alex surveyed the quiet woods and multitude of squad cars lining the road. "You should be safe enough. Take your cell." He pulled out his phone. "It's a miracle, but we've got a signal." He grabbed his laptop off the back seat. "Take your time. I've got plenty of work to do."

Her mouth went dry. How could she not fall for a guy who went out of his way to protect her while also giving her the space she needed to do her job? Just looking at him made her ache. "Tell me you aren't as perfect as you seem, Alex."

"Not even close to perfect." His blue-gray eyes darkened. "Not a complete asshole either."

She huffed out a quiet laugh and opened the door before she did something unprofessional like kiss the guy at a crime scene. Not the sort of law enforcement officer she wanted to be no matter how grateful she was. Or how smitten.

She headed over to the two deputies she knew. "Did you

know the victims?"

"This is West Virginia, ma'am. Everyone knows everyone." Deputy Chance gave her a look that clearly stated this was difficult for him.

It was never easy to work scenes that involved people you knew.

The sheriff waved her over. She excused herself, signed a log, and put on some booties over her shoes before she entered the quaint rustic looking cottage.

"Watch your step. I've got a blood spatter analyst coming in today to help me try and figure what went down."

The bodies had been removed but the sheriff handed her two enlarged photographs as she walked through the entranceway. She looked at the walls and the floor. Heck of a lot of blood. "Did he hit an artery?"

"Yup. Sliced the carotid right through. Bob McCafferty died almost instantly which is more than I can say for his poor wife, Angie."

She followed him down the narrow corridor to the kitchen. She held up the image and stood back, superimposing the body on the scene. "He stabbed her from the front? Think she knew him? Or he cornered her in the kitchen?"

"There weren't any defensive wounds. He must have took them both by surprise. Kitchen knife was found beside Bob's body. We think the killer stabbed Angie first and then Bob came home and disturbed the sonofabitch as he tossed the place. Friends say he was down at the local tavern until about ten."

"You have a time of death?"

"Medical Examiner reckons shortly after he arrived home, between ten and eleven, but that was off the record and his best guess using temperature, lividity and rigor mortis."

"Makes sense though." And in her limited experience MEs only hazarded a guess when they were almost certain they were right.

The sheriff tipped his chin down and folds of skin gathered around his neck. He was a big guy who took up a lot of space. Mallory followed him through to the kitchen. "If I was speculating what might have gone down I'd say some passing scumbag saw the light on and decided to investigate. Saw an elderly woman home alone in an isolated cottage and figured he'd kill her and toss the place. Bob surprised him so he killed him as well and then fled."

It was always easier to think the killer was a drifter rather than someone you might know. Someone you might like.

Lots of blood had pooled and dried on the floor and there were footprints too. "You've got some good impressions here." She looked up. "Big feet. He left through the back door?"

Sheriff nodded. "Looks like. I hope this sonofabitch's fingerprints are in the system."

She raised her eyes to look out the back. "Did you search the woods?"

"Had a couple of teams go out to look for evidence, but there's three hundred acres of forest. Plus, he stole the McCaffertys' car and took off in that. Got a BOLO alert on the vehicle."

She pressed her lips together. Could this be the PR-killer? MO was totally different but to have all these murders in this small sleepy community? A Titanic-sized coincidence. "Where are these woods on the map? Can you show me so I can get my bearings?"

He hitched his belt. "I'll do better than that. Follow me."

He took her out the front door, careful to leave the footprints uncontaminated. She followed him down steps and around a woodpile. The Alleghenies rose all around them, cold and barren. A crow cawed from a branch and a shiver of unease rippled over her flesh. She followed the sheriff along a path through the majestic trunks of oak and hickory and pine, out of sight of the other cops and Alex. The scarlet bark of dogwoods provided the only drop of color on this grim day, the deep red reminding her of the blood smeared all over that rustic log cabin.

"Where are we going, Sheriff?"

"You'll see."

A chill ran down her back. The clouds had that look of burgeoning snow. Chances were they were going to get another dump before the day was over. The sheriff finally stopped at the top of a hill. And pointed northwest, beyond a narrow creek. "See that chimney over there?"

She could just make out some tall red bricks and felt her pulse kick. "Is that Eastborne?"

He nodded. "County line runs through these woods which is why Greenville County Sheriff's Office has jurisdiction for this double homicide." She turned to look down at the cottage belonging to the murder victims and the chill deepened. She'd run wild in these woods every summer until Payton had been stolen. "They were almost our nearest neighbors but I don't remember those people or that cottage."

A squirrel jeered them noisily from its perch high above, and a family of white-tail deer took off through the dead leaves in a noisy rush.

"The McCaffertys only built that place about five years ago and there's no direct road access between your place and theirs. Good folks but not the kind to mix in your parents' social circle."

She slowly turned three-hundred and sixty degrees. She could see nothing but forest and ridge upon ridge of West Virginia mountainside. Her breath froze on an exhale. "How many people live around here?"

"Lots of houses dotted around in the woods. Lot of them are empty. Whole county has about fifteen thousand folks and that number's falling. Not enough coal nearby to attract new folks."

"Which is what keeps this county so pretty."

"Yeah, but the town is dying a slow death without new industry." The sheriff's eyes seem to be trying to pierce the surrounding gloom. "People keep moving out but no one's coming back." Including her family now that her father was selling the family home. "It won't help when people start hearing about serial killers and double homicides." He grimaced. The weight of the whole community on his shoulders. "I'm supposed to keep these people safe."

There was an anger in him that seemed at odds with the uniform he wore.

"We need to catch these criminals," Mallory agreed.

"That we do." His radio squawked and he listened close. "They got a hit on those prints. Let's go see who our killer is."

TURNED OUT THEIR suspect was a nineteen-year-old missing person named Kari Regent from DC. The girl—a history major at Georgetown—was supposed to meet her boyfriend in Gainesville a couple weeks ago. The same night Mallory had hooked up with Alex that first time. But Kari Regent had never shown. The boyfriend had assumed she'd changed her mind because they'd had a fight, her parents had assumed she was with the boyfriend. After a week of failing to contact her, the boyfriend had finally called the parents, and they contacted the cops and filed Kari's fingerprints in the National Missing Person database.

The sheriff let Mallory use his office in the Greenville Sheriff's Office which was crammed from roof tile to linoleum with papers. She waited for a photograph to come through her email. The place was quiet as a mausoleum. It was dark and gloomy because the sun set early this time of year. She switched on the lights. Alex had gone to grab them coffee and something to eat. When the image finally downloaded she forwarded it to Frazer and then called him.

"SSA Frazer," he said as he picked up.

"I just sent you an image of a young woman who's been listed as a missing person."

"You think she's another victim?" he asked, obviously downloading his mail as they spoke. "Huh. She certainly fits the physical type."

"She went missing a little over two weeks ago—totally out of character but she was hitchhiking from DC to Gainesville." Frazer listened intently. Hitchhiking meant she was a perfect candidate for the PR-killer even though she was slightly out of his typical geographical zone. "The twist is they just found her fingerprints on the murder weapon at the site of a double homicide between Greenville and Colby, West Virginia."

He grunted. "Your hometown?"

"Yes. There's more. The crime scene was like a slaughterhouse. They found men's size twelve boot prints. Kari wears a size *five*. They didn't find her footprints anywhere."

"What are the locals saying?"

"They are putting a nationwide APB out on the girl with the warning she's a suspected murderer."

Frazer swore. "She might have hooked up with someone who coerced her into taking part."

"Pretty big behavioral swing for a straight-A student who's a vegan and never skipped a class."

There was a weighty pause. "No sightings of the girl?"

"No. The victims' car is missing. The assumption is Kari and the guy with big feet, took off in that car."

"I'll put out a nationwide alert for the car."

"The sheriff did that... It just feels off."

"A lot of things seem 'off'." He meant her being at the BAU.

She held her silence. Nothing she could say about that. She was following orders and getting nowhere with her and Hanrahan's search for the insider.

"Considering the proximity to both your sister's and Lindsey Keeble's abduction sites, plus the general low crime rate of that area, a double homicide is a little out of the ordinary."

She watched Alex come in the main door and charm his way past the front desk with donuts as he made his way through all the workstations to where she stood inside Sheriff Williams' glass office. She smiled as he winked at her. He was so gorgeous she got tingles just watching him.

"I want you to stay up there overnight. Check in with the locals again in the morning and I'll see if I can come up with anything in the meantime."

"You're kidding." She didn't want to stay up here overnight.

"This could be a good lead, Agent Rooney."

She heard an unexpected hint of admiration in his tone,

but it didn't ease her apprehension. *Ugh.* "Fine. I'll call you if I find out anything."

"Mallory?"

"Sir?"

"If you're staying at your old home tonight you should see if you can remember anything else about the night your sister was abducted." Something she usually tried hard to forget. "I take it Alex Parker is with you?"

Alex opened the door and stood there looking like God's gift. How the hell had Frazer known?

"He's here."

"I found out how he won his Distinguished Service Cross." She unconsciously braced herself. "His Humvee was attacked going to a supposedly peaceful tribal meeting. It was a set-up, an ambush. They were attacked in a valley and cut off from ground support for more than an hour. No air support available. Parker defended their position, killed many insurgents, kept two of his seriously injured friends alive, and stopped the Taliban from mutilating the bodies of his comrades. He's a brave guy and his alibi checked out, but…" Her eyes watched the rim of Alex's irises grow darker and more wary as if he knew they were talking about him. "This killer is serious about getting your attention. Keep up your guard."

"My Glock will help level the playing field."

"Fine. Just don't take any undue risks," said Frazer. "God knows I don't need the paperwork if anything happens to you."

"Gee, thanks."

"Let's get this guy, Agent Rooney. Let's put him in a cage where he belongs."

She took the donut from Alex's hands. "Amen to that."

CHAPTER FIFTEEN

ALEX DID NOT like the situation. At. All.

It was nighttime. They were driving to Mallory's family home in the Appalachians, just a few miles from where the recent murders had occurred and the site of her sister's abduction.

Thoughts exploded in his mind. What were her colleagues up to?

If he hadn't insisted on accompanying her to Lindsey Keeble's funeral Mallory would be up here in West Virginia, alone. So what if she was an FBI agent? This guy had killed over and over and had proved he had no compunction about hurting people to feed his sick appetite.

Some might argue Alex was the same but they'd be missing the point. He worked for the government. Their government. He might be deniable if caught, but it didn't change the fact he only killed people as ordered. The same way a sniper took out the enemy or soldiers killed in combat. Everyone knew what the CIA did abroad. Was it so big a stretch to think the government would also do it on home soil?

Deniability was king.

If an assassin had taken out the warlord ruling a small town in Herat Province the men in his unit, his brothers, would not have been mowed down like bloody skittles. That's why he'd said yes to the CIA all those years ago. To save fellow Americans. He didn't choose targets for revenge. He did not rape, torture or strangle people for jollies. His work was dark and he did it as efficiently and painlessly as possible.

This serial killer had his own agenda and right now he was orbiting Payton Rooney's twin like a satellite about to crash to Earth. Alex wouldn't allow any harm to come to Mallory even though he got in deeper and deeper every time he looked in her eyes.

But he'd rather break her heart than see her murdered. *His* heart didn't matter. The fact he still had one was an unpleasant surprise.

He'd spent most of the day wanting to kiss her and taste her, but couldn't afford the distraction. Now wasn't the time. His instincts were screaming that something was off about this whole situation. Something didn't fit. "We should go to a hotel."

"Local ones are full up thanks to the press." Who'd got wind of the double murder and possible serial killer. "And it's stupid when my dad's house is just up the road."

Up the road was a relative term in West Virginia.

"Plus…"

"What?"

He heard her swallow. "SSA Frazer suggested I might remember more about the night of Payton's abduction if I was at the place where it happened."

And that asshole was willing to throw her to the wolves for a tidbit of information. Or maybe he just trusted her capabilities and Alex was being an overprotective jerk? But if *he'd* wanted to kill Mallory he could have done so a thousand times over—FBI training or no FBI training—and even the idea made him want to puke.

The killer playing this game with Mallory and her family was dangerous. But he didn't know the truth about Alex and that was her secret weapon—she just didn't know it.

"You think the PR Killer is the same person who killed that couple last night, don't you?" he asked.

She darted a glance at him. "The MO's different...but yes. I do."

"You think he's local?"

She swallowed and then nodded. He did too. If not local, then at least living here for the time being.

They turned down a small road, headlights cutting through an avenue overhung by majestic elms. The landscape felt stark, everything battening down the hatches for a long hard winter. He glanced at Mallory's profile rimmed in icy green from the dashboard lights.

If he was the killer he'd have put an electronic monitor on her car so he'd know exactly where she was without her knowing it—assuming he hadn't already seduced her in a bar and planted bugs in her apartment. He rolled his eyes. *Asshole.*

Alex had checked the car earlier and there was no tracker device. That could change at any time, which is why he was always checking and double-checking everything constantly. A guy like him couldn't be too careful and neither could Mallory. Lack of a tracking device didn't make him relax his guard. Just meant the bad guy either wasn't as smart as he thought he was, or hadn't had access to her vehicle yet, or had figured out another way to reel her in. Like a double homicide or the funeral of a local girl.

His brain was firing in all directions.

It was black as coal as they traveled this lonely lane. Who

knew this forest wilderness existed just a few hours outside DC? No streetlights. No neighbors. No moon. No stars. Plenty of unsolved crimes…

Whoa.

Mallory pulled up along the circular drive at the front of a huge house.

"*This* is where you grew up?" He whistled. It was impressive as hell.

They both eyed the red-brick three-story mansion lit up a fiery orange by the headlights.

"It *is* a little over the top for a family of four," she admitted.

"It's bigger than the White House. Fuck, Mallory, you could fit the ranch house where I grew up in that thing about sixty times over."

"Eastborne's been in the family for over two hundred years."

"You come from some serious old money." It was a hell of a motive for kidnapping. So why had they never received a ransom demand? He unclipped his seatbelt.

"I earn FBI wages nowadays so you don't need to be intimidated Mr. *I-own-my-own-security-firm.*" She rolled her eyes and made him laugh. Her irreverence was another of her plus points. She didn't have a lot of use for status and he liked that about her. "It was actually a lot of fun growing up here before Payton was taken. Great place for a game of hide-n-seek when we had friends over to play."

You could be lost for months in a place this size. He didn't say it. It didn't seem appropriate given what had happened to Mallory's sister.

She didn't need to tell him that the fun had stopped when

her sister had gone missing. It was implied by the sadness in her voice. “Lucas Randall lived nearby?”

“His parents kept a summer house about five miles west and we hung out a lot.”

There were no lights on inside the mansion. The whole place had an abandoned feel to it despite the well-manicured lawns and fresh paint.

“Your dad lives in Webster?”

“Yeah, he has a nice little house about five minutes from where he works.” She sat contemplating the house as if it were a living entity. “He grew up here and still comes up some weekends but…” She pulled a face. “It’s just so massive with such a sad association. He wants us all to get together one last time for Christmas, even Mom—they’re still friends—but after that he’s selling up. He’s been talking about it for years, but I think he means it this time. He says it’s time for the house to find a new family.” She crossed her arms tight across her chest and he wanted to pull her to him but there was no room in the damn car. Tears shimmered but didn’t fall. “He’s right. Payton loved this house. She wouldn’t have wanted it to stand empty.”

He took her hand. She had lovely smooth hands with long fingers and short fingernails that felt good on his skin. “Parents who’ve lost children often don’t want to move from the family home. They worry the child will find his/her way back and they won’t be there when they come home.”

She nodded. “I guess after eighteen years Dad finally figured out Payton wasn’t coming home.”

People did get rescued after long bouts in captivity but it was rare. “Do you think he’s wrong?”

She shook her head. “She’s gone. She’s not coming back.” She spoke with such certainty that he looked at her intently but didn't comment. Whatever her reasons, Mallory didn't want to talk about it.

"Let's get inside. It's freezing out here." She pushed open the car door, her face pale in the overhead light. Staying here tonight wasn't going to be easy.

He never left home without a go-bag and obviously neither did FBI agents. Alex took their two overnight bags out of the trunk, along with both laptops. She climbed the steps to the front door and inserted a key. "The housekeeper went to visit her sister for Thanksgiving and isn't back yet."

Alex had forgotten it was heading toward Christmas. Usually he spent the holidays working. "She lives here alone?"

Mallory nodded. There was a beep and she dashed over to an alarm panel and punched in some numbers. "I hope she didn't change the code because this sucker goes straight to the cop shop."

It was a good system but one he could bypass in ten seconds with the right equipment. At least there was some security here because the old-fashioned sash windows and multiple entrances were a security fucking nightmare. The alarm stopped beeping.

The air smelled of clean pine needles with the faint tinge of cloves and old wood smoke. She flicked a switch and a massive black and white marble-tiled entranceway with a huge wraparound staircase was illuminated by the sort of chandelier that wouldn't have looked out of place in Buckingham palace.

He held up his hand to shade his eyes. "I think I've gone blind."

"Funny."

She closed the door and flicked the deadbolt and reset the alarm. Alex looked around. There were antiques and marble statues. Who had life-size statues inside their home?

Mallory grabbed his hand. "Leave the bags at the bottom of the stairs. I'm starving. Mrs. Buxton, the housekeeper, usually stocks the freezer with soups and casseroles, especially this time of year and…" Her voice trailed off as she caught sight of something sparkling in a nearby sitting room. She dropped his hand and went to stare at a twenty-foot Christmas tree. The room was dark but there was enough light coming from the foyer to see a gracious room decorated for the festive season complete with a Martha Stewart worthy tree.

It made his heart clench. He hadn't experienced this sort of Christmas since his mom died and theirs had been on a much more modest scale. The pain of that loss was still a physical ache in his chest.

Mallory reached out and touched one of the baubles. It was a misshaped crystal star. "Payton made this in school." As if unable to stop herself she slipped it off the branch and kissed it, before putting it back on the tree, her touch lingering. "I still miss her." Her voice cracked.

He put his hands on her shoulders and squeezed. He could relate. He still missed his mother and his grandfather and his friends. But he knew they were dead and never coming back. You had to move on. "We're supposed to miss them. That's their gift."

Huge amber eyes met his. "Pain is a gift?"

He nodded. "It proves they meant something to us. That even years after losing them we still feel them. Here." He touched a hand to his heart feeling foolish. He didn't go in for mushy crap and he was straying dangerously close. But she needed this. She needed comfort.

There was one sort of comfort he was good at so he pulled

her flush against him, watched a gasp transform her face just a split second before he kissed her. His mouth coaxed her lips open, aching for a taste. Her tongue hit his in a wet slide and instantly he was hard. *Jesus H Christ, what is it about this woman?*

She wrapped her arms around his neck and kissed him deeper, harder as if she wanted to climb inside him. Maybe sex was better therapy than any shrink could offer. Heat rose up with a wave of lust. His control snapped and all thoughts were gone except one. To get inside her as fast as possible. He yanked her blouse out of her pants, backed her against the wall, undoing the button and zipper on her slacks. He needed her, now. He slid his hand under her shirt and pushed her bra out of the way as he cupped her breasts. Her holster got in the way but it was also a turn on. Her head went back on a groan. Her skin was velvet warm. Nipples tight and beaded. His mouth chased a quiver down the line of her throat to her shoulder and he nipped her just hard enough to make her fingernails tighten on his flesh. He liked that. Liked it a lot. One-handed he shoved her pants down and undid his own as she kicked hers off. He fumbled in his pocket for a condom, taking back control of her mouth. His heart thumped as his blood raced through his veins. There was no time for foreplay. No time for finesse. He covered himself and lifted her, spreading her thighs around his hips as she guided him straight to her center. She wanted this as much as he did.

With one hard thrust he was buried deep in her heat.

She wrapped her legs around his waist, nails bit into his flesh. "Harder."

He drove into her, again and again, nothing but an animal who needed to satisfy a primal urge.

"Oh, God," she groaned and twisted on top of him and he held on tight, trying to lock her in place as she came undone. Muscles clutched at him. He pinned her arms over her head, reveling in the pressure that was building and building and building. Heat and pleasure lashed and she was with him all the way. She cried out and he followed her over that edge like a buffalo on a stampede as his head exploded. Pleasure obliterated everything except this act, this need to take and brand and make her his.

He pried his eyes open. Became slowly aware. Wondering what the fuck was wrong with him when a serial killer was after Mallory. He wasn't fucking Superman and getting caught with his pants around his ankles was a pretty fucking stupid way to die. *Asshole.* His heartbeat slowed. Their breathing quieted and silence roared. He leaned his forehead against hers. "I'm pretty sure I should apologize for that."

"I'll slap you if you do."

"You make me lose control." His words caught and tumbled.

She touched his face and stared into his eyes. "Control is overrated and you just made something right with my world." She grinned, those tilted eyes of hers sparkling. "Now put me down, lover, and let's get some food. I'm starving."

"IS THIS GIVING you the creeps?" She stood in her old bedroom looking at the same duvet covers and blue painted walls they'd had when Payton was alive. Pictures she and her sister had done at school were tacked to the wall, curled at the edges. "It's giving me the creeps." She shuddered.

They'd unearthed frozen pizza and ignored the wine collection and opted instead for soda. Neither wanted to be impaired by alcohol because this guy could turn up to try and kill both her and Alex. She was glad they'd had fast furious sex when they'd first arrived. It had taken the edge off her ramped up tension and no way would they be spending the night tearing up the sheets. They'd take turns keeping watch. It was the perfect opportunity to catch this guy. They were both armed. She definitely felt dangerous.

"Your parents never changed the room?"

Mallory shook her head. "Mama wouldn't let anyone touch a thing. Bought me a new wardrobe and replaced every toy I said I wanted. Parental guilt and the need to honor the dead. It was a messy combination." She propped her hands on her hips. It felt weird being back here. The room smelled musty and airless. "I moved to a bedroom two down from where they slept after that."

"In another wing of the house?"

"Yeah."

"Any idea why you kids were camped out so far away?"

"My mother liked her peace and quiet. I was neither peaceful nor quiet." More guilt. She dropped to her knees and crawled under the bed.

"Something I should know?" Alex quizzed. "A portal to Narnia, perhaps?"

She choked on dust bunnies. Nothing else remained. Not her pillow or her flashlight. Alex squatted down to peer at her curiously.

"When Frazer hypnotized me I remembered I used to sleep under the bed a lot because I was scared of monsters. I saw the kidnapper's feet. Green converse trainers."

"Frazer said being back here might help trigger some memory recall?" Alex asked dubiously.

"Yes." She sneezed.

"Bless you."

She laughed. Then closed her eyes, but she was too aware of this man who'd totally invaded her life and made her feel so safe she was willing—no, *eager*—to take on Payton's abductor.

"Male, female? Young or old?" asked Alex softly.

She closed her eyes and visualized that night long ago. She practiced the deep breathing techniques Frazer had shown her. Felt her heartbeat calm. "Male youth."

"What about scent. Can you smell anything?"

She went to shake her head and stopped. "Rain. It smelled like rain…"

"It rained the night she was abducted?"

"Yes. It did." She frowned. A window or a door must have been left open nearby. There was something else just teasing the edges of her mind. "He said something." The memories were indistinct, like trying to hear underwater. "I think he said not to worry. 'We're not going to hurt you'."

"We?"

"We." She opened her eyes and scrambled from the tiny space that had seemed so comforting as a child. Now it was dusty and claustrophobic. She brushed herself off. Alex stood back.

"So there was more than one of them?"

"I only saw one guy but that's what he said." She rubbed her eyes. "I think. Maybe. Perhaps."

Alex was watching her closely. "Come on. You need sleep."

"Shower first."

He smiled sadly. "As much as I'd like to join you, I'll keep watch." Because a monster might come for her. Might come for them both. His eyes hardened as he read her thoughts. "I won't let him get you, Mallory."

A shiver skipped up her spine and she couldn't speak. Payton's abductor was out there, waiting for her. She could feel him. But she wanted him to come. She had no intention of letting him get away.

HE TRUDGED THROUGH the woods with the girl's naked body over his shoulder. He'd planned to make Kari pay long and hard over the next few days but having Mallory stay at the big house with just that prick of a boyfriend was too tempting. The bruises on Kari's face were testament that he'd made up for lack of time with some serious dedication to the task.

She hung limply, dark hair falling almost to the back of his knees, her skin as white as milk and cold to the touch. He slapped her bare buttocks. The power of having a human being at his mercy was addictive. It hadn't been like that with Payton. He'd loved her. But these bitches? They were like animals. Worthless. Meat. They meant nothing to him.

He stumbled slightly. He was worried no one would ever mean anything to him again. That was why he had to keep looking until he found the perfect replacement.

He skirted the edge of the woods where he remembered watching Payton and her sister play all those years ago. His uncle had planned to kidnap both girls and ransom them off. The parents could afford it. He'd lied about his intent to hurt them though. Hell, he should have known the bastard would rape Payton as soon as he'd got her at his mercy. The old man had done the same to him before he'd been old enough to stand up for himself.

It had been a stupid idea and he'd gone along with it because back then he'd been dumber than a rock. His uncle had slapped him when he'd come out with just one girl and sent him back to find Mallory. But she hadn't been in bed and he sure as hell wasn't searching every room in that giant house for a second girl when they already had one.

While he'd been pretending to go back to get Mallory, his uncle... He swallowed and sweat broke out across his shoulders at the memories. He'd gone back to the chamber horrified to see Payton lying there all bloody and broken and his uncle wiping a sly satisfied grin off his face.

He'd let the bastard think he'd got away with it. He'd had to wait six long months before he got his revenge and the wait had almost driven him out of his mind. But finally, in the spring, he'd managed to pin the rat-bastard underneath the tractor and he could still hear the sounds of his pig-like squeals as he'd been very, very slowly crushed to death. The memory filled him with a sense of righteous satisfaction.

The cops had said it was an accident. His first kill. And the most gratifying.

After that he'd taken care of Payton's every need and he hadn't touched her until she'd been much older and they'd been in love. If he could have released her he would have, but her mind was fragile and she'd been terrified of everything except him. No way could she have lied about how much she loved him. And the world wouldn't have understood. They'd have been separated and he'd have gone to jail.

He shifted Kari's weight. Hell, she was heavier than she looked. He approached the house from the eastern side. No lights were on and a thick mist hugged the ground, clinging to frosty stems of grass. He wore a bulletproof vest, gloves and a ski mask and he had a pistol strapped to his ankle. He went to the door of the mudroom and used the key he'd stolen years ago to open it. He entered the alarm code—the housekeeper was pretty liberal with security and half the town knew the code. Hell, the judge had given him a spare key for the front door but he had no intention of using that today. Dead giveaway. Standing in the darkness he listened intently to the silence. The house was vast, and the idea anyone heard the alarm beeping was unlikely. Still he waited.

He reached down for his gun and headed cautiously into the kitchen.

When he'd taken Payton all those years ago, he and his uncle had propped a ladder against one of the upper windows. She'd weighed nothing at all and it'd been easy to carry her out. Kari was making his shoulder throb like a bitch.

He'd thought about where he was going to leave her. He'd toyed with the idea of dangling her from the staircase which would be quite the sight, but there was no symmetry in it. The drama was all for effect with no subtlety. He moved quietly through the rear of the house where he occasionally had coffee with the housekeeper, glad she was away so he didn't have to kill her too.

He went up the back stairs—the servants' staircase—and trod softly, grateful for the thick carpet over old, thick boards. A slice of light under a door to the right pinpointed where Mallory slept. Presumably with her asshole boyfriend. One of the boards creaked beneath his feet and he moved more cautiously. He wanted them to find Kari's body here—back where it had all started. Then he'd put a bullet in the guy and take the girl he'd wanted all along. No more substitutes.

CHAPTER SIXTEEN

ALEX STOOD BESIDE the bedroom door, listening.

"What was that?" Mallory shot upright in bed.

He held up his hand to tell her to be quiet. He was sure he'd heard something out there in the corridor, but it was so subtle it might just be the house creaking as the temperature dropped.

It was two AM. Mallory had been stretched out fast asleep in bed, fully dressed except for her boots. The urge to curl up next to her had been tempting, but he hadn't wavered from his guard position.

She slipped out of bed, toed on her boots and scooped up her Glock from the bedside table. She came to him and put a hand on his back, holding her weapon pointed at the floor.

"I heard something," he told her quietly.

"Let's check it out," she whispered urgently.

He could practically see her excitement crackling in the air. She wanted to catch this guy. He wanted her safe. He hesitated. If it had just been him he'd have already gone hunting, but *if* this killer worked as part of a team he couldn't risk leaving Mallory alone.

"We stick together. We do *not* split up."

"Okay." Her fingers rubbed his back in reassurance. This hyper-awareness of danger felt a lot like combat. *Okay*. He was better equipped than most to catch this fucker and end this nightmare. But the idea of putting Mallory at risk wrapped around his gullet like barbed wire.

Pistol in hand, he opened the door, looking right and left for targets. Nothing. The corridor was dark and empty. He flicked on the light.

"What did you do that for?" Mallory hissed.

Because if the killer *was* here he wanted the bastard to know they were onto him and run rather than attack. He shrugged.

He moved swiftly along the corridor, Mallory at his back. She kept a firm grip on his shirt, a physical reference point as he concentrated on figuring out exactly what he'd heard earlier. Could have been a cat. A vagrant. The housekeeper returning home unexpectedly. The judge. The senator. He didn't want an innocent caught in the crossfire.

Something drew them toward the room Mallory and Payton had shared as children. Soundless. Cautious. Every sense ramped to high alert. The atmosphere of the house had changed, turned malevolent and hostile. Dangerous. The temperature had dropped.

"Someone's opened a window…" said Mallory.

Someone was here. He could *feel* them. But his pulse never wavered. Hell, the only thing that got his heart racing was sex with Mallory.

He'd trained so well and so hard for combat, killing didn't even affect him anymore. It took years to perfect this sort of combat physiology. He needed that coldness and focus to operate. To kill without hesitation. He didn't want to do it anymore, but if it stopped bad guys like this, maybe it was worth sacrificing his soul.

A breeze tickled his cheek.

All these closed doors were a nightmare, but they didn't have the manpower to search every room.

"I should lead," Mallory murmured into his ear, her fingers tightening on his shirt.

Yeah. No. Way. He used one hand to keep her behind him. They turned another corner. It was like living in a goddamn hotel. Up ahead, there was a light on inside the girls' old bedroom.

Mallory froze behind him. He paused as he surveyed the corridor. Glanced behind him. Nothing. Everything was silent except for the ruffle of a breeze through an open window at the end of the hallway. Was that what he'd heard earlier? Someone lifting the sash?

Once again they moved forward, Mallory a shadow against his back.

He could smell the fear and excitement rolling off her in waves, knew her pulse would be pounding. The predator was near. But where? No sound, no smell, no sign gave the bastard away.

Making sure Mal was to the side of the bedroom door, he pushed it wide.

Christ.

A dead woman lay on the bed. Naked. Battered. Hands resting low over her pubic hair just like photographs of all the other PR-Killer victims. A bloody smear coated her chest where, no doubt, the letters PR had been carved in a macabre love heart. The wind ruffled the yellow drapes and it was bitterly cold.

"There's a drainpipe." Mallory rushed forward to look out the window but he grabbed her arm, checked behind the door and any hiding places without touching a damn thing. He had no desire to put his DNA on this scene. He leaned forward through the open window to check the drainpipe when instinct had him whirling, bringing his gun up as an armed, masked figure in black appeared behind him in the doorway. Alex nailed him twice in the chest and the man fell backward, his shot going wild. It was the same guy who'd broken into Mallory's house in Charlotte.

A woman's low pain-filled squeal made them all startle as the dead woman suddenly rolled over on the bed—*okay, not dead.*

The assailant pointed his gun at the bed and fired. He shot again but his weapon jammed. Alex aimed at his head this time, but the bastard darted out of sight and ran like the chicken-shit he was. The woman screamed in agony. Alex checked to make sure Mallory hadn't been hit, but the victim had been shot in the shoulder and there was blood everywhere. Mallory rushed to her aid and Alex was torn. Leave Mallory alone or end this thing by chasing down the asshole who'd done this?

He went after the killer, running flat-out down the plush corridor, only to be thrown into darkness as the fucker flipped the switch at the other end of the hall.

His legs pumped and his lungs burned as he ran as fast as he could.

Alex had nailed the guy squarely in the chest. He should have been dead but the guy wasn't even bleeding. *Kevlar*. And some grim determination because there was a good chance those shots at that distance had broken a couple of ribs. He should have gone for headshots but had hoped a dying man might reveal Payton Rooney's final resting place. He heard the guy running through the darkness and followed. He didn't want to leave Mallory but this was a chance to get this bastard.

Rounding the corner that led to the main staircase he saw the shadow racing ahead of him. The guy stopped and fired off a few shots. Alex didn't pause, he legged it, full belt, sliding down the banisters and flying after the sonofabitch who was out the door. Big, fit, fast. Running on adrenaline.

Alex burst out the front door in time to see the attacker skidding around the corner of the house. Gravel spit behind his trainers as he ran. He was about to take a shot when the guy dodged behind the eastern wall. He didn't waste time cursing.

He took off running, moving cautiously around the corner. Shots fired, hitting where his head would have been if he hadn't crouched down. He returned fire, heard a grunt, chased the guy's shadow behind an old garage and past an empty pool. He came to an abrupt halt, standing there in the darkness. The trees in the woods rustled at the edges of the wide lawn, beckoning him to give chase. He looked back at the house. *Shit.* No way could he leave Mallory longer than he already had.

What if the guy had circled back? Panic bit into his chest and he started sprinting the way he'd come. He sped around the corner and was abruptly blinded by headlights. He shielded his face with his arm.

"FBI, put the gun down!"

Alex shot out both headlights and dodged to the side. He had the "agent" disarmed, on the ground, face in the gravel when he heard a sound behind him and whirled.

"Oh, God, Alex. That's my boss." It was Mallory. She'd turned the entranceway light on.

"Shit." Alex took his knee out of the fed's spine and stood back. The guy was wearing what had probably been a very expensive pale gray suit and, now Alex had the chance to see, the headlights he'd shot out belonged to a very expensive Lexus that hadn't been there earlier. The guy must have driven up while he was chasing the attacker around the back of the house.

He held out his hand to the man on the ground who was looking a bit shell-shocked. "Sorry."

"No time for that." Mallory grabbed his arm. He holstered his gun while she spoke. Her boss picked himself up off the ground, looking pissed.

"The girl is alive but she's lost a lot of blood. We can't afford to wait for the ambulance. I need help carrying her and we'll drive her to the ER." She pulled him with her.

"There's another victim?" Mallory's boss dropped the attitude and jogged swiftly up the stairs with them.

"Yes, but the UNSUB shot her before he ran away. She was already in a really bad way." Mallory was running up the stairs and both of them stuck to her like honey on bread.

Alex took a quick detour. "Grabbing car keys," he yelled to the feds. He also wanted to get their gear. It took under twenty seconds to stuff everything together and race back out of the room. He met them on the landing with Mallory's boss carrying the battered girl, wrapped in blankets. Her eyes were squeezed shut, and she sobbed in pain and anguish. Alex couldn't imagine what she'd been through and he'd spent plenty of time in hell. Mallory pressed a towel against the gunshot wound which stopped the bleeding a little. Alex strode ahead and opened the car door so the guy could slide in with the girl on his lap. He threw their luggage in the trunk.

“I’ll drive,” said Mallory.

“Not this time.” He got in the driver’s seat and started the engine. He caught the other man’s cold, blue gaze in the rear view. “Buckle up.”

As soon as Mallory had her door closed and belt on, he started driving, foot to the floor, maneuvering the gravel road at extreme speed. “Hang on,” he told them, taking a left out of the driveway that had the tires screeching. Getting Mallory out of danger, getting this critically injured young woman to the hospital was all he gave a damn about. Despite the white-knuckled ride he wasn’t about to let anything bad happen to either of them ever again.

CHAPTER SEVENTEEN

MALLORY PACED THE hospital corridor the way she'd been pacing it for the last hour. *So close.* She'd been so close to the bastard who ripped her sister from her life, she'd looked him in the eye for a moment before he'd run.

For a moment she'd wanted him dead, but more than that, she wanted him to tell her what he'd done with her sister. Where had he buried Payton?

The need to know was so intense it had crippled her ability to actually shoot the bastard.

Alex had nailed him square in the chest only to discover the guy had been wearing body armor. The killer had known they were there and expected they'd be armed so had planned accordingly. There was no mercy in his actions. He'd have killed Alex, left the injured woman for dead and taken Mallory for whatever twisted reason he'd given himself to justify rape and violation.

A burning heat warmed her from the inside. Her fists clenched with anger and frustration. She should have used her Taser. Why the hell hadn't she thought of that sooner?

They were running the injured woman's fingerprints through IAFIS but Mallory was almost positive from her general description that she was Kari Regent. Her face was unrecognizable, but if she survived there was a good chance, once the swelling went down, that her face would return to normal. Although Mallory knew the girl would never be the same.

Why were her prints on the murder weapon at a double homicide? Mallory had no doubt she was a victim in this, but what had the UNSUB made her do before he'd beaten and strangled her?

Was he local? The murders of the McCaffertys and the return to Eastborne with Kari tonight, suggested he was holed up nearby. Maybe he'd been at Lindsey's funeral? Or watching the house?

She made a mental note to talk to the sheriff and check the ID's of the mourners. Maybe they should put surveillance on the grave itself as serial killers often revisited their victims after death.

She shivered.

Without Alex she'd have been a victim.

She'd been taken by surprise in her old bedroom, which is exactly what the killer had intended. Finding the injured woman in her old bed had side-swiped her and changed her priority from hunting to rescue, and he'd damn well planned the whole thing to put her off her game. Smart. Organized. Ruthless. Sadistic.

Alex's instincts had saved them both. She didn't know what she'd done to deserve him but she was grateful he was here. He sat on an orange plastic chair, leaning forward, resting his elbows on his knees.

"You're a hell of shot," she told him with an absurd amount of pride. He hadn't been crippled by emotion and adrenaline. She needed to ramp up her training. He was the civilian—albeit, one who'd earned one of their country's highest honors for valor, she reminded herself.

He nodded like it was no big deal.

He'd also taken Frazer down without breaking stride. Thank goodness he hadn't killed the man because her career prospects were already fried.

Speak of the devil. Frazer strode down the long, white hallway toward them.

"How is she?" Mallory asked.

Frazer opened a door to a waiting room, saw it was empty and nodded his head to indicate she follow him. She stepped inside and Alex was there beside her. Frazer shot him a look but didn't order him out of the room. Progress? She doubted it.

"She's alive. Barely. The fingerprints are a match to Kari Regent." His blond hair was flattened against his skull. Mouth grim. A scrape on his cheekbone, courtesy of Alex's rough handling. He wasn't looking as smooth as he usually did, but she'd noticed some of the nurses checking out the FBI agent. They'd barely glanced at Alex. Somehow he made himself fade into the background—probably because he didn't strut about penis-first. As someone who avoided the limelight, it was another thing that attracted her to him.

"Did she say anything?" she asked.

He shook his head. "They induced a coma until the intracranial pressure goes down and they are worried about internal bleeding. They might need to operate to relieve swelling." He stopped and drew in a deep breath, clearly affected by the young woman's injuries. "Her windpipe is bruised and very fragile. She's been shackled, sexually assaulted, beaten and strangled. Not to mention is suffering from hypothermia and a gunshot wound. It isn't looking great but she's stable and she's here." He ran his fingers over his eyes as if trying to remove some of what he'd seen. "We've got DNA swabs from her body, which have been rushed to forensics. Your father's house is now a crime scene. We all need to give statements at the sheriff's office, then I want to go back and see if we missed anything."

"I don't want to leave until I know she's going to be okay." She felt protective of Kari, as if she owed her a personal debt.

Frazer shook his head. "It could be days before she wakes up. Weeks even. There's a deputy on the door—"

Alex cut him off. "I've arranged round-the-clock protection. No one's going to hurt her again." The energy rolling off him was quiet fury.

"The FBI can protect her." Frazer eyed him down the length of his nose.

Alex took a step into Frazer's space. "One of my partners specializes in personal security and she's sending two of her best people." His upper lip curled and his eyes narrowed. "They'll be here within the next hour. No one will get past them. How long before your guys show up? Long enough for Kari Regent to end up dead?"

Mallory's eyes widened. Her boss and her boyfriend were headed for a pissing contest and she didn't appreciate being caught in the middle.

"What's the problem with additional security? What harm can it do?" She broke in quickly, trying to diffuse the tension that crackled through the empty waiting room.

"I want background checks on anyone guarding her," Frazer bit out between gritted teeth. "And they better not get in the way of law enforcement."

"*They* know how to do their job."

Frazer's mouth firmed at that.

Mallory was already in this guy's bad books. Alex was making it worse. "Why were you there, sir? Not that I don't appreciate the back-up." Although they'd had it handled thanks to Alex. He made a hell of a partner. Better than her so-called colleagues at the Bureau. SSA Danbridge *had* warned her the day she'd left Charlotte.

Frazer blinked at her. His eyes shifted and a weird shiver slipped down her spine. "I decided to come up and talk to the sheriff about that double homicide—"

"You set her up as bait and turned up late for the party," Alex snapped.

Mallory backed up a step. *What?*

Frazer didn't deny it. He smiled tightly. "At least she had *you*, Mr. Parker. Championship marksman, Indy 500 driver. Not to mention hand-to-hand combat aficionado." Frazer's expression turned murderous as he looked down at his torn thousand dollar suit. "I'd say the UNSUB definitely underestimated Special Agent Mallory Rooney's new boyfriend."

And so had he.

Mallory felt winded.

Alex sneered. "I'll repair the car and replace the suit but you are still an asshole."

Definitely not intimidated by the FBI. She'd noticed that trait the first time she'd met him in Charlotte. And civilians were *always* intimidated by the FBI.

"You let an inexperienced field agent take on a serial killer but didn't even have the skills to arrive on fucking time? Were you hoping he took her? Raise your profile on the media stage?"

Mallory froze. Was Frazer disappointed the UNSUB

hadn't taken her? The thought gave her goose bumps. If Frazer was helping the vigilante he might have reason to hope someone shut her up. A serial killer would do it without casting any suspicion on himself. She crossed her arms over her chest. She was inexperienced but she wasn't stupid and things weren't adding up. "Is it true? Did you use me as bait?"

Flinty eyes turned on her. "Are you questioning my decisions, Special Agent Rooney? Or just my ability?"

A wave of uncertainty hit her. "Considering what happened tonight I think we—the FBI that is—could have handled this whole situation a lot better. We should have known he'd turn up tonight. We should have set a trap."

Frazer closed his eyes and held tight to the bridge of his nose. "Hindsight is always twenty-twenty, Agent Rooney. Don't question my authority again."

Right now, Mallory wouldn't trust him as far as she could throw him.

Alex looked ready to punch him but Mallory touched his wrist, reassured by the strong steady pulse beating beneath her fingers. "Yes, sir."

She backed off. Because she'd figured out a way to end her hunt for the vigilante and move on with her Bureau career. She just hoped Alex was there when this was all over.

ALEX SAT IN the main hub of the Greenville Sheriff's Office being interviewed about what happened last night. Inside Sheriff Williams' glass-walled office, Mallory was making her own statement. He couldn't take his eyes off her. Except for a bright patch of crimson over each cheekbone, her skin was ice-white. There was a suggestion of fragility to her face that hadn't been there when he first met her. A hint of vulnerability. Whatever the feelings that had been growing inside him these past few weeks, they had amplified to staggering proportions after the attempt to steal her away last night.

If he hadn't insisted on accompanying her yesterday, chances were Mallory would right now be at the mercy of a sexual predator. The idea made him want to put his fist through something solid. Preferably SSA Frazer's face.

"What happened then?"

Alex glanced at the deputy taking his statement. Deputy Sheriff L. Chance according to his nametag. He fit the general size and shape of the attacker. So did the sheriff and half of his deputies.

"There was a noise in the corridor."

The bodyguards that his partner, Haley Cramer, sent had arrived via company helicopter less than thirty minutes ago. They were taking shifts to watch over the best chance they had of catching this bastard. If Kari Regent survived she could give them a sketch of the bad guy and maybe a description of where she'd been held. Then they'd have a place to begin. Alex was more and more convinced the starting point was somewhere near Colby, and tied back to what had happened there eighteen years ago.

"You were in bed asleep?" Deputy Chance asked him.

Alex shook his. "I was sitting in a chair, wide awake."

"You sat in a chair while Agent Rooney slept?"

"That's what I said." Alex stared at Mallory through the glass. He couldn't relax since that bastard had made a grab for her. There was no doubt in Alex's mind it wasn't the first time he'd tried, and wouldn't be the last. So far Mallory had been lucky, but she couldn't be on guard forever. The only way to end this thing was a bullet in that animal's brain. He drummed his fingers on the desk. The cop was still watching him as if expecting an answer. "We were taking turns keeping watch."

"So you were expecting trouble?"

Alex nodded. Frazer had also been expecting trouble but the sonofabitch had done nothing to prevent it. Why? Alex's eyes narrowed. Was he part of The Gateway Project? The part that had almost gotten him caught last time?

Or maybe he genuinely believed Mallory—a trained FBI Special Agent—could take the guy alone. Alex frowned. He wasn't sexist. He'd figured out one of his fellow assassins was a female and she was one of the best. Women could be operators, damn good operators. But Mallory wasn't there yet. She needed more training, more physical fitness and more ruthless determination to hurt someone.

That's what gave predators and operators the advantage over "normal" people. They worked outside society boundaries and went in fast and hard. No one expected another human being to attack them. It violated all sense of security and made intelligent people freeze and comply when usually they'd fight for their lives.

"Ms. Rooney has stayed in that house many times over the years. Why did she think last night would be any different?"

Alex didn't know what the FBI had shared with the locals about the new evidence turning up. If this guy was supposed to know about the case other law enforcement people could do the honors. He shrugged. "I like to be prepared."

The deputy's eyebrows rose. "Quite the boy scout who carries a SIG P229."

Alex gave him a cold smile. "Wouldn't be alive if I carried

a pea shooter."

"Agent Rooney never fired a shot?" They both looked toward Mallory.

"As soon as she heard the injured woman groan she concentrated on saving her."

The deputy sniffed as if she hadn't done her job very well but Alex wasn't about to tell him he worked better without interference.

"You been seeing her long?"

Alex eyed the cop. The FBI already knew the answer to that question.

He didn't know if the cops and feds had made the leap that the PR-killer and their double homicide were related to Payton Rooney's abduction eighteen years ago. He had. He had no doubt whatsoever. Everything was linked. They just needed to figure out how.

The deputy's pen hovered. "Okay, so, what happened next?"

"You have deputies searching those woods?"

The deputy's lips tightened. "Search parties have scoured every inch and we haven't found a damn thing."

"He knows those woods. You need to keep searching the local area."

The deputy gave him a flat-eyed stare. "We know how to do our job, *Mr.* Parker."

Alex said nothing. This guy would be hard to catch if you followed the rules. Thankfully he didn't have to. He needed to check that algorithm he'd written to compare cell phone information to the dump zones and kidnap sites. He'd add in the local towers from around here and see what popped. Anxious to get away he hurried over the rest of the story.

Mallory was still talking to the sheriff.

"What made you turn around?"

Alex blinked at the deputy. Weren't they done?

"In the bedroom. You said you were looking out the window and you turned around. Why?" The deputy looked interested.

Alex shrugged. "I sensed something."

"Good instincts."

His eyes narrowed. "I got lucky." He didn't tell the guy he got lucky a lot.

"Then you chased him?"

"Yeah. Are we finished?" Pain shot through Alex's head. Fucking headaches. He pulled painkillers out of his pocket and helped himself to a drink of water. *Shit.* Mallory's mother and father arrived. He rolled his eyes, assuming the three-ring circus was following close behind. They swept through into the sheriff's glass office and gathered Mallory into a protective embrace.

A feeling of isolation swept over him. It rooted him to the spot like a nail through his spine. Worse than usual because for a few brief hours he'd experienced how great it felt to be part of something. Now he was back on the outside looking in.

Where he liked it. Where he needed to be.

What he needed to do was rein in his emotions. But there was no way he could back away from Mallory until this asshole was caught. It didn't mean he had to fool himself into believing he and Mallory got to live Happily Ever After.

"Why didn't you follow him into the woods?"

"I didn't want to leave Special Agent Rooney alone for too long, nor the injured woman." Alex was losing patience.

Deputy Chance's lip curled. "And when you went back

you were confronted by Supervisory Special Agent Frazer. Why'd you resist arrest?"

"I was never under *arrest.*" Alex forced himself not to bite the man's head off.

The deputy's gaze was disbelieving. "According to the feeb he identified himself as a federal agent and told you 'to drop the weapon.'"

Alex rubbed his forehead. The guy was killing him. This was why he'd make a terrible cop. Too much monotonous questioning. "For all I knew the attacker had circled around the house and was wanting me to throw down my gun before he shot me."

"So why didn't you shoot him in the head?" the deputy prodded.

"The fed or the attacker?"

The deputy grunted out a laugh and threw a glance at where SSA Frazer was holding court with his team. "Both."

"Knowing the attacker was wearing body armor I should have shot him in the leg."

"Don't they teach you to shoot to kill where you're from?" The West Virginia accent was in full twang now.

Alex didn't smile. He'd taken the lives of too many people to consider it a joke. "Mallory wants to know what happened to her sister. Otherwise he'd be dead." And this whole fuckfest would be over. He'd be free to move on. The knowledge left a gaping hole in his chest.

"You really think it's the same guy who took Payton Rooney all those years ago?" The deputy scoffed.

"Yes." Alex stood as the Rooney family came out of the sheriff's office. The senator caught his eye and jerked her head imperiously to indicate he join them. *Whoopee.* "Anything else?" he asked the deputy.

"Nah, we're done." The deputy sprawled back in his chair. "No taking the law into your own hands again, Mr. Parker."

Sure. Taking a breath, he walked over to where the Rooneys were talking to the sheriff. He stood behind the group like a shadow, but Mallory reached for his hand and dragged him forward. The casual acceptance in front of her parents stopped his breath.

"This is Alex Parker." She introduced him to her father and they shook hands.

"I want to thank you, son." The judge's handshake was firm. "We hear that without you there's every chance Mallory would have been hurt or kidnapped." The man's voice broke. "I know she's an FBI agent, but I can't stand the thought of losing another daughter."

"Glad I was there, sir."

Frazer joined the party and Mallory introduced him to her parents while Alex took a step back. He and Frazer weren't exactly buddies.

"What are you doing to ensure my daughter's safety, SSA Frazer?" This came from the judge.

"I'm about to send her back to Quantico."

Mallory opened her mouth to argue and snapped it closed before any words leaked out. For once, Alex was in full agreement with Frazer, but he'd let the other guy take the heat.

"You're too vulnerable and too close to this case to work the evidence."

"Kari Regent was abducted from just outside DC." Mallory's jaw set at a mutinous angle. "What makes you think I'll be any safer there?"

"I wonder if I could have a private word while they battle it out, Mr. Parker?" the senator asked him softly.

"Use my office." The sheriff waved them inside, even though he clearly wanted to get on with his job, not be tied up with endless politics.

Alex followed Senator Tremont inside and closed the door behind them. She paced—just like Mallory had at the hospital. The sensation of being watched pressed against his back.

"Do you think this killer is the same man who took Payton?"

Alex nodded.

She looked down at her expensive leather pumps. "I want to thank you, for personally looking after my daughter."

He nodded. "I didn't do it because of you."

Her lips compressed together and her eyes narrowed. "Then why did you do it?"

There was no way he was confessing his feelings to this woman, even if he understood them himself. He leaned against the desk, shrugged. "We're involved."

Angry red blotches appeared beneath the flawless foundation. She turned to face the outside window where no one could lip-read the words that passed between them. "I don't care if you two are sleeping together, but if anything happens to her," her voice dropped to below a whisper, "I'll see you back in that Moroccan prison faster than you can spit."

Anger fused with his marrow. He slipped his arm around her shoulders and drew her into a hug. She was as malleable as stone. Her pulse fluttered uneasily in her neck. Good. He put his mouth beside her ear and spoke slowly. "That wasn't the agreement, Senator. Mallory has nothing to do with our bargain. I have five-hundred and twenty days left that you bought along with my freedom and then I'm done. Forever."

The older woman became even more rigid in his arms. To any observers it would look like an embrace with an emotionally stunted female. His voice dropped lower. "If you renege on your promise I will take you down. If you hurt Mallory..." He drew back and let his soulless gaze do the work. She shivered.

He went to break away but her fingers dug into his triceps. Then her eyes filled with a wash of tears as she morphed from powerful senator to powerless parent. "Just don't let anything happen to my baby." She swallowed. "Please."

A ball of emotion threatened to choke him but he couldn't let this woman see his weakness. "I'll give my life to see she's safe, you have my promise." He didn't tell her that he'd sacrifice everything to protect Mallory, including The Gateway Project and the senator herself. "Why did you make that call to the FBI about Meacher?" he asked softly.

Her eycs flared in alarm and then swept over the people watching them through the glass. "I-I..."

"To give Mallory the chance to look good?

"Why shouldn't she be the one to get credit? The animal operated within her jurisdiction." Irritation flashed across her features even as she stared fixedly out the window. "I didn't know Meacher was going to choose that night to take another victim. I didn't know they were going to launch an immediate assault on his house," she hissed.

"Did you make any other calls?" he spoke over her.

"What? No!" She looked shocked by the suggestion.

He assessed her coldly. Like most politicians the woman was a damn good liar. "I still don't trust whoever you have inside the FBI. The warning about the cops going to the Meacher place was so late we almost shook hands in the doorway. Either they're incompetent or they're trying to get me caught. Neither is good for you or your fellow players in The Gateway Project."

She swallowed nervously. "It must have been a technical error. A glitch." Her eyes shot to SSA Frazer who watched them through the glass, but Alex didn't know if he was the inside man or if she was just worried he might overhear something.

It would make sense for it to be Frazer. If the senator had blackmailed the guy into working for their shadowy organization—and Alex wouldn't put it past her—then putting the senator's daughter in jeopardy was an effective way to get revenge.

"Control your dogs, Senator," he murmured in her ear. "Before they bite you on the ass." He turned and opened the door for her then and she swept past him like a queen. Mallory watched him with those soft amber eyes of hers.

"Sorry. What did she want with you?" she asked when he came up beside her.

"To hire my firm to protect you."

Mallory shook her head. "What did you tell her?"

"It's already taken care of." He put his arm on her waist and pressed a kiss to her temple. "I'm not going anywhere while this guy is out there."

His skin prickled as they left the building. It was probably being so close to the justice system he flouted every time he was sent on a mission. The justice system that would fry his ass if they ever caught him.

CHAPTER EIGHTEEN

DECEMBER HAD BITTEN down with the ruthlessness of a gin trap. A couple inches of snow covered the ground and dead leaves shattered under his winter boots. Fury boiled low in his gut and almost choked him. His ribs were sore as fuck. He'd strapped them tight, and had been extra careful not to give himself away even though the pain was excruciating.

Mallory's eyes were the exact same shade as Payton's had been. Her hair one shade off black. Too short but it would soon grow out again. Within a year it would be long and silky against his fingers.

He followed the other man through the woods. Despite last night's monumental fuck up, everything was holding together—just. The media was camped out at the town hall; the mayor looked like he was gonna stroke out if the sheriff didn't solve this thing fast. He liked the sheriff, he was a good man, but he had no intention of easing the guy's burden.

For one thing, he needed to take care of that bitch Kari before she did any real damage. Word was she was unconscious and likely to stay that way for some time.

"Did this area get searched already?" The guy pushed back his beige hat and swiped at his brow. Despite the cold, he was sweating like a hog on a roasting spit.

"Twice." He didn't hide his irritation. Why couldn't the

asshole just let it go?

Sean Kennedy breathed out heavily and then squared his shoulders. "One more time for luck."

"What *exactly* are we looking for?" He heaved out an impatient sigh. He'd been careful to always be the one searching near the woodpile, but Kennedy was doggedly heading in that direction. Fancied himself quite the detective.

"Clothes. Footprints. Blood trail. We'll know if we see it." The other deputy shrugged a meaty shoulder and wiped his mouth with the back of his hand. "Wouldn't it be something if we were the ones that found out what happened to Payton Rooney after all these years? Did you know her?"

A knot of grief twisted his guts. "No, I didn't know her." Apprehension rose with each footstep through the snow. "If there was any evidence it's buried under this snow."

"We should get dogs out here—"

"The killer took the McCaffertys' car. Dogs ain't gonna tell us nothing but which road they took."

"Yeah, but the killer came back for Mallory Rooney last night so maybe he's still in the area."

They were heading ever closer toward the trail to his cabin. Kennedy was a good officer who was getting too close for comfort and beginning to piss him off. "Let's go get something to eat and come back when it gets light at dawn."

"In a minute," Kennedy bit back impatiently.

The temptation of food usually worked on the guy. Kennedy stopped and looked around at the gathering dusk. *Come on, come on. Turn around.* Then the deputy looked over at the woodpile. "Let's check out that area and then we'll call it quits."

Shit.

He moved cautiously behind his fellow officer, checking his shoulder. The other teams had given up for the night and had all headed home. He surreptitiously unclipped his holster.

They followed the faint trail of his earlier footprints into the central clearing where he'd been very careful not to go up to the trapdoor, but instead had concentrated on the woodpile itself. The branches overhead shook as wind whistled through them. Lumps of snow splattered the ground. He glanced down and swore. The snow had melted on the metal ring of the trapdoor, leaving a clear circular impression. He saw the exact moment Kennedy spotted it.

Kennedy turned and caught his eye, excitement filling his gaze. He put his finger to his lips and drew his gun. "Nothing here. Better head back," Kennedy said loudly, then he added in a whisper, "This is gonna get both of us goddamn commendations."

He pulled his gun too, thankful the other officer hadn't called it in. Kennedy obviously wanted to be a hero rather than follow procedure. The guy reached down for the ring, then threw back the hatch which landed with a soft crunch in the snow. It was pitch black inside and almost impossible to see in the gathering dusk. Kennedy grabbed his flashlight and shone it down the steps. "Sheriff's officers. Come out with your hands up," he said loudly.

He checked his shoulder again. No one was nearby.

Kennedy reached for his radio. He had two choices. Let Kennedy call it in and go on the run while they ran forensics. Or…

"You hear that? Like a woman crying?" he whispered urgently, taking a step forward. Kennedy cut in front of him. The guy definitely wanted to be the hero here today.

Kennedy took off his hat and tossed it to the ground before he eased down the wooden stairs, risers groaning under his weight. All Kennedy's attention was front and center. On the third step down, he smashed his service weapon hard into the back of Kennedy's skull. The man crashed to the dirt floor. He scrambled down the stairs, and quickly secured the chain to Kennedy's meaty wrists while he pocketed the officer's keys. He grabbed duct tape and efficiently wrapped mouth, wrists and ankles. He lifted Sean's radio, cell phone, weapon and badge, knowing he should kill him but unwilling to do so just yet. Blood poured down Kennedy's face and his eyes started to open. They were cloudy with confusion, and silently begged questions as his hands jerked against the chain.

"Well hell, Seany, you went and solved the goddamn case." He lifted a couple of things from the shelves. A hairbrush. Kari Regent's backpack. "I lied by the way, when I said I didn't know Payton. I knew her better than anyone. I loved her and she loved me. Sorry you had to be the one to figure it all out." He grimaced wryly. This wasn't what he wanted to happen, but Kennedy had sealed his own fate. He backed up the steps, keeping a lookout for anyone as he closed the trapdoor on his fellow officer and bolted it shut. He spread snow carefully over the top until it was once again invisible.

Sean's disappearance would be one of those unexplained mysteries that people scratched their heads over from time to time.

He headed back to their patrol vehicle, got in and drove to Deputy Kennedy's ranch house on a quiet street in a quiet neighborhood. He let himself in—the guy had never locked a door in his life—put the gun, badge, radio and cell on his kitchen counter top, carefully wiping his prints and DNA from the items. Then he went into the bedroom and stuffed Kari's backpack under the bed. He placed the hairbrush on the dressing table, touched it and remembered brushing Payton's long dark hair until it shone like ebony. He wiped the wooden handle clean and stood back.

What was Kennedy thinking right now? Was he suitably shocked and awed?

He got back in the patrol car and headed to the sheriff's office. If asked he'd say he dropped Kennedy back home after another fruitless search of the woods. When he didn't turn up for work tomorrow, someone would be sent around to the house to look for him. When they figured out he'd disappeared he'd go to the top of the suspect list. The hairbrush and backpack and his sudden disappearance should buy him some time. Long enough to kill Kari and snatch Mallory Rooney from under their noses. Alex Parker had stymied him but not for much longer. He intended to repay the guy by taking his woman. The cops around here weren't exactly rocket scientists and even the FBI was turning out to be a disappointment. But until Kari Regent was dead he needed to start putting together his exit plan, just in case.

Patience, he reminded himself as he drove past all the TV and media vans. Kari was in ICU and everyone was on high alert. As long as he didn't panic it'd work out. He looked out the car window as the snow began to fall softly again, covering the tracks he and Sean had made in the woods.

Patience was his friend.

HER PARENTS MIGHT be powerful people, but there were no

more strings to pull. Eastborne was a crime scene until the feds said otherwise. Mallory had made her parents go home and let the cops do their jobs. Promised to see them for dinner at her mother's house that weekend.

Now she and Alex were back at her father's apartment in DC, and she was effectively kicked to the curb in terms of the investigation. She set her jaw. She could have helped out, but she'd hardly slept in days and was so tired she could barely stand up. It was starting to take its toll on her ability to think straight. Tomorrow she intended to tell Hanrahan her plan for catching the vigilante, but right now she just wanted to sleep and not worry about a maniac trying to snatch her.

The TV was on in the background, muted. It threw flickering images against the wall. The rest of the apartment was dark. Alex came into the room after a shower. He leaned down and kissed her, long and slow.

"You must have better things to do than hang out with me," she murmured against his mouth.

"I like hanging out with you." He pushed her backward until he was stretched out on top of her on the couch. "I like hanging out with you a lot." He nipped her bottom lip and she groaned and then, unable to resist, wrapped her arms around his neck and savored his taste. The guilt of allowing herself to be happy was eased by the fact that without Alex she might be dead. Her sister wouldn't have wanted that.

She pulled back and stared into those pewter eyes. "I can't believe you came into my life at exactly the right moment."

He kissed her again and heat uncurled in her belly, and something else. Something scary. Something amazing. He brushed her hair back from her forehead, framing her face with his hands. "I think I came into your life exactly when it was meant to be."

Fate? Mallory had discounted fate as a fickle so-and-so years ago. Emotion welled up but she didn't want to think about what might have happened if Alex hadn't been there last night. Instead she licked the inside of his mouth, and took control of the kiss, feeling the heady power as he kissed her back. He tasted like strong healthy male and she wanted that strength. She wanted to play with that power, explore the ways she could make him groan. And she wanted to forget that there was a man out there who wanted her as his own personal plaything.

The apartment was relatively safe with good security. One of her Glocks was on the coffee table. The other by the front door in the drawer. Alex wore a weapon in a shoulder holster that looked sexy as hell strapped to that ridiculously honed body.

She rolled him and they landed in a heap on the floor with her on top. They both laughed but the laughter stopped when her fingers moved to the top button of his shirt. He lay unmoving when she worked her way down the length of his torso. He went to touch her but she shook her head.

"I want to do with you whatever I want." There was a challenge in her tone. She needed some control in a life that had gone haywire.

One side of his mouth curled up. "Go for it."

She straddled his thighs and desire blazed through her, reflected in his eyes.

His fingers tightened on her thighs. "Be gentle with me. Or rough. Whatever..." He said it as a joke but as her eyes fastened on his scars she realized people had hurt him, physically and mentally. She lowered her lips to first one mark, then the next. "One day," she said between kisses, "I want you to tell me how you got each and every scar." She pressed two fingers to his lips before he could protest. "Not today. Just one day."

He held her gaze, eyes vibrant with unspoken emotion but he finally nodded.

The warmth of his skin singed her fingers as she smoothed them over his lips, down his throat to broad pectorals and flat brown nipples and six-pack abs that rippled as she touched them. She'd never had a lover so beautiful before. Never touched a body like this. But that wasn't what made Alex beautiful. He called to something inside her. She didn't know what it was but they fit. Perfectly. Her lips followed the sprinkling of golden hair that arrowed south of a navel she wanted to taste. So she did. He was warm and clean and smelled of soap from a recent shower.

She popped the button of his jeans then ran her index finger over the ridge of his zipper. His eyes went dark.

"You like that?" she asked.

"I'm a guy. Touch my dick, I'm happy."

"I like the fact you're a guy." She undid the top button of her shirt and watched him hold his breath as she flicked the next button free. "I like it a lot." She'd said she wouldn't hurt him but she hadn't said she wouldn't torment him until he begged for mercy. Next button. So that he got a glimpse of the lacy black bra she'd put on after her shower.

"You're going to kill me."

"I'm going to try." She undid the last button and slipped slowly out of her shirt, tossing it behind her.

His fingers clenched but he didn't reach for her. "Let me know if I can help." He eyed her breasts.

"I think I've got everything under control." She pressed herself against his zipper and his eyes crossed. She loved the feel of his skin, smooth and taut. Jesus, he was ripped and beautiful. Not bulky, just honed like the blade of a knife.

"You've got a hell of a body for a desk jockey."

"You've got a hell of a body for a government employee." He smoothed his hands up her ribcage to cup her aching breasts and leaned up to take a nipple into his mouth. The rough edge of lace against such delicate flesh made her toes curl; sensations shooting through her body that had her clinging to him. His hands were big and molded every curve. She was supposed to be in charge but somehow having Alex make love to her felt like she'd gotten everything she'd ever wanted.

She shimmied backwards, just enough to break contact and he groaned and lay back with a thump. She eased his jeans down his thighs and he kicked them off. He pulled off his holster and placed his weapon next to hers on the coffee table. His and hers. Lastly he removed his shirt and threw it behind him with a glint in his eye.

His gaze ate her up. She'd worn yoga pants because she'd planned on working tonight, going back over the files she'd been over a million times before. But she needed a break. She needed a life. She needed this. She stood and eased the pants down her legs. Watching his eyes dilate as they took in black lace panties. She'd worn them for him. She wanted to thank him. Not for saving her life last night. But for reminding her she had a life and might one day have a future.

Lust curled through her as she took in his delicious body. God, she wanted him. A red hot fiery want. Damp panties, shaking knees, where's-the-condom want.

He rolled to his feet. “Bedroom.”

She blinked. *Really*?

He grabbed his pistol and then lifted her in his arms and carried her through to the other room and dumped her on the bed, placing his weapon on the bedside table before following her down to rest heavily between her thighs. The blunt tip of him throbbed against damp lace and the temptation to just take him without any protection was almost overwhelming. He slipped down her body taking the bad decision with him.

His lips touched every inch of skin as he kissed his way back to her breasts, laving her nipples until she was writhing on the bed, damn near coming apart from that alone. Strong arms held her wrists down by her sides. She loved the dominant strength of him but that’s not what she needed tonight. She needed to be in control, to know that she could do anything she wanted.

He was about to go lower and god she wanted him to, but… “Alex.”

That one word was enough to bring his head up. “What?”

She pushed with her body and he rolled onto his back. “My rules tonight.” She took him in her mouth and cupped his balls and worked him until his heels were pressing hard against the mattress. Then she licked her way up his body all the way to his sexy mouth. She leaned over to grab a condom out of the drawer and he took advantage to slip a finger inside the edge of her panties to find her wet and ready for him.

“You’re driving me insane.”

“Years without sex does that to a girl—and near-death experiences.”

“I won’t let him get you, Mallory.”

She nodded. “I won’t let him get me either.”

She went to shimmy out of her lingerie, but he stopped her. "Leave it on."

Lingerie fetish. She left it on.

He took the condom from her fingers and covered himself. Eased her slowly over him and shifted her panties aside. He was big, aroused. She sank down just a little bit and he gritted his teeth. She looked down, the vision of him inside her, of the lace against pale skin, was such a turn on she came with a surprised shudder. He held perfectly still as if afraid to move. Squeezing her eyes shut, she sank just a little bit further.

"I know this is your show, sweetheart, and trust me I am not complaining," his voice was low and guttural, "but if you don't start moving soon I'm probably going to start crying." The tendons in his neck stood out. He didn't touch her, except for where they were joined and the thrum of his pulse against her inner thigh.

She leaned forward to kiss his lips. She clenched her muscles around him and he swore. She liked that. Loved that he was doing what she wanted even though he'd do things differently. She started to reward him, moving on him with slow sensuous strokes of her body over the rigid hardness of his. Sweat glistened on his skin, a faint sheen that tasted of salt. He was beautiful, sweaty and hers.

"You're really killing me," he whispered as she lowered her nipple within reach of his mouth. He obliged her, tongue rasping against lace. Pleasure arrowed through her, from her nipple to her core. The need for more, for everything, was building and she reared back, twisting her hips and riding him faster, harder. He held onto her, driving deeper, bucking, every tendon in his body taut with that need for release. "I can't wait any longer, Mallory…" He threw back his head and she felt him come inside her. Her own body reacted, clutching, spiraling into orgasm as a whirlwind of ecstasy exploded through her body. Shuddering, she rested her face in the crook of his neck and he gathered her to him.

Slowly their breathing eased. After a few moments of enjoying the comfort of him against her, she asked, “What are you doing for Christmas?”

He stiffened beneath her. “I usually work.”

She reared back and sifted her fingers through his short silky hair. “Spend it with me.”

Those eyes of his held a funny expression. “Does it involve your parents?”

Despite everything going on in her life there was this weird feeling of joy she shouldn’t be experiencing right now. “I can cancel my parents.” He was more important.

He grunted. “Does it involve food?”

She still needed to go shopping. “Hopefully.”

He took her mouth and rolled her beneath him, pressed deep into the mattress, him deep inside her.

“Is that a ‘yes’?” She laughed, feeling him become aroused again.

His nostrils flared. “We’ll see.”

She cocked a brow. “It could be our first date.”

“We’re not dating, remember.” He thrust inside her and she sucked in a moan. “You didn’t go and do anything foolish like fall for me, did you, Mallory?” he asked.

Emotion welled up inside her. She shook her head and wrapped her legs around his hips. Watched his pupils dilate. “No, sir.”

“Good.” He swallowed. “Me either.”

But as she looked into his eyes she knew they were both lying and it felt dark and dangerous and wonderful.

EARLY NEXT MORNING, Mallory sat opposite Hanrahan in his cluttered office. Alex had dropped her at Quantico, telling her he'd pick her up to drive her home. The weird ache in her chest at his absence meant she was in way deeper than she'd ever thought possible. She was in love.

"It's a good idea," Hanrahan said hesitantly.

"So why don't you look happy about it?"

He grunted and shifted in his seat. "Maybe I don't want to find out for sure that I have someone on my team who is feeding information to a killer."

Mallory sat very still and didn't fidget even though her stomach felt decidedly wobbly. Obviously being targeted by a serial killer was affecting her more than she'd realized. But every time she fidgeted she figured she gave something about herself away to this man. Over the last few weeks she'd wanted to share less and less with the people she worked with. Trust had never been an issue for her before, the Bureau represented all that was good about the American justice system, but she'd never felt as betrayed as she had by Frazer sticking her on that hook and dangling her in front of the UNSUB the other night.

He'd almost gotten her killed.

"You can't tell anyone, this has to remain a secret." Mallory told this man with decades more experience than she had. "Have the IT tech monitor the cell phones. Don't tell them why. You'll have to tell them when they arrive that it's just a training exercise."

Finally he spoke. "There's a cabin we can use...my brother-in-law has a place about an hour's drive northwest of here. It's on federal land so we have jurisdiction." He moved his jaw from side to side. “He and my sister are in Egypt and I’m supposed to be going up there for Christmas anyway.”

“Can anyone trace it to you?”

He stared at her with those seen-it-all eyes. Shook his head. “I don’t think so. It would take a lot of digging. My sister was a widow when she married again so her last name wasn’t even Hanrahan. I certainly haven’t mentioned the place to anyone.”

“How are we going to do it?”

“*You’re* not going to do anything except observe.” He sat deep in thought for a moment. “It has to seem real, but we can’t involve any other law enforcement officers. I want this kept within the unit. If the media gets a sniff of scandal the whole thing will blow up out of control and we’ll never find these people. I’ll drive up there now and use the phone in the local store.” He pulled a digital voice changer out of his drawer. It reminded her she still needed to return Lucas’s call from the other day, see where he was on the Meacher investigation. “I’ll ask to be put through to Frazer—he’s been on the news about the PR-killer so it makes sense someone might approach him for a reward. Frazer will then call me and I’ll tell him to assemble the team and meet me at the store so we can check out the suspect. He’ll bitch and moan but I know him, he won’t be adverse to the idea of us leading the charge on this arrest.”

Her plan had been to report a sighting of the car that had been stolen during the double homicide in Colby. The IT guy would then monitor all cell calls from BAU agents and if someone was in league with the vigilante they’d know—or at least have a good idea who it might be. They could then work backward to collect evidence.

Hanrahan looked at his watch and all the paperwork on his desk. "If the assassin turns up at the cottage he'll find an empty house."

"You don't want a SWAT team sitting on the place?"

Tired eyes met hers. "The most important thing to me is protecting the integrity of the BAU. Once we know who's involved they'll give us the assassin." *To avoid the death penalty*. He rubbed both temples.

His phone rang and he indicated she wait while he took the call. When he hung up Hanrahan's smile faded.

"One of the Greenville deputy sheriffs went AWOL."

She sat forward. "Which one?"

Hanrahan checked his notes. "Deputy Sean Kennedy. Officers found Kari Regent's backpack in his house and are testing a hairbrush for DNA."

"A hairbrush? The guy was bald as a coot, why would he need a hairbrush?" asked Mallory.

"Their thoughts exactly."

Mallory frowned. It didn't make sense. "I knew him as a kid, but he's only about my age, not old enough to have kidnapped Payton. And there's no way he's the guy who attacked me at Eastborne."

Hanrahan shrugged. "He disappeared, so it's suspicious. These attacks have been pretty sophisticated so maybe there's more than one person involved."

She was pretty sure more than one person had been involved in Payton's abduction, but it still didn't sit right. "Any news on Kari Regent?" Her parents were at her bedside, grief-stricken but with that rare commodity of hope.

Hanrahan sighed. "She's still unconscious. The Bureau has a sketch artist on standby at the hospital for just as soon as she wakes up and is able to talk."

"He made his first real mistake with her." She wanted five minutes alone with the killer. Five minutes to try and find out the truth before the lawyers got to him.

"*If* she wakes up. *If* she remembers."

Damn. "True. If we are going to use this ruse we need to do it fast, before they go and catch the guy." Which she prayed was as soon as possible.

Hanrahan smiled. "So let's get on with it. Watch your back, Rooney. Until we catch him remember this killer is gunning for you."

And half her teammates too. "Thanks for the reminder, sir."

"I'm about to start reprimanding you *loudly*. Ready?"

She nodded, it was part of her cover but she could live without the notoriety and drama. He started telling her that she'd taken unprecedented risks…*blah blah blah.* She opened the door, trying to escape. Special Agent Barton was walking past, pretending not to eavesdrop.

Out of nowhere nausea rose up and she bolted out of Hanrahan's office, just making the ladies' bathroom before she was ill. She hung over the toilet hoping to hell she wasn't coming down with something.

There was a knock on the door.

"You okay?" Barton.

Mallory wiped her mouth and flushed the toilet. She came out of the stall and washed her hands, then ran cold water over her wrists. "Must be something I ate."

Barton gave her a wry smile. "Both times I was pregnant I barfed every day for six weeks. Made a hell of an impression on my colleagues" Her smile turned a little nasty. "I even managed to puke on one of my SACs who was a particularly unpleasant man down in Texas."

"I'm not pregnant," she snapped. They'd used protection every time.

Barton looked amused then wistful. "It isn't so bad, you know—having kids—as long as you have a supportive spouse you can make it work with an FBI career."

"I'm not pregnant." *How old were those condoms*? Crap, she'd never thought to check.

Barton shrugged. "Well at least Alex Parker's rich. You guys can afford a nanny."

"And once again, I'm *not* pregnant and it's none of your business." She tried to remember when she'd last had her period. Damn.

"I checked his alibi. Jane Sanders says they're old friends who went out to dinner the night Lindsay Keeble was abducted so he's definitely not our PR-killer."

Which she already knew.

She almost missed it, she was so freaked about skipping her period. She jerked to face the other agent. "Jane Sanders?"

"Yeah, your mother's aide. What are the chances?" Those black eyes of Barton's gleamed like jet. "I'm going to the cafeteria for some orange juice. Can I get you anything?"

"No. Thank you." Mallory headed back to her desk. A ball of ice wedged inside her lungs and made it hard to breathe. Had her mother gone to some elaborate lengths to insert a man into her life—a man who could also act as her part-time bodyguard? That was ridiculous but…what were the odds of it being a coincidence?

She needed to call Alex and ask him outright. The feelings she had for him swamped anything she'd ever experienced before and maybe those feelings were screwing with her mind. And there was something even more important she needed to check before she spoke to him. She grabbed her keys and headed into town.

She drove to the nearest pharmacy, bought a pregnancy test, headed into the nearest McD's and spent five long minutes waiting in the bathroom stall. Sweat beaded on her upper lip as she watched the line in the window turn blue. She closed her eyes and felt a flutter of panic in her chest. She wanted to scream. What the hell was she going to do?

The idea of a baby scared her to death. She was in a career where she put her life on the line on a regular basis and the man who'd stolen her sister had targeted her for the same treatment. What the hell would she do with a baby? What would the killer do?

In the space of five seconds she went from being horrified she was pregnant to knowing she'd kill to protect her child. What would Alex say when he found out? Christ, what if he was only seeing her because of some scheme her mother had set up? Her stomach turned over and tears welled in her eyes. Being pregnant certainly explained the recent swings of emotions and rapid onslaught of tears and nausea.

Great. At least it wasn't terminal.

What if Alex wasn't interested in long term? The idea cut to the bone. He'd told her at the start he wasn't a good bet for a relationship—that he let people down. Maybe he'd been in this position before. For all she knew he already had a child somewhere and didn't like the kid.

She loved Alex. She was pretty sure he loved her. He couldn't be someone who worked for her mother. That was insane. But no way did she want him to feel obligated toward her. She had money. She had a good career. She laid her hand over her flat stomach. And it was early days and the test might be wrong.

She stood and whirled in a circle. Her phone rang but she ignored it. She didn't know what to do. Did she tell him so they could deal with the situation together? Or did she keep it to herself for a few days while her brain processed the idea and she helped deal with the vigilante and the serial killer?

The door squealed as someone came into the restroom. Her phone vibrated again and she remembered she was still a target of the PR-killer. And now she didn't just have herself to worry about. Her hand slipped to her Taser because she wanted him alive if possible.

Heart pounding she checked through the stall door and saw a woman pushing a stroller. She stuffed her Taser and pregnancy test in her purse to figure out later. Maybe it was a false positive. Maybe she'd read the instructions wrong. She came out of the stall and washed her hands, looking at the woman struggling with a toddler and a baby. "Do you need any help?"

The woman looked unsure and so Mallory flashed her badge. "I'm an FBI agent so I can watch junior if you need a minute."

The woman nodded. "Thanks. Most people don't get how difficult it can be."

Mallory's throat tightened. She had a feeling she was about to find out. The woman and toddler disappeared into a stall. She looked at the sleeping baby, so content, so…vulnerable. The idea of a child felt weird, alien. Amazing. Thrilling. Christ—like she'd been handed a miracle. A chance to make things better. But first she needed to make sure Payton's killer was dealt with. And how she dealt with him was going to tell her everything she needed to know about the type of human being she really was.

CHAPTER NINETEEN

SINCE HE'D STARTED doubting the integrity of their inside guy at the FBI, Alex had set up his own alert system regarding the PR-killer investigation that was now being run out of the FBI's Washington Field Office in conjunction with the BAU and Greenville County Sheriff's Office. To make things easier, he'd bugged Supervisory Special Agent Frazer's phone.

This particular report was so fresh Alex barely had time to unlock his office door before he turned around again and left. He had a lead on the PR-killer and a good hour head-start on the BAU. He took the metro and walked the rest of the way to his storage garage. He went in the side door. Security was state of the art with reinforced steel doors. This was where he stored his weapons, his transportation, his disguises. He wasn't about to leave it vulnerable to thieves.

As always he swept for bugs. Time was tight, but he worked best when he followed routine.

He took his favorite SIG P229 and suppressor from a floor safe. He opted for the beard disguise and a woolen hat that covered his ears. Ears were as individual as prints and he kept his obscured as much as possible when he was on a job. Hell, even blue jeans had been used to ID perps.

Mallory had left a message on his voice mail to say she was

going out on a bust and that she'd be working late tonight. She assured him she wasn't going to be alone for any reason at any time. With luck he could be back at Quantico ready to pick her up when they were both done.

If everything went to plan, her problems would be over and he'd then have to find a way to get the hell out of her life. The alternative was too tempting and she deserved better.

The thought made him stop dead.

For the first time in his life he wanted the normal things people wanted. A wife, a house, a family. All the things he couldn't have because of the bad decisions he'd made. He was sick of lying, sick of killing.

But right now he had no choice.

This one was for Mallory. To keep her safe.

He got in an innocuous silver sedan and drove for an hour and twenty minutes. Most of the snow had melted but the occasional patch lingered deep in the trees. Winter was coming—ready or not. Unstoppable—a bit like this serial killer who started abducting young girls at least eighteen years ago and was still killing today. Wasn't much of a moral dilemma to put a bullet in this guy's skull.

Alex couldn't underestimate the guy. He was smart and Alex didn't have time to plan anything more sophisticated than a quick double tap. Head shots this time. No pissing around with body shots even though that meant Mallory would never get the answers she craved. Better to be alive and grieving than dead.

The roads got narrower and narrower and less congested the further north he got. He pulled over at a small convenience store on the lakeside about quarter of a mile from his target's location.

"You rent out canoes?" he asked the guy behind the counter.

"Sure do. Not much call for it this time of year though."

A little too much daylight for Alex's plan but sometimes it was better to hide in plain sight.

"You on vacation?" the man asked. He had shrewd eyes beneath bushy eyebrows. This guy wouldn't forget a face.

"Driving to Denver to start a new job, but couldn't resist one last paddle before I hit the Midwest."

"It's beautiful country. Guess it wouldn't do any harm to take one out. No ice on the lake yet. That'll be fifty bucks an hour with a hundred dollar deposit. Canoes are around the side." He jerked his head in the general direction of the lake. "If you need a hand, let me know."

He handed him a life jacket. Alex thanked him and paid cash. Small bills. He didn't worry about fingerprints. He didn't have any. Contact DNA was another matter but hard to prove given how many people had handled those notes over the years.

He carried the canoe down to the small dock and went back for the paddle. He climbed in, placing a small backpack between his knees. The water was clear and flat. The only leaves on the trees were yellowed and stubborn. It was cold out on the lake and his breath froze, but it was so peaceful the quietness washed over him like a balm. A fish jumped.

He scanned the properties along the shoreline. A pretty part of the world but not that isolated. Neighbors *would* notice if someone was using a cabin that was supposed to be empty. Alex spotted the property and glided on past. The place looked quiet, curtains drawn. No fire despite the November chill. Didn't look like anyone was around. He paddled up to an inlet around a small headland and pulled up on a small man-made beach. The lake looped around and the ridge above him would provide a clear elevated view while allowing him to keep his distance. He hopped out and pulled the canoe up the beach. No one was home here either which was a definite plus. He climbed the ridge, hidden by trees until he could survey where this guy was supposed to be holed up. The property was still a ways off, just visible through the trees. Minutes ticked by, but he didn't see anything.

He sat quietly. No hint of smoke in the chimney. No car this side of the building. He waited. Feds took their time in these situations and got lots of back-up. He checked his cell phone to make sure it was set to vibrate. There was a new message from Mallory. She needed to talk to him but nothing urgent she assured him.

His heart gave a twinge. What the hell was he going to do about Mallory? He'd fallen for her like a HALO jump gone bad. Worse, she'd fallen for him and he didn't want to see her hurt.

At some point she had to dump his ass because she was incredible and he was a lying asshole. But until this guy was dead—one hundred percent categorically not breathing with no hope of resuscitation dead—he wasn't going anywhere.

A quiver ran down his back and he frowned as he scanned the area. Something didn't feel right. Rodman hadn't felt right either and he'd been a pedophile who fucked kids for fun.

Silence of the woods pressed down on him. It was *too* quiet. The whole situation felt like a trap. But *if* the PR-killer was here it could be over in minutes. Over like Meacher was over. Over. Finished. Dead.

The headache was back. *Shit.* Something really didn't feel

right. He backed up slowly, careful not to make a sound as he got back in his canoe and paddled further down the lake, going all the way around before hitting the far shore. Then he powered back to the shop and jetty. No way was he ignoring his instincts. They might be flawed but the fact he was still alive was a testament to their veracity.

He returned the canoe to the store and collected his deposit with a polite smile. A silver-haired guy was perusing magazines at the back of the store. Alex's nape prickled. He bought a packet of chips and a can of Coke, got into his car.

Seconds later a convoy of three vehicles with government plates rolled past. Mallory was in the last vehicle and he sat there frozen like a two-by-four, but she wasn't looking at him.

A rush of emotion filled him. Despite the certainty that they were here to arrest him he sat there looking at her. The first two cars emptied but instead of surrounding him, the agents rushed up the steps and confronted the silver-haired man. Through the glass he could hear them complaining about "training exercises".

And Alex realized what was going on. It was a trap, but not for him.

The trap was for whoever was working inside the FBI.

Taking it slowly, having no doubt that they'd already checked his plates, he drove away. Cover should hold. It was a good one, designed to protect the same government the FBI served. He didn't think they suspected him else he'd have been on the floor with his hands cuffed, waiting for another rescue that wouldn't come from people who were supposed to have his back.

Out of the corner of his eye he saw Mallory turn and lock onto his profile. Sweat ran down his spine. Not from the fear of getting caught, but from lying to the woman he loved down to his poor worthless soul.

He knew he couldn't lie to her anymore.

He drove west, cutting down back roads. Then he pulled over and called Jane on the secure line. "It was a trap."

"What do you mean?"

"I mean the FBI turned up, but the house was empty. A decoy."

"The killer might have just fled. The FBI could just be arriving. You knew there wouldn't be much lead time—"

"No. You don't understand. I think this was a set-up to ferret out whoever is working with you inside the FBI. If they contacted you, they are about to be fucked. Any way you can warn them?"

"They didn't call. No one called. Maybe they knew it was a trap?" Her voice trembled. "If I call them to check that could compromise us all." The encryption was excellent, but everything could be broken if you had a starting point.

"Then maybe we're safe. But someone is onto us and we need to change everything about how we operate." Shit, *Mallory*. She'd been onto them and then transferred to the BAU. She was working with someone inside the BAU to bring down The Gateway Project. She was a smart cookie. Another reason to love her.

Love? *Crap*.

"Dump your cells and destroy the SIM cards just in case. Lay low until this is all over…I'll be in touch."

Jane sounded tentative. "You should disappear for a while…"

"I can't." He hung up. He couldn't even remember how many days he had left on his contract. He just knew he couldn't leave Mallory until the PR-killer was dead or arrested.

Then he realized it was only a matter of time until she figured it out—she was too smart not to connect the dots. Sweat broke out on his back. He had to tell her. Lying to her face wasn't possible, he'd figured that out almost the moment he met her. But going to jail and leaving her unprotected wasn't an option either.

Idiot. He slammed the steering wheel with the bottom of his fist. He'd known someone was onto them and he'd been arrogant enough to think he could get away with it anyway.

His phone rang. Mallory. He picked up because he needed to hear her voice.

"Alex?"

There was a motel up ahead. "I need you to meet me. It's not far from where you are right now." He gave her the name. "Come alone."

"How do you know where I am right now? Did I just see you here?" Her tone held a healthy dose of suspicion.

He hung up. She either trusted him or she didn't. He pulled into the motel parking lot and dug into the data his programs had been sifting. He might be going to prison for what he'd done for his country, but first he was going to save the woman he loved.

HOW DID ALEX know where she was? Mallory stood outside the store and stared at her phone in confusion. Had she seen him here at the store? In disguise? Driving a car she'd never seen before? And he'd just hung up on her.

What the heck?

Hanrahan was busy telling his people they'd wasted a day driving up to this spot, on his whim. They were pissed too.

She didn't care.

The fact Alex knew Jane Sanders, her mother's aide, and hadn't mentioned the connection, was getting more and more suspicious. She got that horrible feeling in the pit of her stomach—like nausea only a hundred times worse because it wasn't going away. Like maybe he *had* been watching her all this time simply because her mother had paid him. If that were true no wonder he'd been so hard to get into bed. God, she felt sick.

Or was he simply following her today to protect her?

That was the sort of thing he'd do too.

There was another theory tugging on her brain. An insidious idea that, now it had taken root, wouldn't go away.

He'd come into her life the day after Meacher had been murdered in North Carolina. He'd shown up here again today when they'd baited the trap with another serial killer. Could he be…?

No. It was ridiculous. He consulted for the FBI. He was good with computers. He was a hell of a marksman. He'd been in the military—those damned scars… He'd taken Frazer down without breaking a sweat. *No. No. No.* He ran a security firm. He wouldn't do that. But he was in a unique position…to be the vigilante.

Her hands shook. *Why* had he hung up on her? *Why* was he driving that old wreck of a car when he had his Audi? Her brain was arguing with itself and yet suddenly all the pieces snapped together. Him being in Charlotte. Him not freezing when they were attacked, instead reacting like he trained for such things even harder than she did. He was the man she was after.

She was in love with a trained assassin, and having his baby. *Oh, God.* Her mouth went dry.

Hanrahan stood arguing nose-to-nose with Frazer.

"...what do you mean it was a training exercise...training for what?" fluttered across the clearing.

"...my decision, not yours..."

Barton was also on the phone. Maybe she was in league with the vigilante? Was she right now warning him? Was it Alex?

And then it struck her—if Alex was the man they were looking for, a man who took the law into his own hands and dispensed justice as he saw fit, she'd just set into motion a sting operation that might end up implicating herself. *She'd* been in contact with the "vigilante."

Hysterical laughter bubbled in her throat and she needed to get away.

She wished she'd never had this stupid idea. Wished she was sitting in her office dodging verbal darts from Henderson and searching through wastepaper bins. Palpitations fluttered in her chest.

Did she turn him in?

There was no evidence—just a hunch.

She stumbled around the front of the car as if drunk. Frazer frowned at her. "You look like shit. You need to go home." He ran an agitated hand through his blond hair that made it stick out in disarray.

Was it him? Was he the mole?

She met Hanrahan's gaze.

"If you're not feeling well, Special Agent Rooney, you should go home."

Recognizing he was giving her the out she desperately needed she went with it. "Something I ate for breakfast I think, sir. What's going on?" she asked rather desperately.

"This was apparently just a training exercise." SSA Frazer's eyes cut back to hers. He looked volcanically pissed. Christ, she couldn't wait for him to find out this was all her idea. Her stomach roiled.

"You can leave," he said. "Make sure you check in when you get back to Quantico. I don't want you falling off the map with this UNSUB still at large."

Barton went to get in the car with her.

"Not you, Barton," Hanrahan stated. "I want you to ride back with us. I'm going to need your phone." He held out his hand and Barton looked at him like he'd gone insane.

"What? *Why*?"

"We need all your phones. We're doing an update." It was so obviously a lie that Barton planted her hand on her hip.

"In a store parking lot?" she sneered.

"It'll only take a few minutes." Hanrahan probably wanted to check the call logs and see if anyone had tampered with them compared to the cell tower data. It was a good idea.

"What about her?" Barton jerked her head toward where Mallory was just sliding behind the steering wheel.

"Agent Rooney's not a full member of the team. She doesn't need the upgrade. She's also a federal agent who I'm sure can drive herself back to the office without a bodyguard." Hanrahan snapped at her but his eyes held apology. If she hadn't felt like puking she'd have high-fived him. Barton pinched her lips and then with a glare at both Hanrahan and Frazer she tossed him her phone and stood fuming with her arms crossed.

Mallory kept moving. When the SSA held out his palm for Frazer's phone, Mallory thought the guy was going to explode. Instead he handed his cell over. She put her vehicle in reverse to turn it around, and he stood watching her like he could see inside her brain. Mallory's heart pounded harder and harder though she never stopped driving. She needed to get out of there. She needed to think.

CHAPTER TWENTY

MALLORY HAD NEVER understood the need to fall off the grid. Until now.

The motel was some fifty miles east of Colby, West Virginia. Alex had texted her a room number. She looked up at the uninspiring building, grabbed her purse, and climbed out of her car in the parking lot. A noise behind her made her spin, hand firmly on the butt of her weapon.

Alex.

Christ, just looking at him hurt, but his expression was cold and remote.

Was this the real Alex? Or was the real Alex the guy who made love to her until she gasped out his name? She'd thought she'd known him but looking into those guarded eyes she knew she'd been kidding herself.

He turned his back on her and walked to a silver sedan—the one she'd seen at the store. Started the engine and waited, both hands visible on the steering wheel. She stared at him for a full ten seconds before she walked over and stood there. Drunk on lunacy.

"Take the SIM card and battery out of your phone," he told her quietly.

"So you can take me somewhere quiet to kill me and dump the body without anyone following?"

He held her gaze. "If I wanted to kill you you'd already be dead."

A sharp pain shot through her chest. "Are you the vigilan-te I've been searching for?"

He just looked at her and she felt small and stupid.

"I need the words, Alex."

There was a wild look in his eyes, so far removed from the cold stare he'd met her with she almost took a step back. "How about these words, Mallory. I love you. I've loved you since the moment I saw you with that black eye, and no room for anything in your life except looking for your sister's killer. I love *you*, Mallory Rooney, and I will tell you everything you need to know, but on my terms." His eyes cut back to the road, looking for her back-up.

She sucked in a breath. Those words of love were ones she'd wanted to hear but what did they mean now? He didn't deny any of her accusations. Blood thumped through her veins with an aching thud. They had no future. She'd been sleeping with a killer. Sharing her body, worse, her heart, with a murderer. Her hand touched her stomach and she swallowed. Did she tell him about the baby?

A shudder of revulsion moved through her. Would he kill them both? Or would she turn him in and one day have to confess to her child that their father was serving life in prison—or worse, on death row—and she'd been the one to put him there?

His eyes softened and almost begged her to get in the car. Her throat hurt from locking down a sob. Maybe she was the world's biggest fool. She couldn't believe that the man who'd fought so hard to keep her safe would harm her now. Of course she hadn't suspected the truth about him until today and he'd probably assumed she'd continue in blissful ignorance. Her whole life was built on ignorance and now it was crumbling. Crashing like a stack of cards in a hurricane.

"Mallory." His voice softened. "Get in the car, please. We'll go somewhere and talk. I promise I'm not going to hurt you."

Something in his expression snapped another piece of her heart. She loved him but she didn't want to be stupid. She rested her hand on the rim of the window and he reached out and touched her finger, as if he couldn't *not* touch her. She felt the connection to the tips of her toes.

"It's only a matter of time before the FBI figures out you're involved. The FBI was monitoring all calls made by their agents when we set up that sting. He or she will give you up. You know that."

"Whoever works inside the BAU doesn't know my identity any more than I know theirs. And no one called me with this information, I bugged Frazer's phone."

Her heart cracked wide. "So you *are* the vigilante."

He wouldn't say the words but his eyes told her everything. Maybe he worried she was wearing a wire and had fifty agents waiting in the wings to swarm in and arrest him. That's what a true FBI agent would have done.

"I'd never hurt you, Mallory. You have to believe that. And I will turn myself in, but not until you are safe from the asshole hunting you. After that I don't really care anymore. I'm done." This dead tone scraped away another layer of her heart. How could she love this man? Worse. How could she not?

She was a fool to believe him but she got in the car any way. Then dismantled her cell proving she wasn't just stupid, she was stark raving mad. He started driving. Several miles to another motel, the silence crackling with tension. He parked at the end of a row and walked around to open her door.

Nice manners for a stone-cold killer.

She followed him up the stairs and to the end unit. He stepped inside and closed the door. She didn't know whether to be terrified or furious. Both emotions warred inside her and fury won.

Her jaw set. "You used me."

"No." He put the car keys on the desk beside the TV and sat in a chair, resting his face in his hands. "I didn't use you. You seduced me and I fell like a fucking rock."

Hot blinding tears filled her eyes. She wanted to believe him. She couldn't. "You knew I was looking for you. You knew I'd searched ViCAP for vigilantes."

He didn't deny it.

"Who are you working with in the BAU?"

"I told you, I don't know."

"I didn't come here to listen to lies, Alex. I have to turn you in"—her voice cracked but she ignored it—"don't you dare lie to me about this." She took a step toward him and he lifted his head to look at her. Her career was fried when the powers-that-be found out about their relationship. She was having his baby for God's sake. She needed her job to help find out what had happened to Payton, but it all faded to nothing when weighed against losing this man she'd fallen in love with.

"It doesn't work that way," he said.

She narrowed her gaze at him. "*What* doesn't work that way?"

"The Gateway Project. We aren't told the identities of the other people involved in the organization. We deal with an intermediary." His eyes were full of secrets.

He knew a hell of a lot more than he was saying. Or he was

insane. Or maybe that was her. "Gateway Project?"

"It's an off-the-books government organization that uses people like me to deal with violent offenders in an expedient manner."

"Expedient? You shoot them in the goddamn head!" Her knees wobbled and she dropped to the bed. His words sank in. "It can't be government-sanctioned. We have prisons and the death penalty to deal with these cases—"

"Is your sense of justice still so black and white? Is there no room for gray, even after everything your family has been through?"

She refused to answer. Refused to engage.

"You know how long most victims' families wait for death penalty sentences to be carried out? After the lawyers get through the postponements, the trial, appeals system, *habeas corpus*? It can take as long as twenty-five *years*. These aren't even cases where guilt is in question. The justice system is supposed to balance the scales but instead it tortures the victims' families for decades."

"There's no morality in murder."

"You think *I* don't know that?" He closed his eyes, but not before she spotted the pain there. "Every individual is responsible for their actions—including me. I don't like killing but it's what my country asked me to do, and I do it." He drew in a big breath, voice calm again. "Do you know what it costs to pursue capitol cases? Seventy percent more than non-capitol cases. Since 1978, enforcing the death penalty has cost $4 billion in California alone."

"You can't put a cost on human life." Mallory shoved her hand into her short hair.

"Sure you can. There's a cost to health services and law

enforcement, isn't there? How many more cops could have been hired to patrol and make California safer with *four billion dollars*?" The curve of his mouth gutted her. "Is it really easier to believe the man who's fallen in love with you is a cold-blooded assassin rather than just another form of law enforcement?"

"Alex...what you're doing isn't law enforcement. It's murder."

"I serve my country. The same way I served it in uniform. And I don't carry out orders unless I am personally one-hundred percent sure the target is guilty. I'm not saying it's right, I'm just telling you how it is."

Mallory realized he was either running an elaborate scam, nuts, or this thing was much bigger than she and Hanrahan had ever imagined. "Who's in charge of The Gateway Project?"

They exchanged a silent look. He wasn't going to tell her. *Damn.* Cold sank through her clothes and her skin felt dipped in ice.

"Now you have a decision to make," he told her.

Instinctively she touched her abdomen. His eyes followed the movement but she doubted he understood its significance. "I can't pretend I don't know, Alex."

Lines appeared between his brows. "Shit, I know that. But before you tell your FBI bosses I want to help you find the man who abducted your sister, the man who is after you. Then you can bring me in. That should save your career."

Her eyes shot to his. How did he know the heart of her so well? He was offering the opportunity to go after the man who'd destroyed her family, destroyed her parents' marriage and her sister's life with no comeback on herself. The idea of making the killer hurt, making him suffer and maybe pulling the trigger was seductive.

What did that make her?

A hypocrite.

But where was her sister's body? She had no doubt Alex could help her get that information. It was so tempting. He was offering her everything she thought she'd wanted. Now she only wanted him and their baby and the sort of ordinary life most people took for granted.

She tried to catch a breath and failed. She felt like she'd been kicked in the chest by a horse. She wanted that serial killer dead, but there was no way she'd let Alex kill him for her. Vengeance sounded petty. Retribution sounded so much better.

Sadness swirled through her mind. After all these years she was finally getting closer to the truth about what had happened to her twin, but now she was going to lose the man she loved. But she couldn't think about Alex. Thinking about Alex hurt. He'd lied to her. Betrayed her.

"Did you know about Payton before we had sex?"

He watched her. His eyes were the same silver smoke she always found so irresistible. The handsome face and broad shoulders were not the way a merciless killer was supposed to look. Finally he nodded and pain sliced through her.

"What else?"

"I was one of the men you confronted in your house in Charlotte." He held up his hand as she went to hit him. "I was staking out the place and saw the other guy jimmy the lock. I followed to stop him from hurting you. I think it was the same guy who's been after you all along."

"So you rescued me by scaring me half to death?" She breathed in deep through her nose. "What else?"

He stood abruptly. "I bugged your father's apartment and your laptop and cell."

Her eyes widened and it hurt to breathe. Fury rose up inside her like a dragon snaking through her lungs. The violation of her life and her privacy was nauseating.

"I watched you working every night, looking for this bastard. Never resting, never having a life."

"That was my choice, Alex. My choice. You had no right to spy on me." She'd never felt this angry before. Her skin felt tight, head heavy with a dull pain throbbing against her skull.

He closed his eyes and swallowed. "I know. I did it anyway."

There was a blinding flash of realization. "You were the one who sent me the box of information on those other cases?"

His smile twisted. "For all the good it did."

The fury burst, leaving desolation in its wake. "Did you pursue a relationship with me because I was looking into vigilantes?"

His lips tightened. Lips that had tasted every inch of her skin. "I told myself I did, but that was a lie." He glanced at his wristwatch. "Listen, you need to decide. We don't have much time before this guy runs. Doctors were planning to try to rouse Kari Regent from her coma today."

"Maybe he's already gone?"

Alex's mouth hardened. "I don't think so."

Goosebumps flashed over her skin. The killer was waiting for her and if it wasn't for Alex she'd already be at the guy's mercy.

"I won't let him get you." He took her hand in his and she saw the glitter in his eyes before he looked away. But it could all be a con. A way of manipulating her.

Thoughts whirled in her head. She was torn. Confused. She'd fallen for this oddly vulnerable assassin, but she had to turn him in—didn't she? "The scars on your body? How did you get them?"

"Courtesy of an arms dealer in a Moroccan prison where the CIA left me to rot when a mission went wrong."

"You were CIA." That explained a lot about what he did and how he did it. The Agency operated by its own rules. No wonder Alex knew how to bend them. No wonder he didn't respect the FBI—interagency rivalry demanded nothing less.

"They won't acknowledge anything I did for them. The Gateway Project offered to get me out of prison if I gave them three years of similar service."

Did that make him a vicious killer or a patriot? "It's illegal to act against American citizens."

His laugh lacked amusement. "All assassinations are illegal but somehow most people can live with the CIA taking out unknown threats on foreign soil. At least working for The Gateway Project the only people I killed were scum of the earth and not just anti-American."

"Meacher?"

He nodded.

"What does Jane Sanders have to do with this?"

"She's a friend, nothing more." His eyes looked blank. "After I met you there was never anyone else. There never will be."

She couldn't tell whether or not he was lying. "She works for my mother."

"I know who she works for and, no, I didn't sleep with you because your mother paid me to. There isn't enough money in the world for me to prostitute myself that way."

"But you're okay with murder?"

He laughed and nodded to her Glock. "What's that on your hip, a laser pointer?"

She wrapped her arms over her chest. "I'm a federal agent. I get to carry a gun to protect people."

"And I shoot serial killers and pedophiles for the same reason." His words were clipped.

She paced. He'd put her in an untenable position. But her heart was aching because like a fool she believed every word he said.

"Did you have anything to do with me being transferred to Quantico?"

He shook his head.

"What made you join the CIA?"

"Revenge. I wanted to get back at the people who'd caused the men in my unit to die."

"What made you join this Gateway thing?"

"Survival. I was in a shithole prison and I wasn't getting out any time this century. CIA denied all knowledge of me. The Gateway Project offered me a deal."

"So all the talk about balancing the scales of justice is bullshit because you'd probably have agreed to shoot the President to get out of there?"

He shrugged. "Maybe. Probably."

"So why protect these people? You can turn state's evidence and maybe get immunity from prosecution." And their baby might have the chance to know its father.

His eyes shuttered. "I don't break promises, Mallory. When they came to me I guess I figured I could live with their terms. That was before I met you." He moved his hand toward his pocket and she flinched in sudden fear.

"Christ, Mallory." He swallowed repeatedly as if he was having trouble breathing. "I would never hurt you. *Never.*" He stood and then dropped to his knees in front of her. Before she saw him move he had her gun in his hand and was pointing it to his temple. "I would rather die than let anything bad happen to you. You have to believe me." His eyes burned. Hands shook. The cool assassin was gone. The man in front of her was a mess of pure emotion.

Her heart hammered. "Give me the gun, Alex."

"Do you understand yet? Do you *get* what I am telling you? I don't care if I die. I only care about your safety. I love you. I love you and I haven't loved anyone. In years. I know we don't have a future together. I know you hate me. I'd turn myself in right now but I can't take the chance that this killer might get his hands on you."

The fact that he really did seem to love her made her heart crack wide open. The fact he gave her this opportunity to betray her ideals—and that he knew she wanted to—Christ, she didn't know what to think. It made her no better than him.

"I don't hate you." But she wanted to. "Please put down the gun." She ran a hand over his face, wanting to make the moments they had last forever, knowing it was impossible. "We can't take the law into our own hands."

"I have government sanction to wipe this motherfucker off the face of the earth." Those beautiful eyes went cold again. He handed her the gun and she put it back in the holster. "The law is handicapped by bureaucracy."

"Vigilantism is *wrong.*"

"It's justice." He climbed to his feet. "But I'm sick of killing. Sick of lying. Sick of working for a government that won't acknowledge the system is broken."

Mallory was torn. By not phoning this information in, by not talking to Hanrahan she was throwing away her career. But why had she joined up in the first place? To find out what had happened to her sister. Maybe her career didn't matter anymore. Maybe Alex was right. Maybe this was about justice.

She kissed him hungrily. The overwhelming desire to have him one last time raced through her, making her throb and want. All the things they could never have, all the things they'd lost because he wasn't who she thought he was. She loved him. Her kiss said it all and Alex kissed her back with the same intensity.

She pulled away, knowing what she had to do. Determination grew inside her. She reached into her purse and pulled out her Taser. She shocked him before she could change her mind. She knew how fast he could move and wouldn't risk him disarming her. He jerked and fell to the floor, hitting his head and convulsing. Despite the pain she was causing him she shocked him for another five-second cycle until he was truly incapacitated before she took her finger off the trigger. Damn, he was unconscious, probably from hitting his head. He groaned and Mallory sat back on her heels. Chances were he'd be fine and she'd gone too far to turn back now. She dragged out a pair of flexi-cuffs and attached his wrists around the bed leg which was conveniently bolted to the floor.

She checked his pulse—strong and steady. A light sweat coated his forehead. She kissed him and turned him on his side into the recovery position, then grabbed his car keys.

For the first time in her life she wanted to really hurt someone. Ironically it wasn't Alex Parker, trained assassin. No matter what, she loved this man. But she needed this over. She needed to figure out who she was. A dedicated FBI agent? Or exactly the same as Alex, but hiding behind a badge to commit murder?

She needed to know.

And she had an advantage that no one else had when hunting this killer. She didn't need to find him. He'd find her.

CHAPTER TWENTY-ONE

THE WHOLE TOWN was on edge when they found out Deputy Sean Kennedy had disappeared. He made sure he'd defended the guy at first, but inside he was pretty damn happy about Kennedy becoming a suspect in the attack on Kari Regent and in the other murders. It bought him some time.

Except time was running out.

He'd just heard Kari Regent was awake and recovering in the hospital. No matter how desperately he wanted to wrap his hands around her throat and crack her hyoid bones, the bodyguards that asshole Alex Parker assigned were unwavering, as was her parents' presence at her bedside. Maybe he'd have to let Kari live with her nightmares and console himself that at least she'd never forget him. Maybe wait a year and track her down when she was just starting to feel safe again.

He finished the report he was writing on a speeding ticket he'd handed out that afternoon. Tomorrow was his day off, but given the shit going on around here, chances of getting it was about as probable as the FBI figuring out this mess on their own. Not fucking likely. He turned off his computer and grabbed his coat and headed to the diner for something to eat.

"The usual?" The waitress asked him with a big smile. The place was packed but one of the waitresses on a break gave up her stool for him. It was still warm.

"Make it extra-large. I'm starving." He'd barely eaten or slept over the last few weeks. Time to sleep when he was dead.

"They found Kennedy yet?" She chewed gum as she topped off customers' coffee.

"Not yet."

"Is it true what they say? He might be the serial killer?"

He shrugged. Although he was always happy to get away with his crimes it was disappointing people didn't realize how cunning he was. Not until it was too late anyway. He wondered if Sean was still alive. He should probably go check before the guy started to stink. On the other hand why bother?

"Can't say."

He looked over at a table of reporters. One brunette was eyeing him like a mark. The idea of taking her, of killing her was potent. He looked away. Easy boy. Plenty fish in the sea, and only one fish he wanted. He could play later.

The bell over the door jingled and the waitress's eyes bugged.

He swiveled to face the door and damn near fell off his chair. Mallory Rooney stood in the middle of the diner. Her arms were wrapped tight around her chest and her eyes flicked over everyone but never stopped to rest. When she was sure she had everyone's full attention she walked to the cashier and ordered a burger to go.

His breath caught. She was so close. What the hell was she doing here? Her gold shield gleamed on her hip and her weapon was clearly visible. The press was abuzz. On their cell phones and yakking to editors. If Mallory had wanted to make a statement that she was in town she couldn't have picked a better spot.

Were other agents outside? Where was the dickhead boyfriend? Her order was clearly for one. She got a coffee to go and was out the door before his plate of food arrived.

"Wonder what she's doing up here?" The waitress muttered, making sure he had everything he needed.

She'd come for him. The knowledge unfurled happily in his stomach and spread a warmth right through his flesh. She'd come for him. But she was expecting him which wouldn't make things easy.

"Will you do me a favor?" the waitress asked.

He frowned. His life was a little complicated for favors.

"One of my waitresses, Mandy," the woman nodded toward a blond girl who was waiting tables. "I promised her mom I'd give her a ride home but I'm going to be here for a few hours what with all these reporters hanging around." She smiled. "Would you mind giving her a ride home for me?"

He looked at the young woman and found a fierce sense of rightness with his world. One minute he'd been worried how the hell he was gonna catch Mallory, and the next moment the answer was handed to him on a platter. He remembered what had happened last time clearly enough. A live victim would distract the crap out of her. And she certainly wouldn't be expecting it. He hadn't been. "Sure."

The waitress's gaze was clouded with worry. "I want this whole thing to be over with. I want my town back."

He placed his hand over hers. She felt cold so he gave her a rub. "Don't worry. It'll all be over soon."

Her lips trembled, and the skin around her eyes crinkled. "Promise?"

"Cross my heart."

"Dinner's on the house." She kissed his cheek and

squeezed his shoulder. "You're a good man. A very good man."

He made a show of looking at his cell. "Ah, sh-crap. Got a call out." He stood and grabbed his burger and wrapped it in a napkin. "I gotta go. If the girl wants a ride she's got thirty seconds. I'll wait outside in the cruiser." With that he was gone.

The engine was just turning over when the girl came flying out of the diner, carrying her jacket and a bag. She threw herself into the front seat. He blasted hot air at the windows to clear the frost.

The young woman shrugged into her jacket and grinned. "Thanks for the ride, Officer." There was a glint in her blue eyes that was older than her years.

He smiled. She was perfect for his needs. "Can't be too careful these days. Buckle up. Roads are slick and I don't want any accidents."

She did as she was told.

He sure as hell liked a woman who did as she was told.

ALEX CAME AROUND slowly. There was a bump on his skull that throbbed viciously. What the hell had happened? His arms jerked to a halt from a restraint and his eyes popped wide. For a split second he was terrified he was back in that North African hellhole. Plastic, not shackles. Cheap musty carpet rather than dirt floor. He blinked.

Mallory. She'd shocked him and left him here. He shook his pounding head, trying to clear the haze. It didn't make sense.

Oh, shit. Yes, it made sense.

He checked his watch. Thirty minutes had gone by with him passed out. She'd electrocuted the fuck out of him and considering what he'd done he couldn't say he blamed her. He looked around for the car keys but she'd taken them. He stretched out his legs and dragged his laptop case to the floor using his feet. He winced as it crashed but his priority was getting out of these cuffs ASAP. Maneuvering the bag between his knees he ripped the Velcro open with his teeth. He shoved the bag closer to his hands and un-zipped a side pocket that held some basic tools. A pair of snips was all it took to get free from the bed. Three seconds later he'd repacked his tools, grabbed his coat and laptop and walked out the door. Then he stared at the parking lot. Shit. No car.

He considered his options. Although stealing a car was the easiest he didn't want to end up in some stupid car chase. He went into the office.

"That your *Focus* out there?" he asked the girl behind the desk.

"Yeah. Why?" She eyed him warily.

"I'll give you five thousand dollars if you lend it to me for twenty-four hours."

"Get out."

"You on the Internet?"

She nodded.

"Look up the number for the FBI's Charlotte Field Office and call and ask for Special Agent Lucas Randall." He had her attention and she did as he asked. Five grand was probably a lot of money to this woman.

She put her hand over the mouthpiece of the receiver. "They're putting me through. Is this for real?"

He showed her his driver's license. "Tell him that a guy named Alex Parker is offering you 5K to borrow your car and ask him if I'm good for the money."

She did so. "He said to tell you to make it ten."

He shook his head. That's what friends were for. But Mallory was out there and he didn't have time for haggling. "Fine." He handed her his card. "Call my office and tell them what I told you. Someone will courier you a check. I'm good for any damages. Tell Special Agent Randall to call me immediately on my cell. He has the number."

"Okay…"

He held out his palm for her keys and she handed them over. No fuss, no panic. People were crazy.

He got into the car and adjusted the seat. He booted up his laptop which thankfully still worked, looking for Mallory's positional GPS from her cell or laptop. Nothing. He closed his eyes and counted to ten. Her laptop was back at Quantico and she'd dismantled her phone because he'd told her to. But she might turn it on again later. Seeing as he hadn't been arrested as yet, her plan was probably to go to Colby and hope the killer showed up. It was reasonable under the circumstances. But if the UNSUB ambushed her along the way or overpowered her… He might never see her again. He started driving.

He needed to figure out who this killer was.

His phone rang. Lucas. "I can't believe you just did that."

"Mallory took my car."

"You're seeing each other?" Lucas sounded pissed.

Alex felt numb. "Not exactly. She's pretty angry with me at the moment and took my car."

"She stole your car?"

"Borrowed." Without permission. "I need your help."

Lucas remained quiet but Alex knew he was listening. "Lindsey Keeble. She was murdered by this so-called PR-killer."

"I know who Lindsey Keeble is," Lucas's voice deepened.

"Did they find anything new from the autopsy, or in her car?"

"That's privileged information, Alex. I can't give that out."

"You sent me privileged information to look at when you sent me that cell phone data…"

"This is different." Lucas wasn't budging.

"Tell me what they found and I'll tell you who killed Meacher."

"You know? You don't know."

"I figured it out."

"Shit." Alex could practically see Lucas raking his fingers through his hair. Then he heard him tapping buttons. "Okay, DNA isn't back. According to the report they didn't find any prints except from Lindsey, her dad, and the cop who found the car in the woods. They did identify flecks of black car paint beneath her nails. Forensics are trying to narrow it down to make and model."

Alex swore. "The prints, were they from the deputy who went missing?"

"Nah. A guy called Leo Chance."

That was the guy who'd interviewed him at the sheriff's office.

He pulled over and ran Chance's cell data through his algorithms and got a couple of hits. Not conclusive but… "What color car does Leo Chance drive?"

There was a long hesitation, then a sigh and more tapping. "Black SUV."

Alex thought about it. Could it be him? Could it be a cop? He was the right size and shape. Age would fit. And something about that interview had bugged him, he just didn't know what it was.

"Is Kari Regent out of her coma yet?"

"That's what I heard," said Lucas.

"Can you email me a photo of Leo Chance?"

"You really think the killer is a cop?"

"Can it do any harm for me to ask Kari Regent if she recognizes the guy?"

Lucas grunted. "Fine. But no heroics."

"Not my style."

"Done. Okay. So who killed Meacher so I can put this baby to bed?"

"I did."

"Ha, fucking ha, Alex. Shit. If anyone finds out I told you anything about this case..."

Lucas didn't believe him. That was funny. "You told me nothing, Lucas. But it might just be enough."

He called his partners and got them to wire money to the girl at the motel. Didn't want her getting cold feet and calling the cops.

It was a thirty minute drive to the hospital and every muscle in his body was knotted with tension. The sun was dropping out of the sky and darkness was not his friend.

He'd screwed up so badly with Mallory. He'd betrayed her on every level, personally and professionally. The idea of forgiveness was ridiculous. And he couldn't even threaten to turn in his superiors because that would destroy what little was left of her family and no way in hell would he do that to her. He'd rather hang. Or suck back some pentobarbital which was more than possible in the great states of North Carolina and Virginia.

Cold mist clung to the mountains and drifted through the trees like cobwebs among the spindly branches. He didn't dare contemplate what he'd lost. But whatever they might have had together was dead. The only thing that mattered was getting the willowy brunette with the soft amber eyes safely through the night. She needed closure to move on with her life and he intended to provide that and at the same time give her the biggest break in her career. Capturing—dead or alive—a serial killer and a vigilante would look pretty fucking good on her résumé.

Assuming he found her before the PR-killer did.

He got to the hospital and found one of the men he'd assigned standing guard. He knocked on Kari's door and the guy followed him inside.

"Can we help you?" An older man in a blue button-down shirt climbed to his feet. A woman held Kari's hand and a young man of about twenty sat on her other side.

"My name is Alex Parker—"

"You're the gentlemen who arranged security?" the father asked. "The one who got her here?"

"Yes, sir." He hadn't come for thanks. He looked at the bed. Kari's head had been shaved and she was wrapped in bandages, tubes inserted into her nostrils, intubated. Her eyes were open and she watched him. "I need to ask you a question, if I may?"

She nodded slightly and winced. Headaches. He could attest to the fact she'd have lots of headaches in her future. The bump on the back of his head throbbed but he deserved it. He moved closer and held up his cell phone with Leo Chance's smiling photograph on the screen. "Is this the man who hurt you?"

Her pupils dilated and her pulse revved on the heartbeat monitor. The nod was unnecessary.

The father grabbed his arm. "The cops are going to catch this guy, right?"

"Yes, sir. I have to go now." Alex gently unhooked the man's fingers. On the way out he showed Leo's photograph to the man on the door and told him who he thought the guy was.

"He's been by a couple times," the bodyguard told him. His eyes narrowed. "I didn't let him in."

"Good." Alex nodded to the guy. "Don't let down your guard until this fucker is locked up or dead. Not until you hear from me, okay?"

"Sure, boss."

Kari Regent was too vulnerable and had suffered too much for them to get complacent now.

He had to get to Mallory. Right now she was probably sitting in her father's house waiting for this bastard. He texted her the killer's identity in the hopes she'd turned on her cell and then raced back to his car. Alex intended to be her back-up whether she liked it or not.

DID THE KILLER know she was here? Had he stuck around or had he already run?

Mallory didn't know what else she could do to advertise her presence in the West Virginian community where she'd grown up. Maybe hire a marching band or place a flashing neon sign on top of the hills? Put out a newsflash on local radio?

Snow was falling harder now, batted away by the wipers only to cling to the windshield again in icy desperation. She peered through the glass, keeping a slow steady speed along the unplowed highway. He had to be local. She didn't believe it was Sean Kennedy—at least not acting alone—although to say her instincts were screwed was an understatement. She was in love with an ex-CIA operative who took out serial killers in his spare time.

Crap. A serial killing cop was almost pedestrian in comparison.

Her meal from the diner sat in the passenger seat, wafting out aromas that were overpowering enough to turn her stomach. Only the awareness that she needed to keep up her strength for the challenge ahead stopped her from throwing the lot in the garbage. She needed to eat, so she'd eat.

She popped a French fry in her mouth. It tasted like salted cardboard.

She hoped Alex was okay. The motel staff would find him eventually and with luck he'd have time to escape before Hanrahan tracked him down. The FBI would never catch him. Hell, if he was telling the truth about working for the government they might not even try. She needed to talk this over with Hanrahan. Needed to get a handle on all the smoke and mirrors that were going on with this organization, but not until Alex had a chance to get away. Inside she felt numb. Numb with grief over losing Alex. Numb for the life together they wouldn't have. She touched her stomach. She had to put him out of her mind and move on, but that was easier said than done when she needed him now more than ever.

But her gun was a solid entity on her hip, her back-up weapon strapped to her right ankle. Her trusty Taser in her pocket. She was as prepared as she'd ever be. A damn sight more prepared than any little girl. She turned onto the family estate—the driveway had been plowed by some kind soul, probably the gardener—and drove up the long curved path to her childhood home.

The red-brick three-story mansion was a dark hulking shadow, no longer familiar and dear, but creepy and secretive. The windows glinted malevolently as the moon started to rise above the trees. Snow covered the front steps. No one had gone inside that way since the snow had started to fall in earnest that afternoon.

She parked the car, turned off the engine, and then looked up at the grand Georgian edifice that had witnessed so much drama. Officially it was still a crime scene but that worked for her. Fewer innocent bystanders at risk of being hurt. She grabbed her bag of food and got out, snow immediately covering her ankle boots and soaking into her black pants. She went up the steps, stomping off as much of the wet stuff as she could.

The front door was dressed in a wreath which was strangely incongruous next to the crime scene tape. Taking her gun in hand, she unlocked the door and pushed it wide. The alarm system wasn't armed. It didn't seem to do much good anyway, or at least the killer sure as hell knew how to bypass it. Looking inside she didn't know what to expect. Blood trails? A man standing behind the door with a meat cleaver?

The moonlight revealed the foyer as its usual elegant and dignified self.

Taking her phone battery and SIM card she put them back

in her cell, only to notice the signal was non-existent. “Damn.” Must be the weather.

She flicked on the chandelier and remembered Alex’s reaction to her family home. It tied another knot in her heart. Spying the landline her father still maintained she went over and called Hanrahan. He answered on the first ring. “Where the hell are you?”

“Colby. Did you figure out who was working with the vigilante?”

“No.” She could almost hear him scrubbing his face. “There were a few calls but the IT guy needs time to trace them and he’s been overrun by a pedophile doing live broadcasts. Priorities… Anyway, the worst that will happen is they’ll bolt and we’ll go after them. You with Parker?”

“Yes.” Her voice cracked like a scratch on a vinyl record. Did Hanrahan know about Alex or was that just a normal question? “We’re just at my father’s house to check something and then we’re going to the hospital to see if Kari Regent remembers anything.”

“She woke up?”

Mallory didn’t know but she lied anyway. She was getting good at it. “We’ll wait there until she can give us a proper description.”

“Don’t do anything stupid, Agent Rooney.”

She looked around the empty house. Too late. “No, sir.” She rang off and ate a cold French fry. Bleh. She headed to the kitchen to reheat her food. She’d thrown down the gauntlet. Now she had to wait for someone to pick it up.

CHAPTER TWENTY-TWO

MALLORY SAT ON the kitchen floor, Glock beside her, staring at the table where she and Payton had often sat and begged cookies from the housekeeper. Loneliness crowded her. Her sister's ghost had been with her for years. At school. On dates. All through her FBI training. On the gun range. Especially on the gun range.

But her sister's spirit hadn't haunted her when she was with Alex. He'd taken away the grief that resided inside her heart like a cavity. She'd found peace with him in a way she had never known before. Now he was gone.

There was a noise at the back door.

She wasn't scared. She picked up her pistol, relishing the cold weight of it in her hand. No, she wasn't scared. She was determined. And deep down, she was furious. This guy had ruined her sister's life and wanted to ruin hers.

What he didn't know was her life was already in tatters. Nothing he did would change the fundamental truth that she could never have the man she loved. The knowledge made her want to fall to her knees and weep, but it wasn't just her life at stake. And she wasn't about to let this creep win. She wanted to make him pay. Quietly, she moved through the corridor into the mudroom and found the back door wide open. It had been locked so the bastard must have a key.

She poked her head out and looked around, drawing quickly back inside. But he wasn't going to shoot her. He wanted her alive. A single set of footprints headed to and from the woods.

Making a decision, Mallory ran toward the woods—his domain. But she wasn't an unarmed kid. She was a trained federal agent. She headed into the trees and along a wide path that white-tailed deer often used. Her boots were soaked through in seconds. Branches scratched her face. It was a clear night with a full moon and she had to concentrate on where to place her feet because the ground was rough and uneven beneath the snow, and she had no desire to twist an ankle. The tracks were easy to follow. Maybe too easy. She slowed, taking her time. Knowing she couldn't plow into this guy head-on.

For the first time since meeting Alex she felt utterly alone. She wanted to tell him about the baby, but couldn't stand the look on his face when he realized he wouldn't share their lives.

She finally reached the top of the hill. Footprints were scattered. Too confusing to track. Her fingers were numb from cold as they gripped her gun. Temperature dropping rapidly. She looked around, just making out the roof of the property where the McCaffertys had lived. They must have got in his way somehow.

No one knew where she was going or why, she realized. No way would she let this guy get away with his crimes regardless of what happened to her. She was in a bit of a clearing and whirled making sure no one was creeping up behind her.

Her phone buzzed. She had a signal. She checked and saw she had a text from Alex. "KARI SAYS KILLER=DEPUTY SHERIFF LEO CHANCE."

Her first thought was relief that Alex had escaped the motel. Her second was the memory of meeting Leo Chance and not having a clue he was the man who'd killed all those innocent women. Bastard was going down regardless of what happened in these woods tonight. Kari would have her revenge, and so would Payton, and Lindsey, and all those other girls whose lives he'd destroyed.

She dialed Hanrahan.

"Hello?" The line was terrible.

"The name of the PR-killer is…" *shit*, she still had no solid proof except Alex's word, which was probably gold when it came to this kind of thing. "Deputy Leo Chance. A local cop. I'm in the woods behind Eastborne tracking him right now." She hung up before he could give her different orders, and slipped her phone into her pocket.

An owl hooted, sending a shiver through her body.

She started forward then heard someone cry out in pain. A woman. *Ah, shit.* She gritted her teeth as she inched forward, Glock in a two-handed grip. Heartbeat steady. Mind focused because being distracted now would get her killed. She dodged around a wide tree and froze. A girl with a rope around her neck dangled on tiptoes from the branches of the old American oak.

Mallory's heart gave a giant *whumph*. She knew this was a trap, she knew it was a distraction but there was no way she could leave that poor girl hanging there. And the bastard knew it. She ran over to the terrified young woman. Gagged. Bleeding. Hands tied behind her back, rope tight, scared to death.

"You're okay." Mallory fought with the knots but they were pulled tight. She needed both hands. The girl coughed and choked and Mallory tried to support her with her torso as she fought to undo the ropes one-handed because no way in hell did she want to let go of her weapon. Finally the knot loosened and the girl dropped to her knees in the snow, gagging and breathing hard. A sound made Mallory's heart clench. She got her gun up but was struck by a bolt of electricity that threw her to the ground. Her finger squeezed off a shot, but she couldn't even see straight, let alone aim. The gun slipped from her fingers.

God, it hurt! She writhed with agony that fused her teeth together, prayed it wouldn't hurt her unborn baby. Snow was frigid against her face, in her nose and mouth, icy water trickling against the bare skin of her neck. She swallowed and turned her head slowly to come face-to-face with her sister's abductor.

LEO COULDN'T BELIEVE how easy it had been. Fucking amateur. As soon as she saw someone suffering she turned all weak and pathetic. Had she forgotten her last lesson so quickly?

Yeah, she had.

Too bad it would be her final one.

He searched her pockets, tossed a cell phone and Taser into the snow. He grinned when he saw the latter. Great minds and all that. It no longer mattered if they found the chamber. Part of him welcomed the idea. The horror it would evoke. The enormity of his deception.

He hauled Mallory over his shoulder and headed toward his cabin. The waitress was curled up in a pathetic heap in the snow and would probably die of exposure before she managed to free herself. He didn't care. His identity was out, but with Mallory in his possession he could get away like planned. He ran his palm over her ass. She was the exact same size and shape as Payton. He squeezed her tight. He had her back and he wasn't ever letting her go.

He jogged around the front of the cabin and dumped her into the cargo space of his SUV. Back porch light was on and flowed over her features. *Payton.* He bent down to put her foot inside when she lashed out with her boot and caught him squarely in the mouth.

He staggered back. And was looking down the barrel of another Glock. *Shit.*

"Back the fuck up," she demanded. He took a few steps away and she swung her legs out of the car, turned on her flashlight, and shone it in his eyes. *Bitch.*

"Throw down the Taser and service weapon," she ordered.

He did so, cocking his head to one side. "Where's your boyfriend?" he jeered.

She ignored the question. "Get out your handcuffs and put them on."

He put the cuffs on but was careful not to lock both sides. "You going to kill me?"

"Maybe."

She even sounded like Payton and it gave a little twist in his gut.

He must have moved.

"Stay where you are! You think I wouldn't love an excuse to put a bullet between your eyes?" Her eyes went hard.

"Do it." He leaned toward her. "You think I give a shit? You think I can stand to live without your sister?" Her fingers tightened on the trigger because he'd just confirmed he was the man she'd been searching for all these years. So she hadn't been certain. He filed that information away.

"Why did you do it? Why'd you take her? Why did you kill her?"

"I didn't kill her, you stupid bitch. I loved her."

A shiver wracked her body, teeth rattling like bones. She didn't believe him. "I want to know where my sister's buried." Skin was icy pale. Lips more white than pink, heading toward pale blue. "I want her back."

A smile started inside him but he didn't show it. He needed a little more time for her reactions to slow further and he could get the advantage again. She wouldn't shoot him. She was a federal agent with a stick up her ass. And she wanted to know where he'd buried Payton. He'd show her.

"I'll take you there but I need my flashlight." She nodded that he could get it out so he did, relishing the feel of its weight in his hands. Despite playing tough cop she knew not to get close enough to allow him to overpower her. Meant she couldn't search him and she wasn't the only one who carried a back-up.

He started to walk, deeper and deeper into the forest, following the trail he'd been walking almost daily for the last eighteen years. Trees cracked as the temperature dropped and he could hear her shivering. A branch snapped under his feet. If he could get her into the close confines of the chamber he had no doubt he could get the gun off her and subdue her.

"It was you who broke into my house in Charlotte, wasn't it?"

He shrugged. "Don't know who the other guy was though." He looked over his shoulder. "Looked a lot like your boyfriend now I come to think about it."

Her lips narrowed.

"I almost got you by letting the tires down on your car at Quantico too. Borrowed a recovery truck from a friend of mine to whisk you away but again you blew it for me."

She huffed out a soft snort. "Sorry. My manners are dreadful when it comes to serial killers."

His mouth firmed this time. He wasn't some psycho asshole. He'd been looking for something—someone. And now that he'd found her he'd better figure out a way to turn this thing around.

"Where are we going? How far is it?" she asked angrily. But there were nerves too. She shone the flashlight back in his face and the light burned his retina.

Bitch. "It isn't far. I'll show you where she's buried." *Then I'll end this thing.*

"I have back-up coming so don't try anything."

"Sorry to break it to you, Special Agent, but I know you came alone."

She stopped moving. Would she have the balls to shoot him in the back? He doubted it. He got to the woodpile, eyed the ax out of the corner of his eye.

He reached down to undo the bolt to the trap door.

"What are you doing?" Nerves made her voice vibrate, along with the cold. Wouldn't be long before she was incapable of holding the gun.

He had to get closer. "You wanted to know what happened to your sister and where she is?" He flipped the trapdoor wide and shone his flashlight into the darkness.

He watched surprise then horror stretch her features.

"You kept her down there?" Her voice rose. "All this

time?"

He didn't like her tone. "It's not so bad." Although at night it had a sinister feel.

"It's a dirty hole in the ground. It's worse than a cage in a zoo. How long? How long did you keep her locked up like a dog?"

A vague feeling of shame wrapped around him and he didn't like that either. "I looked after her." He carefully slipped one wrist out of the cuffs.

"You treated her like an animal!" She shouted at him, out of control in her rage. He lunged, grabbing her arm and thrusting the gun sideways as she fired off a shot. He landed flush on top of her and it shocked him how much she *felt* like Payton. He smashed her hand against the ground until she dropped the weapon, then he held her immobile as she tried to fight him. Her angry eyes and spitting mouth told him she wasn't really Payton but, if he closed his eyes and cut out her tongue… He forced his knees between hers and her thighs wide open, ground himself against her. She felt…right.

Her breath was hot against his ear and he shivered with memory.

"You disgust me." She bit down hard on his lobe and he screamed.

He reared back and slammed his fist into her jaw. "Bitch. Now you're going to find out what the others found out. But no matter how much you hurt or suffer, I'm never letting you go. Never."

CHAPTER TWENTY-THREE

HEADLIGHTS OFF, ALEX followed tire marks through the snow, wishing the girl from the motel had been driving something more substantial than a compact. The rear end kept sliding in the six inches of fresh snow that covered the ground. He corrected the skid, and then again as he forced himself to slow down going up the single-lane track through the bush. He got to a narrow spot between dense bush and stopped, getting out and locking the vehicle to block the guy's escape.

He jogged up the road, sweat starting to form on his back. Up ahead was a tidy looking cabin built in the middle of nowhere that his GPS told him was where Deputy Sheriff Leo Chance lived. On the southern tip of the forest that bordered both the McCaffertys' property and Mallory's dad's estate. It had previously belonged to Leo's uncle who'd died in a farming accident six months after Payton Rooney had been taken. Leo had been seventeen and the only witness to the man's death. Alex didn't think it was a coincidence.

He listened for a moment but the silence told him no one was here. There was a police cruiser parked to one side, and an SUV with the rear door wide open, a thin layer of snow coating the black carpet inside. Several sets of footprints led in and out of the cabin, and also into the woods. Instinct made him want to search the woods first but the cabin made more sense. First, he quietly disabled the SUV by disconnecting the battery and did the same with the patrol car. It would slow the bastard down, and all he needed was one clear shot.

He tried the cabin door, which was unlocked. Inside he found a meticulously neat home. Big ass TV. Men's clothes in the dresser. Men's size twelve shoes near the door. He cleared each room. There was no attic, no basement. No "guest" room.

There was a noise outside the front door and Alex moved into position ready to take the fucker out. Supervisory Special Agent Frazer stepped inside the cabin, gun drawn.

"Don't shoot," said Alex, moving into view.

Frazer lowered his weapon. "Where's Rooney?"

"I'm not sure." Alex ignored his dry mouth, pulled out his cell phone and tried dialing. No reply from Mallory and no tracking data. Shit. "What are you doing here?"

"Mallory called Hanrahan who is on his way here in a chopper along with Senator Tremont." Frazer sounded pissed. "I was on my way to visit Kari Regent, hoping to get more information out of her when Hanrahan said Mallory had identified Deputy Leo Chance as the PR-killer and to get my ass out here."

So she'd got his text about Leo. *Good.* At least she knew who she was dealing with. Alex wondered what else she'd told Hanrahan but right now, as long as the FBI didn't try to stop him, it didn't matter.

"Where are the locals?"

Frazer narrowed his gaze along that fine blade of a nose. "I don't know if they'd take my word or warn the son-of-a-bitch."

"You didn't tell them?"

Frazer shook his head.

"We need to search the woods."

"We should probably wait for back-up."

"And yet you're already here, Agent Frazer. Hero complex?"

"Just want to catch a killer, Parker."

He moved past Frazer. "Then let's go."

Frazer gave him an assessing stare as he followed him outside. "Who the hell are you? Really?"

Cold air hit him afresh. Mallory wasn't dressed for a winter storm. His fault. He'd fucked up and never expected her to Taser him. He'd smile if he wasn't so damn scared he'd never see her again. "I'll tell you everything *after* we find Mallory."

"Fine." Frazer followed him out of the cabin. "What makes Mallory think Leo Chance is the PR-killer?"

"Kari Regent ID'd him as the killer." That gave him an idea. He called the bodyguard standing outside Kari's room. "I need you to ask Kari a couple of questions for me. Did he keep her in a building?"

The bodyguard relayed the questions. "No. She wrote 'underground'."

"Underground? Like in a mine shaft?"

The bodyguard answered, his voice gruff. "No, she says in a chamber, in the woods."

It turned Alex's stomach to think about what she'd endured. He hung up and turned to Frazer. "He's got some sort of underground hidey-hole out here. We need to find it."

The footprints through the snow were their best bet. Alex walked to the side of the tracks, trying to preserve the integrity of the evidence. Frazer was in dress shoes but didn't baulk. He went up a tiny notch in Alex's estimation.

"I did a little digging on the drive over from the hospital.

Leo inherited this place from his uncle and moved in when he was seventeen. Never left the area, never went on vacation until January this year when he went to Cancun. Guess what else turned up in Cancun at the same time?"

Frazer raised his brow.

"Couple of dead brunettes."

Away from the cabin they were plunged into a snow-lit darkness and neither had a flashlight. They moved cautiously. Mallory was somewhere nearby with this sonofabitch. He knew it. He could feel them out there in the darkness. What would happen if she shot the guy in cold blood and Frazer witnessed it? He grimaced because the idea of them both being on the run held a grim appeal and he didn't want her to have to live like that. And not that she'd want him now, not after he'd lied to her about something so horrific.

But she wouldn't kill this bastard. She might think she would, she would be tempted, but Alex recognized her pure heart. She was a good person. An amazing person. He was not. He'd kill anyone who got in the way of protecting Mallory, which made him no better than the scum he hunted.

He heard someone cry out and they started moving swiftly through the woods toward the sound. He pulled Frazer to a stop and listened intently. To have any hope of surprise they needed to circle around and approach from the other side. And they needed to do it quietly because he wasn't about to watch the woman he loved die at the hands of a maniac.

THE SENSATION OF wetness seeping into her clothes roused Mallory from her daze. Someone grabbed at her wrists and started binding them together. No way. She leveraged her legs up and kicked him hard in the balls, twisting and springing to her feet. He toppled face-first to the ground and she used one foot to immobilize an arm, her other foot pressing hard across the side of his throat, both her hands grabbing his other wrist, twisting his arm behind his back.

He started to buck and she pressed harder with her foot, cutting off his air supply. The flashlight he'd dropped on the ground showed his features half-buried in snow, contorted as he started to choke.

"How do *you* like it, Leo?"

Maybe Alex was right. Maybe vengeance was the only form of true justice in a world full of sadists and killers who showed no mercy to those under their control. She pressed her foot down harder, watched him gasp for air as his lips started to turn cyanotic. Hatred surged inside her. This was a fraction of the pain and suffering he'd caused. He went still and silent. Crap. She released the pressure, thankful when he drew in a shallow breath. A flash of realization shot through her and she shuddered in relief. She didn't want him dead. Personal retribution wasn't her idea of justice. The idea of the government sanctioning such a thing was unbelievable, but she already knew the CIA and NSA, even the military, did things she'd never condone.

So, if Alex was telling the truth, what did it make him—vigilante or soldier?

She spotted her gun in the snow and grabbed it before Leo Chance decided he had nothing left to lose by fighting back. She pointed it at the man who lay hacking in the snow. Finger on the trigger.

"Don't do it, Mallory." A quiet voice in the darkness. *Alex.*

He'd come for her when he should have run. "He isn't worth a piece of your soul."

She barked out a laugh to cover her sorrow. "A little ironic coming from a government assassin don't you think?"

"I understand the cost better than most." Alex walked up to her.

She swore when she saw Frazer behind him. Sent Alex a wry smile as if her heart wasn't shattered. "Guess I blew your cover, huh?"

"I promised to tell him everything after we found you anyway. I told you I wasn't going anywhere." Leo Chance lay on the ground panting and cradling his neck. He watched them carefully between slitted eyes. "Want me to kill him for you?"

"Frazer?" she joked. Frazer's eyes went wide at her quip. If she had to make a guess she'd bet Frazer wasn't The Gateway Project's inside man.

"Funny." Alex seemed unperturbed.

She knew Alex would kill for her if she asked him to, but she didn't want blood on her conscience. The knowledge made her stand a little bit taller.

"I want the justice system to do its job. I want this man who betrayed his uniform to stand trial for everything he's done, and to get justice for all the women he hurt. For Payton." Alex took the gun from her hand so she could bend down and cuff Leo. The guy lay meekly on the ground. Alex held two weapons at his head and the man seemed to realize Alex would have no hesitation pulling the trigger if need be. *Coward.*

When she was done, Alex handed her back the weapon and then shrugged out of his jacket. She shook her head but he wrapped it around her anyway. It was still warm from the heat of his body. He might be an assassin, but since the moment she'd met him he'd been nothing but supportive and protective of her. Not in a smothering sense, but as though she was the most important person in his world. She knew that Alex Parker would make the best father a child could ever hope for. The fact struck her like a knife in the heart because she was still going to lose him.

It had stopped snowing and the clouds had cleared. Silvery moonlight hit the snow, bouncing back to light up the whole woods.

In the distance flashlights bobbed. Anxious voices drifted. Cops? The crunch of footsteps got louder as people drew closer. She tensed with anticipation. Mallory shone her flashlight over the new arrivals.

Christ, was that her mother?

Her mother ran toward them, breathing heavily as she lugged herself through the thick snow. Agent Hanrahan followed at a slower pace.

"Mom?" *What the hell?* "What are you doing here?" asked Mallory.

But her mother wasn't looking at her, she was staring at Alex, fury blazing in her eyes. "I order you, Parker, make him tell me where my baby is."

And then Mallory got it. Her mother was the powerful figure who'd got him out of that Moroccan prison. Her mother was the reason he'd never give up his superiors. Not because of his loyalty to The Gateway Project, but because of his loyalty to *her*. "Jesus Christ, Mom. You started your own private vigilante organization?" Crap.

"I was doing what law enforcement failed to do for eighteen years—find justice for my baby!" Her voice rang out for miles. Her mother looked like she was about to lunge for a weapon and Mallory kept a close eye on her, and the others. The only person she really trusted was Alex who guarded her back like a shadow.

"Is this the man who stole Payton? Where is she? Is she alive?" Mallory grabbed her so she didn't get too close to the deputy.

"She died you stupid bitch!" Leo cried out from the ground. "She fucking died and it wasn't my fault."

The senator's gaze never left the man in the snow. "Parker, if you don't shoot that bastard, I will—"

Alex said, "It's over, Senator Tremont."

"What's going on, Agent Rooney?" SSA Frazer asked carefully.

"Come on, Margret." Hanrahan tried to comfort her mother but the senator made a grab for Hanrahan's gun and the two ended up grappling.

Frazer stepped in and jerked her mother away from the other agent. "Someone needs to explain to me exactly what is going on or so help me…"

Mallory squirmed. Her explanation might get the people she loved most facing the death penalty. "It's complicated."

His eyebrows rose. "I can usually keep up," he said wryly.

Alex touched her shoulder. "He needs to know what's going on, Mallory. This thing has to end."

She touched his fingers for just a moment and then let her hand drop away. "The reason I was recruited to the BAU was because SSA Hanrahan and I both suspected someone inside the FBI was leaking information to a vigilante group who were systematically murdering serial killers."

"Is this true?" Frazer asked Hanrahan.

Her silver-haired boss nodded. He looked uncomfortable in the spotlight.

"The Gateway Project had official backing from the top but no one will ever admit it." Her mother's lip curled when she looked at Leo Chance.

He returned her stare with such coldness Mallory wished she'd kicked him harder.

Alex started talking. "I used to work for the Agency. The senator recruited me to work for an organization called The Gateway Project which specializes in identifying serial killers and pedophiles and…neutralizing them," Alex explained. Frazer's face got paler and paler.

"This is fascinating, guys." Chance jibed from the ground. "We could start a club."

"Except *we* don't kill innocent women and children. We only dispose of the dregs like you."

"But you got busted, asshole, and now you're gonna die just like me." Leo's lip curled, but Mallory remembered the young woman in the woods. How could she have forgotten her? "Oh, God. There's a girl out here somewhere in the snow. She's scared, but alive. She needs help."

"I'll go look for her," Hanrahan offered.

Alex grunted.

"Wait." Frazer was struggling to take it all in. He wasn't the only one. "Why didn't you tell me about your suspicions, sir?"

Hanrahan frowned. "I didn't know who to trust—"

Frazer shook his head. "We could have run phone taps and set up a sting operation." His eyes widened. "That was what this morning's fiasco was about?"

"That was my idea," Mallory admitted. May as well get it all out there.

"And yet we still never made any arrests? You took our phones and wiped the call history, but you didn't take anyone into custody?"

"No one called!"

"Then why wipe the call history?" asked Mallory. Why would he do that?

"He's the inside man," said Alex. His gaze never wavered from Leo Chance who was watching the proceedings with glee from his prone position on the forest floor. "But he'd started to lose his nerve."

"Is it true?" she asked Hanrahan, the man she'd admired. The man she'd trusted—and one who'd successfully isolated her from her colleagues, she realized now. "You were feeding The Gateway Project information?"

He'd drawn his weapon and the tension ratcheted up by about a million. "Your mother persuaded me to give out profiles and other classified information before the cops got it. We devised a warning system so her assassin wouldn't get picked up by the cops, that was all." His gaze swung wildly between them. "I didn't know the assassin was your boyfriend." He rubbed his hand over his brow. "Look, I served the justice system for nearly three decades and nothing ever got better. At first I thought killing these guys was the right choice to make, but then I kept worrying someone would shoot an innocent person and I couldn't live with that."

Wind rustled the dead leaves. Mallory felt cold down to her marrow.

"I wanted a way out." He shrugged, his eyes holding an apology. "I figured the easiest way was if the assassin was caught."

"So you started sending out the warnings later and later," said Alex.

"Why didn't you say something to me?" her mother asked Hanrahan.

Hanrahan shook his head, tears glistening in his eyes. "You wouldn't listen to reason, Margret. There was nothing but vengeance in your heart and the hunger for blood in your soul."

They meant something to one another, Mallory realized. Something special. "You're all guilty of conspiracy to murder," she stated. *Christ.* Should she arrest them? It was obvious they thought themselves so much better than Alex. But just because they didn't do the deed didn't mean they were any less culpable.

Hanrahan's expression turned bitter. "You spotted the trend when no one else had. I had you transferred so I could keep an eye on you."

"But the whole thing backfired when Rooney fell in love with your assassin," Frazer said quietly.

She exchanged a glance with Alex and felt like her world was being torn in two. Frazer was the only one here not knee-deep in this mess. Her mother and the man she loved both faced possible execution if convicted. Her hands curved over her stomach. Frazer was too rigid to bend the rules. She felt sick. This was her worst nightmare.

Alex squeezed her shoulders. She quivered under his touch. "We need to find that girl who's lost in the woods and get this asshole into custody. It's time to decide who to trust and what you want to do, Frazer."

Mallory grabbed Alex's hand and pressed it to her stomach. "I love you."

Alex smiled slowly and touched her face. "That's more than I deserve."

Frazer ground his teeth. "This is hardly the time."

Tears flooded her eyes but she refused to let them fall. She forced out the words. "It's probably the only time we have left. Or haven't you figured that out yet?"

DAWN BEGAN TO spread over the Appalachian Mountains. Special Agent Lincoln Frazer stood in the middle of a West Virginia forest holding a gun on a serial killer who'd killed at least seven people they knew about, an assassin who'd probably killed more, a corrupt senator, a dirty FBI SSA he'd spent his whole career trying to emulate, and a rookie agent whose instincts were a damn sight sharper than his own.

"Got your handcuffs, Rooney?"

"Deputy Chance is wearing them, sir."

The "sir" was added as an afterthought. He hadn't earned her respect. Hell. His mistrust had almost got her killed. He'd been way off in his judgment of her. Of everyone. He had one pair of cuffs and didn't know which of his adversaries was more dangerous. Parker, in theory, but having spent time with the man he didn't think he'd do anything to put Rooney in danger. He seemed like a good guy, for a killer.

"I need your weapon," he told Hanrahan, hoping the man didn't try anything stupid. "Empty the chamber and remove the clip and throw it over there in the snow."

Hanrahan's hands shook even as he obeyed.

"You're all going down." Deputy Chance was on his knees

now, laughing. "I cannot wait to see what happens when the media gets hold of this shit. Every one of you can be charged with murder or conspiracy to murder. Except you." His eyes turned to Mallory. "Payton would have been proud of you for not killing me. She loved me. She wouldn't have wanted anyone to hurt me."

Narcissistic prick.

The pain on Mallory's face took his breath. But Frazer saw an opening when everyone else was too busy hurting. "Someone will need to tend Payton's grave when you're in prison. Where is she?"

Deputy Chance's eyes flicked to the woodpile.

"She's under there?" Frazer asked.

Deputy Chance nodded and swallowed hard. "I didn't kill her. She died."

"You killed her! You stole my baby." The senator lunged for the man and Hanrahan grabbed hold of her.

"She got sick and died you stupid bitch! If she hadn't died I wouldn't have killed anyone else." Deputy Chance spat out.

Now it was the girl's fault? A girl he'd robbed of her freedom and ultimately her life?

"If you'd taken her to the hospital she might have survived. You never gave her that chance. You kept her like a dog for your own pleasure." Mallory's voice cracked and Alex Parker wrapped his arm around her and pulled her close. Protecting her as much as he could for as long as he could.

God. All his years of service were being tested and he just wanted this mess to go away. The idea of locking these people up sat like gasoline in Frazer's gut. But he didn't make the rules, he followed them.

"I'm going to make a phone call. It's in your best interests for you to let me." The senator had regained her usual arrogant composure. She pulled out her cell phone, careful not to make any sudden moves. "Just wait a moment."

They stood, freezing their asses off in the snow as she explained to someone what was happening. Then she held the phone out to him. Frazer frowned and slowly placed it to his ear. The person on the other end of the line identified himself even though his voice was easily recognizable. All the saliva in his mouth dried up.

"If this gets out the whole government could fall." The voice on the phone was a low rumble. "Our enemies across the world would pounce on the scandal and it will destroy the BAU and the FBI." Damn, Frazer wanted to close his eyes but didn't dare let the players out of his sight. This would destroy the BAU's reputation, something he cared deeply about. All their actions would be reviewed. All their cases would be reopened and reexamined. Lives dissected…

"No one else can know about this," the man hissed.

Frazer looked around the group of five people who were all pretending not to eavesdrop.

"Do you understand?"

Shit. Was this guy serious? Frazer swallowed hard. "I'm not sure I do, sir. You want me to…"

"Make sure there are no loose ends, Assistant Special Agent in Charge Frazer." The tone was harsh. "*No* loose ends."

Assistant Special Agent in Charge? "And I do this with your blessing?"

A pause, probably pissed for making him spell it out even though he'd just had a crash course in reasons not to trust his superiors.

"Under my direct orders. And do it before the local cops

turn up, else this will be the shortest promotion in history."

Frazer stared at the phone. What this man was asking was inconceivable. It would make him just as flawed as the rest of them. Could he do it? Could he compromise his principles like that? Throw away his moral high ground? At what cost? But what would this scandal cost them? It might be enough to shut down the BAU forever.

Alex Parker shifted in front of Mallory. He still gripped his weapon and Frazer had no doubt he'd use it before he let anyone hurt her. The guy had amazing instincts. He considered himself a soldier, but he was working for the wrong team. It struck Frazer that Alex Parker could have shot him to protect himself at any time since they'd met up in the cabin, but he hadn't.

The senator looked as if she was in a stupor, a broken woman as her plots and schemes came unraveled. At least now she knew where her daughter was buried. That was something. Hanrahan's shoulders sagged, no doubt picturing his public disgrace and the very real danger of death and injury once incarcerated.

Leo Chance staggered to his feet and laughed. "You're all finished. You're all gonna die before I do, but don't worry, I hear it's relatively painless."

Because the Bureau always followed the rules.

The killer's lip curled. He was a big man. Six-two. Solid with muscle. The women he'd taken had never stood a chance. A man of reasonable intelligence but emotionally stunted by the events of his past. Probable abuse by someone he should have been able to trust, twisting his mind, destroying his ability to empathize. Some might feel pity, but he was a monster who'd made very deliberate choices to inflict pain and would never be rehabilitated. Serial rapists and killers were not redeemable. Killing for pleasure was not the same as killing because you were ordered to do so. Frazer's gaze flicked to Alex Parker, and he finally understood what made a man kill in cold blood. He understood Alex Parker.

Frazer raised the gun.

Chance sneered. "You don't have the balls."

Frazer pulled the trigger and the sound ricocheted off the 480 million year old Appalachian rock. Crimson blood splattered against the snow. The air stank of piss and excrement.

He expected to feel remorse for taking a human life, but this man had been evil. He turned and looked Parker in the eye. "He shouldn't have tried to escape."

Parker said nothing. He eyed Frazer warily. Parker knew how this usually worked. No witnesses. He knew that the higher up you went, the more you could get away with. Frazer wasn't that guy. He had better methods that didn't involve more killing.

"The CIA agreed to transfer you to a consultancy position in the FBI, Mr. Parker."

"What?" Mallory stepped forward, eyes wide.

Alex pushed her back behind him and huffed out a breath that might have been a laugh. "The CIA did?"

The sound of a siren wailed in the distance. The cavalry were finally coming.

"To plug certain holes in FBI security." He nodded. "Are you going to accept the position?" Frazer asked him.

"Work for the feebs?" Alex eyed the gun in Frazer's hand. His lips twitched. "Sure, if Mallory can stand having me around."

She turned the man toward her and took his face in her hands and kissed him. Parker still kept one eye on him though. Smart man. Frazer figured he had their silence.

He looked at the senator. "You will step down due to ill health. You will hand over to me every piece of information you have on The Gateway Project and you will never interfere with law enforcement policy again or you will be arrested for conspiracy to commit murder."

Her eyes drifted to the woodpile. "I'm done. I just want to bury my baby. You don't need to worry about me any longer."

Hanrahan stood looking at him like he'd won the lottery. Frazer pointed his finger at the man. He felt sickened by his betrayal.

"You just retired. You can go on your book tours and your fucking media circus but if you ever mention this, if you even hint at vigilante justice or corruption in the BAU, I will put a bullet in you myself. Now get your gun, and go with the senator to look for that missing girl. You weren't here when Chance died. You know nothing about what happened. You went searching for the girl as soon as you heard she was out here. Go."

They stumbled away.

He faced Mallory Rooney. What did he say to a woman who'd known something was going on from the moment she'd seen her first dead serial killer? A woman who'd been hunted by a madman, betrayed by her family, her lover, her boss? And had survived to prove she was a better person than all of them.

Judging from the way she clung to Parker's hand, she'd managed to forgive him. Frazer had just executed a man in front of her in cold blood. Would she forgive him too? Or had he gone too far?

"Special Agent Rooney."

"Yes, sir?" She stood straighter, bracing her shoulders, a defiant expression on her gamine face.

"Welcome to the team."

She smiled at him, a sunburst of hope and thankfulness. He figured he had his answer.

Five days later…

MALLORY STUFFED HER hands deep in the pockets of her new down winter jacket and stood at the top of the hill, looking down the track that led through the woods to her childhood home. The sun was rising to the east and she thought of her twin who'd been nearby for so many years, but oh so far away. One day she might be able to forgive herself for not finding her sooner, but not yet. Not yet.

She started walking down the hill toward the crime scene tape that surrounded the pit, wanting this to be over, needing this to be over.

Newly promoted ASAC Frazer had shut her and Alex out of the investigation and she was grateful. She was grateful to Lincoln Frazer for many things.

Deputy Sean Kennedy had been found alive inside the pit. Weak from dehydration and hypothermia, he'd survived his ordeal and was recovering in the hospital being praised for being the first to solve the case even though it had almost cost him his life. Amanda Collie—the young waitress—had managed to make her way to Eastborne and had called the cops. She was shaken up but Leo Chance hadn't sexually assaulted her. He probably hadn't had time. The town was aghast. The sheriff had been to see Mallory three times and every time he looked more distressed.

Hard to cope with the fact you'd been fooled so completely when you were supposed to be in charge of keeping the town safe. She knew he wouldn't run for office again. She'd seen it in his eyes. Leo Chance's crimes had destroyed many lives. Not only his victims and their families, but his remaining family who bore the brunt of the shame.

Bryce Keeble had spent many hours keeping her company during her vigil. They didn't talk but they understood one another implicitly.

The buzz of a generator grew louder, industrial lights spilling over the area where the woodpile had once stood. The feds had relocated the whole thing a few hundred yards west, carefully examining each piece of wood for possible evidence. Yesterday, they'd used ground penetrating radar to target the most likely resting place for Payton's remains. Today they'd start digging.

The snow had melted again and Mallory trudged through the dark mud to resume her place on the sidelines. The only reason she went home was to sleep. Finding her lost twin was all she could think about right now. Alex took care of everything else, from procuring clothes suitable for standing in the winter woods all day long, to bringing her food, to making sure no evidence could rebound on them and destroy the bargain Frazer had so cleverly put together. He even dealt with her mother, who now deferred to him about everything from what to tell the press to how much caffeine to drink. Sublime to the ridiculous.

She arrived at the clearing and noted they'd already begun excavating. The crime scene technicians shot her a glance. Her mouth went dry. They'd told her they wouldn't begin until noon and it was only dawn. They'd lied. They'd probably started as soon as she'd left around midnight. Part of her was furious but she understood them. She made them uncomfortable but she couldn't stay away.

She felt Alex's presence before she saw him. She still hadn't told him about the baby but they were entering new territory now. She wanted to navigate it carefully. Her feelings went deeper than she'd believed possible. Knowing someone would kill for you, would give up their life for you, was sobering. It put their passion in a different light. Made it deeper, brighter, bolder, stronger.

She didn't think he was a monster, just a man who'd gone off course while suffering the terrible effects of guilt and PTSD. She knew there could still be fallout. Knew they may never be completely safe from the shadowy figures who'd helped her mother set up this terrifying organization. But Alex said he'd arranged certain safeguards for their protection, and whoever ran the thing must know he was not the sort of man to take on unless they were willing to die for the cause. Given they all had so much to lose should the conspiracy come to light, she figured they were safe, for now.

He handed her a cup of steaming coffee in a travel mug.

"Promise you'll never lie to me again," she said quietly. By tacit agreement the five of them had agreed not to talk about what happened in the woods that day, but this was about the future not the past. "Not even for my own good."

"You have my word." He kissed her temple, his lips warm and soft.

She caught his hand in hers. It was time to come clean. "Do you remember, before everything went to hell, that I called you and told you I needed to talk?"

His eyes crinkled infinitesimally at the edges. "I remember." Although he'd obviously forgotten in the ensuing chaos.

"I figured out why I felt so nauseous." She watched his

skin pale, his gray eyes widen.

"You're…?" His Adam's apple bobbed up and down. He dragged a big hand down his face. "You're pregnant? That whole time you went after Leo Chance, you were pregnant and you knew it?"

"Are you angry?"

He looked at the sky. "Fuck. Yes! At myself. At you." He squeezed his eyes shut and gathered her close. "Are you sure?"

"As a dime store pregnancy test and one missed period."

"Pretty sure then," he mumbled into her hair as he held her closer.

She gave a soft laugh, clinging to his shoulders. "Think you can cope?"

He drew back and looked her in the eye. "You're my one shot at a normal life, Mal, which doesn't sound flattering unless you know how fucked up I am. If you can trust someone like me to look after a child—"

"I'm not worried about you hurting our baby, Alex. But I am worried you might do something stupid with some archaic notion of protecting us. I don't want any secrets between us. I want a fresh start—"

"You want that first date we never went on?"

She touched his face. "Yes. But only after we lay Payton to rest."

He nodded soberly, but there was a light in his eyes she hadn't seen before. She wanted to give him hope for the future. She wanted to give him all the joy he'd missed over the years. She turned around in his arms and watched a group of feds return blurry-eyed to the scene. They looked at her and then went down the pit. They were cataloguing evidence. DNA. Trace. Diaries, photographs, and notebooks that probably belonged to Payton. She wanted so badly to look at the documents and see what they said but it wasn't possible until they'd been processed. She knew that. That was her job too. It didn't make the wait any easier.

The technician bent over the excavation site nearest to them, looked up and called over one of the other techs. "I've got something."

She froze. "Do you think it's her?" she whispered.

Alex's hands squeezed her shoulder, fingers digging in. "Yes. I think it's her."

Moisture gathered in her eyes. The long ago sound of Payton's laughter flitted at the edge of her mind. She rested her hand over his. Determined to wait it out, determined to show her sister the love and respect that had never stopped, no matter how many days and years they'd been apart. "I think it's her too." She squeezed his hand. "It's almost over."

Alex slid both hands over her stomach and she leaned back against him. Something fluttered inside her. The sun started to rise over the tree tops, filling the dawn with dramatic reds and pinks. She smiled through her tears. It seemed somehow right that Payton would finally see the sunrise again. "Just keep holding me, Alex," she whispered.

He squeezed her tight, and his warmth engulfed her. "I'm never letting go, Mallory. I'll never let you go."

USEFUL ACRONYM DEFINITIONS FOR TONI'S BOOKS

AG: Attorney General

ASAC: Assistant Special-Agent-in-Charge

ATF: Alcohol, Tobacco, and Firearms

BAU: Behavioral Analysis Unit

BOLO: Be on the Lookout

BUCAR: Bureau Car.

CIRG: Critical Incident Response Group

CMU: Crisis Management Unit

CN: Crisis Negotiator

CNU: Crisis Negotiation Unit

CODIS: Combined DNA Index System

CP: Command Post

DEA: Drug Enforcement Administration

DOB: Date of Birth

DOJ: Department of Justice

EMT: Emergency Medical Technician

ERT: Evidence Response Team

FOA: First-Office Assignment

FBI: Federal Bureau of Investigation

FO: Field Office

IC: Incident Commander

HRT: Hostage Rescue Team

HT: Hostage-Taker

LAPD: Los Angeles Police Department

LEO: Law Enforcement Officer

ME: Medical Examiner

MO: Modus Operandi

NAT: New Agent Trainee

NCIC: National Crime Information Center

NYFO: New York Field Office

OC: Organized Crime

OCU: Organized Crime Unit

OPR: Office of Professional Responsibility

POTUS: President of the United States

RA: Resident Agency

SA: Special Agent

SAC: Special Agent-in-Charge

SAS: Special Air Squadron (British Special Forces unit)

SIOC: Strategic Information & Operations

SSA: Supervisory Special Agent

SWAT: Special Weapons and Tactics

TC: Tactical Commander

TOD: Time of Death

UNSUB: Unknown Subject

ViCAP: Violent Criminal Apprehension Program

WFO: Washington Field Office

COLD JUSTICE SERIES OVERVIEW

A Cold Dark Place (Book #1)
Cold Pursuit (Book #2)
Cold Light of Day (Book #3)
Cold Fear (Book #4)
Cold In The Shadows (Book #5)
Cold Hearted (Book #6)
Cold Secrets (Book #7)
Cold Malice (Book #8)
A Cold Dark Promise (Book #9~A Wedding Novella)
Cold Blooded (Book #10)

COLD JUSTICE – CROSSFIRE

Cold & Deadly (Book #1)
Colder Than Sin (Book #2) Coming 2019

Cold Justice Series books are also available as audiobooks narrated by Eric Dove. See Toni Anderson's website for details (www.toniandersonauthor.com)

ACKNOWLEDGMENTS

Even though writing is a solitary endeavor I had a lot of help with this manuscript. Biggest thanks, as always, go to my amazing critique partner, Kathy Altman. Thanks also, for encouragement and beta-reads, to Laurie Wood, and my lovely hubby, Gary. Much appreciation to JRT Editing and Ally Robertson for helping me make this story shine. I also want to thank my agent, Jill Marsal for all her help and support.

ABOUT THE AUTHOR

Toni Anderson is a *New York Times* and *USA Today* bestselling author, RITA® finalist, science nerd, professional tourist, dog lover, gardener, mom. Originally from a small town in England, Toni studied Marine Biology at University of Liverpool (B.Sc.) and University of St. Andrews (Ph.D.) with the intention she'd never be far from the ocean. Well, that plan backfired and she ended up in the Canadian prairies with her biology professor husband, two kids, a rescue dog, and one chilled leopard gecko. Her greatest achievements are mastering the Tokyo subway, climbing Ben Lomond, snorkelling the Great Barrier Reef, and surviving fourteen Winnipeg winters. She loves to travel for research purposes and was lucky enough to visit the Strategic Information and Operations Center inside FBI Headquarters in Washington, D.C. in 2016, and she also got to shove another car off the road during pursuit training at the Writer's Police Academy in Wisconsin. Watch out world!

Sign up for Toni Anderson's newsletter:
www.tonianderson author.com/newsletter-signup

Like Toni Anderson on Facebook:
facebook.com/toniannanderson

See Toni Anderson's current book list:
www.toniandersonauthor.com/books-2

Follow Toni Anderson on Instagram:
instagram.com/toni_anderson_author

Printed in Great Britain
by Amazon

56713579R00213